Also by Jean Davis

The Last God
Sahmara
A Broken Race
Destiny Pills and Space Wizards

Forthcoming Volumes for *The Narvan*

Chain of Gray (2020)

Bound in Blue (2020)

Seeker (2021)

Trust

Trust

The Narvan • Book One

Jean Davis

TRUST: Book One of The Narvan

www.jeandavisauthor.com

ISBN-13:   978-1-7345701-0-6 (print)
                  978-1-7345701-1-3 (ebook)

First Edition: April 2019
Second Edition: February 2020

Printed in the United States of America
Published by StreamlineDesign LLC
Distributed by Ingram

Prologue

I

Loud voices inside the house brought me to a pause on the front step. One belonged to my brother. The other to a woman, likely the one he'd been seeing that I'd never met. My hand hovered over the door controls. Staying outside and out of their argument would be wise.

The last time we two brothers had gotten into it, the neighbors had called the enforcers. I hoped they didn't feel so inclined this time around. I didn't need any additional questionable behavior tainting my otherwise commendable record.

I glanced up at the sky. A few fluffy white clouds dotted the vast blueness, giving no indication of the war raging on outside the atmosphere. There hadn't been any ground attacks in a couple weeks. I prayed to Geva that Artor was finally making some progress against Jal. The war had already taken my parents and so many others. We needed to end this, soon, before I lost my brother, too.

Out of school early thanks to a canceled class, Chesser wouldn't have expected me to be home yet. Did he bring Anastassia here often while I was gone? He was only on leave for another two days. Her too, for that matter, since he'd recruited her to his team.

It would be a month or more before I saw him again. His off time was supposed to be our time together, to pretend we were still a family for a few days, a little dose of what I vaguely remembered as normal. But since he'd met Anastassia, they were inseparable. Elsewhere. They were together the whole time he was on duty. Wasn't that enough?

I wasn't opposed to him seeing anyone and I'd made that quite clear, but he still made no effort to get the two of us in the same room. Maybe she was ugly, but it sure didn't sound like his friends gave him any grief about her.

The argument inside elevated to all out shouting. I leaned in closer to the door.

"Why wouldn't you want children?" Chesser asked.

"Why would I? I'm not about to give up my life to sit around here and personally replenish your homeworld's population. Besides, who knows if we're even compatible that way."

"We are. I received a confirmation from the inquiry I had submitted to the University."

"You made a fucking inquiry?" Her voice rose, breaking from the steady malice she'd been slinging at my brother.

Something hit the wall next to the door and thudded to the floor. Great, one of them was throwing things. At least it didn't sound like anything breakable.

"Bearing children is an honor. This isn't some little rustic utopia like Veria Prime where everyone reproduces on a whim. I'm cleared to continue my family line, and I'd rather not see it end with me and Vayen."

My teeth ground together. He hadn't even seen fit to introduce me to this woman, but he intended to join with her and they were talking children already? Oh Geva, that meant he'd bonded with her! That wasn't something that could be undone.

She wasn't even Artorian for Geva's sake. Similar, and naturally telepathic like us, but not the same. My mother would have had a fit about him even considering bringing half-breed children into our line.

If any of what he told me about the missions he did were true, he probably had gained a few favors from fairly high up the chain of command, but I rather doubted even that was enough to get the government to overlook Anastassia's genetics.

"Then Vayen can continue your family line. Leave me out of it," she said with all the finality of an official decree.

"He's only sixteen." There was a single loud thump that I hoped was Chesser slamming his hand on the countertop or table and not a fist through a wall that I'd have to fix. "It will be another six years before he's eligible for the procedure. With the war going on, who knows if he'll make it that long. At this rate, I won't. Anastassia, I need to know this is taken care of."

Chesser couldn't die. He was all the family I had left.

As I stood outside, heart pounding, ear pressed to the door, I became increasingly aware of inquiring gazes from those passing by on the street. One of the round news feed bots whizzed by, hopefully chasing down some celebrity or government official and not an indication that another attack was about to happen. Traffic overhead was minimal at this hour, but if I stood here much longer, someone was going to file a suspicious activity report.

Despite the continued shouting, I keyed in my entry code and stepped into the kitchen. Already modestly sized, it was not near large enough to contain the tension that skyrocketed upon the two of them spotting me.

Chesser halted mid-curse to force a smile in my direction. "You're home early."

My mind raced, debating whether to join in the fray or escape to my room. The red-faced woman with narrowed green eyes gripping the countertop as though she wanted to tear it from the wall decided it for me. If this went any further beyond shouting, someone would be calling in the enforcers and it might even be me.

I slid the bag off my shoulder and dropped it onto the table in the middle of the room. "You're supposed to be ending this war, not dying in it," I said. "How can you even consider having a kid right now? Half the cities on Artor are running at half power thanks to the last round of ground attacks. Ours is one of them, which is why I'm home by the way. Not that you've probably even noticed the power rationing in that dingy hole of a bar that you'd rather hang out in than be here."

The subtle smile that spread across Anastassia's lips interrupted the venting spree I was just getting started on. She wasn't ugly, but not exactly stunning either.

Not being familiar with her kind, I could only guess her age, based on her appearance, was somewhere between Chesser and I. Now that she appeared calmer, it became clear her skin was naturally pale, a stark contrast to our coloring. Chesser had mentioned finding her on Veria Prime but she didn't appear to be related to them either. She came from one of the transient races. I half-remembered Chesser saying that her kind always looked for home elsewhere or something bigger and better. Which made me seriously wonder why she was here, with him, in the middle of a war.

A braid of light brown hair dropped below her shoulders. She wasn't slight, but she didn't have the bulk or height common in Artorians. There was no way in all the nine hells she would ever pass for one of us. If anything, she held more resemblance to a Jalvian, except that they shared our build. I wondered if that bothered him on some level, being with a woman who looked like the enemy.

Anastassia raised one eyebrow and smirked at Chesser. "You should listen to your brother."

He took a few steps forward, almost as though he were trying to get between me and Anastassia. "Don't bring him into this."

While I held no delusions of holding my own with Chesser, him being twelve years older and in top form, I wasn't about to be dismissed like a little kid.

"As I recall, *you* brought him into this," she said.

I crossed my arms over my chest and nodded. "From what I heard, she's right."

Chesser ran both hands over his close-cropped hair, as though he wanted to yank it out but there wasn't enough to get ahold of.

"Is this why you've been keeping us from meeting?" Anastassia asked. "Because we'd gang up on you when you started spouting off idiotic notions?"

"You see this place?" He snarled. "It's a dump. Maybe I didn't want you to see that."

From the muscle twitch in the right corner of his upper lip, I knew it was time to shut up. He could be a nice guy now and then, mostly sullen and quiet, but he could also fall into a really foul mood that was to be avoided at all cost. That's when fists went into walls and bottles or anything else within reach flew through the air.

The soft whirring of our lone cleaning bot teased the heavy silence as if it could anticipate that there would soon be a mess to attend to.

The bot adequately performed the tasks its low budget model provided. However, with the war dragging on and constant efforts at recovery, power wasn't the only thing being rationed. Chesser's pay had been cut three times in the four years since our parents died. We weren't going hungry and the bills were covered, but that was about it.

I had another year of school before I could join the ranks and earn an income of my own. I'd offered to enlist now, but Chesser insisted that I finish my training first. He refused to let me join what he called the "fodder" teams that some of my friends had gone into.

The bot trundled across the worn rug under the table that sported no shortage of dents on its wooden surface. Our house wasn't a dump. It just held a lot of old things. Things that had fuzzy histories because I hadn't been listening when my mother would ramble on about where this or that had come from. But they were important, not junk. They meant something: my mother's prized weaving on the wall of the common room, the chair with the carved legs that my father had sat in every night after dinner, even the chipped grey-green dishes with hand-painted leaves around the edges, most of which were dirty and scattered across the counter behind Anastassia.

Sure there were a few cracks in the ceiling and up the wall beside the front door, and the windows in the room that had belonged to my parents had shattered. Our city had been bombed several times over the years. It would be hard to name a building that didn't show some degree of damage.

Our family had never been wealthy, but we hadn't been poor either. It had never occurred to me that Chesser might wish to have something better. Was he embarrassed by the things our parents had loved and left behind? Maybe all those accolades had gone to his head and now home wasn't good enough. Was I good enough? He hadn't been in a hurry to show me off, either.

Anastassia's hand on my shoulder caught me off guard. I'd been too wrapped up in my own head to notice her bridging the gap between us. Good thing one of my instructors hadn't been there to witness my lapse in awareness. I'd have been hearing about that for days.

"I've got this," she said as she let go and walked up to my brother to land a heavy slap across his face. "Quit being an asshole."

Chesser's face went as red as hers had been when I'd walked in. "How dare you strike a superior—"

She stood her ground. "We're off duty, remember? And I'm a volunteer, so unless you'd like me to leave and take everything I have to offer with me, I suggest you cool off and spend some time with your brother before we get back to it."

I didn't care what she looked like, I quite liked her just then.

"You should leave," he growled.

"Planned on it."

She turned to me for just long enough to offer a slight nod before raising one hand and twisting two fingers together in what I gathered from Chesser's tight lipped snarl was an obscene gesture.

"Anastassia," he called after her.

She walked out the door without acknowledging him further.

"Not a word," he growled at me and then stalked off to his bedroom.

I watched his door close in cautious silence and wondered if I'd ever see Anastassia again.

II

When Chesser came home two months later, he seemed happy with his latest mission and his team, but there wasn't a word about Anastassia that led me to believe he regarded her as anything but one of his soldiers. Using the intelligence she'd shared, they had managed to take out several key Jalvian ships and he'd led an attack on the Jalvian controlled world of Rok. He went out drinking with some of his men one night, and Geva's knows what he did during the day while I was in training, but he was at home all three nights. For a little while, life was normal and good. Then he left again.

Being alone for long periods of time lent itself to focusing intently on school and excelling in my training. Having the memories of my parents all around me kept me company when friends were busy. There were neighbors available if I needed help, but I preferred to take care of the house myself and wait for Chesser if big chores came up, like when the wall crack started spreading and my patch job was no longer doing the job.

The days ticked by and then the first day of scheduled leave was followed by the second and third without any message. My stomach began to twist and turn. I pored over the news feeds but didn't see any mention of an event that would explain his delay. Every time a transport stopped near my house, I waited for the tap on the door from someone in uniform to tell me he was dead. But the transports all continued on their routes.

I lay awake at night, wondering if he'd been taken prisoner

or was he on some secret mission gone wrong that no one would learn about for years. The only reassurance I had was that his credits kept rolling into our family account each week.

Two and a half weeks late, he showed up sporting a fading bruise on his face and a big grin. He carried a large bag in each arm and his usual pack over one shoulder.

"Where have you been?" I asked.

"Calling in favors and earning a couple more. Nothing to worry about, everything is fine." He set all the bags down by the door and took off his coat.

"Fine? You're over two weeks late. You didn't send word. I thought—"

There, in the middle of the kitchen, he pulled me into a rare but quick hug. "Not to worry. Just had to go silent there for a little while. We're close to winning this. Finally."

The relief of having him home, of not being alone in the known universe, eased my raw nerves. "That's great."

He nodded. "Hope you don't mind, but some of us are having a little celebratory dinner tonight. I promise I'll make it up to you tomorrow."

A tap sounded on the door. Chesser ran to open it. Anastassia stood there in a red dress that was so long it hid her shoes. But what made my throat go dry was the silver band around her neck that looked exactly like what one would give a prospective mate as a joining gift.

I reached behind me for one of the chairs by the table and sank into it.

"You're not changed? We're going to be late," she said.

"I just got here. The debriefing went longer than expected and I had a few stops to make." He shuffled the large bags and his pack away from the door. "Might as well come in for a few minutes. You can keep Vayen company while I get ready."

Tearing her gaze from him, she seemed to notice me and smiled.

I couldn't stop staring at the band around her neck. When had he done that and why hadn't he said anything? Had they completed the ceremony? Had my brother joined with her and neglected to mention it? I was too confounded by the utter lack of courtesy or anything else to even form a coherent curse.

Chesser headed for his room while Anastassia settled into the chair next to me. She ran her fingers over the band, tracing the swirling lines of the engraved design he'd chosen for her. She licked her red lips and her gaze darted toward his closed door.

"I told him not to get this. I know you two need all the credits you can get. I hope you don't hold it against him." She nodded toward the bags Chesser had brought in. "We got a good bonus. That should make up for some of it at least. He said he'd get you some new clothes. I think he managed some extra food rations too."

"Are you joined?" I blurted.

"He keeps talking about it, but no. He said something about gifting being part of it?"

Her hair hung lose, longer than I remembered. The thin straps over her shoulders did nothing to hide the sinewy muscle of her arms. The more I noticed the dress, the more absurd it looked on her. She belonged in a uniform.

"It's stupid isn't it?" She rubbed her forehead with the palms of her hands, the only part of her face not touched by cosmetics. "I borrowed the dress. I would never own something like this, but he was so excited about looking the part for the medal ceremony and I'm not allowed to wear your uniform, being an outside consultant."

"What ceremony?"

She rested her hands on the table, palms down and fingers splayed. Anastassia cast a suspicious glare at the closed door. "He didn't tell you about the ceremony?"

"He just walked in the door."

"He sent a message, surely. He's known about it for weeks. We poured through four jump gates in five days to get here in time. I think my stomach is still back at the second one."

"He said something about maintaining silence."

A single finger began to tap on the tabletop. "I see. That would explain why you aren't dressed to go with us."

"I don't—"

Chesser's door opened. He came out wearing his dress uniform. He took one look at the two of us and scowled. "Is it too much to ask that you two don't join forces against me every time you're in the same room together?"

"All both times?" I said, shooting to my feet. "When she moves in, you might as well move out."

"I don't plan on moving in." Anastassia stood, carefully gathering the skirt around her as she moved away from the chair.

"You didn't plan on joining with him either the last time I saw you, but here you are with his gift around your neck, and he's bonded to you, so don't expect him to leave you alone. Hells, next time either of you feels the urge to stop by, you'll probably have that kid you didn't want in our arms."

She swallowed hard and looked between me and Chesser. "So this *is* more than just a necklace. Like an engagement ring?"

Anastassia started shuffling toward the door. She probably would have moved a lot faster if it wasn't for the dress made for an Artorian woman's height getting tangled up in her shoes.

"I told you, it's a gift," he said.

"A joining gift," I clarified loudly.

"Anastassia, wait," he ran to the door as she slipped outside.

"Dammit, Vayen. Can't I have just one good night at home?" he said over his shoulder before slamming the door behind him.

III

We didn't talk much those last three days of his leave. His deceit ate at me. He'd never been like that before and other than Anastassia being in his life, I couldn't pinpoint any other reason why he'd slipped into using half-truths and omissions as a standard. As much as I wanted to blame her for turning my brother into someone I couldn't trust or depend on, she'd been just as upset with him both times. Only seeing him a few days every month or two didn't give me much information to go on. He hadn't been in any mood to offer any explanation beyond a barely audible mumbling of an apology this time either.

When he gave me his next leave date, I didn't bother recording it. We said our wooden goodbyes and he left.

It wasn't until a couple weeks later that I began to miss him and tried to remember the date he'd told me. But I'd been too mad at the time to commit it to memory. I highlighted an estimated two week span on my datapad and tried not to pay much attention to it. At night, in the silent house, I stared at the ceiling and imagined hundreds of conversations where I'd get to the bottom of what was going on. When he came home next time, we'd figure this out and get past it. Things would go back to how they used to be with or without Anastassia around.

By the time my estimated dates had passed and then a couple weeks more had gone by, I was alternating between angry and depressed. Neither of those extremes were helping me at school or in training. Instructors had called me in several times to ask what was going on. None of them had answers for Chesser's delays, but the sympathy in their eyes was crushing. They knew what I knew deep inside. We'd all seen the same scenario happen enough to not know how it ended.

Mine ended with a tap on the door, much like everyone else's. Except that it wasn't the uniformed official. It was Anastassia. The somber look on her face was the same one I'd imagined Chesser had encountered upon hearing the news of our parents when the ship they served on had been destroyed.

My legs forgot how to work. My stomach went cold. The next thing I knew, I was sitting on the floor of the kitchen with Anastassia next to me.

She was paler than the last time she'd been over. Dark circles lingered under her eyes. While she still wore Chesser's gift around her neck, she didn't caress it like before. We sat in silence, side by side, both lost in our thoughts.

"I hope you don't mind that I came instead of someone else," she said finally. "I thought it would be easier for both of us."

Numb, I could only nod.

"It's not." She managed a half smile that faltered a second later.

"We wanted you to know, his team I mean, that you'll be taken care of. Your expenses will be paid as usual until you finish school. This house is in your family name. You can stay here indefinitely. I'm told you had a social services check in before. They're putting you back on that list."

That was some relief. I'd seen other orphans taken off to group homes or auto-enlisted if they were my age. Though I'd been happy upon my last birthday to have my services rep sign off on my living status, it wasn't surprising they'd put me back into the system now. All hope of normalcy had officially flown out the window. Tears threatened to fall, but I had no intention of crying in front of Anastassia. If she could hold it together, I could too.

"I'd like to say he died for a good cause. But is there really any cause good enough for that?"

I found my voice, though it sounded hollow and distant. "Did it at least make a difference?"

"Yes. It's all classified right now, but hopefully, some day, you'll see that it definitely made a difference, and not just for what's going on here in the Narvan. We brought home something big, something your University is working on as we speak."

"Was it a Jalvian?"

"No, but I can't say more."

Plenty used to the classified excuse, I nodded.

"We set up a memorial service for tomorrow. His team is heading back out afterwards."

"But not you?"

Her gaze moved slowly around the room, over the chaos of dirty dishes I hadn't had the energy to deal with and the clothes thrown over three of the four chairs at the table. It was a good thing she couldn't see into the common room from there or the view would have been more of the same.

Anastassia focused on the still frame of the four of us on the wall from when I was much younger. We were standing outside behind the house by the garden my mother kept before the war broke out. It was nothing more than an overgrown square lot now. Chesser called it our natural landscape. The neighbors politely ignored it.

Anastassia got up and went over to the still frame.

"I have to say, your people really have their genetics nailed down tight. You two could pass for identical twins, a perfect mix of both parents." She cocked her head. "Do your women actually give birth or is it all engineered in a lab?"

It occurred to me that she might really not have any idea, having only been here on Artor with Chesser for the grand equivalent of two or three weeks since she'd joined his team. I imagined her off time was spent relaxing rather than researching her prospective mate's culture and history.

"Most choose the lab with a simulated pregnancy experience. Our mother gave birth."

"Amazing that you're both still so similar then. Doesn't it get boring with everyone looking the same? I mean, what happens to the random mutation? Do you hide the albino Artorians in a lab underground?"

Her questions offered a welcome distraction. I managed to get up and block her from going around the corner to the mess in the common room. "What does a military consultant care about genetics?"

"My father was a botanist," she said quickly. "I used to assist him. The consultant job wasn't my first choice. Or even second. It just sort of happened."

She backed away from the still frame and me. "I hope better

things happen for you."

I realized she was making a break for the door again. Her hands shook at her sides and her voice had taken on an uncertain tremble. "I'll have someone send you the details of the service. I have to go."

She escaped as efficiently as she had before, leaving me alone in the house that now held one more lifetime of memories tied up in things.

Chapter One

"Could you kill someone if I asked you to?" asked Anastassia Kazan as she thrummed her fingers on the plain hotel room table between us.

The woman who sat across from me was harder than the one I'd last seen at my brother's memorial service eight years before. The green eyes and braid were the same, but she now wore a full-length armored coat and no few weapons, if I judged the lumps beneath it correctly.

"You mean, if they attacked you?"

When she'd contacted me out of the blue to interview for a bodyguard position, I'd jumped at the opportunity. She'd had a hand in ending the war that had plagued my homeworld and I owed her for that. All of Artor did. However, her question sounded more like she was looking for someone eager to commit murder at her whim.

"If anyone attacks me, yes of course, but also if I give the order. Without questions," she said.

My gut reaction was to say no, but having read the brief she'd sent with the invitation, I realized that anyone who had managed to work her way into the position of advisor to the entire Narvan System under some confidential organization, had likely made quite a few enemies and questionable arrangements along the way.

This wasn't the sedate head of security job I'd managed to work myself into. Working for Anastassia was going to have legal risks and moral compromises.

She sat back, opening the top latch of her black armored coat to reveal the neckline of a plain grey shirt beneath. There was no sign of the neckband she'd once worn. Her intent gaze seemed to note my every movement down to the length of each breath.

I wondered why she chose this place for our meeting rather than her office or even a restaurant or some other public place, but questioning her choices didn't seem like a wise idea if I wanted the job. When the war with Jal had ended shortly after Chesser's death, my military future ended with it. Too many experienced people stood between me and making a decent living in that arena. I'd taken the best job I could get, but the pay was minimal and the opportunity for advancement slim.

Chesser had trusted her, and undoubtedly, he'd followed similar compromising orders issued during the war. I wouldn't have been any different had that opportunity still been open to me. Besides, the compensation offer she'd proposed had enough zeros to make me ignore my gut.

"Yes, I can do that," I said, forcing myself to mean it.

"Then I suppose you're hired." She sighed and looked a fraction more relaxed. "You'll start immediately."

"But I—"

"Don't worry about your current job. I'll take care of favorably closing out your employment record."

I leaned forward, realizing that if I didn't speak up now, she'd roll right over me. Anastassia was clearly accustomed to being in command.

"I have a home and someone waiting for me. I traveled halfway around Artor for this meeting, but I can't just drop everything right this instant."

Sonia would be expecting me to get back from my supposed business trip soon after midnight, and I had people I wanted to say goodbye to at work. I hadn't anticipated that Anastassia would hire me on the spot, or really, that she would hire me at all. I'd figured the interview was more of a favor given her past relationship with my brother. But we'd talked for well over two hours and she'd asked serious questions right from the beginning with little effort to catch up or speak of the past.

She held up a hand. "We'll deal with all that. First though, I need to make a connection with you."

I nodded, opening my mind to hers so we could create a natural connection for telepathic communication. The light-skinned face of a Jalvian man with long, white hair and a determined gleam in his eyes popped into my head.

"If you see this man, kill him," she said.

Killing a Jalvian without question wasn't much of a compromise. I'd been waiting for an opportunity to do that for years.

"Second order of business..." Anastassia reached into one of the many pockets of her coat, this one at her hip. She produced a gun and slid it across the table. "Once Kess finds out you work for me, he'll want to kill you too."

Great. From bodyguard to target all in a matter of minutes.

"The good news is that you won't be working alone. I'm putting together a team. Come on." She stood, the heavy armored fabric rasping against the chair as it fell into place just past her knees.

Not wanting to be seen with an illegal firearm, I tucked the gun away and covered it with my shirt. Lagging a few steps behind as we walked down the hall gave me a chance to guess how many other black market weapons she had hidden between the military-issue boots and the collar that reached the base of her skull. Before I'd gotten to her waist, she stopped at a door and palmed the security panel. The door slid open.

The hotel room, identical to the one we'd met in, contained two narrow beds and a round table flanked by two chairs. A muscle-bulked Jalvian sat in one of them. He tossed a long mass of blond hair over the shoulder of what resembled a casual version of the standard Jalvian military uniform. He looked young enough, maybe she'd plucked him right out of his last year of training. His bright blue gaze met mine. My fists clenched.

"This is Jey Te." Kazan placed herself between us. "Yes, your people have a war-ridden past. For all your gods' sakes, I helped put an end to the last one." She shook her head. "That was seven years ago. Neither of you was involved in the fighting. Get over it."

Getting over it wasn't an option. My parents were dead because of his people. Many of my friends had died. That war had taken Chesser away, leaving me mostly alone the last years of his life. My fingers itched to hold the gun tucked into the waistband of my pants.

A dark scowl spread across Jey's face, marring the perfect symmetry his people had attained through centuries of genetic alteration. We had done the same thing, making it simple to tell us apart from the aggressive bastards who, long ago, had been the other half of our race.

Kazan gave us each a stern glance. "I need you both to work together."

I forced myself into a state of calm. The opportunity held too much promise to throw away over one inconvenience, major, as it might be. "Fine."

Jey grunted his agreement.

"Good. Then, as I have already covered with Jey, you need to understand that it won't be safe for you to stay in your home. I have homes throughout the Narvan, you will stay there with me."

"I'm sorry, what? You neglected to mention that detail."

"She does that," muttered Jey.

"Remember what I said about Kess? I wasn't kidding. He will use anything to weaken me or you. By anything, I mean the people you care about. You'll need to cut all ties."

"I don't know if I can do that." Or that I wanted to. Sonia and I had been seeing each other for two years. I planned to join with her someday, buy a big house, start a family. This job was my ticket to making that possible.

"Once you are fully trained, you'll be able to visit, but I wouldn't recommend drawing any attention to your presence."

Visits didn't sound promising, but maybe I could make this work. Chesser and I had made the most of our four days once a month for years. Not that a monthly visit was exactly what I'd envisioned my joined future looking like, but this job didn't have to be a lifetime career. I just needed to fill my account and then I could quit and we could live comfortably on a salary like the one I was leaving behind.

"All right then, but I didn't pack for an extended stay and I do have some explaining to do at home," I said.

She nodded. "I'll bring you there in a moment."

"In a moment?" It had taken me six hours in a high speed transport to get here and that was in the early morning hours before traffic got heavy.

Jey chuckled. "Oh, you're going to enjoy this. Wish I could see your face on the other side."

Kazan kicked the leg of his chair, nearly knocking him out of it. "Your face was pretty green too. Everyone's is the first time."

She looked me over from head to toe in a way that made me feel like I was a prized prantha on the auction block. A faint tickling in my mind flared into a split second of sharp pain. Was she fucking probing me?

I slammed my defenses down. The breach of privacy wasn't near as aggravating as the ease by which she had plowed through my head.

"Sorry, I needed a jump point. The probe was easier than explaining exactly what I needed." She closed her eyes and put her hand on my arm. "Jey was right, you won't enjoy this."

The room turned black and the sensation of a sucking void pulling at every fiber of my being overtook me. The next thing I knew, we stood outside my house, or rather, the one provided by my soon-to-be-previous employer. My stomach threatened to heave my breakfast onto the front step.

"What in the name of Geva did you just do?"

"That was a Jump. Sort of like the gates used by ships, but on a personal level. You'll be able to do it on your own once you get a link implant." She squeezed my arm. "Are you feeling all right?"

No, but I wasn't about to admit it. "I'll be fine."

"This is part of the technology your brother died for. Your government has kept it under strict restrictions. They started to market it to the elite over the past several years to help pay for the rebuilding efforts on Artor and your other colonies."

"I'm hardly one of the elite."

She shrugged. "You're with me. I helped test it."

If she could go anywhere in a matter of minutes and had been in on the project from the beginning, that went no small way in explaining how she'd managed to earn her current position.

While I waited for a couple calming breaths to settle my stomach, I glanced around to see if we were noticed. The windows of the identical modest single-family homes lining the street remained empty of staring eyes. The factory where I'd worked stood tall and sprawling behind the trees and the five-minute walk of park space between it and the first house on the street. Gleeful shouts of children emanated from the park, assuring me that life as usual was carrying on for those with less ambitious aspirations who weren't skulking about on their doorsteps with an illegally armed, and mythical system adviser.

Confident I had myself back under control, I let Kazan inside. Her gaze darted over the few worn weavings on the walls, the glass case of medals my family had earned during the war, including the last one Chesser had received, and the scattered chaos of clothing and food wrappers.

"Looks much like your old family home," she said.

"I wasn't expecting company. Then or now."

"If you say so." She shook her head and waited in the common room in front of the medal case while I tossed clothes into my pack. My hand lingered over a still frame of Sonia, but I left it. I'd be back to visit. The silver flask she had given me for my last birthday sat beside the vid screen. This day was definitely going to require a drink. I shoved the flask inside and sealed my pack.

"If you want time to talk to anyone, we're going to have to hurry."

"She lives right down the street," I said.

"I know."

A chill settled over me along with another aggravating tingle. I had good defenses dammit, she shouldn't be able to just rifle through my brain like I was a four-year-old just coming into his telepathic abilities.

I found myself vomited out of the disorienting blackness onto Sonia's front step.

Kazan stood at my side. "You've got five minutes."

Gathering my scattered wits about me, I opened the door.

Sonia looked up from the couch, her deep brown hair rippled over one shoulder as she set aside her datapad and stood. "I wasn't expecting you back for hours. How did your trip go?"

I stepped away from the door and the woman who waited outside it. "Good, I guess."

"Did you happen to bring me anything?" Her excitement vibrated along our natural telepathic connection.

The pack weighed heavy on my shoulders, and it had nothing to do with the contents. Setting it down, I cursed myself for not remembering to pick up a shell for her collection like I always did when I traveled. Then again, maybe giving her less ammunition to throw at me was a good thing.

"Not this time."

"Are you sure?" She gave me a hug. "No trinkets, no shells, nothing," her eyebrows rose, "special?"

I returned her embrace, all the while praying she didn't notice the prohibited gun nestled against my back. The projectile weapon was a far cry from the stunner I usually carried.

Special. Oh Geva save me, with my sudden excuse of a business trip, she'd assumed I'd gone to commission a joining gift. My stomach churned again.

"Sonia, I'm sorry. It was a job interview."

Her grin vanished. "You have a job. Here. With me."

"I know, but I got a better one, one that can get us the future we talked about. I'm going to be a bodyguard for Anastassia Kazan." After the words were spoken, I wondered if I should have said even that much.

She threw her head back and laughed. "Yeah, right. She's a myth the politicians propagated so they'd have someone to blame their problems on and an excuse to drag their feet." Sonia jabbed a finger in my chest. Then her lips quirked at the corners and she winked. "If you think this wild story is going to get you out of buying me a joining gift, you are sorely mistaken, Vayen Ta'set."

I opened my mind to her, just enough to show her I was being honest about my new employer.

Her mouth dropped open and her hands fell to her sides. "She is real?"

I nodded.

"And she hired you."

"Yeah."

Sonia bit her lower lip. "And what about us? What about our bond?"

Though she was a smart woman, kind and beautiful, all that I could have asked for, we didn't have one. That was part of the reason why I hadn't used my chit to get her a joining gift yet. I wanted to let the bond form, to feel the intense protectiveness, the urge to be near her. The sense of peace and well-being other men assured me I would enjoy sounded good, but despite my efforts it hadn't happened. Maybe I was too hung up on my financial situation or the lack of satisfaction with my mind-numbing job to truly relax into it. Working for Anastassia would solve both of those problems. A little distance between me and Sonia might also help the driving urge to be near her to surface.

"We'll work it out. I promise." I kissed her on the forehead.

Sonia leaned into me, her chin resting on my shoulder.

"I have to leave for a while for training. I'll be back as soon as I can, but Kazan is talking short leaves rather than being here full time."

She stiffened.

"I know, but it's not a forever thing. Just until I get enough credits saved up."

Boots scraped on the doorstep. Could Kazan hear us or was she growing impatient?

Sonia glanced toward the door, a scowl as much in her voice as on her face. "Who's out there?"

"She is. I should go."

Her eyes widened. "You didn't invite her in? You left her standing outside? What were you thinking?"

"That I wanted a few minutes alone with you and she could wait outside for a few damn minutes if she insisted that I leave in such a rush."

Sonia laughed again. I loved that sound. It convinced me that everything would work out.

"I'll be back as soon as I can. Oh, and don't mention any of this to anyone. Leave it at I got a new job and that's all you know, all right?"

"Got it."

I kissed her once more and went to the door with my pack in hand. Sonia opened it to see Kazan waiting, annoyance heavy on her face.

"That part about hurrying? I wasn't kidding," she said to me. "For your own good," she said to Sonia, "forget I was ever here."

Sonia nodded, giving me a wide-eyed stare.

That was the last thing I saw before Kazan grabbed my arm and pulled me back into the black sucking void.

Sonia's doorstep dissolved into a paved street corner. A larger than life, stone statue of one of Artor's prominent scientists masked us from immediate view. Traffic flowed overhead and a few land transports sped past.

Nausea shuddered through me. Would I ever get used to traveling this way? I drew a deep breath and let it out slowly. Still the moist salty air of home, but it had been late afternoon when we'd left Sonia's house just a moment before. Now, late morning sunlight winked at me in the windows of a shop across the street. Great Geva, we'd traveled far around Artor again. The possibilities of the link sent my mind racing.

Kazan dropped her hand from my arm. "I have one more interview tonight. I'd feel safer with someone standing guard at the door."

I looked up and down the street. Businessmen in pressed suits with datapads tucked under their arms, mothers with children in tow, a couple of food vendors, no one that appeared to pose any threat and no one close by. Nothing suspicious on the rooftops. Traffic glided overhead, moving along in an orderly pattern. Fairly safe, but I would have preferred walls and a ceiling.

"You're meeting someone here?"

Kazan shook her head. "I have a limited number of jump points I keep per planet. The rest are more of a one-time use. There are only so many I can keep track of reliably. This just happens to be the closest point to where I need to be."

She stepped around the statue and pushed the button on the pole beside the street to summon a public transport. Kazan moved with calm assurance as she came back to stand beside me on the empty corner. The rough surface of her armored coat rubbed against the thin fabric of my shirt. Unease rippled through me. Unarmored and with a single projectile gun that I could only assume might be fully loaded—which I'd not practiced with in the seven years since I'd left military training—I prayed for the transport to arrive faster.

A white puff spouted from the statue in front of us as a bullet hit the stone just above Kazan's head. I knocked her aside. "Get down!"

I dropped my pack onto the sidewalk, yanked the gun from my pants and ducked behind the statue. People around us scattered with the silent efficiency of those who had lived through a war.

Keeping my head down, I scanned the rooftops behind us. A lone shadow darted from view. Kazan might be nothing but a myth to the general public, but someone believed in her enough to want her dead.

"Get out of here. I'm going after the shooter," I said.

"Don't bother. They're already gone."

I noticed she had a gun in her hands too, though she kept it by her side, far more inconspicuous than mine.

Following her example, I put my gun down, grateful to see that my momentary display of an illegal firearm hadn't gained us an audience. The sidewalk was empty, though it wouldn't be much longer before a vid bot showed up to document the disturbance someone had no doubt reported by now.

"If they found me that quick, they're linked too. Besides, you're going to need armor before you go chasing after anyone. I didn't hire you so you could be killed on your first day."

I put my gun away. "Do you have a different day scheduled?"

She smirked as her gaze drifted over the rooftops and the traffic overhead. "Remind me to establish a new jump point. This one is compromised. I'll reschedule the interview elsewhere."

I picked up my pack. "If most people don't think you even exist, who wants you dead?"

"Most of the people that do know I exist, and I hope that one day, you won't be one of them." She wrapped her hand around my wrist and pulled me back into the void.

Chapter Two

The Jump spit us out in the open foyer of a standard-issue Artorian home. "Where are we?"

"One of my houses. Wait here." Kazan vanished only to return moments later with Jey, who carried his pack on his shoulder and didn't look as uncomfortable with Jumping as I felt.

Her trembling hand grasped a low-walled cubicle that stood beside the foyer. With the push of a button, the lights turned on throughout the house.

Kazan caught me watching her hand and frowned. "Jumping someone without a link is taxing on the system, not to mention doing it several times in a day and adding luggage into the equation."

I nodded and focused my attention on my surroundings.

"The common room." She waved to the room behind us that contained a smattering of plain formed furniture with tan cushions. "The kitchen is through there." She pointed toward an archway off the common room. "And those," she waved toward a hall lined with doors, "are the bedrooms, where I will be going in a moment."

"And that?" I eyed the cubicle lined with vids and a terminal that closely resembled the workspace at my previous job. Except that had covered security for an entire factory complex. This was one house.

She motioned for us to come around. "This is the security station. One of you should always be here when I am in the house unless I say otherwise. The system is much the same in all of my homes." She demonstrated how to adjust the vid views and use the controls for the cameras, locks, and grids.

"Jey can take the first shift," she said.

He settled into the chair in front of the vids and smiled at Kazan. "Sleep well."

Me, he ignored completely, and that was fine. I followed Kazan to the hall of closed doors.

"This one will be yours." She nodded to the second door.

"Settle in and get some rest; we have many long days of training ahead. The kitchen is stocked if you get hungry." She opened the door across the hall and went in.

A glimpse into her room as she ducked inside yielded a view of similar bland furnishings. There was nothing on the bare floor, the storage doors were all closed. A dark blue blanket covered her bed, tucked at the corners with perfection. Her door shut.

I opened mine. For a woman who held such a powerful position, albeit a quiet and private one, I'd expected more flaunting of wealth.

The room contained a bed with two blankets folded on the end, an empty desk along one wall and a closet and chest along another. I set my pack on the chest and flopped down on the comfortable bed. The sheets smelled new, as did everything else the more I thought about it. I wondered what had motivated her to buy a new house.

As I stared at the ceiling, Sonia's face swam before me. I closed my eyes, but even at this distance there was no tug, no feeling that I had to speak to or see her. Maybe I was too overwhelmed with the excitement and uncertainty of it all.

Kazan's warnings about Kess got me thinking. I opened a natural connection with a couple members of my security team, offering an apology for my sudden exit and asking them to watch over Sonia while I was away in training.

Then I pulled out the flask from my pack and took a long drink. I settled onto the bed and opened my connection with Sonia. We talked for nearly an hour, debating ideas on how to make the best of this new position before it became clear that her earlier acquiescence about my job choice had worn off.

Kazan was no longer standing on her doorstep and the only reality was that I'd left without any warning. She began to throw accusations at me. She claimed I was trying to get out of joining with her and that maybe I'd been planning this for months.

"I don't want to fight," I said. *"It's a great opportunity."*

"For you. Not for me and not for us."

"In the long run, it will be. You've just got to trust me."

She sent a sharp burst of annoyance. *"How can I when you walked out on me like that?"*

"I didn't. I came to explain."

"Care to explain why you're assigning your people to watch me now?"

I eyed the flask, but decided against it. Patience had never been my strong point. Keeping busy was. *"So I know you're safe. Look, I have to make it through this training or I'll just end up back behind a desk, and while you might like that, it's not what I want. I'm going to close off our connection for awhile so I can focus here."*

Her aggravation spiked. *"You can't be serious."*

"I can't be interrupted, not if I want to make this job work. Send me a message if you need to talk before then, and I'll respond when I can."

She cut contact hard and fast, rather like a punch to the gut. I sealed off our telepathic connection before she decided to return and throw anything else my way. Once I had a link, I could go to her and reestablish our connection. A little time to cool off would be good for both of us.

✂

Knuckles rapped on my door. My eyes opened to empty walls and a clean floor. Not my house. The job. Kazan. It all rushed back to me as sleep fled my mind. After a moment to pull on fresh clothes, I opened my door.

Kazan stood in the foyer with another man, she in her armored coat, he in plain clothes like myself. From his dark complexion and hair, I surmised he was a fellow Artorian. Thank Geva she'd had the sense not to hire another Jalvian.

"Vayen Ta'set, this is Merkief Ma'tep."

Merkief and I exchanged amicable nods.

"Jey went to bed. You're up for a shift. Would you mind showing Merkief the controls? Now that there are three of you, I could use a few more hours of sleep before we head to the University to get you all linked."

"Sure."

Kazan yawned and headed to her room.

Merkief leaned against the wall behind me as I took my place in front of the vids. He shifted from foot to foot, taking in the general bareness of the house and finally resting his gaze on Kazan's closed door.

"She's not what I expected," he said.

"Me either."

While she'd been plenty confident when she'd been with Chesser, it was the authority she exuded now that drew my attention most. I wondered what had happened in the eight years since we'd last met that had turned her into this. Was it the link or something else?

My stomach rumbled. "Would you mind finding us something to eat?" I pointed Merkief toward the kitchen.

He returned with a handful of packaged meal bars. "Pick your flavor."

"This is her idea of a stocked kitchen?" No in-house cooks? Not even pre-made meals?

I plucked a blue foil-wrapped bar from his hand, tore it open and took a bite. If I wasn't so hungry, I would have spit it out. "How can anything so tasteless still manage to taste bad?"

Merkief laughed. He ran a hand through his short, spiky hair, a standard military cut that reminded me of Chesser. "Interesting team she's assembling." He picked a bar for himself and set the other aside.

"How so?

"Jey's served a couple years in the Jalvian fleet, you've been in security and I've been working in a lab."

I pointed to his head. "You've got the training though."

"Same as you, yes."

I rather doubted it was the same as mine, having earned the honors with which I graduated, but I nodded in favor of not coming off as a nitpicking ass. "Since it sounds like you got more background than Jey and I did, did she offer any insight as to why we're here instead of anyone else already linked and more qualified?"

"Feeling inadequate?" He chuckled. "But no, she didn't and she didn't offer any background. I looked." He reached into his back pants pocket and waved a small datapad at me before putting it back.

"Been a bit busy for that." And I'd been too tied up with Sonia to even think about doing any research of my own. That further solidified my confidence in the decision to seal off our connection.

"Would you mind showing me the controls?" he asked. "Kazan said I should get some sleep before we leave."

I gave him the rundown of the control panel along with an overview of the handwritten notes Kazan had provided, outlining passwords, protocols and various intricacies of her security measures beyond the vids and grids. We were expected to memorize everything so she could destroy the notes as soon as possible. The compiled information, even though it was off any network, seemed to make her edgy.

We chatted a bit once business was concluded. I was glad to find him good-natured and easy to talk to. I had a feeling Jey and I wouldn't be sharing many deep conversations.

After Merkief went to his room to sleep, I spent the next six hours in silence with only the flipping of vid views to keep me company. At least at my old job, there were techs to observe, a staff to give orders to, log records to fill out and the ever-present grinding and squeaking of machines churning out whatever our current contracts demanded. Here, I sat with my cheek resting on my fist, watching three people sleep. Wind blew through the four trees in the yard, the front door remained closed, and every window remained shut. The grids remained inactive. I almost jumped for joy when Kazan woke up.

Moments later, she stood beside me with the meal bar Merkief had left at the station in her hand. She ate methodically and stared at the vids. She expanded the view of the one focused on her bed.

"Some changes are in order. I'm not used to having to deal with bodyguards."

"Why? Do they usually die before you get them settled in?"

She scowled. "I've never needed them before. Sane people know better than to screw with me."

"Oh." Apparently she'd missed my attempt at humor. I averted my attention to the controls before I got myself fired.

She went back into her room. The vid view ended abruptly. Kazan returned to the station.

"Are you sure that's wise? What if there is someone in your room?"

"If there is someone in my room, I've invited them there." She picked up her wrapper and frowned upon seeing mine crumpled next to the controls. "What condition you keep your room in is up to you, but I expect the rest of the house to be kept clean. The bots will do most of the work, but you will have to make more effort than we both know you're used to."

"Sorry." I snatched the wrapper and shoved it in my pocket. "How large is the staff in the other houses?"

This being a new acquisition and small, it didn't surprise me that she'd opted for cleaning bots here. They were top of the line models, fully capable of keeping everything in order even down to the dishes and laundry.

Kazan let out a hollow laugh. "I don't trust anyone, least of all strangers, with my personal belongings or access to my food."

"Your collection of meal bars, you mean?"

She shrugged. "I don't cook. Once you get your links, the three of you can take turns importing meals. Just keep it healthy, would you? I can't afford to have any of you out of shape. And don't frequent the same place with any regularity. Predictability will get you killed."

No cooks, no cleaners, no personal assistants—not what I'd expected in the least, but that also meant fewer people I'd have to watch over. One ultra-paranoid woman seemed enough at the moment.

Kazan's face took on a distant cast. "I've called a transport. We need to get to the University to get your links implanted. We won't be coming back here for a while, so go pack your things and wake the others."

Twenty minutes later, the four of us lugged our belongings into the waiting automated transport. Two cushioned seats faced each other. Kazan took the one at the front and reached over the seat to program our destination. The three of us took the other. The low, tubular vehicle hummed to life and accelerated down the road.

Jey stretched out, crowding me and Merkief. "You've not really said, why the need for bodyguards now?" he asked.

She studied the dusky red interior of the transport. "I've had some issues lately."

Merkief leaned forward. "Just lately? I thought, you know, being in your position, that you'd be rather susceptible to *issues*."

"You have no idea what position I'm in." Kazan glared at him. "Until recently, I had a partner, Kess Atta. Our separation didn't go so well, and now he's out to kill me."

That explained the man's face she'd shown me at the interview. I shifted against the seat, assuring myself that the gun she'd given me was still there.

"How long has he been threatening you?" Jey asked.

Her fists clenched in her lap. "Too long."

I hated to be blunt, but we needed to know what we were up against. "What's stopped him from putting a bullet in your head so far?"

Jey frowned. "Only the military has access to projectile weapons and their use is closely monitored."

Kazan's fists clenched tighter, her knuckles went white. "That's what your people would like you to think, that they're all so civilized by using their stunners. But there are guns out there, the real kind, and lots of them." She laughed but there was no humor in it. "I'm lucky because heads with link implants holding the kind of valuable information that mine does, don't get top payout on the assassination market when they're filled with bullets."

Her gaze locked onto mine. "The big problem is that Kess seems to have stopped caring about that aspect. He only wants me dead."

Had it been Kess himself on the rooftop, or had he hired the job out? If it had been Kess, he now knew I existed and exactly what I looked like. And if he was anything like Kazan, it wouldn't be long before he'd know every detail about me, including the fact I was very new to this job. I stared out the tinted, narrow window, forcing myself to take several quiet, calming breaths.

After seven years of recovery efforts, signs of the war had dwindled. Buildings sported new exteriors, some the light brown stone that was abundant in this area, some the smooth white of high-end plascrete. The walks were full of people on their way to work or shop and children played outside. Street and air transports quietly hummed along their paths. It was as if the years of bombings from Jalvian ships and pulse pistols in the hands of clashing ground troops happened in distant memory.

The transport came to a stop. We spilled out onto the white stone steps of the Artorian University—the stronghold of our brightest scientific minds and home to the technology that operated the links. Sideways glances and muttered words greeted Jey. Perhaps the memories of war weren't so distant.

We followed Kazan through the initial security scans and stations, traveling deeper into the maze of corridors. She led us into a ward-like room with white walls, a table and chairs sat at its center. Six cots lined the walls. The door closed behind us.

"I am about to make a large investment in your futures. Don't make me regret it."

The three of us took a seat at the table.

"We'll stay here overnight. Kess is known to University security. I have put them on alert."

"Would he dare bother you with the three of us around?" Jey asked.

"Until you learn to use your links and get more specific training, yes."

"He's not invincible," I said.

"True, but I know what Kess is capable of. Get comfortable, pick a bed. I'm going to speak to the Link Experts. One of the LE's will be coming for Jey within the hour."

Kazan left us alone in the room. Thoughts of the ominous Kess swirled in my mind. I hoped she knew what she was doing with the three of us and that the link and the abilities it allowed would be enough. She was one of the few reasons the Narvan was holding together in a state of peace. I didn't want to dwell on what life would return to if someone took her out.

I woke with an aching head and reached up to touch the bare spot on my scalp. My fingers brushed over the tender, raised line of an incision. Kazan sat on the edge of Jey's bed, speaking in hushed tones. Merkief was still asleep. A rush of excitement passed through me. My link.

Jey's voice rose enough that I could make out what he was saying. "They'll both hear me."

Kazan shook her head. "Calm down. Link speech is similar to telepathy. Can you hear when Vayen and Merkief are talking to one another?"

Jey's gaze passed over me. "No."

I found this amusing because Merkief and I had not yet become comfortable enough with one another to create a telepathic connection.

She said, "Internal speech is more limited than vocal speech. You have to reach out to the person you want to speak to and maintain a connection. With the link, you can connect with more than one person at a time, but you still control those connections. This means you need to work on your defenses so that you can withstand probes and block connections if you so wish. Though, I don't recommend ever blocking me."

She patted his shoulder and walked toward me. *"Everything feel all right?"*

Unlike our previous telepathic exchanges, her voice now came from a different place in my head. "Yeah." I grinned like a kid given endless credits at a toy store. I tried out my link speech. It didn't take near as much effort as my natural telepathy and the connections were clear and simple to establish. *"This is amazing."*

"I told you so." Kazan sat down on the edge of the bed and showed me how to access a seemingly endless number of information sources. When Merkief woke up, she left me to my own experimenting.

I spent hours lost in maps of places I had never been, examining records and even locating my lacking credit account. Every bit of recorded information was there for the taking. All I had to do was know where to look and how to worm my way through security.

Unlike my natural mind speech, which only worked between two telepaths, the link allowed for simultaneous conversations with multiple users. I sought out Jey and Merkief's links. Touching them without words gave me a sense of their whereabouts and mood. Merkief's excitement rushed toward me along with the sensation of a big grin.

Examining everything now at my disposal kept me busy far into the night. We all practiced again after breakfast until Kazan called for a break.

"Before we move on, I want to make it clear that just because we have link speech, we will not be giving up vocal comunication." She glanced between Merkief and me. "You two might be used to it, but the majority of the known universe isn't. I understand Artorians use vocal speech as a common courtesy, and I expect you to continue that."

Kazan focused on Jey. "I want you to spend extra time working on your link speech. I'll work with you when I can, but Merkief and Vayen can also teach you how to build your defenses."

Jey, being the only one in the room without natural telepathy, appeared mortified. The mighty Jalvian was brought low, and by

Kazan's own lips nonetheless. I couldn't help but smile.

"Now that you understand information accessing, you're ready for the next step. You have all experienced a Jump. Now you need to learn to do one on your own."

The thought of traveling anywhere with a thought was exhilarating. I could grab a few more things from my house and visit Sonia without Kazan's impatient hovering or Kess seeing me there. I made a note to myself to remember to bring a shell this time. Maybe even one from another world.

Kazan paced in front of the table where the three of us sat. "Your links take energy which comes from you. Information searches will not be much of a drain, but Jumps will. You'll need to practice and build up your stamina. I have meetings all over the Narvan and traveling by ship is not an option. We will often be Jumping many times a day."

She drew a deep breath and let it out. "I'm sorry we don't have more time. You'll have to learn on the job. Finding the three of you has put me days behind schedule. Now, close your eyes."

I listened to her smooth, commanding voice. "You will need a visual. Details are important. Get as many of them as you can." Her link opened to mine, showing me the image of a paved walk surrounded by lush green grass. "The majority of my usual jump points feature a small pattern such as this one to make them easier to remember." She focused on a faint pattern of diamond shapes scratched into the stone.

"It is always safest to use a jump point you have established in person so you can be sure of what you are Jumping into. Flashed images, such as this one, will do if you have no other option. Keep in mind that if you don't get it right, you'll stay right where you are. Today that means nothing more than a headache, but in the future, it could mean getting stranded in the middle of gunfire and your death.

"Now, stand and sink into your link. Shut out everything around you except the sound of my voice. Visualize yourself in the image I flashed you and pull yourself towards it. You will feel the sensation of a snap when you have it right. Step into the void, and when you open your eyes, you will be outside the Narvan, in the Rakon Nebula on a world called Merchess."

My head throbbed with the effort to pull myself toward the vision in my mind. Something crackled and jolted within my link. My eyelids flew open.

The grey walk now lay beneath my feet. Merkief and Jey appeared beside me. I'd traveled from my homeworld to a planet outside my own star system in the matter of a single minute. The realization made me lightheaded.

Kazan appeared seconds later with our belongings. She set them down and started up the walk. "Welcome to the friendlier end of the Rakon Nebula. This is Merchess, my only holding outside the Narvan."

I took my pack from the pile and looked up to find a grey dome rather than a blue sky. Artificial light shone down upon a mansion fronted with sculptured, bar-lined balconies. Tall, narrow windows accented with priceless prism glass reflected a myriad of rainbows onto the lawn.

Inside, the expansive foyer opened into a three-story room filled with rare ivory-hued prantha hide furniture. Carved stone pillars rose to the upper levels.

This was a home worthy of Kazan's position.

She led us through the foyer to a room boasting a wall of vids. "This is the security station. Being that the Nebula is often under Fragian attack, people here don't abide by the anti-violence laws like the good citizens of the Narvan. More security is required."

Merkief gawked at the expansive control panel. "I take it Kess doesn't abide by the laws either?"

"Hardly," Kazan said. "Those laws apply to the general public, not the rest of us."

I raised an eyebrow. "Us?"

"Not you, not yet. Me, Kess and others." Her subtle head shake silenced the next question on my tongue.

Jey turned from the vid wall. "These Fragians, will they be bothering the Narvan?"

"They hold seventy percent of the Nebula right now. The Narvan is rich in resources. My guess is that once they conquer the Nebula, they'll head there next. So as far as showing up at the front door with guns in hand, probably not, but I expect a full-scale war over Merchess, its moon, Twelve, and the settlement on the hunk of ice known as Thirteen in the next year or so."

Another war. My excitement faded. The last one was far too fresh in my mind. The Narvan wasn't in a position to fend off an attack from the outside. Not to mention expecting the Artorian and Jalvian worlds to work together as a unified force.

"I've heard the Fragians have forged into advancements far

different from ours," I said.

Visions of their long, scaly faces with deep-set, round, black eyes came back to me from training. Their hands and feet were outfitted with long, sharp claws and they even sported a thin, scaled, prehensile tail that we were told they used to help fly their fighters like an extra hand. They looked like five-foot-tall, emaciated, demonic rodents.

Kazan's eyes took on a determined gleam that reminded me of Chesser when he'd talked of defeating the Jalvians. "Alternate paths of advancement, yes. I have private forces targeting Fragian ships within the Nebula. We harvest their tech, run it through the Artorian University and alter what we find to meet our needs. Which is how links came into being."

The links. The tech that Chesser died for. It was Fragians that had killed him. I caught Kazan's gaze. She nodded.

"Will your private forces be enough?" Merkief asked.

"Since I took hold of Merchess four years ago, they've tested our resolve several times, but they've not made it past us. I intend to keep it that way. War tore the Narvan apart once before. I'll not see it happen again."

Chesser's dream stood embodied right before me. Peace for my homeworld, for the entire Narvan. This one woman meant to uphold it, and I meant to do everything in my power to help her.

We left the security room and climbed the wide, open staircase to the second floor. Our footsteps echoed through the empty house. A soft clicking brought my attention to the rounded, chrome surface of a cleaning bot at my feet. Its eight legs plucked debris from the carpet at the top of the stairs and placed the particles in its mouth-like receptacle.

Bots could be reprogrammed. "Do they get sent out for servicing?"

"I have a service bot. This is a self-sustaining force," Kazan said.

I nodded, coming to fully appreciate how much her paranoia made my job easier. We followed her down a hall with widespread doorways.

"These are the bedrooms the three of you will use. Mine is down the opposite hall. I will give you half an hour to settle in and then we'll meet in my office downstairs." She headed back the way we'd come, leaving the three of us in front of the seven available closed doors.

The closest one seemed as good as any. I went in. A bed with its token blankets folded at the foot, a desk, a chest, all the same basics as before. A blank slate for me to do with whatever I wanted. All I needed to do was earn my credits so I could start filling my rooms. And time to Jump to my house to get the rest of my stuff. And, of course, visit Sonia.

I reached into my pack and pulled out the silver flask. My fingers traced the etched whorls, a pattern Sonia had drawn up herself. The same one she'd hinted at wanting on her joining gift. I sighed and set the flask on the desk.

Once I'd unpacked my things and put them away, it was time to meet downstairs. I glanced at the flask one last time and then closed the door to my room in Kazan's mansion far from Artor, Sonia, and everything I'd ever known.

Chapter Three

Kazan's office turned out to be a sparse box of a room, all hint of the opulence in the rest of the house stripped away. The only decorations were three daggers mounted on the back wall. My boots scraped across the bare brown stone floor. I sat in one of the three grey, comfortable chairs. A standard terminal and vid adorned the corner of her black, marble-topped desk behind which Kazan was seated.

It occurred to me that having nothing permanently distinctive, this room would make a horrible jump point. Maybe I was meant to keep my room plain for the same reason.

"What I am about to tell you does not get repeated. Ever." Kazan peered across the desktop at us, her lips drawn into a straight, thin line.

"Everything has a price, your life, your freedom, and the peace your homeworlds currently enjoy. And because there is a price, you can then infer that there is someone whom must be paid."

Her dead serious tone made me uneasy. I shifted in my chair.

"It is not your gods that control the known universe, but a high council who shroud themselves in secrecy and orchestrate their whims through an organization of operatives known as Kryon. I am Kryon."

The chair offered little comfort in light of the knowledge that we were all nothing more than puppets of some hidden mortals with unknown agendas. "What does that make us?" I asked.

"For now, employed by middle management and dead if any

word of this gets out."

Jey cleared his throat. "And later?"

Kazan's chair creaked as she leaned forward to rest her elbows on the desktop. "I've examined your profiles extensively. Each of you is capable of doing the things I will ask of you. You've all had training with a multitude of weapons. You know how to take orders. You have ambitions. Through me, you can realize them and become Kryon."

Merkief crossed his arms. "And just what are you asking of us?"

Kazan sat back and pulled a knife from her coat, her fingers tracing over the scrollwork etched in its silver grip. The pattern struck me as familiar. I realized it was similar to the pattern Chesser had chosen for the neckband he'd gifted to Kazan. She'd worn it to his funeral ceremony. I wondered if she's sold it or if it lay packed away somewhere, forgotten.

"Kryon approached me during my attempt to help end the war between Jal and Artor. Through them, the High Council gave me the backing I needed to bring peace to the Narvan. The Council also wanted peace. Your war had interrupted their plans and the flow of resources for too long."

So it wasn't just Kazan working some sort of magical show of power that had reigned in our armies, but this nebulous council. If they wanted to keep the Narvan at peace, I supposed I could deal with following their whims as much as Kazan's.

"The Council gave me the go-ahead to gather up the Narvan as opportunities presented themselves. We are no longer floundering in interplanetary bickering but going forward along the path the High Council has set before me. The entire system is at peace. That is an end we can all agree on, can't we?"

I nodded.

"But at what price?" asked Merkief.

"People who want to cause trouble need something to occupy themselves with—be it drugs or a smaller controlled crisis than the one they'd create if left unattended. Credits and resources must be made to flow in the correct directions. Conflicts must be mediated or dealt with quietly. Sometimes the price for peace is silencing certain voices. Permanently."

My mouth went dry. The question she'd asked during my interview echoed in my head. *Could you kill someone if I asked you to?*

"You kill people for them?" asked Jey.

Kazan put her knife away. "I do what their contracts tell me to do. Because of that fact, you have enjoyed seven solid years of peace and prosperity."

Jey sat back in his chair, staring at his hands and then the desktop, but not at Kazan. Their methods sounded rather like bribery or blackmail to me, but she had a point.

"And Kess, was he Kryon too?" I asked.

Kazan nodded. "Their contracts are involved. My position requires that I deal with the planetary governments. I can't be everywhere at once. I needed help."

Help that was much more qualified than we were, and now he was out to kill her.

Merkief grasped the arms of his chair. "And what if we say no?"

"I hope you won't. It would be a huge waste of talent that could go toward serving your people." She sighed. "You now have knowledge of the High Council, which means I must follow Kryon rules. I hate to sound overly dramatic, but unfortunately, I'd have to kill you."

~

My first real shift began with me standing in Kazan's office on Merchess, weighted down with a long armored coat and wound up in a web of holsters containing a small arsenal I prayed I'd never need to use.

"We're going to go do a job."

The way she said *job* set my nerves on edge. She planned to kill someone. I kept my hands off my weapons and loose at my sides. "Where?"

"Here on Merchess, but first we need to stop and meet a friend on Twelve." She flashed me an image. A pale blue hallway marked with four fine black lines, no longer than my little finger, along the baseboard beside a polished wooden door. Two chairs covered in smooth burgundy fabric sat outside it. Tan carpet with rust colored specks that reminded me of dried blood lay beneath them.

"When we get there, commit this point to memory. We'll be using it regularly," she said.

Kazan Jumped. I followed. She rapped her knuckles on the

door once and went in.

A man wearing a beige suit sat behind an expansive wooden desk topped with polished black stone. He bore the smooth yellow-brown skin common to Arminites but the flat facial features of a Verian. Neither were races I'd met in person before.

He smiled at Kazan and stood. His stature remained true to both sides of his heritage, bringing him up half a head shorter than Kazan.

I stepped up behind her.

His smile died. "Who is this?"

Kazan nodded toward me. "Vayen Ta'set, one of my bodyguards. Vayen, this is Marin, leader of the Assassins' Guild."

We sized each other up until Kazan cleared her throat. I tried not to hold the fact that he couldn't come up with a more original name for his organization against him.

"Bodyguards? Really, Anastassia, I don't understand why you put yourself through all this. You have a suite here that is perfectly safe. Surrounded by fellow assassins, who would think to threaten you?"

"We've talked about this, Marin."

He scowled and returned to his seat, clasping his hands on the desktop.

I revised my assessment of Kazan yet again. Not only did she do dirty work as part of Kryon, she also dabbled as an agent for Marin's lamely named guild? Whether that should have surprised or disappointed me, I wasn't quite sure, but it did make me extremely hesitant to piss her off.

"Do you have any open contracts for an Atashi Ka'opul?"

Marin consulted his vid screen. "Doubling up on your contracts again?"

"The credits all add up. If I'm going to take him out, I might as well please as many people as I can."

"I doubt that after all this time you need any more credits. What's to stop you from retiring a rich woman and enjoying the comforts of your suite here with me? We don't spend near enough time together. You've done enough — relax. Let me take care of you." He returned to the too-warm smile he'd put on when she walked in.

Kazan glanced back at me, her fingers flexing into fists and opening again. I tried to imagine her and Marin together, but I kept seeing her with my brother instead.

"We'll talk about it later," she said. "Do you have anything for Atashi or not?"

"Small. He's only a minor member within the Ka'opul family."

"Fine. I'll take it. What is needed for proof of completion?"

He scanned the vid. "You're in luck. Public acknowledgment of his death is enough. I'm assuming you need physical proof for your other contract?"

"That's none of your business," she said.

Marin locked her in a challenging stare. "In fact, it is. I like to know my competition."

I found it somewhat amusing that Marin might have an organization of his own and be intimately familiar with Kazan, but I, the new-hired bodyguard knew of the High Council and her Kryon position. He thought he had a measure of control over her, but he was only being used.

Did she make a habit of using people? I didn't mind being used as a shield, that was my job, but this level of deception used on someone who thought himself close to her, made me wary of her true nature. Had she been deceiving Chesser too? I searched my scant memories of her. Her grief had seemed real at the time, but she'd changed in a many ways since then.

"I have work to do," Kazan announced. She flashed me a location and we Jumped.

I stepped into a plain room with a mosaic tiled floor depicting a night sky full of stars. Two armed men nodded to Kazan and took note of me as we passed by.

"What is this place?" I asked.

"One of the Ka'opul strongholds on Merchess. They're the largest of the three operations here. At last count, they had thirty thousand slaves and a solid hold on the drug market throughout the Narvan, the non-Fragian colonies in the Rakon Nebula and into the Verian Cluster. They also control various other lucrative black market dealings."

"And you're fine with slavery?"

She cast me a sideways glance. "Not in the Narvan, but out here, that's how things are done. I'm not about to upset the balance of an already precarious arrangement by liberating the workforce. The families provide me with an abundant income from my cut of their profits. Usually."

"Where do those profits go that makes this excusable?"

"They keep people paid off, fund the research the High Council demands from your people, and finance the extra weaponry upgrades on the Jalvian fleets." She came to a halt. "And you can quit looking at me with that disgusted glare and be grateful the Narvan is happy and quiet and that the Jalvians are equipped to keep it that way. That was part of the deal I cut with them to get them off Artor's back."

I shoved my distaste down my throat and followed close behind as she made her way past closed doors and others that stood open, revealing small conference rooms. A woman, bearing a red slave-star tattoo on her neck, passed by with downcast eyes and a tray of half-eaten food in her hands.

Kazan came to a halt. "Here we are."

Though his family name hinted at Artorian roots, this man was of a descent so mixed that I couldn't begin to guess at the components. He sat at a rectangular table with two chairs opposite him. He stood up and offered us a tight smile. "Welcome, Kazan."

"Save the welcome, Atashi. Where are my credits?"

"Perhaps we could sit and discuss the matter?" He indicated the empty chairs and planted himself back in his seat.

"Oh, by all means, let's." Kazan sat on the table right in front of him and pulled out her knife. "So, now that we are seated, where are my credits?"

Atashi licked his lips. His gaze darted upwards. I spotted a camera in the tiled ceiling.

"The credits are tied up in investments. We need a few more days."

Kazan tsked. "You know I don't work that way. Your cousin Siro knows, too." She leaned in closer. "Did you stop to wonder why you're sitting here giving me excuses instead of him?"

Sweat broke out on the marked man's brow.

She looked over her shoulder into the camera. "His blood will not buy you more time, Siro. My cut goes into the usual account by the end of the day or you're next."

In the time it took me to blink, she'd slid off the table and moved behind Atashi to grab his chin in one hand. She slit his throat with the other. His eyes bugged out as he gasped in a futile attempt at a last breath. She let go. He slumped forward and limply tipped to the side of his chair. Blood dripped from his throat and onto the floor. Anastassia wiped her hand and her blade on his shirt and put it away. A fine spray of blood covered the table where she'd sat only a moment before.

A location flashed into my mind: a gaping black hole, steam, and plascrete pipes bearing another scratched pattern. She clamped a hand on Atashi's arm and Jumped.

When I arrived a minute later, she scowled at me. "You need to be quicker."

"I'm sorry. I'm trying."

Her scowl stayed in place. "This is one of the places I use to dispose of bodies. You'll want to remember this jump point as well."

A howl of wind came from the black pit. "You drop them down the exhaust tube to be vaporized? I thought you needed the body?"

"Good. I hope Marin does too. He doesn't need to know as much about what I do as he thinks he does." She tossed the body down the tube. "Now, we've got other, more diplomatic meetings to attend to. Let's go."

⁊

I dove into the chaotic frenzy of Kazan's life—standing behind her during droning meetings with planetary heads, sitting at the security station staring at the vids, and endless hours of listening to her mumble to herself as she read reports and evaluated requests for funding. My days were interspersed with moments of conscience-twisting uncertainty each time I accompanied her as she did the High Council's dirty work and a little of her own. I still hadn't gotten used to that. I didn't know if I ever would.

As weeks turned into a month, it felt like every time we left the safety of one of her homes, the odds infinitely increased that we'd face the next attempt by Kess. There were enough by other people to keep us on high alert. From the tense looks on Jey and Merkief's faces when we saw each other in passing, I wasn't the only one expecting a bullet with every next breath.

Jumping between planets left me with no true sense of day or night. I'd begun to think in eight-hour increments. Eight to sleep, eight to work, eight to train—they all proceeded one another in the only regularity I'd found.

Meals shifted in flavor between Artorian, Jalvian, and Kazan's occasional request for Friquen or Verian fare. My stomach didn't know what to make of half of what entered my mouth.

My head throbbed from absorbing the abundant knowledge my link offered, not to mention the constant Jumping. Every muscle ached from sparring with Kazan or Merkief. At least she'd been kind enough to arrange our rotation so that Jey and I each slept when the other was off duty.

If my previous employer hadn't sent me a message to remind me that my company-provided home was nearing the end of its obligatory two month transition status, I wouldn't have even noticed I'd been working for Kazan that long. I didn't have time to notice.

I sat on the edge of my bed in the Merchessian house, suddenly short of breath and dizzy. There hadn't been any messages from Sonia. Then again, I hadn't sent her any either. Could we recover from this?

A few minutes with my link yielded her schedule. She was due home from her shift within the hour. Having just finished my shift, I'd planned to go to bed, but that would have to wait. I owed it to Sonia to at least speak to her, and I needed to get what belongings I wanted to keep out of that house and into this one or maybe into the family home I still retained ownership of. The company home had been fully furnished so there wasn't anything big to deal with. But I wasn't supposed to be seen around my own homes. I'd have to Jump anything I wanted to keep, and I'd hadn't had much practice with transporting things yet. I was just getting fast enough Jumping myself that Kazan didn't scowl at me every damn time.

Jumping into my own home wasn't too difficult. I knew my belongings and where I'd left them well enough to form a jump point. Deciding which things I wanted to take with me was more difficult. What I didn't remove within three days would be donated or disposed of. I could only Jump so much.

Most of the next hour passed with me deciding that the majority of what was in the house didn't define me. Except for a few things I'd brought here when I'd taken the job, the important things were still in my family home. I gathered up the case of medals and the wall weaving that had been in my mother's family for generations. Some smaller belongings I put into two bags: clothes, trinkets and the like. A still frame of my parents with me and Chesser hung on the wall in the common room. I deactivated the fastener and took it down. All three of them were in uniform. I looked out of place in plain clothes, but it was the last image of us together. I paused to touch them one by one before setting the still frame on top of the clothes in one of the bags.

With my paltry pile of items assembled, there was nothing more to do than wait by the window to catch Sonia as she passed by on her way home. She lived down at the end of the street. We'd talked about consolidating into one house, but had never quite come to an agreement as to which one of us would be moving.

As I stood there, watching for her, trying like all hells to figure out what to say that might get me back in her good graces, it hit me that in months since I'd left, I'd still felt no flicker of the bond. I tried to tell myself it was because I'd been too busy, but I'd not even had the urge to need to send her message, to make sure she was all right, not even to check in with the people I'd asked to watch over her. What in the hells kind of person was I?

She deserved better, a man who could form a bond with her without it taking years, who wanted to join with her and maybe raise a kid or two. The more I worked with Kazan, even in the uncomfortable moments, I knew that wasn't me.

Maybe the years of living mostly alone had screwed with my head. Not having the predictable days and safe and secure nights I sort of remembered from childhood, I'd thought having that again would make me happy. But it turned out that I'd been a sleepwalker here, going through the motions of a normal life. Now I was wide awake, and even though several of my nights had been sleepless, the thought of forcing myself back into this place made me feel prickly all over. I shook off the sensation, and seeing motion outside, searched for familiar faces in the crowd flowing from the factory.

Employees walked by, some in groups, talking and laughing, others alone. Sonia walked behind one of the groups, one of my people lagging behind her. She carried a black bag, the one she kept her test logs in, just as she had every day we'd walked together. Head high and her lab coat fluttering with each brisk step, she passed me by. Her gaze did not drift over my house, my door, or my face resting against the window.

Despite the realization I'd never be happy here, a lump formed in my throat. Maybe it was the finality of seeing that option removed or just the unpleasant way in which it had ended.

The best thing I could do for her was to leave her alone and let her get on with her life. I'd wasted enough of it. She'd be safer without me around anyway.

Leaving the window, I picked up my bags, the case, and the weaving. I closed my eyes and stepped out of the void into the foyer of the Merchessian house. At least I'd managed to get that right. Merkief gave me a questioning glance as I passed by the security station. I ignored him and made my way up the stairs to my room.

With the remains of my life spread across one half of my bed, I sat on the other with blurred eyes. The lights, detecting no movement, eventually turned off. As she did now and then, Kazan brushed over the linked connection we shared. It wasn't as close or personal as a natural connection so I didn't mind. She was usually brief, just getting a feel for what we were doing, keeping an eye on us keeping an eye on her, I guessed. But this time she lingered.

"Are you all right?" she asked.

"I'm fine."

"You don't feel fine."

"I was just going to bed."

"If you say so." She sent the sensation of a shrug and vacated my head.

She had an odd way of doing that, seeming like she was a decent person who cared, like she still might be the same woman who had sat with me on my kitchen floor after Chesser died. But then I'd remember the things I'd witnessed her doing. Those two women couldn't resolve themselves into a single body.

Sleep sounded good, but after laying there awake for an hour with Kazan's if-you-say-so voice, Sonia walking by, and everything I'd left behind at the house whirling around in my head, I decided that wasn't going to happen. Merkief's shift would have ended by now. I went to see if I could catch him before he got busy with something of his own.

As it turned out, he was busy drinking in a small nook off the common room that was well out of immediate view of Jey, who was on duty at the station. It wasn't that the two of them didn't get along, but we all liked some space. The vids may have picked up most everything we did, but the illusion of privacy was a welcome one.

The scent of alcohol made my mouth water. "You mind?" I asked.

He shook his head and reached into the cabinet next to him to pull out another glass. An assortment of bottles of various colors and sizes sat on the lower shelf.

"She notice we're drinking her dry yet?"

Merkief chuckled. "She said that if we're inclined to drink, we should do it here where at least she knew we wouldn't do anything too stupid. I took that as she noticed, but didn't mind."

"Fair enough."

I gestured for the bottle, which he pushed toward me. I filled my glass to the top.

He nodded toward my glass. "Bad day?"

I was free of Sonia. She was free of me. As much as I kept trying to tell myself that was what I wanted, and what was best, I didn't feel at all good about it. I drained half the amber liquid in a single swallow.

"Get kicked out finally or did your housing contract expire?" Merkief sipped at his drink without looking at me directly. "I got an ultimatum when I said I was leaving for training. Took that as a sign it wasn't meant to be. I left for good that first night and sent my stuff into storage."

"Housing contract," I said.

Whether he believed me or not, he didn't push. We had both refilled our glasses before he said, "We've all had bad days. Even Jey."

I didn't really care what Jey's days were like but kept my mouth shut. Merkief's family hadn't been impacted by the war like mine had. He'd become the neutral territory of the three of us. Since Kazan had stopped nagging at us to get along, I gathered she was pleased enough with our arrangement.

A welcome, numbing warmth seeped through my body as I emptied my second glass. "It's all worth it, though, right? What she does? What we help her do?"

He stared at the bottom of his empty glass. "I have to believe the answer is yes or we've thrown everything away for a one way express trip to the ninth hell."

I nodded and went back to my room to stare at my ceiling until my body finally gave in to sleep.

❧

Kazan waited for me in the common room of her house on Jal. While I'd accompanied her to meetings on Jal a few times over the five months we'd been working together, she hadn't moved us here until now. I supposed it had to happen eventually, but since arriving three days before, I'd been unable to kick my foul mood. The homeworld of my enemies was not one of the places I'd longed to visit, at least, not without a fully armed fighter and the clearance to launch as many missiles as it took to even our losses.

If Jey had cared about all the time we'd spent on Artor in between everywhere else, he'd not visibly shown it. I conceded that as the one thing he was better at than me.

Though fairly plain like the house she had on Artor, the Jalvian house was stark and angular in design. At least she had a single unit house here rather than a suite in one of the towering plexes that loomed over the cityscape. Most of the Jalvian elite preferred plex living so they could look down on everyone else.

Bright blue walls, the same damn color as Jey's eyes, stared at me as I reported for my shift. "Where to today?"

Kazan stood up from her desk in the small office that was much like all the others she maintained. "I took a job on Merchess. It's a local one. Which means it's through one of my contacts rather than Marin or Kryon. For the most part, local contracts are quick and easy. I use them to keep in practice, try out new things, and to keep contacts indebted."

She patted down the contents of her coat. "Today we're using the contract to see what you can do."

My breath caught in my throat. I wanted to sit down, to process this announcement, but she barreled on with her instructions.

"This is your target."

She flashed me the image of a blond haired man wearing an armored coat similar to mine. His eyes were hard and his neck thick.

"He's an enforcer for the Keefe family—rivals of the Ka'opuls. Several merchants have banded together to produce enough credits to put out a contract on their overzealous tormentor."

Couldn't she sit back down and read over reports for an hour or two while I came to terms with this? I wasn't ready to take this leap.

Kazan raised a single eyebrow. "You've been looking like you wanted to kill something since we got here. I thought you'd appreciate the opportunity. What's the problem?"

Great. Now she was going to think I wasn't cut out for this. Had Merkief and Jey already passed her test?

I was really going to have to work on keeping my shit to myself and getting my face under control. Hells, Kazan had a near permanent mask of indifference. I needed one of those.

With my shoulders squared and my best impersonation of her mask, I said, "No problem, but won't his death impact your cut of Keefe profits?"

"To a small degree," she said. "The ruling families are greedy. They like to find ways to collect enough credits to offset paying me. Knowing some harmless merchant has been antagonized over protection money to the point he can't feed his kids is not something I'm comfortable with."

"But you accept slavery. I'm having a hard time following your standards."

Kazan took a step toward me and didn't look at all pleased. Though I did keep an eye on her hands, I did my best to keep my newfound mask in place while internally willing my mouth to keep my opinions to myself.

"Keeping Merchess in order has proved to be a challenge, but the High Council wanted an outpost planet to keep an eye on the Fragians."

"The Council doesn't control the Fragians?"

"Not yet, but they'd like to." she said. "If we were to go to war against them and bring them low—"

"The High Council could swoop in and do whatever it is they do."

Not that I wanted to be involved in another war. There had to be some way to prevent it.

"Exactly." She smiled and looked me over. "I know you can do this."

That made one of us. I took a deep breath, readied my Jump and prayed to Geva that Kazan was right.

The Keefe's domed city resembled the Ka'opul one Kazan lived in. The air was clean, as were the streets. However, the buildings showed chipped exteriors, slaves sported worn clothing, and the artificial light lacked a convincing luster. With Kazan trailing behind, I followed the information the contract had provided regarding the enforcer's credit extortion schedule.

He was due to arrive in a local pharmacy—a business owned by a partner in the contract and a place offered as suitable for taking the man out. Kazan had specified that we were to strive for locations out of the public eye, clean up any evidence whenever possible, and dispose of the body unless the contract stated otherwise. I wrapped one hand around the gun in my pocket and opened the door with the other.

The enforcer stood with his back to me. He leaned toward the man behind the counter. "Hand it over."

The victim's gaze darted to me, alerting the other man that he had an audience.

I pulled the gun from my pocket, not the plasteel stunner I'd carried for years, but a real black market gun loaded with bullets. Bullets that would kill a man, ending his cycle of harassment forever. Pulling the trigger of this far more permanent solution proved more difficult than I'd thought. Self defense was one thing, or protecting Kazan, but this...

A sense of urging flowed from Kazan's link to mine.

This was a small time contract, meaning I could go for a head shot. It should have been easy. I was accurate as all hells and I'd practiced for this, but he wasn't a training target. Thank Geva my hands weren't shaking, but I hoped Kazan didn't pick up on my sudden cold sweat.

The enforcer spun around. Another man sprang from one of the aisles with a pistol in his hand. I fired at the target. He crumpled to the floor with a hole in his forehead.

There, that line was crossed. The man behind the counter still appeared to be damned edgy but maybe it was just the sight of the guy getting killed in front of him. I glanced at Kazan.

"He doesn't seem too relieved."

A bullet thwacked into my coat, distracting me from her answer. The spent round fell to the floor as the impact spread across my chest, driving the air from my lungs. I fired, but that only earned me a sneer from the man I recognized seconds too late. Kess. He leveled his gun at Kazan.

Training overrode the pain in my chest. I dodged in front of her. Kazan's arm swung around me to let loose a spray of gunfire into his coat. A bullet tore into my neck. I fell back against her, gasped, and dropped to the floor.

Another shot rang out; whether it was his or hers I couldn't tell. I focused on the place where he had stood, but it was empty. A sense of distance crept over me, muffling sound and blurring the edges of my vision. The wetness on my neck didn't bother me as much as it had seconds ago. Even the pain faded.

My first contract and I'd failed. I'd killed a man, so I guessed it was fair in some universal sort of way that I'd been taken out too. I'd find out soon enough of Geva was going to call it even.

Kazan's face appeared over mine. Her lips mouthed, "Hang on."

The sensation of a Jump surrounded me. Then nothing.

Chapter Four

I woke up on a narrow bed in a cold room.

"Vayen?" Kazan sat in a chair beside me. Concern flowed from her link into mine.

My hand flew to my neck to find no evidence of my wound other than a dried, flaking substance on my skin. "I'm not dead?"

"Not today. How are you feeling?"

Like I took a bullet to the neck. Like my chest was covered in a giant bruise. But as I took a moment to bolster myself for the pain, I realized there wasn't any. I itched all over, but other than that, I felt fine.

I sat up, letting the sheet fall away to examine my bruise-free chest. "What in the—"

"You took a bullet for me and almost died." She cracked a smile. "I'd love to tell you that means a raise, but it's all part of the job."

I'd almost died. I clung to the almost part of that statement.

"How did Kess know..." I played the last moments before I'd been shot over again in my head.

"Your instincts were spot on. Kess had offered a sum large enough to entice any common Merchessian citizen to let him know where I might be."

"And you know this how?"

"I took a few minutes while you were recovering to interrogate those involved with the contract. I also made an example that should make anyone else considering turning on me to think twice."

Taking care of the problem didn't surprise me, though I wished she hadn't done it without me. I had a few choice words in mind to share with the double-crossing bastard behind the counter. Too late now.

"Speaking of recovery, how long have I been out?"

"Around seven hours."

I didn't feel like I'd been cloned, but would I? That seemed the only logical answer. "Cloning is illegal, you know."

"And I'm so concerned with being legal and all." She laughed. "Don't worry, you're not a clone."

"Then you must have some really damn good doctors."

"Something better. I'll show you." She waved me to my feet.

As I slid to the edge of the bed, I realized I was naked. The dried flakes covered my entire body. "What is this stuff?"

Kazan motioned for me to follow.

With the sheet wrapped around my waist, I followed her down a long, narrow corridor. "Where are we?"

"My private ship. No one else knows about it."

Except me. I smiled to myself as I ran my hand over my neck again, still amazed to find no hint of the bullet hole.

Stopping outside an open door at the end of the corridor, she turned to face me. "You were willing to die, so I'm going to trust you. Don't make me regret it."

I nodded and entered the brightly lit room. A sprawling piece of equipment filled most of the space. Two gurneys stood against one wall. A monitoring system took over another.

"Have you ever heard of a regen tank?" she asked.

"I've heard they don't exist."

"You owe your life to this one."

I reached back to the wall behind me to steady myself. "A working regen tank?"

"You're alive, aren't you?"

"I think so." Dead or dreaming seemed more likely.

Kazan ran her hand over the long clear tank of bubbling liquid. It rested atop a waist-high stand that was covered with small doors, indicator lights and dials. An array of tubes and wires ran from the tank and stand to a nearby terminal.

"I'm not perfect, Vayen. Jobs go wrong, unexpected things happen, and even I have bad days. I picked this up four years ago from a trader while on a job far from the Narvan. It cost me a fortune, but it's paid for itself many times over."

"How long was I in there?"

"About three hours. It was a pretty straightforward wound. The resting afterward is what eats up the time."

A silver metal platform lift attached to the tank caught my notice. If we were alone on the ship...

"How'd you get me in there?"

"Not very easily," she said. "The gurney helped. Once I got you on that, I raised you up and rolled you onto the platform, but you're heavy." She shook her head. "Thankfully, the tank healed any bruises from when I dropped you."

I stared her down. "You dropped me?"

Kazan headed for the door. "Well, once I got you undressed, with all the blood—Sorry, you were slippery."

She'd undressed me. I'd been floating naked in a clear tube for three hours. Medical staff dealing with such things wouldn't have bothered me, but this was my boss. I clutched the sheet around my waist.

Kazan glanced over her shoulder, but not fast enough to hide the smirk on her lips. She led the way back to the room we'd come from.

I willed the heat from my face and managed an indignant, "You dropped me."

"I said I was sorry."

Though I couldn't see her face, I swore the smirk was still there.

I cleared my throat. "So how does the tank work?"

"It doesn't without a profile. I had the University create one for each of you when you got your links. Get cleaned up then I'll show you how to operate the tank. If I'm ever wounded beyond the ability to Jump myself and set up the sequence, the tank is useless." She pointed across the hall and then ducked out of the room before I could ask anything further.

The bathroom provided a long, hot shower. The shower provided enough time for a hundred questions to form. And so when the steam cleared to reveal a blood-free change of clothes waiting on the counter, I got dressed and went to find some answers.

Kazan sat in the chair beside the bed with a distant look in her eyes. "Feel better?" she asked.

"Not big on privacy, are you?"

"I thought you'd be more comfortable in clean clothes rather than dashing across the hall naked."

"About that."

She rolled her eyes. "Yes, I've seen you naked. Kind of hard to avoid that when you were dying and all. I've seen naked Artorian men before."

Had she and Chesser ventured beyond our natural telepathic pleasure sharing into full physical relations? I wondered if he'd managed to receive the correction procedure even though they'd not yet been joined. Without it, he'd remain impotent. Though, I supposed there were other ways of pleasing non-Artorian women. I shook my head and tried to banish the thoughts of whatever my brother had done with the amused-looking woman before me.

"Something on your mind?" she asked.

I sat down on the bed. "Kess killed me. How am I supposed to protect you?"

"But he didn't kill you, and you did protect me."

I remembered the pain of the bullet in my neck quite vividly. The tank may have saved me this time, but would I be so lucky again? "Yeah, right."

Kazan took a sudden interest in a latch on her coat, picking at it with her fingernails. "Train more. Get better. Don't let him win. I'm counting on you."

Kess's win would mean Kazan's death. Her death meant less resistance on the Fragian front and Jal and Artor would be back at each other's throats in no time.

Protecting Kazan from random attacks by disgruntled political parties, I could handle. The distant threat of a Fragian war would happen when it happened, and I would stand beside Kazan while she called out orders in a safe bunker somewhere. But this damned Jalvian who had killed me on my first job, he would haunt my dreams until one of us was dead. And if I managed to kill him, I wanted to make sure he stayed that way.

"He doesn't have a tank, does he?"

"I highly doubt it. Working ancient tech like that is hard to come by. I'm sure most were dismantled to engineer the easily-manufactured topical version of healing gel most everyone is familiar with now. As you can see, the tank is far more effective. I've never found another one on the market, and I've looked. The last thing I need is for Kess to get his hands one."

"Anyone he would be working with that I need to know about? Any other exes?"

"None that are living anyway."

"Well that's reassuring. I think."

Kazan cracked a smile. "You remind me so much of him."

"Who?"

"Your brother. You even share the same sarcasm." She closed her eyes for a long moment before regarding me again. "He'd be proud of you."

A lump formed in my throat. I swallowed it down. "You too. You helped end the war, just like he fought so hard to do."

Tears gathered in her eyes. She blinked them away. "I owed him."

Witnessing her mask dissolve caught me off guard. I shifted on the bed, resting my back against the wall, trying to put a little more distance between me and the unsettling visage of the woman I'd known before in the form of the one with my blood still on the sleeve of her armor. In fact, it was all down the front of her coat.

She seemed to notice my gaze and come to the same realization. "I guess I'll need to get that cleaned."

Kazan stood and peeled off her armor. She carefully draped it, less bloody side down, over the chair and stood there, looking around the room. I'd seen that look before, the same one the softer woman had worn just before she'd bolted out the door.

"Seems to me he owed you," I said, hoping to lure her into staying for once. Without the coat and uncompromising expression, she wasn't quite as intimidating.

She moved to the door, but didn't open it. Instead she leaned against the wall beside it. That was progress, I supposed.

"It was more of a mutual owing," she said slowly. "I'd ended up in the Verian army during the Jalvian invasion of Prime. They were using us for additional food and supplies while they fought you since Artor was no longer supplying them."

"Veria Prime didn't put up much of a fight from what I heard. No offense."

She shrugged. "Prime isn't known for its military prowess. It made for an easy target. As did Veria Minor, which put up even less resistance."

Kazan eased off the wall and took a couple steps toward me. "You've probably noticed that I look far more Jalvian than you do."

"A spy? I asked.

"By necessity, yes. Again, not my first choice of occupations. After a crash course in the language, I was a passable half-breed as long as I didn't bring too much attention to myself. I'd returned to the port station above Veria Prime where I'd lived previously. That's where the Jalvians had set up command to control their exports and where I met Chesser. He wanted what I knew."

"And what did you get out of the deal?" I asked.

"Your forces were much better suited for a resistance. Once we did end the war, Jal pulled out of the Verian Cluster, making my people nearly as happy as yours."

She took another couple steps forward until she was at the bed. I moved over and nodded toward the open space.

"I suppose I owe you a bit too for taking his attention away from you." She gingerly hoisted herself up onto the bed.

Her cautious movements urged me to give her a quick once over. "Were you wounded?"

"Just sore from lugging you around. You're not exactly light." She laughed softly.

After sitting there, examining her fingernails for a couple minutes while I tried to think of something to say that wouldn't send her rushing for the door again, she said, "If you want to, I'd like to share a few memories of Chesser with you. Through the link, I mean. It's easier than your way."

"Yes, of course," I blurted. It hadn't occurred to me that she would know how or want to do something so personal. I opened my link to her, my excitement removing any reservation about giving her open access to my head.

Flashes of memory began to play like vid clips in my mind. At first it was disorienting, being behind her eyes, hearing what she had, and feeling what she felt at the time, but then the illusion of being in the moment settled in around me.

Chesser, out of uniform, stood at a bar. A Jalvian harassed him. Anastassia felt bad for him. She spouted off a string of insults that convinced the Jalvian to leave.

In another, Chesser sat across from me at a table, eating and laughing. "Vayen's pissed at me again. He really wants to meet you."

Caught up in seeing my brother, eight years gone, brought to life again, sent me reeling. These weren't my glossed over memories, they were hers, her perceptions of a man she knew very little about. She liked the look of him, how he smelled. That struck me as an odd thing for her to remember so vividly in that moment. Apparently she hadn't been hanging on his every word either.

"You'd like him," Chesser said. "He's going to show me up one of these days, too damn smart for his own good."

Outside the memory I couldn't help but snort. Show him up? Hells, I'd all but ceased to exist except for the select few people that saw Kazan in person while I was on duty. I couldn't recall him ever saying anything that complimentary to my face.

That memory flickered to another where Chesser sat beside me in a cockpit, patiently explaining the controls.

It was so strange to see this other side of him. I didn't remember a time where he'd patiently done anything. But for her, he had.

Another flicker. At a table again, this time dressed in a crisp white shirt. With a nervous grin, Chesser handed me an ornate square box.

The pounding of her heart was mine, as was the excitement and then confusion as he spouted off a barrage of formal sounding words I didn't understand. I hadn't taken into account that Chesser might have slipped into Artorian when he'd gifted her rather than the common trade language Kazan used.

Her faltering voice broke the stream of memories. "The details of his death were classified at the time, but we're beyond that now." She glanced at me. "Do you want to know?"

"I do."

She'd dropped enough hints that I knew the general circumstances, but she'd been there. She could show me and then I'd know once and for all if I could really trust her in spite of what she did in her Kryon work.

She rested her head back on the wall. "We were on our way home after completing a mission near Jal. Chesser talked endlessly of enjoying some time off and spending it with you." She offered me a sad smile. "He said that he hadn't left on good terms."

I shook my head, not wanting to think about the last leave we'd both squandered.

"Near Artor's space, we ran across a wounded Fragian vessel. We figured it was scouting and got caught in the crossfire somewhere along the line. Chesser knew Artor was losing the war with Jal. He was convinced that the ship full of Fragian tech might sway things back in Artor's favor. We detected life, but he felt the risk was worthwhile."

She shook her head. "For the record, I tried to talk him out of it. I even used you to try and change his mind."

While I appreciated her sentiment, I knew how stubborn Chesser could be, especially when it involved anything to do with the war. It was the topic of the argument that had gotten out of hand and got the enforcers called on Chesser and I.

Kazan drew a deep breath. A wave of sorrow through our shared link connection warned me of what was to come. Her memory flooded over me, taking my breath away with its intensity.

A heavy rain of gunfire filled my head. Chesser stood beside me, shooting at a crowd of oncoming Fragians. His eyes narrowed, a determined look carved into his face. He bled from numerous small wounds. One Fragian after another dropped until only a few remained. A voice cried out beside me. I turned to see Chesser on the ground with his hands clasped over his stomach.

Despite the gunfire around us, I dropped down to pull him behind cover. I held him, with hot tears streaming down my face as the life faded from his eyes and he went still, a limp, unbearably heavy weight in my arms.

A torrent of grief, both hers and mine, collided within my mind, knocking me out of her memory. The warm wetness on my face remained after I came back to myself. I raised my hand to wipe my own tears away, only to find it was firmly entwined with hers.

"Sorry," we said simultaneously. Our fingers released.

Kazan stood and kept her back to me. Her voice was stiff and forced. "I have to go check on a couple things. Give me a few minutes."

She grabbed her coat and made her long delayed exit from the room. The door closed behind her, leaving me alone once again.

I basked in the joy and grief of her shared memories and the pleasant sensation of her hand in mine. It had been months since I'd touched anyone in such a manner. I didn't realize until just then how much I'd missed even common trivial touches.

Kazan returned fifteen minutes later with clean armor and her emotions tucked back under her mask of control. "We need to get back soon."

"All right." I slid to the edge of the bed.

"I need to ask you something first."

Her gaze once again darted around the room before settling on me. I didn't know what she intended to ask, but after what she had shared, I felt better about possibly agreeing to it. I'd seen without a doubt that she did in fact have feelings. Intense feelings, that she kept buried deep inside. She wasn't the jaded and soulless killer she portrayed to everyone else. The woman I'd first met and liked was in there.

All I needed to do was almost die to bring out that part of her. How often did I feel like getting killed so I could enjoy an honest and open conversation?

Kazan took my armor off the hook beside the chair and tossed it at me. I caught it before it hit the bed.

"I'm not accustomed to bodyguards, but I have always worked with a partner, someone I can depend on and trust, at least to some degree. Are you ready for a promotion?"

∼

When we returned to her Jalvian house, Merkief and Jey were sitting in her office, waiting. Both of them watched her like she might explode at any moment. I don't know what kind of reaction she'd expected upon making her announcement, but I was glad I wasn't sitting next to either of them. I'd elected to stand by the door in case I needed to make a quick exit to help diffuse the situation.

"Partner?" Jey shot from his seat to stand beside the desk. Fury shown in his eyes.

"Sit down," Kazan demanded. "Things are going to change for all of you. Vayen and I work well together, that's why I chose him. Merkief, I have several projects on Moriek that would benefit from your attention."

I endured Jey's blatant glare while Kazan spoke silently with Merkief.

Kazan called out, "Jey."

He turned back around to face her.

"You will be my new liaison with the Jalvian military."

The protruding veins on his forehead subsided somewhat.

"Your shift rotation schedule will remain the same. Whatever other duties I may ask of the three of you, they will not interfere with your primary function as bodyguards. Once Kess has been dealt with, we can move on to further opportunities.

"Kess targeted Vayen on our last job. You will all need to be extra careful, which brings me to the tank." Kazan rubbed a hand over her face. "I've never given anyone else access. Kess was there once, but he was unconscious and I Jumped him elsewhere before he woke up. I'd prefer the three of you didn't know about it either, but I'd rather not have to hire more bodyguards. Keeping you alive with the tank is the most logical option."

She went on to explain the ship and the regen tank to Jey and Merkief. "We will need to practice Jumping one another so that if a dire need for the tank occurs, we can Jump in seconds rather than minutes. The more familiar you are with each other, the easier it will be. Feel free to practice going to the ship; it's the one safe location I've got."

My neck itched. How many more times would I die for her?

Chapter Five

When I reported for my next shift, I found Kazan in her office straightening a stack of datapads on the metal desktop with one hand and kneading her right temple with the other. If she'd slept, it hadn't been for long. She'd seemed brittle and on edge. I stood, waiting silently rather than stepping into that minefield.

She finally acknowledged me with a heavy sigh. "As my partner, there are certain people you'll need to know. That means additional jump points. Are you ready?"

How many of the damned points did she keep in her head? It had taken me months to master the first batch.

"Sure."

She flashed me the image of a wall of crates, a peeling grey floor covered in dirty boot prints, and a girder-lined ceiling with an etched pattern above my head.

We Jumped into a corner in a vast warehouse filled with the beeping of automated mover units stacked high with crates bearing Jalvian labels. Three armed men in blue uniforms stood nearby. They nodded to Kazan.

Men and women ran their fingers over datapads as they walked among rows of sacks and long lines of various metal and formed plas parts that I didn't recognize.

"New inventory." Kazan pointed me toward a hallway.

The wide passage bridged two warehouses and was lit by a long row of windows. While the people around us were mostly Jalvian, the city had a dome. We were on one of the engineered

planets within the Narvan. The sky projection was fairly convincing and the generated light was of a natural spectrum, marking
it of Artorian quality. Jal had made a couple passable attempts
at altering planets, but they'd never bothered to fabricate domes.
That might make life comfortable for their citizens and that
wouldn't spur them on to conquer new worlds.

From the glimpses of other warehouses surrounding us and
the deep hum of large amounts of traffic, I gathered we were in
a port city. Somewhere, far above us, through a system of air-
locks, massive spaceships loaded and unloaded freight into a
hub station. The transports that flew overhead within the dome
distributed goods to the correct storage facilities.

"Are you done ogling the scenery?" Kazan asked.

"Are we on Rok?"

She nodded.

I'd been here on meetings with her, but they'd all been inside.
The war had begun here with Jalvian forces exterminating the
Artorian colonists. We'd upset the equal balance within the
Narvan by claiming one world too many, according to them. Not
like they knew how to alter them properly. Visions of the Jalvian
world of Syless and its perpetual whipping winds filled with
orange sand came to mind.

We came to a stop at a closed door. Kazan knocked and went
in before anyone answered. I tried to block out where we were in
favor of focusing on who I was supposed to meet.

A Jalvian teetering on the far reaches of middle age glanced
up from his littered desktop and grinned. "This is a welcome surprise." He stood and motioned for her to sit in the chair across
from his desk.

"Vayen, this is Gemmen. He runs Cragtek for me."

I sought any mention of the company but found nothing.
"And what would that be?"

Kazan grinned at Gemmen. "Your security measures seem
to be working just fine." She waved me to the empty seat beside
her. "Our company of re-appropriated goods. They make forays
into trade routes beyond the Narvan and Rakon and also raid the
Fragian forces in the Nebula. This is the private army I told you
about."

After learning about everything else that Kazan was involved
in, the knowledge that she employed an army of thieves didn't
exactly shock me. I rather wished it had. Each morning my con-

science objected a little less to what I'd learned and done the day before.

Kazan turned back to Gemmen. "Find anything good in this last batch?"

"Nothing the University hasn't seen before, and the few Fragians we've managed to capture all took their medicine before we got to them."

I glanced at Kazan. "Medicine?"

"A mind wipe pill they take. It would seem that they don't count on their soldiers to be zealous enough to take a suicide pill so they issue an eraser instead. We believe it's in the hopes that if they escape, they'd remember enough to know where to return in order to relay what they've learned while they'd been held."

"How much does this drug wipe?" I asked.

"We can't tell exactly," Gemmen said. "Estimates are somewhere between a month and a year. Certainly long enough to lose their mission, and often, enough to lose any helpful knowledge of the supplies or tech we've taken from them."

Kazan scowled. "It's been an ongoing aggravation."

She turned to Gemmen. "I'd like to take a quick look anyway and have a word with the scouts. That should give the two of you a few minutes to get acquainted." She got up and walked out, sealing the door behind her.

Close-cropped blond hair on Gemmen's square head and a scarred face distinguished him from the average vain Jalvian. His eyes held the same unyielding strength as Jey's, but they lacked the arrogance. He sat back and offered me an easy smile.

"So she picked an Artorian? Have to say, I didn't see that coming." He jutted his chin at the door. "Rather partial to Jalvians, that one."

I shrugged. "She knew my brother."

His eyes nearly disappeared in the deep creases surrounding them as he laughed. "Kazan's known lots of men."

I gritted my teeth. "They were to be joined."

"Really?" He let out a low whistle. "And here I thought Marin was the only one stupid enough to try to tie her down." He shook his head and shifted a few things around on his desk. "And here you are, her partner. She owe some huge debt to this brother of yours?"

"Excuse me?"

"I've not heard of you before, and she's usually one for picking a partner with an established reputation. Keeps the rabble quaking, if you know what I mean."

'She's desperate' didn't sound like a stellar endorsement. "Maybe she's trying something new."

Gemmen chuckled. "You might be on to something there." He looked me over. "I won't call myself an expert on Artorians, but with that bonding trait bred into you, I'd think this situation would offer all sorts of problems."

My hand rested on a gun at my side. "Just what do you mean by that?"

"Relax. I'm just saying that I know how you lot get attached to your mates. Kazan's not one you want to do that with. She's not your typical good-natured Artorian woman, ingrained with urges to settle into blissful monogamy."

"I'm not an idiot."

He held up his hands. "Didn't say you were. Just remember that I warned you. She's a good woman, in her own way. I'd hate to see another partner turn on her, especially over something as simple as incompatible urges."

Gemmen continued with his futile efforts to create order on his desk. "Now then, if you ever need a ship, come see me. Our company ships are better equipped than any of the planetary forces."

"I'll keep that in mind."

He struck me as odd for a Jalvian, maybe because I'd not met many who had moved past their younger, violent years. It was hard to believe we'd all been one people once, yet Gemmen proved we shared a middle ground, something between conquering and a driven desire for expanding minds and tech.

Kazan's voice interrupted my thoughts. *"Next stop."* She flashed me a jump point.

"I'll be right there."

Her presence left my head. "It seems I'm needed elsewhere."

He nodded, his smile returning. "Good luck to you. Keep her safe." His voice dropped to a mutter I wasn't sure if I was supposed to hear. "I wouldn't wish that job on anyone."

Despite him being Jalvian, I didn't mind Gemmen. Too bad Jey wasn't fifty-some years older; we might have been better off than tolerating one another.

I concentrated on the image Kazan had given me. A stand of tall trees, brown leaves under my feet, a wooden house and sunlight filtering through a canopy of leaves.

A step into the black void later, I found myself next to her. She stood with her eyes closed, her face lifted to a beam of light shining through an opening in the leaves overhead. The Narvan's smallest planet, Frique.

She turned to me and smiled. "Beautiful, isn't it?"

"The word that comes to mind is hot."

Damn humid and hot. And smelly—heavy and pungent, like a herd of prantha lurked close by. My nose twitched and I sneezed. Sweat trickled down my brow. Leave it to backwards-minded, tech-despising Artorian rebel extremists to skimp in the initial planetary alterations and refuse to correct their mistake afterward. How did these people put up with the heat?

Kazan cast me a questioning glance and then shook her head. "Oh yes, I'm speaking to one of those climate-conformist Artorian minds. Not everything has to be totally engineered, you know." She headed toward the single-story house. "I suppose you'd rather cover this natural sky with a dome or move civilization underground so you'd have control over every little detail?"

As if a planet full of prantha herders and farmers warranted use of the word *civilization*. "You'll notice there are no domes over Artor."

She stopped at the door and rolled her eyes. "Of course not. You've got the entire planet rigged for perfect weather and maximum crop production with your thousand satellites and an army of agri-networks. I'm talking about every other planet your people have touched that didn't quite conform to your ideals."

I tried not to let her tone get under my skin. "We didn't touch Jal or the settlements on Syless. Blame them for their substandard efforts to mimic our tech."

The lock on the door clicked and she opened it. "Them? They were you until your great and all-knowing civilization fractured."

Arguing history with Kazan wasn't something I yearned for. I let her words dissipate while I examined her home. An extreme departure from the luxury of Merchess and the cold manufactured blandness of her homes on Artor and Jal, this house boasted wood floors with thin grass rugs that did little to absorb the sound of our footsteps. Bare wooden walls lined with tall windows echoed our every sound. One stone wall with a fireplace at its center broke the wooden monotony. At least the air was cooler inside. I sat down on the couch and found it more comfortable than expected.

Kazan stood at one of the windows, gazing out into the forest.

"And who are we meeting here?" I asked.

She turned to glare at me. "No one. After all your peering around on Rok, I thought you might like to see Frique."

The Artorian worlds, Moriek, Karin and Artor itself, provided ample lumber, livestock and food supplies, enough even to supplement what the Jalvian worlds' inferior systems failed to provide. Frique was so small and inconsequential that it garnered no interest by Jal or Artor, even though we'd colonized it long ago. It offered no rare minerals or gasses, no caches of metals suitable for weapons or shipbuilding, nothing that warranted Kazan's attention. Its scattered population of farmers and tradesmen weren't the sort to yield contracts on any level, and even its politicians had few demands of her.

Was I missing something important? I'd figured out Rok from a few visual cues but this backwoods hothouse refused to share its significance, even after a few minutes of rampaging the local networks with my link.

"How is it that you can be so observant, yet so blind?" She sighed and turned back to the view of trees, dirt, and beating sun. "We have another stop to make."

The disappointment in her voice gnawed at me. I prayed the next stop yielded something redemption-worthy.

The flashed image solidified into a steel alcove with a narrow line of symbols etched in the wall. We stepped out to find two men in grey uniforms with guns at their sides. They nodded to Kazan and looked me up and down once before resuming their blank-eyed stare at the alcove.

"High Council guards," she said as she led me down the wide hallway.

No windows, no particular shift in temperature or smell. Sere, the Kryon base, I deduced, but I wracked my brain for a hint of where that might actually be. According to all the information I had access to, Sere didn't exist. Neither did the High Council and there definitely weren't any maps available to help me look like I had an idea of where we might be going.

She led us into a small room where two men stood talking. The men halted their conversation as we drew closer.

"And who is this?" The thinner of the two looked me up and down. He appeared to be Artorian, but he sported several feature alterations—light brown curly hair, high cheekbones, and deep blue eyes.

"Fa'yet, this is Vayen."

"Ah. I've heard quite a bit about you." He offered me a friendly smile. "Finally letting you out, is she?"

"Shut up." Kazan swatted his shoulder. "I need to go check for contracts."

"Go on. I'll make sure he doesn't get into any trouble."

I turned to watch her leave. The other man followed her out the door.

"You're younger than I pictured. Not that she gives me much solid information to go by."

Standing next to Fa'yet, I did feel young. Not necessarily because I guessed him to be twice my age, but because he carried a sense of power and absolute confidence coiled in his wiry frame.

"It's not just me then?" I asked.

"Hardly." Laughter filled his artificial eyes. "Your first Kryon contract?"

"I suppose."

He grinned and shook his head. "She's really got you in the dark, hasn't she? Can't say as I blame her after Kess. Come on, I'll give you the quick tour."

Plain, steel halls greeted me at every turn. The rooms we passed were small, unadorned and entirely utilitarian in their furnishings. Men and women in grey uniforms shared the halls but never paid us more attention than a passing glance.

Fa'yet followed my gaze as one of the grey-suited men passed by. "Don't call any attention to yourself, and they'll leave you alone. High Council puppets," he muttered. "Trust me, you don't want their notice."

He stopped in front of a clear plaz door. I spotted Kazan inside, sitting across from a grey-suited woman at a desk. A vid screen sat between them.

"This is where we are assigned contracts."

Fa'yet pointed to other rooms as we passed. Rooms where trials were held for errant members, rooms where one should not go unless summoned, the room where we were to report when a contract was completed, and at last, Kazan's quarters.

"I let her know she could find us here." He palmed the pad on the wall and opened the door. "You look like you could use a moment to let this all sink in before heading out to whatever she's picked up for the two of you."

"Thanks."

Five months ago, my days consisted of filling out daily logs, breaking a good sweat in the gym, going home to dinner, and maybe spending a couple hours in front of the vid before a full night's sleep. It was boring and predictable and I'd dreamed of more. More, at the moment, was pretty damn overwhelming. I took a seat in Kazan's quarters on a secret base full of advisors, assassins, thieves and whomever else the High Council employed to do their bidding throughout the known universe.

Fa'yet sat and adjusted his long coat, similar to mine, though well worn and far past any hint of stiffness in its dense armored weave. "I've known Kazan a long time. She can be difficult to work with, as I'm sure you know by now." He gave me a quick smile. "I'd rather not see another partner turn on her, so if you ever feel the need to talk, come see me."

His link opened to mine, establishing a connection so that we could contact one another without Kazan. Then he flashed me the image of a tall home sandwiched between two others against a skyline. I recognized it as being on Artor's moon, Karin, the one place in the Narvan Kazan held no official control over. Maybe Karin was too insignificant to bother with, or more likely, since she had her hand in tiny Frique, she'd just not gotten around to it yet.

Since I sat alone with someone who had information about Kazan and the seeming willingness to share it, I didn't waste time. "You mentioned Kess. What happened between them that has her so worried?"

Fa'yet licked his lips and glanced at the closed door. "Not really my place to tell. In fact, I wouldn't ask her just yet either. She took his defection quite hard. Never know what that woman will do when she gets upset."

"How many have there been?"

"Two."

So she'd managed to kill one. At least that gave me some hope of survival at her side.

"What happened with the other one?"

"Another time maybe." He kept an eye on the door and seconds later, it opened.

Kazan walked in. "I hear you got the tour. Ready to go?"

"I guess."

"I'll leave you to it then." Fa'yet nodded his farewell in my direction and brushed his hand over Kazan's shoulder as he passed by.

She cast a smile at him and then focused on me. "I picked a simple job for your first Kryon contract."

Somehow I doubted that any contract worthy of a Kryon member was simple, but I Jumped to the location she flashed me all the same.

Flanked by two stone columns, we stepped from the void into a long hall with high ceilings and several matching pair of columns lining the distance to a wide set of doors at the far end.

"What's our objective?" I asked.

"A Sylessian official needs to be silenced."

I'd accompanied her on several Kryon contracts, but this was the first time in an official capacity. Before, I'd watched her back while she went about her business. This time, she expected me to take part.

Music struck up somewhere on the other side of the door. When I strained to listen, I made out the muffled conversations of men and women. "What's going on?"

"Party of the rich and influential. He's a guest."

"We're going to walk into a party and kill the guy?" Maybe Kryon standards were a little more relaxed than the ones she'd impressed upon me before.

"Do we look dressed for a party?" She gave me a dry stare. "No, we're going to get close to the entryway and wait for him to step out for a smoke. He's got a good addiction going. I doubt the allure of rubbing elbows all night is enough to keep him from it."

"How do you know about his addictions?" She'd just taken the contract ten minutes ago for Geva's sake, not near enough time to dive into a full rundown of the target's history and routines.

"Through Kryon, the High Council often disperses or controls the flow of drugs to those under their watch. It's always good to have something to use to your advantage when needed."

"A bit all-knowing of them, isn't it?"

Kazan patted down her coat and shrugged. "I don't ask questions. Just do your job and try not to over-think things. That's the best policy."

"I'll keep that in mind." I ran my hands over my own coat, feeling for the right bumps in the right places. With everything in order, I followed her.

The hallway proved to have a decent collection of art set between more of the thick stone columns. Further down and across the hall, two guards stood near the set of doors, more interested in trading stories of their weekend conquests than actually guarding anything. The music grew louder, a mellow refrain that masked all but the general murmur of conversation inside.

"How many people are in there?"

"Doesn't matter. The point is to keep any of them from seeing you and to kill the target the moment he's out of their sight so we can get paid."

Put in her terms, the job did seem pretty simple. I stuck to the shadows against the wall and positioned myself behind a column to remain hidden from the guards.

Kazan kept one hand on a gun at her side and her gaze locked on the open doorway. The guards yammered on about a woman they discovered they'd both been with.

After forty minutes of waiting and two false alarms, the man we'd been sent for walked through the door. I checked his face against the image Kazan had shared with me—pale skin, shoulder-length, straight blond hair, long nose, wide-set eyes and a pair of ears that made him unmistakable, sticking out as they did.

"That's him." Kazan slipped back to watch him walk past us and out the way we'd come. "After he turns the corner from this main hall, we've got about ninety seconds before he reaches the outside doors. Not much time for error. Follow me."

Sticking close behind her, I listened to the guards, making sure they kept to their conversation and that no one else left the room. Kazan drew her gun, as did I. We followed as the target rounded the corner.

He stood ten feet away by a pair of columns and appeared to be admiring a large still frame mounted on the wall. Kazan fired.

The target leapt back. The bullet chipped off a shard of the stone column. The sound echoed through the hall. How could she have missed such a perfect shot on an unsuspecting target? I raised my gun, readying a shot to take him down the second he popped into view. The heavy thunder of boots pounded toward us. Damn guards.

A hand snaked around the column, pointing a gun right back at us. What in the nine hells was our targeted government official doing carrying a projectile gun, let alone at a public party? I gave him a second, waiting for a shot at his head when he peeked around to fire at us. Seconds stretched into ten and then twenty, turning the guards' footsteps into a nightmarish drawn-out hammering that fell in sync with my heartbeat as it thudded in my ears.

Kazan fired again and again, expending her rounds as did our target. Stone shards filled the air all around our heads and his. My ears rang and I lost track of the sound of the guards.

Keeping the target in sight, Kazan reached into her coat for a new clip.

He didn't peek. He fired.

Kazan stumbled back, crashing into me. I let loose a bullet and a prayer that it would find a home in the bastard's flesh. She faltered on her feet and slid to the floor.

Oh Geva save me, she'd been shot. She wasn't supposed to get shot! I was supposed to be in front of her, protecting her. But I thought she knew best. She certainly seemed capable. She'd been doing this on her own for years. Now she lay limp at my feet with blood dripping from the collar of her coat onto my boots. Shit.

I opened my link to her and was bombarded by pain and shock. I had to get her to the tank.

The target stepped out from behind the columns with his gun trained on me. He froze for just a second as he took in Kazan on the floor. I shot him, or at him anyway. He vanished before the bullet made contact. She'd made no mention that the target might have a link.

Time set itself to rights in a rush of barely audible shouts as the guards rounded the corner. I shoved my gun into a holster. With shaking hands, I grabbed Kazan and formed a Jump to the ship.

Half an hour later, I sat monitoring the tank displays while rubbing my throbbing temples. Jumping her hadn't been easy. I wasn't used to her being wounded, not to that extreme. At the edge of my vision, Kazan floated above the platform, naked and submerged in the clear gel.

I couldn't help but go over those gunfire-filled moments. They played in an endless loop, showing me how I'd failed to keep her safe, how the target anticipated her moves, and how I'd failed to get off a single worthwhile shot. Would Jey have done a better job? Or Merkief? My fingers formed fists, near ripping the hair from my scalp.

The pain didn't help anything. It didn't make Kazan heal any faster, and it didn't make the memory of my failure fade.

The tank required no action on my part other than getting Kazan on the platform and activating her profile, yet I couldn't leave the room. The display wasn't enough. I needed to see her healed. If she died, I had no idea what kind of hell the Narvan would become.

Over three hours had passed before the platform rose from the tank, bringing Kazan's gel-drenched body within my grasp. I draped a crisp, white sheet over her, covering everything below her still face and wet hair.

I left the cold gurneys against the wall and instead scooped her into my arms, doing my best to ignore the curves in my hands and sorely failing. Kazan's head rested against my shoulder as I carried her from room to room. Her hair left wet streaks on my coat as I walked. The ship was fairly small, with only four rooms containing beds and a handful of others used for other purposes. I found the one that contained enough of her things to signify it as the one she slept in. After laying her on the bed, I covered her with a blanket and sat back to wait.

The waiting ate at my nerves. I went back to the tank room and gathered up her clothes, weapons, and armor and brought them to her room. Cleaning the blood off her armor didn't take as much time as I hoped. Nor did cleaning the gel off of mine. If her recovery was similar to when I'd been shot, it would be several more hours before she woke. I settled back into the chair.

Jey's voice popped into my head, waking me from the uneasy sleep I'd drifted into. *"You're late. Everything all right?"*

I didn't want to be the one to tell him our boss was sleeping off a near fatal bullet. She could set him straight if she wanted to.

"We're finishing up a contract. We'll be back in a few hours."

He grumbled and broke contact. I was cutting into his Kazan time. Too bad.

"What are you looking so annoyed about? I'm the one who got shot."

Awake at last. I grinned. I couldn't help myself. She was alive.

Kazan wiped the dried gel from the corners of her eyes. "I see you got the tank figured out." She sat up a little, tugging the blanket up with her. "I'm not used to this deluxe treatment. It sure beats waking up freezing out there on the platform."

As happy as I was to hear her voice, there were things that needed to be said. "I'm sorry, I didn't—"

She shook her head. "I should have realized it was him when I saw him standing there."

"You knew the target?"

"That wasn't the target." She sighed. "That was Kess. We trained together, worked together, he knows how I move."

"But the description matched. How could that be?"

"Temporary enhancements? Prosthetics?"

"And he's never done anything like this before?"

Kazan sank back into the pillow looking for all the world like she wanted to go back to sleep and wake up with a different realization. "No, but he'd not tried anything like on Merchess before either." She shook her head. "He put a good deal of work into the whole disguise. Kess was hoping to catch us off guard and it worked. He knew I'd have you out on a contract, a less involved one, and he placed a bet."

"That's one hell of a bet. Is he still in Kryon? With you being at odds, I thought he'd be on the outs with them."

She pressed the heels of her hands against her eyes and took a deep breath. "He's no longer on their payroll. That much I know for sure."

"Then how would he even know about the contract at all? Does he have a spy on Sere? He'd have to know what contract you would be assigned in order to prepare."

Her gaze locked onto me with an intensity that might have incinerated me on the spot if such a thing were possible. "He would. I need to get dressed. Do you mind?"

I waited outside her room, wondering how I'd managed to piss her off.

She dashed across the hall to the bathroom I'd used after my dip in the tank with her arms full of everything I'd brought back to her room.

Kazan emerged a short time later, settling the last of her weapons into place. Water dripped off the end of her braid where it hung over her shoulder as though she'd just finished it seconds before.

"Sere. Now," she said.

The steel alcove and grey-suited guards materialized before me. I dashed after Kazan who strode down the corridors at a pace just short of running. Fa'yet stood in the doorway to Kazan's Kryon quarters.

He stood aside so we could enter. "How'd it go?"

I took an offered seat across from Fa'yet. Kazan paced beside us. Other than the faint wheeze of the air vents and her boots thumping on the carpet, the room was quiet. Glares between Kazan and Fa'yet confirmed my guess that they were holding a private conversation.

As their link discussion progressed, Fa'yet's brows lowered and his lips took on a pinched look. His fist pounded the arm of the chair.

"I assure you, I've had no contact with that viscu you once called your partner," he said.

I began to wish I'd turned my shift over to Jey when I'd had the chance. Getting stuck on the outside of their conversation left me feeling awkward and useless.

Fa'yet turned to me. *"I don't suppose you could call off your charming partner?"*

"Like I have any say?"

My palms became clammy. If the two of them got to physically fighting, would I be able to break them apart before they took me out for trying? I might be bigger than either of them, but I still rather doubted it.

He turned back to Kazan.

After a good ten minutes, her pacing subsided. With her scowl still firmly in place, she leaned in close to Fa'yet. "If you find out anything, even a whisper, I want to know about it."

"Ana." He reached for her arm.

She pulled away before he could touch her.

Fa'yet dropped his hand to his lap and sighed. "I'll let you know if I hear anything."

Kazan gave him a curt nod and headed for the door. Fa'yet watched her leave. He glanced at me. "Keep her safe."

"I'll do my best."

He nodded. "You better get after her then."

Her footsteps were already fading down the hall. I shot to my feet and caught up in short order. All the tension and rushing around did little to ease the pain in my head. I squeezed my eyes shut for a moment, trying to find some relief.

Kazan halted her high speed march down the corridor and turned to me. "Are you all right?"

"Just a headache. Not used to Jumping you when you're bleeding all over."

A faint smile chipped away at her scowl. "Hopefully you won't have to get used to it."

I took a little comfort in the fact that she'd neglected to berate me for allowing her to get shot. At least she was sort of smiling about my effort to get her to the tank instead of yelling at me for not being prepared for it.

"Fa'yet can do the digging here, and I'm fine thanks to you. Now, you need to relax and knock that headache, and I need a drink." She flashed me a jump point and vanished before I could argue.

We arrived in an alley. A quick glance at the surrounding bunker-like buildings revealed we were on Twelve, Marin's home base in the Rakon Nebula. Frequent Fragian attacks promoted the benefits of squat, sturdy structures despite their lack of visual appeal.

She scanned the area. I did the same. The few men across the street wore coats similar to ours, though likely of lower quality. They stared, gaping at our sudden appearance. I gave them the menacing glare I'd perfected for intimidating people while on duty. The men turned away as we headed down the street.

"Is this a safe place to be?" She'd already been in the tank once on my watch. I didn't want a second time on my conscience.

"Safe as any."

After the day we'd had so far, that statement offered little assurance. I kept my eyes on everything, which did absolutely nothing to help me relax.

She stopped in front of a graffiti covered building emitting a pulsating, thudding noise. She pulled the door open.

Cacophony washed over us. Two naked Jalvian women danced on a distant stage to a throbbing beat. Voices fought to be heard over the music, creating a general din, and dense smoke filled the air with the musky scents of common drugs.

The music didn't help matters at all but a few deep breaths of the drug haze did loosen the muscles in my neck and shoulders. Kazan sank into a chair at a table near the back wall. The majority of the crowd sat near the stage, cheering for the dancers.

She didn't strike me as the sort who liked women. I gave her a questioning glance.

"No one looks back here, and the drinks are strong and cheap, which I thought you'd appreciate since you're buying." She pointed to the bar.

"Right. Thanks." I gave the room another once over. Nothing

suspicious stood out. I went up to the bar and ordered our drinks. As the bartender mixed them, I kept an eye on Kazan and the crowd. I'd much rather have gone back to one of her houses and made her a drink myself, but she wanted to be here and she was the boss.

That didn't mean I couldn't try to talk some sense into her. I slid her drink over as I sat down. "Are you sure this is a good idea? Kess just about offed you, and here you sit in public having a drink."

She took a deep swallow. "I need to relax or I'm going to kill someone. Unless you're volunteering?"

I shook my head and slid my chair a little further away. So much for the sense talking.

"Both Marin and Fa'yet are keeping their eyes and ears on the Kess situation. You're here. The only place safer would be with the three of you at home, but I don't feel like subjecting Jey and Merkief to my crap-ass mood."

Lucky me. More likely, she didn't want them questioning what put her in that mood to begin with. I sipped my drink, kept my thoughts to myself, and enjoyed the show.

One of the dancers flipped up onto the crystalline rainbow-filled pole made of prism glass and spun around to the floor. Whistles and shouts filled the air.

Kazan shoved her empty glass in front of me. I went to get her another.

Setting down the fresh drink, I said, "How many of these do you plan on having?" Not that I was worried about going broke over a few drinks, but we were on Twelve, which wasn't the most friendly place to be on a good day.

"Enough."

I watched the dancers again, giving her time to suck down yet another drink while I sipped my first. "What happened between you and Kess?"

"Looking for ideas?"

I shook my head. In fact, I was looking for pointers so I didn't fall into the same trap, but in her current mood, I doubted she'd believe me.

She sat back, putting some welcome distance between herself and her nearly empty third drink. "I don't even know. Not really."

"How can you not know why he wants to kill you?"

Ignoring the dancers and the crowd, she stared at the table.

The pitted and sticky surface offered little of interest beyond a ring of condensation from her glass. The droplets reflected the flashing lights from the stage.

"We were getting along just fine," she said. "Working together, we even had a decent personal relationship going. Then he started wanting things, Cragtek, to oversee a planet, things I wasn't willing to hand over. I thought he understood why."

She stirred the dregs of her drink with her straw. "He grew distant, and then one day, he closed our linked connection and left without a word. A month later, the attacks began."

I wondered how Marin took sharing Kazan with Kess. From what little I'd seen of them together and Gemmen's comments, it was clear they were in a long-term relationship of some sort.

"Kess has been after you for a while now and you've not managed to kill him?"

She stabbed at the ice with her straw. "Kess might be alive, but you'll notice he controls nothing."

Alive without power was still alive. And still after her, which seemed to have a negative power all of its own.

"I see that."

She grabbed her glass and gripped it tight. "Killing me isn't quite that simple. My contacts have their orders should I disappear."

Her partners had turned on her. But she knew me. She knew my brother. "You have to know I'd never—"

"Save your breath. You all do it eventually."

My heart dropped. Did she really think I was just another partner waiting to betray her?

A slight slur edged her words. "Quit with the sad face already and get me another drink. While you're at it, get yourself another too. Enough with nursing that lukewarm thing."

I found myself in true need of a drink to wash down her accusation. When I returned to the table, her chair sat closer to mine.

"You need to relax more. Smile once in awhile. Go out and enjoy an off-shift with some friends," she said.

"I'll keep that in mind." I'd given up the few friends I had when I'd hired on. Training and learning all I could to help her filled my off-shift hours. The only person I had left to relax with was Merkief, which we did manage to do from time to time.

While I did sip more avidly at my second drink, I didn't plan on having another in our current surroundings. "We should get back soon. Jey is already ticked that I took most of his shift."

"In a while. You need a couple shots first."

"Jey and I have enough issues without him catching me drunk with you." Not to mention, getting drunk with my boss screamed bad idea.

Using the link, I checked the shift schedule. Mine had ended five hours ago.

"Are you going to let him know?" I asked. Jobs did go over shift changes on a regular basis, but I thought it considerate to keep each other up to date.

"How about you let him know. Probably not a good idea for me right now."

She had a point. If Jey sensed she'd been drinking, he'd hold me accountable for not making sure she was safe at home while in a vulnerable condition.

I opened my link to Jey. *"Kazan picked up another contract. She's in a mood. You're better off with a down shift."*

"Are you all right to keep going? I don't want to hear about some mishap because you got tired."

"I'll be sure to let you know if I need to trade off."

"You better." He cut contact.

"There. That's done."

"Good. Shots." She pointed to the bar.

"I don't think you need any."

"They're for you." She slapped a credit chip in my hand. "Get a couple. Relax."

"But if I'm drinking, who's going to watch your back?"

"I've gotten by on my own before."

Be that as it may, I rather doubted she'd been well on the way to drunk while doing so. I started to get up in the hopes of getting her to leave, but she grabbed my wrist.

"Oh sit down." She signaled to someone behind me. A waitress walked to Kazan's side and leaned low, exposing considerable cleavage. She nodded and left. Kazan grabbed the credit chip from my hand. When the waitress returned, Kazan swiped it through the reader.

Three shots appeared in front me.

"One would be fine."

"I doubt it," she said. "You're big. I know. I had to lift you."

Heat rushed up my face. She wasn't going to let me forget that anytime soon.

I tossed back a shot. It burned. Whatever she'd ordered, it was strong as all nine hells.

"Just the one." I slid the others toward her.

Her hands slammed down on mine, splashing alcohol from the glasses. "Don't argue with me. Drink."

The first one had dulled my headache nicely. Or maybe that was the drug haze. I was starting not to care as long as the pain was gone.

"Only if you promise that we're leaving when I finish these."

She grinned. "Agreed."

Rather than give her the chance to order another for either of us, I slammed the remaining shots and prayed to Geva that she'd agree to leave before they kicked in.

I indicated the empty glasses. "So?"

Kazan got to her feet. She stood, wavering there. I reached out and took her arm. She didn't shake me off, rather, she stepped closer.

"Artorian house," she said.

"We're on Jal."

She poked me in the chest. "I know, idiot."

Behind us, the crowd roared as a foursome of dancers took to the stage. It seemed like a good time to leave without drawing any notice. I led her out the door. By the time we reached our previous jump point, the effects of the shots had fully unfurled in my gut.

Kazan looked up at me and grinned. We Jumped to Artor. The dark, empty foyer greeted us with silence.

"Why here? I'd feel better about you being safe with Jey and Merkief on watch." I could feel my reflexes melting. I'd be little good if any call to duty arose.

"I'm not big on audiences." She winked and staggered toward my room.

I froze. Getting drunk with the boss was one thing, but this was a whole new level of bad idea.

She turned on the light in my room and poked her head out. "You waiting for something?"

Yeah, sanity to kick in. Though the longer I stood there, the more warmth flowed through me and the more blurred my search for reason became. I headed for the rectangle of light and the woman waiting there.

Kazan hung her coat on the hook beside the door. I found that if I leaned against the doorframe, remaining vertical was much easier. She split into two Kazans, then merged into one, and then doubled again. I blinked. It didn't help.

"What in Geva's name were those?" My words came out far more slurred than hers had.

"Those were Chesser's favorite. I figured you'd like them too. Let me help you with that." She came around behind me and pulled my coat down my arms. She hung it on the hook beside hers.

I had no idea what Chesser had liked to drink other than the quantity was high when he went about it. If he'd remained coherent and standing after three, his tolerance had been much greater than mine. He won.

The effects were only going to get worse. At least my headache was gone.

She took my hands and pulled me inside. Her mind opened to mine, not over the link, but along my natural paths. Sensations flowed from her, fingers on flesh, lips joining and electricity that tingled in all the right places in my hazy brain.

All hint of moisture left my mouth. I stumbled and fell to the floor, dragging her with me.

Kazan untangled herself from my numb limbs and knelt beside me. She kept one hand on mine, our only true physical connection. With the other, she pushed the stray hairs from my face. Even with a clear line of sight, there were three of her. The room spun.

"He was the only one to never betray me." A vague sense of emptiness accompanied the barrage of blissful sensations she threw at me.

I filled her mind with the only thing I was capable of at the moment, flooding her with pleasure-filled energy, images, and sensations. She gasped.

Her defenses lowered, offering me a glimpse at her physical responses to my mental stimulation. Through the haze of alcohol and pleasure, I became dimly aware of her hands grasping my shoulders. My mind filled with her racing pulse and the building warmth within her.

Part of me wanted to reach out and touch the fine sheen of sweat covering her body, but her burning presence in my mind demanded all my attention. Her breath quickened. Her fingernails dug through my shirt and into my flesh. A flash of white light filled my mind as her forehead dropped against mine. Waves of light emanated from her mind, sending my own over the edge.

Anastassia brought herself closer, her cheek resting against mine. Her warm breath tickled my ear as her breathing resumed its natural rhythm. Our connection closed off.

"Come on. You can't sleep here." She got to her feet and offered me her hand.

I reached for it but found only air.

Her hands snaked under my arms, hauling me toward the bed. I helped the best I could and fell against the soft mattress. She hefted my feet upward and pulled a blanket over me. "Get some sleep."

"Stassia..." I felt I should say something, but great Geva the room spun. My eyes closed and refused to open.

"Good night, Vayen."

The door closed behind her.

Chapter Six

I woke to the beat of the throbbing bar music. As my bedroom on Artor came into focus, I realized the throbbing was in my head. The bar, the shots, me and Anastassia on the floor. I threw my hands over my face.

Merkief's link nudged mine. *"You awake yet?"*

Nausea swirled within my stomach, and not only from the drinks. What did last night mean for my job? Were things going to be awkward between us? Was this a one-time thing for curiosity's sake or something else?

I slid out of bed and spotted a small white pill on the bedside table. A stim. I'd seen Kazan popping them from time to time. She must have left it for me. I popped it in my mouth and swallowed.

"I'll be out in a few."

By the time I'd showered and dressed, the stim had banished the groggy hangover haze. I poured myself a glass of water and went in search of Merkief. I found him sitting in the common room.

He glanced away from the vid feed. "I hear you had a busy night."

She'd told him? Heat rushed over my face.

"I can't believe you managed to complete two contracts in one night. She must have been driving you hard." He shook his head.

Something like that. At least she'd had the good sense to come up with a story.

"She was in a mood to work, and who am I to argue?"

"Smart man. I'm just glad we're back to staying on Artor for the moment," Merkief said.

I sat down at the other end of the couch, staring blindly at the local vid feed. Memories of the night before played over in my mind—Anastassia's smile and the sensations that had passed between us. All of it remained in memory with surprising clarity given my level of drunkenness at the time.

"Where is she?"

"With Jey on Rok. Then they're off to do a job for Marin."

I checked the time and found I'd slept through most of Jey's shift. "Looks like you're on soon."

Yet he wasn't dressed for duty nor appeared in any hurry to go do so.

Merkief slouched into the cushions. "Kazan told me they'd be working late. Since she only slept for a few hours before they left, I gather I'll get sleep watch."

"Is that a bad thing?"

"I'd rather be out overseeing her sanctioned experiments on Moriek or here at the University. I hate when shifts get screwed out of our usual rotation," he said.

"We have a usual rotation? Seems like things are always pretty screwed around here." I took a drink of the cool water, grateful for the relief it brought to the desert the alcohol had left inside me. The stim sent surges of energy coursing through my body.

Merkief turned to face me, looking like he'd just eaten something unpleasant. "Do you think Kazan is sleeping with Jey?"

I choked. Water shot up my nose. A wracking round of coughs set things back to rights. I set the glass aside and regarded Merkief with watering eyes. "What?"

"I'm sure you've seen the way he fawns over her. He's on watch when you and I are sleeping or busy elsewhere, and he's the only one who is physically compatible at the moment."

"I have noticed." The thought of Jey touching Anastassia like in the images she'd shared with me the night before made my teeth grind together.

Merkief sighed. "I mean, I know she's capable of Artorian sex, but I get the impression she prefers the physical variety."

I was glad I'd put the glass down. Had she sampled all of us? "What do you mean, you know she's capable?"

He gave me a sideways glance. "She's naturally telepathic. Didn't you say she was gifted by your brother? I figured that meant she knew how we worked, that's all."

"Oh. Right, yeah."

She knew how we worked all right. Knock our defenses down with a few drinks and come on strong. No single Artorian male would think twice about turning that down. Without the responsibilities associated with physical sex, we were free to be as promiscuous as we wanted. Except for having sex with some-one in a bonded relationship. Which Kazan had been. With my brother. Who she often compared me to. Who liked the shots she fed me. Who I was a near dead match for.

I slammed my head back into the cushions and closed my eyes. Idiot.

She'd been drinking too. Had she even known it was me or had she been off in some drunken delusion?

I forced my voice to a neutral calm. "Has Jey said anything about being with her?"

I didn't expect that Jey would utter a word of it to me unless I pushed him to toss it in my face, but he and Merkief had seemed to fall into a viable friendship.

"No, but maybe he's following orders not to."

Maybe they had a story just like her and I did. At least it didn't sound like Merkief had been with her. Or maybe this was his attempt to divert attention from himself. In which case, I could play that too.

I shrugged. "Does it matter who she's sleeping with?"

"No, I suppose not."

From his less than energetic response, I had a feeling that it did.

Her relationship with Marin was one thing. Whatever it really was, it had been going on since before Kess and maybe her other partner too. Being with one or all of us shouldn't have surprised me, but so soon after we'd been together, the thought of it stung. For all I knew she was out taking Jey to a bar and hopping into bed with him at one of her other houses at that very moment. I wanted to think she was above that, but maybe I was still too naïve for this job.

My stim-infused body refused to sit in one spot any longer and I needed a more productive place to focus. "I'm going to go work out."

Merkief nodded and went back to watching the vid.

Four hours later, I spotted Kazan standing in the doorway

of the training room that filled the entire basement. Dark circles underlined her eyes. Whatever she'd been doing, actual sleeping hadn't been involved. I finished my last lap and jogged over to her.

She looked me over and scowled. "Don't tire yourself out too much, that stim will only carry you so far. We've got another Kryon contract tonight with Merkief. I'll need you to be able to work."

"What about you? Looks like you could use a long rest before doing anything."

"You worry about you and I'll worry about me." She stormed up the stairs before I could catch my breath enough to say anything else.

⁂

The Kryon contract involved two members of a research company who were impeding the progress of certain projects the High Council felt were important. At least that's how Kazan paraphrased it in our briefing. I hoped the impeded research involved advancements in the bio-engineering that Moriek was well known for. I'd sleep better knowing that the deaths I was about to cause would free up the cure for someone's illness or at least better the lives of other Artorians in some way. Then again, whatever line Kazan fed us might only be to soothe our consciences. Or her own.

The Artorian world of Moriek greeted us with an ordered and engineered splendor that almost rivaled Artor itself. The air smelled clean, the sky overhead was a deep shade of blue and a row of spire trees lined each side of the street, adding stripes of green to the eye-pleasing, natural-toned structures that housed families and businesses.

Kazan had left Jey behind to sleep. I wished she'd taken a few more hours for herself. Merkief and I stood on either side of her, waiting while she located our targets on the local network.

She turned to Merkief. "You have the address?"

He nodded.

"No one sees you. Clean up any mess and bring the body to Sere. Got it?"

Without a backward glance, he stepped to the roadside, hailed an automated transport and was gone.

"Ours has dinner reservations. We might as well get to his house and wait."

"No quiet place to hit him between now and dinner?"

"Not with your nosey public surveillance satellites and roving news bots in action. I'd rather not interfere with the feeds unless circumstances become dire. That gets messy."

"We're on the feed already just standing here," I pointed out.

"Are we doing anything illegal?"

"Standing here, talking? No. Why couldn't we just Jump right to the location?"

"It's unverified, as most contract locations are. That's why we use my jump points. If you want to take the chance of Jumping into a room laced with mines, automatic weaponry or a field of lasers, you go right ahead. I'll take a transport, walk in, and wave to your splattered guts."

Where was the woman who had done wonderful things in my head the night before? "I know you're tired—"

She halted a transport and tossed a glare over her shoulder. "Drop it. Get in."

The fifteen-minute transport ride passed in strained silence. Her link offered nothing but barbs of annoyance when I sent a tentative thought her way. By the time we'd reached our destination, a three-story home with a vast lawn and manicured gardens, I'd given up any hope of resolution.

She took care of the cameras while I bypassed the multiple door locks. The house lay shrouded in darkness, but the network provided floor plans detailed enough to keep us from bumbling into security measures. We made our way up the stairs to the second level to wait. Our target took his sweet time getting home to his impending death.

The door opened on the floor below. I drew my gun. Cautious footsteps sounded on the stairs. A head ducked into the doorway. The lights flared on in the room.

The face didn't match the target. Dammit, he had a bodyguard.

"Take him. I'll get the target." Kazan stepped back, giving me room to work. The room was large enough, but there was too damn much furniture to deal with. I began to appreciate Kazan's sparse furnishings in terms of keeping a target from reaching cover.

I fired two shots while the element of surprise was on our side. One missed, but the second hit home. He staggered backward, but his armor kept the bullet at bay.

Kazan slipped out of the room to hunt the target. I gave her a few seconds to get down the stairs before I dared fire again.

The guard gasped for a deep breath and pulled a gun. I kicked a chair out of my way to clear some space to move freely. He fired twice before I managed to shoot his hand. His gun fell to the floor and he clutched the bloody mess I'd created.

A shot sounded below us followed by a heavy thud.

"It's done." Kazan's voice cut through my concentration. I glanced over to see her leaning against the wall, watching us.

The man whirled around to face her. "You killed my brother!"

Not a bodyguard. A brother. I glanced at Kazan. She shook her head.

With an anguished growl, he leapt to clear a couch that stood between him and a fairly clear path to where she stood.

Though I secretly wished Kazan would pull the trigger, I knew she expected me to do it. She'd already done her job, this one was mine.

I fired. He collapsed, sprawling face down across the yellow couch. His arms hung over the back while his feet touched the ground on the other side.

She stormed over as I checked him to make sure the bullet in the back of his head had done its job. "Are you trying to get us killed?"

I took a step back. "Of course not. It was just that—"

Kazan shook her head. "We've covered this. No involvement. We walk in, pull the trigger, clean up and leave. That's the job."

"The job sucks."

She backed up a step and gazed down at the dead man. "I know the rules seem harsh, but we can't afford to be soft." She sighed. "Try not to let them talk. That makes it easier."

"If you say so."

Kazan's hand rested on my shoulder. "I'll take care of him if you want to take the target to Sere and file the completion. How about I meet you on Sere when you're done and we can discuss last night?"

In light of her radical mood shifts, I needed some time to sort out what exactly I wanted to say. "I'll dispose of the guard. You take the target. Merkief is waiting for you on Sere."

Kazan cast a somber glance at the body on the floor. "All right then."

I Jumped the body to one of our usual disposal zones. The man gazed up at me with dull, empty eyes. I reached down and closed them. He had only been defending his brother. No more than I would have done for Chesser. I'd dreamed of killing the bastard who had fired the shot that had killed him more times than I could count. Tonight, I was that bastard.

I lowered the dead man into the black void and mumbled a few words to Geva on his behalf. His body vaporized halfway down the tube. As much as I wasn't ready to talk to Kazan, I also didn't want to get caught gazing down an exhaust shaft by patrolling guards. I considered my options of quiet places to think and formed a Jump to a secluded section of shoreline on Artor.

After a quick check to make sure my spot was indeed deserted, I sat down in the sand. The first stars shone down from the dusky sky as the white globe of Karin rose just above the horizon. Waves lapped at the pebbled shore, offering a soothing song to my troubled mind.

My father had taken me and Chesser fishing here when he had time off. He'd been an officer like my brother, but peacetime had assured his duty was served mostly behind a desk and that he was usually home each night.

What would he think of me now? Would he be proud of my position or question my role at Kazan's side? Maybe he would despise me for my actions, or perhaps he would understand their necessity. I tried to listen for him, but couldn't remember what my father's voice had sounded like.

Chesser's voice still haunted my dreams, but for now he remained silent. I pulled the flask Sonia had given me from inside my coat, running my fingers over the whorled pattern. The endless series of spirals mirrored my life.

Was I rising up or spiraling downward? It was hard to tell.

After a prayer to Geva for some guidance, I raised my flask to my departed family and shivered as the potent liquor slithered down my throat. I drank again to the brothers who had met their end on Moriek and then put the flask away. Kazan was waiting for me.

I Jumped to Sere. Jey looked up from his plate as I walked in the room.

I stopped dead. "What are you doing here?"

"Kazan left a message saying you were all on Sere, so I grabbed some breakfast and Jumped over."

Great. I'd hoped for some time alone to talk to her. Now I had both Merkief and Jey underfoot. "And where is she?"

"She left with Merkief to get a drink. She said she'd talk to you later. You in trouble or something?" He grinned.

"Something." I trudged to my room, leaving his bemused face behind.

◆

Later never happened. Kazan spent the majority of her free time with Marin. In light of which, I wasn't overly broken-hearted that I'd been nothing more than a drunken one night stand. She took Merkief or Jey on contract work and relegated me to bodyguard duty during her whirlwind sessions of private meetings with planetary heads and her sleep shift. Days dragged into weeks and by the third month of generally being ignored, I began to wonder if I'd been demoted and she'd just never got around to informing me.

I finally asked Merkief about Kazan avoiding me. He mumbled something about her fighting a lot with Marin. He claimed she'd been in a rotten mood so I was better off not being around her any more than I was. Then he promptly left with her.

A few hours of working out only left my mind to fume while my body was busy. Merkief's near repeat of the same damn excuse I'd used on Jey further reinforced my theory that Kazan was having sex with Merkief. Her being with Marin or even Jey, I could shake my head at and accept, but being blown off for Merkief was entirely different. He couldn't do anything more for her than I could.

She had gone after me for Geva's sake. It certainly wasn't my fault that I'd been dead drunk. Maybe she'd learned her lesson and only plied Merkief with two shots instead of three.

Maybe I was better off alone. I didn't need her temper or her moods that seemed to change by the second. I should just focus on my job, save my credits and make a name for myself so I could branch out on my own eventually.

With that settled, I got into bed.

Jey's voice popped into my head. *"Meet us on Twelve, Kazan's room in Marin's compound. Five minutes."*

Nice advance warning. Thankfully I wasn't sound asleep. I reloaded up my weapons and pulled my coat back on. Four minutes later, I stood in the middle of Kazan's quarters with the three of them already in deep conversation. I cleared my throat.

Kazan gave me a brief glance before returning her attention

to the datapad in her hands. "Marin has an emergency job for us. One of his people botched a contract on Karin's Premier. The target has six bodyguards, all linked, all high caliber." She shoved the datapad at me. "Any problems with these?"

I committed the target's face to memory and moved down the file. Still frames of the six bodyguards scrolled down the screen. One caught my eye, a woman, Janeel. We'd gone through military training together, but I'd not seen her since. Bowing out on my first contract in months over a past acquaintance would only put me further out of her favor. If I stuck close to Kazan, we'd be going after the target, not dealing with putting down the opposition.

"No."

"Good." Kazan snatched the datapad back. "We'll be working in her office." She flashed me the closest jump point. We took a transport from there and arrived in a lobby next to a fountain of burbling water surrounded by low-lying greenery.

She nodded to Merkief and Jey. "You two wait here. Pick off the guards from behind as they go in." She pointed to the plaz doors bearing the etched triangular seal of Karin. "Vayen and I will take out the front guards or the target depending on how they enter. I need the target alive, at least enough to talk."

I didn't recall seeing anything about the target remaining alive during my brief glimpse of the contract, but I figured she knew Marin's stipulations. Within ten minutes of taking our positions, a faint ding sounded as a lift in the hall opened its doors. Multiple footsteps marched our way. The doors swung open as two men walked in.

Kazan dropped one. I took out the other with a clean shot to the head. A single shot rang out from behind before the Premier was thrown to the floor with a man sprawled over her. The four remaining guards, one of whom was injured, yelled orders between them and fired out into the lobby.

Merkief swore in my head. *"I'm hit. I can handle it alone if I get to the tank now."*

I glanced at Kazan, who was busy exchanging fire with the nearest man, now on his feet and shielding the Premier behind him. Jey seemed to have two of the other bodyguards occupied, one of them limping. That left one for me.

"Go on. We'll take care of the rest."

"Good luck." Merkief cut contact.

Bullets thudded into my coat. I fired back, moving in closer to Kazan's side. The fourth guard aimed directly at my head.

I let off three shots in her direction and a few more at the man firing on Kazan. Both of them dropped. Kazan dashed after the fleeing Premier. Jey swung a man into a wall. His wounded opponent had gone missing.

A shot hit the back of my neck. The collar of my coat may have deflected the bullet but not the chill that spread down my spine at the near-fatal hit. I spun around.

Janeel's eyes widened, but the gun in her hand didn't waver. I cursed my job as I fired. Nothing happened. Shit. I tossed the empty gun aside and kicked.

Her gun went flying. She stumbled sideways, clutching her hand. She teetered there, keeping the weight off her bloodied leg. If only Merkief or Jey had done their job, I wouldn't have been put in this damned position.

I connected a hard hit to her jaw. She fell backward.

Gunfire filled the room around us. I tried to get a fix on the situation as I dragged her behind a desk. She seemed stunned and didn't fight back when I pinned her down.

Janeel's voice slithered along the natural paths we'd formed years before when we'd shared classes and friendly talks over lunch. *"I looked for you at your old job a while back. Sonia had a message for you."*

Don't let them talk. I wanted to punch myself when my heart beat faster and I asked, *"What message?"*

Janeel's eyes refocused. *"She said if I ever ran into you, to make sure I had a knife in my hand."*

That didn't strike me as something Sonia would say...unless she really hated me. She had every right to, but it still hurt to consider that she'd want me dead.

I glanced over the desktop. Jey exchanged blows with the guard and Kazan fought the target. The Premier wore top grade armor and appeared to be far less defenseless than I'd anticipated.

Janeel bucked beneath me, smashing her head into my chin. *"She was a pretty one. A shame what they did to her."*

"Who? What happened to her?"

Janeel bared her teeth and slammed our connection shut. Her fingernails dug into my wrists.

My hands circled her throat. *"Talk, dammit."*

She gasped. Her face turned deep red.

Gunfire continued around us. Another deep bruise blossomed under the shield of my coat. Kazan cried out. Shit.

Janeel had to die, but at least I could make it quick. I snapped her neck.

Jey's heavy footsteps thundered by as he dashed after the remaining bodyguard and knocked him down.

The target stood near Kazan, who lay on the floor grasping her stomach. Blood dripped from a deep gash on the Premier's forehead. She held a gun in her hand. Red-faced and staggering, she headed for the door.

Kazan screamed in my head. *"Don't let her leave!"*

I yelled at Jey to get out of the way, pulled my pulse pistol and flicked it to the lowest setting. A wave of energy shot forward, knocking the target off her feet and shattering the plaz doors.

Plaz fragments pierced Jey's opponent. He screamed. Both of them fell to the floor. Jey got up, scowling as he shook off the plaz shards that had showered him from fifteen feet away.

We both ran to Kazan's side.

"Is the target dead?" she asked through clenched teeth.

I knelt down to check. "Not quite yet."

"Good." With Jey's help, Kazan sat up. "Jey, go to her desk. Pull up the current contract I have with Artor."

Jey ran to comply, getting clearance codes from her as needed to gain access.

"Change the name to Karin and date it two weeks ago. Vayen, bring her over here."

I dragged the semi-conscious woman to Kazan's side. "What are you doing?"

"Taking control of Karin."

"Now?"

"Yes, now." She shot me a contemptuous look. "She wouldn't agree to it without a bullet in her, but now she doesn't have a choice. I can use the signed contract to sway the rest of the governing council later."

Jey handed Kazan a datapad loaded with the information.

"Vayen, deep probe. She should be weak enough that you can make her sign this. We'll also need her access codes and her identity confirmation."

Squeezing my eyes shut to block out the distractions around me, I reached into the woman's mind. I recoiled instantly. Her pulse was too faint.

"She's dying. If she goes while I'm so deep in her mind, I could lose my own. I won't be much use to you locked in a padded cell. Get the contract signed by the new Premiere later."

"You're not much use to me right now. I said, do it!"

"It's too risky. No." What was she thinking? She'd put off Karin for years. What was the rush now? I reached out to Kazan through our linked connection, but her thoughts were moving too frantically for me to follow. The only concrete thing I picked up was urgency.

Jey, not having any natural telepathic abilities, was unable to help. I'd thought I'd averted the situation but, Kazan pulled herself closer to the dying woman and closed her eyes. She began the probe herself. Damn woman.

Jey knelt behind Kazan, supporting her. I held the datapad so the target could finalize the contract under Kazan's influence. The woman's body strained as she and Kazan fought for control. Her hand tapped a mad frenzy of codes on the datapad and then fell to the floor.

I checked the target. No pulse. Kazan's head lolled back into Jey's chest. Only time would tell if she'd wake with her wits intact. I looked to Jey.

He pulled Kazan's coat open. Blood seeped into her shirt from the hole in her stomach.

"What the fuck were you doing? Having a quick mind fling?" Jey pointed at Janeel's body. "This is your fault. You call that protecting her? You couldn't follow orders and now look at her. This should be you." His voice held even more disdain than Kazan's had.

"That wasn't an order. That was reckless insanity."

I could still feel her presence through my link. She would live. Her condition wasn't my fault.

Jey scooped up Kazan in his arms. "I'm sure she'll want to hear all about why you weren't watching her back. Partner." He snorted. "Take the target to Marin for confirmation. I'll take care of Kazan."

Chapter Seven

After a hefty sigh and a check around the room to make sure we hadn't left any traceable weapons, I grabbed the target and Jumped to Marin's complex. Following the delivery instructions in the contract, I went to his office.

His door was closed and my hands were full.

"It's done. I've got the body."

Marin's voice grated in my head. *"I'm busy at the moment. You'll have to wait."*

Wait. In the hallway, with the dead Premiere of Karin. Sure, why not.

I placed the body in one of the two chairs beside the door. He could deal with a little blood on his furniture.

After pacing the hallway for a short while, I took the other seat and kept my gaze locked on the wall in front of me.

Half an hour later his voice returned. *"Come in."*

I picked up the body and went inside. I didn't see any sign of anyone else having been there, and the surface of his expansive wooden desk was clean. I couldn't help but think that he was just fucking with me.

Marin sat behind his desk, his hands not courteously visible. He didn't offer me a seat, and I didn't take one.

"You send us off on this contract in a Geva-forsaken rush and then have the nerve to keep me waiting when the job is over?"

He kept me locked in an unblinking gaze as he got to his feet. "I'll be back in a few minutes." Marin took the body from my arms.

"Sit. We're going to talk."

An inkling of what had transpired during that last half hour pried its way into my brain. Jey had contacted Marin and had given Kazan's deadly, long-time lover his views on how the job had gone down.

I kicked one of the chairs aside and sat in the other.

Jey wanted me gone so he could take my place, and I couldn't have given him better evidence to discredit me. Kazan and I were already on the outs, and I had little doubt she'd be pissed as all nine hells to learn why I wasn't at her side when the Premier had managed to shoot her. And if Kazan didn't buy Jey's story, she'd certainly listen to Marin.

I rubbed my hands over my face and waited for his return.

Janeel's face floated before my eyes. Not the red, straining face, but the one I'd known years before. I killed one of my friends. I stared down at the tiled floor. Not only had I killed her, but the act of doing so had nearly killed Kazan, whom I had sworn to Chesser's memory to protect so my homeworld would remain at peace.

And Sonia, what had happened to her? It could have all been a ruse, but what if it wasn't?

Marin reappeared. I scrambled to put my work face back in place, hard and indifferent. He took a seat behind the desk. This time he kept his hands where I could see them.

"We both know that today didn't go well. Anastassia suffered because of your actions," he said.

As much as I didn't like the guy on a personal level, he did genuinely seem upset about Kazan being wounded. Marin's morals were questionable, but if I had to place a bet on one thing he had actual feelings about, it was her. From the daggers he was glaring at me, I was damn glad I wasn't Kess after whatever had gone down between him and Kazan.

"She was reckless," I said. "She disregarded my advice."

"Your advice." The muscles along his smooth jawline quivered and his nostrils flared. "You're not ready for this partnership you've been pulled into. You can't protect her. You have nothing to offer. Everything you have, she's given you."

That was true. All of it. Any angle of defense I tried dried up on my tongue.

Kazan was reckless today. Was her promoting me any different? The drunken night on the floor argued that it was not. She seemed to have her life in order and her shit together on all other fronts. Was there something about me that brought out her bad decisions?

He slammed his palms on the desk, startling me mid-thought.

"This is how you thank her? You sit there mind-screwing some bodyguard while Anastassia is in the middle of a fight? You didn't follow her orders and drove her into doing a probe while she was wounded? What were you thinking? She could have died!"

My efforts at indifference shattered. "Then maybe she should have listened to me and not done the damned probe!"

He shook his head. "Since you've been afflicting Anastassia with your presence, she's been so distracted by watching out for you that she's not able to take care of herself."

"I didn't afflict anyone. She chose me."

"I have no idea why." He waved one well-manicured hand in the air. "She tells me you're qualified, that you have experience, that she can trust you."

Whatever she'd told Marin about me, it was the last one settled like lead in my stomach. Her drunken words about Chesser rushed at me with sudden clarity. *He was the only one to never betray me.*

Marin shook his head, scowling. "Don't get me wrong, you do have skill and you seem smart enough. But you're inexperienced in her dealings. Go out and make a name for yourself. Give it a few years and then maybe you'll be ready for her."

"She'd kill me if I just walked away. Did Jey put you up to this?"

His hostility eased a few degrees. "We all want what is best for Anastassia. You want her kept safe. She's got two men left to do that, and I'm not going anywhere either. But be honest, are you the best partner she could have right now? Can you help undo the damage Kess caused in her life? Can you work with her or only for her?"

Considering the past eight months, I had to say no to all three. If anything, I was the distraction he accused me of being. Maybe with a little more of a push, she would take Marin up on his offer to move into his compound, where she would have plenty of protection while keeping the Narvan together.

A push like my resignation.

Exhaustion I'd been holding back with stims and alcohol crept over me. Kazan didn't want me around. She'd made that clear. If she couldn't bring herself to admit her mistake in promoting me, in hiring me to begin with, I could take that burden from her.

"If I were to resign, how do you propose I do so in order to remain living after the fact?"

"As I said, we all want what is best for Anastassia. I'll make sure she doesn't take your departure the wrong way."

If Jey had made that same offer, I would have laughed in his face, but recent quarrels or not, Marin had been with Kazan since before Kess. She trusted him. Whether I liked him or not didn't really matter. We didn't have to be friends to have a common goal.

"All right then. I'll start working on my resignation."

She'd be in the tank for a couple more hours. That would give me plenty of time to sort out what I wanted to say.

Marin sat back in his chair, his intensity dialed down to a moderate level as he pulled a datapad out of a drawer on his desk. "I have a place you can stay until you get established on your own. There are plenty of local jobs, and if you need me to, I can toss a couple your way."

"Sounds good." I watched Marin typing with bleary eyes. "I should get my things before she's back on her feet."

"On that note, send your resignation to me. I'll broach the topic safely so she doesn't leap to conclusions before fully understanding your honorable motivations. After Kess, she's liable to leap after the first line."

I nodded. He really did seem to have her best interests at heart. Maybe I'd judged him too harshly.

He handed me the datapad bearing the still frame of a blue three-story building lined with symmetrical rows of windows. I swiped the screen to get the address and found a standing reservation in one of the suites.

"I picked a name at random. Hope you don't mind," he said.

"It's fine." Given my current state, I probably would have picked one of my recently created aliases that Kazan knew. Staying off any network until Marin had time to talk to her would be best for my health.

A touch of his usual condescending tone crept back into his voice. "You do have some credits of your own, I hope?"

"I'll get by. Thank you for your assistance." I never thought I'd be thanking Marin, let alone meaning it.

It only took a few minutes to drain my account. I moved a good sum, Kazan did pay well, to the unmarked credit chip I had on me and then transferred the rest into a couple investments I'd had my eye on for a few months.

I spent the next hour jumping to my rooms in Kazan's homes and transferring my belongings back to my family home. Though part of me wanted to stay there, it would be one of the first places Kazan would look if she didn't take my resignation well. Even if she did, I fully expected her to need some time to cool off about it. Kazan wasn't the quiet and accepting type.

With the essentials crammed into a single pack, I Jumped back to twelve and made my way to the hotel. Checking in required nothing more than confirming the name Marin had given me at the front desk terminal.

As I stood in the suite, which ranked right in the middle of opulent and revolting, it occurred to me that I should close off my connections with Kazan. Jey wouldn't bother me other that possibly to gloat once Marin made my announcement, but I blocked him too. Merkief, assuming he'd gotten through his tank cycle before Kazan had needed it, would also no doubt be contacting me soon. Though I did terminate our linked connection, I hesitated to seal off our natural one. If I needed to make contact, he was the safest point. I muffled him to the point of almost sealing the connection and left it at that. If Kazan was going to hunt me down, Marin would warn me.

Unpacking consisted of dropping my pack on the floor as I dropped onto the bed. It didn't have much give, but I wasn't in the mood for comfort.

The room was too silent as I composed my resignation. The words fought me at every turn. It was hours later before I'd come up with two succinct paragraphs I prayed wouldn't get me killed. With that sent to Marin, I considered what I wanted to do with the rest of my life. First order of business was to visit Sonia and see if what Janeel said was true.

Before I got to that, I needed to sleep. Now that the letter was done and everything was in Marin's hands, my mind wanted nothing more than to forget recent events for a few hours. But I didn't dare take off my armor or disarm, not alone in a random hotel room with no security. With no one on watch. My mind raced with imagined scenarios of Kazan not believing Marin and forcing him to tell her where I was. In some of those, we talked it out, but in most, I ended up dying in various unpleasant ways.

Exhausted and drained, but unable to sleep, I gave up on the bed and went for a walk outside the hotel. The city didn't have the chaotic frenzy of one with a port, but there was enough activity that as long as I kept to the edges of the crowds, the pointing and murmured comments about my attire remained at a minimum. This was Twelve, after all.

Dinner, alone and eaten inside a restaurant instead of out of a box, tasted bland but filled my stomach. When I returned to my room, I finally fell asleep while thinking about what I wanted to say to Sonia. Even if something had happened to her or she hated me, was it too late to do anything about it?

❧

In order to avoid being seen, I formed a Jump into Sonia's common room. The void refused to swallow me and my head started to ache. Left with no choice but to get out of sight as quickly as possible, I Jumped to her doorstep and tried my code. It didn't work.

The door opened just far enough for a stunner to be aimed at me.

"Who are you?" asked a male voice.

Thrown off by the unexpected presence of someone else inside, I didn't answer fast enough for his taste. He opened the door a bit farther, blocking my entry with his body. "I'll use this."

"I'm looking for Sonia?"

"She's not here," he said.

"I see that. Who are you?" From his only wearing loose pants and the left side of his hair sticking up on end, I gathered that he'd been sleeping. Sleeping here, in Sonia's house.

He stared down at me, finger resting on the trigger.

"Sonia and I used to be together," I said, hoping that didn't also give him a reason to stun me.

He nodded slowly. "Ah, so you're the one to blame."

"Apparently so." I didn't like the sound of that at all. "Can I come in? I shouldn't be out here."

"You're right. Enough people have died on your account." He swung the door open and nodded me inside. "She's been notified that you're here. Have a seat."

He pointed to a new couch in an unfamiliar common room. The walls had changed color, the furniture was all different. The collection of shells that had covered most of one wall with all its cases was missing. Even the floors and light fixtures were new.

An ominous feeling settled over me as I sat on the spongy couch. People had died. Because of me.

I tried to contact the men I'd asked to watch over Sonia, but couldn't reach any of them. I prayed it was because they'd sealed off our natural connections. None of them had notified me that there had been any problems.

He stood there, stunner in hand, barely blinking until the door opened and Sonia came inside.

I leapt from the couch and then froze mid-step, unsure whether to hug her or keep my hands to myself in light of the perturbed man still focused on me.

She'd cut her hair shorter, but otherwise, the same woman I'd left stood there before me with wide brown eyes.

The dead silence amplified her soft voice. "You're really here."

Everything I wanted to say vacated my mind.

She closed the distance between us with a few quick strides and promptly slapped me across the face.

I deserved that so I didn't hold it against her. "Sonia, I—"

"Do you have any idea what my life has been like since you left?" She stood with her arms crossed.

"I'm sorry, I meant to come back and explain, but it wasn't safe."

"Safe?" The man snorted.

"Put that away," Sonia said, pointing at his stunner. "I've got this, thank you."

He looked dubious but shrugged and went into the spare bedroom Sonia had previously used when working on projects from home. She watched his door close and then spun back to me.

"So what are you here to explain exactly? How you left me to become a cold-blooded assassin?" She came very close to spitting in my face. "Oh yes, I know all about that."

I backed away until my legs hit the couch. She knew I worked for Kazan, but knowledge of my other activities had no business in her head.

"Do you know how many times someone showed up at my door looking for information on you? People threatened me, Vayen!"

"Who?"

I'd hunt them down. How dare they threaten her? I'd stayed away. They should have had no reason. And if this was Kess, I'd find a way to kill him without Kazan's help.

"I don't know who! Thug types. Men in long coats like yours.

People with illegal weapons and no care for anyone standing between them and the credits on your head."

Janeel's taunts haunted me. "Did they hurt you?"

Sonia turned away. "Yes, Vayen, they did. That's what you people do for a living, isn't it?"

"You know I'd never do anything to intentionally hurt you."

"Well then, I'd hate to see what you do when you do intend to hurt people." She huffed and after a long moment, glanced up at me before turning away again. "Is that really what you do? Kill people for a living?"

"Not exactly." How much did I want her to know? "I really did get hired as a bodyguard for Anastassia Kazan. Sometimes, my job requires that I do things. Unpleasant things."

Her voice shook. "So she's to blame for turning the caring, brilliant, quietly commanding man I knew into a killer, no better than the brutes who did this to me." She held up her hand, revealing two missing fingers.

My mouth went dry. "It's really not like that. I mean, I do, but it's not random. There is a purpose."

"These men had their purposes too."

"I'm so sorry." I reached for her, but she swatted my hand away. I took a deep breath and let her have her space.

"Sonia, did you speak with a woman named Janeel after I left?"

"A friend of yours from training, right?"

"Was she one of the ones who—" I pointed to her hand.

She shook her head. "She and several others accompanied a few members of Karin's council when they visited the production facility to check on a host of projects they'd commissioned from us. I seem to recall her asking about you and then prying about the bandages I had on my hand."

She had been telling the truth, at least some of it. I swore.

Sonia raised her eyebrows and took a step backward.

I took a deep breath and let it out. "What did these people want from you?"

"To know where you were, when you'd be back, and if I knew anyone else that they could use against you."

"What did you tell them?"

She tugged her sleeves down to cover her hands. "What could I tell them? I didn't know any more than they did. Less, actually."

I stared at the new thick rug on the floor where her tormentors had likely also stood. The walls with their weavings and smattering of still frames of Sonia's family seemed to close in around me.

"I see you have a new...?" I nodded toward the spare bedroom.

"Live-in guard? Yes. Some of your people had been checking in on me, but two of them were killed a few months ago when I was attacked here. It looked like a big stunner, but the blast, it destroyed this room. I'd have been dead too if one of them hadn't thrown himself on top of me. I ended up with this though." She pulled up her sleeve to reveal a vicious scar from what I guessed to be residual effects of a pulse pistol.

Not only had she been hurt, the two men I'd asked to watch over her had been killed. And she'd been attacked again. Instead of finding someone to enjoy her evenings with, she had a guard living in her spare bedroom.

I'd done this, me and my ambition for something more exciting, something bigger and more meaningful than the life I'd had here. Now Sonia had scars inside and out and I was living out of Marin's hotel on Twelve with, according to a quick network search, a very comfortable lifetime-supply of credits on my head. That all had worked out so well. I swore again.

Company guards weren't equipped to deal with men like us. Like me. "Let me help you get away from here, somewhere where you'll be safe."

I tried to reach for her, but she batted my hand away.

"I don't need your help. I have a good job here that I enjoy very much. I thought you did too."

"I'm sorry. Really." But even as I uttered those words, my mind was already busy scanning the local vid feeds and sending inquiries to the monitoring systems connected to the vid bots and planetary surveillance feeds. Her house was tagged for observation and my arrival on her doorstep was noted for Kess or any other credit happy would-be assassin to act on. I resisted the urge to cause great amounts of damage to the nearest inanimate object, instead, putting my frustrated energy into erasing all mention of my sighting.

"I'm a complete idiot."

Sonia let out a bitter laugh. "I had a stronger word in mind, but I'll go with that."

"I need to get you out of here before anyone shows up."

"What are you talking about? I can't leave. This is my home!"

"I'm not going to let anyone else hurt you." Was I afflicting Sonia with my presence too? "I understand that you don't want to leave, but you have to. Right now."

"But all my things." She spun around, her gaze darting around the room. "My research. My job. I have responsibilities here."

Through the window, I could see darkness creep across Artor's sky, casting shadows that set my nerves tingling. "Really, I'm sorry, but we need to go."

"No, I can't just leave."

"Fine. Pack. Quickly."

Sonia chewed her lip for a moment, looking me over and following my glances out the window. She dashed into her bedroom, emerged with three empty bags and tossed one at me.

"You used to know what was important to me. You can at least be useful while you're so intent on ruining my life."

I didn't feel particularly useful to anyone at the moment, but I ran through the house, gathering up her things. The guard emerged from his room.

"What are you doing?" he asked Sonia.

"She's leaving. You should too," I said. Backup would be welcome, but he didn't have armor and the stunner would only get him so far. I didn't need another death on my hands.

Multiple sets of heavy footsteps sounded outside. The hair on the back of my neck stood on end.

"They're here. Get out the back." I shoved the guard toward the rear door.

He looked at me like I was crazy. "You're going to need help. I saw what the last ones did."

His call. I'd tried.

"Sonia!" I dashed into her bedroom. "We're leaving. Now." I took in her details and those of the bags she had frantically packed. The Jump formed in my mind. I reached out to grab her.

She dodged aside. "You're not making me vanish like you did last time. That was—"

The front door crashed open. A barrage of gunfire filled the common room.

"He's here," someone yelled.

I glanced over my shoulder. "Find some cover, and for Geva's sake, stay there."

She dropped the bags and ducked down between the bed and the wall.

Gunfire ripped through the house, shattering still frames on the wall and tearing into the furniture and the newly repaired walls. I stepped into the doorway in the hopes that my coat would keep anything from reaching Sonia. The guard lay face down on the floor, the stunner still in his grasp.

With a gun in each hand, I made quick work of the attackers.

Three bodies lay on the floor. I ruled out Kryon. They wouldn't have acted against me unless Kazan announced my defection, thereby releasing me from the 'no Kryon shall act against Kryon' rule. From their inferior armor, I guessed them to be locals looking to make a name for themselves. No matter what I did with my future, I'd be dodging their like for the rest of my life. Kazan had afflicted me with her presence too.

The echoes faded, giving way to Sonia's frantic breathing behind me. She spotted the guard and sobbed.

"Get your bags. Now."

She returned to my side seconds later with all three bags and a look somewhere between dazed and terrified.

I reached out for her. This time she didn't move an inch.

Not knowing if Marin was keeping an eye on me on Twelve, I Jumped Sonia to Karin and secured a hotel room using an alias. She'd be more comfortable there in semi-familiar surroundings than in the rough city I'd set up in on Twelve.

Sonia hadn't reacted well to the Jump, getting sick several times on the way to the hotel. Now I sat in the chair by the bedside trying to block out the stifled sobs coming from the bathroom, feeling worse by the second about everything, including myself.

When the door finally opened, Sonia's red-rimmed eyes took in the room. She bit her lip and came over to me.

"Sonia, I am sorry."

She smiled weakly.

I pulled her down onto my lap and held her. She sat rigidly against me. I was about to let go when she heaved a great sigh and wrapped her arms around my neck.

Her lips brushed against my ear. "I missed you."

She smelled of home. "I missed you too."

Our minds opened naturally to each other, reestablishing the connection I'd severed. Sorrow mixed with fear and wonder crept from her mind into mine. As much as I would have liked to fall back into the relaxed openness we'd once shared, I kept my mental defenses up and my thoughts carefully guarded.

"I thought they'd killed you. There were so many shots."

"Them?" I chuckled to put her at ease. Her body pressed

against the mass of bruises on my chest and shoulders. I was glad she couldn't see me wince.

"I can't go back, can I?"

I couldn't watch over her, not all the time. Sonia didn't belong in the world I'd chosen. "No."

She sat back to look at me. "Are you really all right?"

"Honestly, I could use a few hours of sleep."

Sonia slid off my lap and followed me onto the bed.

I fell back on the hard pillow. The exhaustion from Jumping her and her baggage above and beyond the long day before and the few rough hours of rest I'd managed earlier convinced my eyes to close. It wasn't until her familiar weight settled in next to me that I realized I was still armed and armored. My chest and arms hurt too badly to consider the effort to take it all off. That had all become a familiar weight too and perhaps, sadly, it brought me just as much ease of mind as knowing Sonia was safe.

Sleep demanded my full attention. If Sonia had it in her to murder me while I was at it, well, I deserved that. But I didn't think she would.

❧

I woke with a mass of soft hair against my cheek. I'd missed that, but what was I going to do with her?

Karin's network didn't offer any mention of me and no one had busted down the door. That was one positive step first thing in the day.

Footsteps passed up and down the hall outside our room. Each set matched Kazan's gait for a few seconds before I discounted it.

Relocating someone off any network wasn't something I had experience with. I was going to need help if Sonia was going to have a chance at a new start. Fa'yet came to mind. Being Kryon, like Kazan, he would have resources I didn't currently have access to.

He might also be looking for me, with or without threats from Kazan, but that was a chance I'd have to take.

I opened the connection we'd established and sent a tentative inquiry his way. He offered to meet us at his home in two hours. He cut contact rather abruptly, but I got the impression he was in the middle of something rather than annoyed with me. I hoped it wasn't the middle of getting an earful from Kazan.

Ten minutes later Sonia woke beside me. I watched her stretch languidly, her eyes still half closed. Then she sat up, taking in the room and her bags on the floor.

"We're going to see a friend of mine after breakfast," I said.

"Why?"

"Because I need to know you're safe, and as you've seen, that's not anywhere around me."

She bowed her head and nodded.

After a quick breakfast grabbed from a vendor cart, I hailed a transport. Jumping would have been far faster, but we had time and she hadn't enjoyed the experience whatsoever the day before.

We arrived at Fa'yet's address with only minutes to spare. His house looked like all the others on the street, tall and tucked into one of the many groupings along a tight row. The reengineering of the surface of Karin had focused on providing fertile spaces for crops rather than green spaces in residential zones.

Fa'yet opened the door before I could knock. "Come in then. No need to have her seen."

We followed him down a hallway and into a large room filled with unexpected richness when compared to the humble exterior of his home. Karin had no building resources of its own. Everything had to be imported, but apparently Kryon contracts paid extremely well.

Warm lighting hung from the high ceiling on long cables. Deep brown Moriekian wood inlaid with narrow rows of polished Artorian firestones covered the walls. Wall weavings, far more intricate than those that had been in my family, stretched from ceiling to floor, flanking his expansive liquor display. The black cabinet filled half the wall. Hundreds of tiny prismatic lights illuminated a vast array of bottles of every shape and color. Thick plaz doors kept his treasure safely confined.

There were no windows and only one other door, which I assumed led into the rest of the house. Thick rugs that swallowed our footsteps covered the floor. He brought us to four chairs sitting around a prism glass table that twinkled in the light of the convincing but artificial fire that crackled in the stone fireplace.

Sonia looked to me and Fa'yet and then sat, tucking her hands into her sleeves.

Fa'yet nodded to Sonia. "So what do you want me to do?"

"She needs a new life. I seem to have ruined the old one."

"I see."

"You have more resources than I do for this." I explained quickly over our linked connection what work she'd done previously and what had befallen her.

He offered Sonia a reassuring smile. "Don't worry. I have the perfect place for you. I think you're just what they're looking for." He turned to me. "Here are my terms. First, when she leaves, it will be with me. You will not see her again. No contact of any sort. Got it?"

"No contact?" Sonia said. "You can't be serious. We just found each other again."

I'd missed her familiar breathing beside me at night, her smile, her ability to turn most everything into an interesting conversation. However, I couldn't keep her safe, and despite all of the things I liked about her, I had no urge to form a bond and join with her.

The way she sat with one hand over the other, covering her missing fingers in the long sleeves that also hid her scars, forced my answer.

"No contact, got it."

Sonia gasped, but I made myself focus on Fa'yet. This was for the best, for both of us.

"Secondly, this is a favor, Vayen. I will not tell you where she is or anything about her. You will not ask. You will not look. I would take it very badly if you jeopardized this favor by fucking it up in any way. Do you understand me?"

I swallowed hard and nodded my agreement, all the while wondering how badly he would take the news that I'd defected from Kazan's service. I didn't plan on enlightening him or hanging around to find out.

"Then that's settled. I have to consult with a few people before we leave. That should give you adequate time to say your goodbyes and retrieve any belongings."

We all stood and he left the room. Sonia hugged her arms to her chest. "So just like that, you're leaving me again?"

"He'll set you up with a new life somewhere. I've told him what you do. I'm sure it will all be fine."

Her voice rose. "Fine? How is any of this fine? People filled my home with bullets. Real, honest to Geva bullets in my walls! What about the laws?" Her gaze dropped to my side. "That didn't look like any sort of stunner in your hand either. You really are one of them."

My mouth went dry. I nodded.

"So where does that leave us?" she asked.

"There can be no more us. You make the best of whatever life Fa'yet gives you. Find someone who will treat you better than I did and be happy." I shrugged.

"Don't let her ruin your life too. If the rumors are true, Kazan may have done good things for our people, but she's not good for you."

"I know. I quit yesterday." There, I'd said it out loud.

While the words made Sonia smile, they only made me feel hollow. Quitting sounded a lot like admitting defeat. Jey, Marin, Kess, even Kazan, they had all beaten me. Merkief, Gemmen, and Fa'yet, what would they think? What would Kazan tell them?

Sonia wrapped her arms around me. "You'll be all right then. Won't you? Those men will stop looking for you now that you're not working for her, right?"

Not a chance. "Yes."

"Good." Tears welled in her eyes as she pulled away. "Take care of yourself."

"You too."

If only it were as simple as telling Fa'yet that I wanted a new life too. But I didn't. Not exactly. I just wanted some time to fig- ure out Kazan's world without feeling so damned inadequate at every turn.

"I'll be right back." I said.

I Jumped to the hotel room and gathered up her bags along with the few things I'd brought and returned to Sonia's side. She made no move to take them from me so I set them down.

Fa'yet returned. Sonia wiped the tears from her eyes. This time it was her that sealed off our natural connection. She gave me one last look as she picked up her bags and walked to Fa'yet's side.

"Go," he said.

She would be fine now. Safe. I Jumped back to my room on Twelve to begin my new life. Alone.

Chapter Eight

Marin held up his end of the deal, throwing a few jobs my way. Piloting anything beyond an automated transport had never been one of my better skills so I had to decline his first offer. Helping to quell a riot in one of the rougher districts over a medical supply shortage left me feeling redeemed for the two simple shot-to-the-head hits I'd done the week before. When he didn't have anything else useful for me to do, he set me up as muscle in a club of a friend. While I wasn't fond of the services offered within those walls, they paid me well enough to stand there and look menacing. Unfortunately, a few days into the job, I couldn't ignore the services any longer and I looked too menacingly at a few of the clients. They asked me to leave. That must have ticked Marin off, because he didn't offer me anything else.

I didn't hear from Kazan, assuring me Marin had smoothed things over adequately. There had only been two attempts on me since I'd taken up residence on Twelve. One had been a very large woman with an artificial arm, the kind the mercs out on the fringe got, ugly and over-amped. Thankfully, because I no longer had the tank at my disposal, she hadn't snapped my neck or broken my face before I managed to pulse her directly in the chest. It was only because one eye was still swollen shut that the second attempt nearly got me one night as I went out to find dinner. Word must have gotten out to any interested local parties after I dealt with that one because the attempts halted for a few days.

Without Marin's referrals, the job market on Twelve had

nothing to offer beyond thug or thief unless I wanted to enter the general labor pool. None of those were going to earn me the name Gemmen and Marin had mentioned. Not unless I spent a long time working my way up the social underbelly ladder.

Pursuing the military career I'd trained for would lead to a background check, which would trigger countless questions I couldn't answer without implicating Kazan or the High Council. That would get me killed in short order.

I considered going elsewhere, but Thirteen was worse than Twelve. One of the Merchessian families might have been a viable opportunity, except that even if I could swallow the slavery, the families reported to Kazan.

I wasn't ready to face her. I might never be.

She held the Narvan, all the worlds I was familiar with, everything I knew. Shipping off with a crew to the fringe or landing a job on a freighter would earn me a living, but not a name that Kryon or anyone else would give a shit about.

By diving in full force with that damned woman, I'd screwed my slower track options. I'd tasted what she had to offer, the pay, the work, being on the inside of the planetary head meetings. Stepping back to a security desk job was a move I couldn't swallow. Her life was too much. Everything in between wasn't enough.

Unable to block out Chesser's disparaging voice in my head or to sort out the mess I'd made for myself, I found that drinking large quantities of alcohol at least granted me a few hours of blissful reprieve. I did use a jump point rather than walk from the hotel, varied which bar I claimed a stool in each day, and kept my face and name off any network, but by the third week of my departure from Kazan's employment, that was the extent of using the skills she had given me.

Days and nights melded together, broken on occasion by the locals, who had started to try to cash in on me again. Even not directly attached to her service, it seemed that someone thought I had enough worthwhile information stored on my link to pay out a hefty sum.

It was keeping that information, Kazan's houses, her security measures, her tank, out of anyone's hands that convinced me to Jump back to my room each time rather than letting them put an end to the mess I'd made. Kazan had driven me to learn to Jump fast and on reflex. Which was good, because taking anyone out or fighting back wasn't an option in the perpetual drunken condition I allowed myself to maintain.

One blurry evening, as I was busy staring at the traffic passing overhead in the reflection of my half-full mug at a sparsely-occupied over-priced outside bar, I felt someone looking at me. Not in the usual conversational observance of betting on how drunk I might be, or the prickly back of my neck sort that triggered my reflex to Jump, but just staring. Had I become an easy mark for Twelve's roving street thieves now?

I gave everyone outside the plascrete half-wall that separated the bar from the sidewalk a good dose of my glare. No one stood out. Maybe I'd finally drowned enough brain cells to start losing my mind.

I finished my drink and signaled for another. The hazy face of the woman who had been filling my mug for the past few hours said something about promising not to cause any trouble, to which I nodded so she'd pour the damned liquor already.

That drink was nearly gone when someone came up beside me. That prickly feeling didn't come with them so I figured it was just one of the other customers I wasn't supposed to cause trouble with. I did my best to ignore them, and that was working quite well until he started to talk.

"What are you doing?" a man's voice asked.

"Drinking. Leave me alone."

He put his hand on my shoulder. "Do you have a room around here?"

"Fuck off." I might be drunk, but not that drunk.

I tried to get off my stool, to get away from him before I did cause trouble, but came to the belated realization that I might have lost track of how many I'd had because I couldn't seem to get my feet under me. I tried to catch the edge of the bar, but there were several of them and none of them were solid.

My mug fell, shattering on the stained plascrete. I found myself next to it, palm bleeding from a gash with a transparent brown shard sticking out of it. That was going to hurt. Eventually.

I yanked the shard out and tried to form a Jump, but with everything around me spinning, it was difficult to focus.

Someone tried to help me up. I swatted them away. "I'm fine."

"Sure you are," said the voice that had been next to me. It was a voice I knew, one I wasn't prepared to put a name to just then. Even the thought of doing so made my stomach turn. If he was here, so was she. I vomited on the floor.

The woman at the bar said, "You can't take him without paying his tab."

"Holy hells, how long has he been here?"

"All day."

The rasp of a chip sliding through a reader registered. He knocked me in the back of the head.

"You owe me," Merkief said.

Everything lurched sideways. I realized I was standing again, or leaning. It was hard to tell beyond all the spinning.

"Let's get you cleaned up. You have a lot of explaining to do."

At least my link was safe if Merkief got it. With my last conscious thought, I prayed to Geva for a terminal case of alcohol poisoning.

❧

I cracked open one very dry eye to find myself in the hotel room on Twelve. Merkief sat nearby, watching the local vid.

"Did she send you here to kill me?" I asked.

He didn't turn around. "Yeah, that's why I paid your ungodly tab, bandaged your hand, and have been wiping vomit off your face for the past twelve hours."

I connected vague snippets of memories. "Right. Thanks."

"And in case you forgot from the last twenty times you asked, Kazan doesn't hate you, and she doesn't want you dead."

"Sorry." I had been saying that word a lot lately. "I honestly didn't think she'd take it so well, not even with Marin talking to her instead of me."

That got him out of the chair and looming over me, looking mightily annoyed. "Take what? I don't know what you're rambling about, yet again, but she's going to demand answers and you better have them ready. If I have to share another off-shift with Jey, I'm going to kill someone. And not the someone I'm supposed to."

He made a disgusted sound. "Nevermind. Just fix whatever the hells it is you fucked up with Kazan and get back into rotation."

"Get back into rotation? Why would I go back?"

Merkief exhaled loudly. "Look, I get that Jey was an ass about the Karin job. He laid it on hard with Kazan. Marin didn't help on that front either. If you were hoping for him to stand up for you, your hopes were very misplaced."

Why were the lights so damned bright? I covered my eyes with my arm and tried to time the throbbing in my head with my breathing. "You don't happen to have a stim on you, do you? I don't know where mine are."

"I suppose you're coherent enough now not to choke on it." He tossed his tin at me.

It hit my side. I fumbled with it, my hands shaking. Once I got one out and in my mouth, I found I didn't have enough saliva to swallow it. Merkief handed me a glass of water.

"You're going to want to drink a lot of that. When was the last time you ate?"

"I have no idea." I drained the glass and set it down before collapsing back onto the bed. "Not that I don't appreciate you dropping by, but why are you here? I resigned. I don't work for her anymore."

Merkief laughed. It faltered and trailed off to an uncomfortable silence.

"Marin was supposed to give her my resignation, not stand up for me," I said.

He sat back down heavily and kicked at a tangle of clothes on the floor. "We haven't been able to get a ping on you for over a month. Kazan has worked herself into a frenzy, thinking someone offed you. I've been hunting for you for weeks. Just happened that I caught a notice of you sitting there for long enough to get a solid location before it vanished. How the hells were you still covering your tracks while that drunk?"

"Talented, I guess. Can you talk quieter?"

"Really though, what is this about a resignation?" he asked at the same damned volume. "You can't quit. She needs you."

It was my turn to laugh.

"Can you make up something about nearly getting killed to explain your absence? If you tell her the truth she's going to... Geva I don't know, but I don't want to have to clean what's left of you out of the rug when she's done."

The stim started to work, clearing the haze from my thoughts. "Does she know that you found me?"

"Yes, but I didn't tell her about your condition. I said that I'd bring you in as soon as I could. She's been on my ass for the past eleven of the twelve hours since we've been here, and I honestly don't think I can hold her off from showing up here herself for much longer. So if you could shower and change so we can get on with this, I would greatly appreciate it."

I sat up slowly. The spins had subsided to a slow twisting and swaying of the room and my stomach. The room was littered with crumpled clothing, empty bottles and overturned furniture. When had I done that and why hadn't room service done anything about it? I vaguely remembered threatening someone who had entered my room. How long ago had that been?

Imagining Kazan's revulsion at the sheer chaos of it all convinced me to get in the shower. The pelting of the water on my skin woke me up a little further. By the time I got out and found something to wear that didn't smell too horrible, the room was again stable and my shakes had subsided. Thank Geva for stims.

Merkief helped gather up my stuff. I crammed it back into the pack.

"You're not going to bolt, right? You'll go talk to her?" he asked.

"No, I'm not going to bolt."

"You want to practice your story? You came up with something, didn't you? Please tell me you did."

"I'm not giving her a story."

He sighed. "Your choice. Not a good one, but yours. After you then. Merchess, by the way."

I carried my coat and weapons. Arriving armed seemed unwise if she was wound as tight as Merkief made it sound. He took the pack from me. Likely not to be helpful, but because he hoped that I wouldn't run off without my stuff. As if the loss of a bunch of dirty clothes would compel me to meet with Kazan. It was more that I didn't have running in me and nowhere else to go.

❧

I Jumped to the foyer of the Merchessian house. Merkief arrived seconds later. Jey stood behind Kazan with a hand on the gun at his side. Merkief made a show of shouldering the pack and taking the coat and weapons from my hands before taking a few steps back.

Back in close proximity, Kazan reestablished our linked connection. Her concern and anger bombarded me. I dialed her down but didn't shut her out.

Jey stepped forward. "Where in the nine hells have you been?"

Kazan was one thing, but after the last conversation we'd shared, my tolerance for Jey had bottomed out.

"I don't believe I work for you."

Kazan pushed him aside. "I was beginning to wonder if you still worked for *me*."

I tore my gaze from Jey to Kazan. Her concern wavered to uncertainty; she was waiting for me to attack. The tension flowing from both of them made it hard for me to think clearly. I needed to get her alone.

"Can we talk?" I asked.

Kazan looked over my shoulder to Merkief and then nodded. Jey walked between us until we reached her office. He followed her inside.

She put her hand on his chest. "You can go."

"I don't think that's wise." Jey stood his ground. "He's been gone for thirty-eight days without a word. Neither of us knows what he did or who he talked to on Twelve. You shouldn't be alone with him."

"Your concerns are noted. If you don't trust him, wait outside the door." Kazan shoved Jey aside and clamped her fingers around my wrist. She yanked me forward and closed the door. "Sit."

I sat, but remained at the edge of the chair, every muscle screaming at me to get back on my feet.

She backed away, putting just enough space between us that she could lunge or retreat as necessary. "So, are you here to kill me?"

"No. Are you going to kill me?" I asked.

Her gaze darted about my person before coming to rest on my empty hands clamped down on the arms of the chair. "Not at the moment."

I let my muscles ease a minute fraction.

"Then, as Jey put it so nicely, where the hell have you been?"

Maybe Merkief was right about going with a story, but all I had was the truth, or a version of it anyway. "I had to take care of some personal things."

"Personal things?" Her voice rose. "Why don't you start by explaining why you dropped out of contact?"

The betrayal of her past partners was surely racing through her mind. She didn't have a weapon in hand, but she was armed and armored, so that could change any second.

Marin hadn't delivered my resignation, no doubt for a damned good reason. Until I knew what that reason was, I didn't want to shake her trust in others any further by pulling him into the fray with me. Jey, on the other hand.

"I'm sure Jey told you about Janeel," I said.

"The guard that Jey claims you were busy mindfucking while I got shot?"

I stared at my hands, seeing them wrapped around Janeel's throat. "We were friends once."

"Why didn't you tell me about the personal conflict before we went in?"

"I didn't expect to have to be the one to—"

Kazan turned away. "I see. So he was right. You were off sulking."

"I was what?" Maybe depressed and even wallowing by the time Merkief found me, but I took great offence to sulking. "Jey is a—"

"He's done enough name calling for the both of you." Her stare remained intent and unwavering. "So what were you doing with Janeel when you should have been killing her, other than letting her talk, which I expressly told you not to do more than once?"

"She told me Sonia had been hurt."

"That was considerate of her, you know, while you had your hands around her throat."

"Hardly, but I had to go see if there was anything I could do, if it was because of me. You were in the tank. Jey and Merkief were with you. She didn't have anyone."

"And?" Her boot tapped an impatient rhythm on the stone floor.

"Yes, it was because of me. They pulsed her house, killed the two guards I'd asked to watch over her, and took two of her fingers."

"I warned you."

Her lack of compassion brought me to my feet. "I never went back there until now! I dropped her to work for you, and she still got hurt anyway."

She stepped backward, readjusting her stance. When she spoke again her tone had softened. "I see. So you spent some time with her."

"One night. I spent one night with her, and not for the reason you're thinking, but because her house got shot to shit while I was there and another guard got killed. We went to Fa'yet and he helped to relocate her."

"You went to him and not me?"

I couldn't believe she was offended over that, not in light of how she'd been treating me for months. "I'm sure you had better things to do, what with taking on Karin on top of every other damned thing you have going on."

Seeing that she'd gone distant for a few seconds, I sat back down. If we were going to both leave this room alive, I needed to remain calm in order to keep her calm.

"He says you were there, but that was over a month ago. What were you doing on Twelve?"

Her stance screamed suspicion. Her hands hovered over the slits in her coat.

"Sit down, would you? I'm not out to get you. I told you before that I wouldn't do that."

"So you've said, but they're just words, and I've heard them before. Knowing you, you'll eventually find some way around them so you can keep your precious conscience intact." Kazan waved my unspoken protest to silence. "Who recruited you? What were you doing? Talk. Now."

So much for a story. All I had left was the other end of the truth.

"Why don't you ask Merkief what I was doing when he found me?"

She grew quiet and distant again, and then her eyes widened. "Is this really you?"

The image of a very unkempt, very drunk me staring at a mug on a bar popped into my head. No longer drunk enough to drown him out, Chesser's voice goaded me with disparaging remarks. I made a pact with myself right then and there not to provide him with any more fodder. The answer to my mess of a life was to embrace it and make the best of the choice I'd made until the day I didn't Jump fast enough.

"Looks like I'm up to some serious plotting against you, doesn't it?"

"I knew I shouldn't have dragged you away from her." Her hands relaxed and she rolled her neck and shoulders. She held up her hand and went distant again.

When she came back to herself, she said, "I cut the vid feed for the room. They don't need to hear or see this. Between you and me now, honestly, was there a bond involved?"

"I wouldn't have left if there was."

Relief washed over her face. "But you still care about her."

"Why, is that against one of your damned rules too?"

"No, but it's easier if you don't."

"Look around, Anastassia. Nothing in this life is easy, no matter what you say about not letting the condemned talk or not caring about anyone." I got up, determined to leave before I totally lost my temper and talked my way out of getting my job back.

She grabbed my arm before I could get past her. "I never said this life was easy, and I never said I didn't care about anyone."

"You don't have to say you don't care, you do a fine job of showing it."

Like a sudden break in the clouds, her mask dropped and she was that woman who had sat on the bed next to me sharing memories of Chesser. Her grip on my arm loosened to become a simple familiar touch. She stepped forward until she stood against me, forehead resting on my shoulder.

"I'm sorry, it's complicated," she said.

What was this now? I didn't know how she flipped her emotions on an off like that but it gave me whiplash.

"Everything about you is damned complicated."

The weight on my shoulder increased. "I'm glad you're all right. I was worried."

"I heard. Though it's why you're glad now, after you didn't hardly speak or look at me when I was here, that I'm having a hard time with."

I put my hands on her shoulders and gently pushed her away. "If you want me to be your partner, quit treating me like an afterthought. If that promotion was a mistake, then fucking say so."

Kazan stiffened and her mask fell back into place. "It wasn't."

"Good. Then whatever you feel for Marin or any of the others you pull into your bed, is your business. Leave me out of it and stay out of mine."

"I see," she said. With her emotions back under lockdown, if she was relieved, upset, or seconds away from deciding to kill me, I'd never know it. "Then know that if you pull this unannounced leave of absence shit again, we'll be having this discussion in a far different manner."

"Understood."

She shifted her weight, the fingers on one hand rubbing

together. A swallow. A slow blink. Then she met my gaze once again. "Now that you're back, we'll resume rotation. You're on in two hours."

🙞

My big return to partner duty turned out to be another one of her damned sleep shifts. I settled in at the security station, hoping that maybe Merkief would wander out and keep me company for a little while before he went to bed. Unfortunately, as I surveyed the feeds, I noticed Merkief in bed and then Jey's face glaring at me in another camera. She might of had the courtesy to let me know rotation had changed. Especially knowing how well Jey and I got along.

I wasn't surprised when he came through the archway and into the security station a few minutes later. His hand clamped down on my chair and spun it around.

"Why the hells did you come back? She was getting used to the idea that you were gone," he said.

"I'm sure you helped that idea along."

"Marin assured me that you were agreeable to disappearing. What did it matter what Kazan chose to think?"

"He assured you? You were working with Marin?" That conniving bastard. Both of them. "Did you really think she would promote you to partner in my place?"

"You didn't want to be here!" he said.

"I thought I had other places to be. I was wrong." At the sight of his clenched fists, I stood too. "I'm here and I'm staying, so you better get that through your thick Jalvian skull."

He took a swing at my face. I managed to dodge his fist and catch him under the jaw. It didn't slow him down as much as I'd hoped.

Jey swung again. Ducking under another heavy-handed swing, I rushed him. My shoulder connected with his chest and sent him over backward. His head hit the edge of the archway with a heavy thud. The sound must not have carried because when I glanced over my shoulder to check the vids, Merkief was still blissfully sleeping and Kazan's door remained shut.

His eyes had a dazed look to them. I pinned him down while I had the chance.

"If I ever catch wind of you conspiring with Marin to get rid of me again, I'll kill you."

That seemed to snap him out of it. He struggled beneath me. "I'd like to see you try."

I would have too, but without concrete evidence against him, Kazan would never forgive me. "Your scheme put Kazan's safety at risk."

"It wasn't a scheme. You set it in motion, Marin and I just went with it. We all want what was best for Kazan, and we all want her safe. You weren't up to it so you left."

More like Marin dangled an out in front of me and I ran with it. He wasn't my friend on any level, and I was beginning to doubt that he was Kazan's friend either. She was playing him to a degree, but did he have his own game?

"Kazan may have been distracted, but in time she would have given up her search and gone about her business," Jey said. "Merkief or I stayed with her the entire time. I never lied to her about you," Jey said.

"It sure sounded like you were planting suspicion in her head when I showed up."

"We didn't have the right to be suspicious? You left and then showed up out of nowhere. Even Merkief wasn't entirely sure of your intentions. We are all concerned about Kazan's safety." Jey's gaze never wavered, and when he said Kazan, he appeared every bit as zealous as he had when we'd first met.

"You told Marin how the job went down when we split up."

Jey nodded.

"What did he tell you?" I asked.

"That he'd take care of it. After he talked to you, he told me that you'd quit and that I should do everything I could to keep her safe. He suggested that we bring her to his compound for a few days until she calmed down. So we did." He bucked beneath me. "Let me up, dammit."

I got up and returned to my chair. "How's your head?"

"It hurts, you bastard. What do you think?"

"I think you deserved it."

He got to his feet and rubbed the back of his head. When he pulled his hand away, I was relieved to see that there wasn't any blood. Kazan would be pissed if I sent him to the tank, whether he was the one that swung first or not.

"And unless you'd like our forgiving and lenient boss to learn that you knew what was going on but chose not to say anything,

I would suggest you back the fuck off and respect my position," I said.

Jey's jaw went tight and his eyes narrowed, but he offered the slightest of nods before turning on his heel and making for the stairs.

I watched the wall of vids until his footsteps finally retreated. Even after he'd left, I couldn't relax. What Jey had said about Marin kept bouncing around in my head. If he wanted what was best for Kazan, why hadn't he given her my resignation? He'd gotten his way. She'd come to him for solace, but he still didn't tell her the truth. If I was going to have a chance at figuring out what he was up to, I was going to have to talk to him.

After giving the vids a thorough look, I buckled down everything in my head and opened my link to Marin.

"Thank you for your assistance, but I've chosen to come back."

"I heard. Damn selfish of you."

"You made it quite easy since you didn't give her my resignation," I said.

He kept his tone level, as though I were nothing more than a minor annoyance. *"She wasn't out to kill you. That was your concern, and I said I'd keep it from happening. I upheld my end of the bargain."*

"The deal was you telling her plainly that I was quitting. I even gave you the words to say. She should have been working, but you let her stew and worry. You were wasting her time."

"Just like you do every day that you remain there," he said, sounding far more aggravated now.

"What the fuck is your problem with me?"

"We covered that. In detail. I tried to be civil, but you threw that in my face by slinking back. Don't expect the same courtesy in the future." Marin cut contact.

Whenever Kazan did feel inclined to return me to work duty, I hoped to all hells it didn't involve anything with Marin. No matter how much of a work face I might plan to put on, I rather doubted I could fake my way through any level of politeness where he was concerned. What did she see in that manipulative lying bastard anyway?

❧

Almost a month and a half later, without any explanation,

Kazan rearranged our schedules, which put me back on working contracts with her again. Whatever her reasoning, I accepted my good fortune and kept my mouth shut. Her previous mood of avoidance had vanished, leaving only a zone of silence over my disappearance that enveloped any half-asked question on her part or mumbled answer on mine.

Having promised myself I would make more of an effort at living up to being Kazan's partner, I'd spent the last few weeks seeking out something to make me more useful in her eyes. My search led me to the perpetual stack of datapads that consumed a good deal of her time. Once we were back to working together again, I'd offered to review Gemmen's company reports and she'd smiled. There hadn't been many smiles between us in quite some time. It was a nice change.

I spent a week of my off shifts going over the details of all the reports before asking if she minded if I met with Gemmen to discuss them. With her blessing, I then Jumped to Rok.

Gemmen sat in his office, examining the vid screen in front of him. When he noticed me standing in the doorway, a friendly smile broke out on his weathered face.

"Good to see you. Have a seat."

For the next two hours, Gemmen went over my suggested new scouting patterns for the Nebula and beyond with enthusiasm. Once we hammered out the details, I sat back to see what other information he might hold. If I was going to stick around, I needed to know where my predecessors had gone wrong.

"How is it that Kazan managed to kill one partner, yet Kess is still around?"

Gemmen chuckled. "Doing a little digging, are we?"

"Maybe."

"Between you and me, I think it comes down to one thing. She hated Zsmed more."

"I don't know as that could be possible," I said.

"Well, Kess tried to kill her. She deals with that every day. Zsmed went after her on a more personal level."

I shook my head. "How can you get more personal than attempting to kill someone?"

"By killing someone else." Gemmen sighed and sat back in his chair. He rolled his head slowly left to right, his neck making crackling noises as he winced.

Kazan's solemn face when she'd heard of Sonia's disfigurement, came to mind. "Who did he kill?" I asked.

"She didn't share the details, but I gathered it was someone innocent. Did a real number on her." His chair creaked as he shifted his position. "Zsmed got the Fragians involved in the bloody mess too. She doesn't talk about it much, and if you value your life, I wouldn't dig any further."

That explained her sympathy. Thank Geva, Sonia hadn't suffered a similar fate.

His serious demeanor faded into a smile. "You've got a good head on your shoulders, kid. The best way to keep it there is to keep your mouth shut around Kazan."

"I'll try."

He laughed. "That's all any of us can do."

Chapter Nine

Kazan leaned against the wall of the security station. "Would you like to get something to eat?"

I glanced back to the vids, giving myself a few seconds to save the extended Cragtek planning I'd been working on in my spare time. I'd been handling the reports for a few months now. Gemmen seemed happy with having my attention and Kazan a little more relaxed with having one less thing to deal with on a daily basis.

"What do you want me to get?" I asked.

"Merkief and Jey are doing some set up on a contract. It's just the two of us for a few hours. How about we both go?"

The last time the two of us went out to spend time alone together, I ended up drunk on the floor with Anastassia doing wonderful things in my head. Fun as that one night was, I thought I'd made it pretty clear I wasn't interested in repeating it.

"I don't think so. Just tell me what you're hungry for and I'll get it."

Her eyebrow quirked. "Vayen, it's dinner. What's the difference if we eat together here or somewhere else?"

"There's a difference, and you damn well know it."

"It's just dinner. There may even be conversation involved if that doesn't violate your personal space rules."

At least she acknowledged my decree. "Fine. Get your coat."

She stayed put. "I was thinking we could go somewhere nice, where people who don't wear armor eat."

"That sounds an awful lot like a place that people who are doing more than just having dinner might go." I crossed my arms and remained in my seat.

"You're damn difficult, you know that?"

I shrugged and turned back to the vids. I expected her to storm off in short order, but she didn't. When I turned to see if there was a gun in her hand or a curse waiting to be flung in my face, I found her mask wavering instead.

Dammit, real moments of Anastassia were rare. Did I really want to squander this one when we were finally settling into a productive work relationship? A little outside of work conversation with someone other than Merkief might not be so bad.

"This isn't going to require me changing my clothes, is it?" The hesitant look on her face informed me that it did. I sighed. "Give me a few minutes then."

Kazan smiled as I passed her to head for the stairs. I went to my room, hung up my coat, and found a reasonably pressed shirt in my closet. At least I had a few weapons in my work pants, and if she was demanding no armor, the shirt was the only concession I was willing to make.

I found her right where I'd left her, but she had changed as well. She wore a black shirt and fitted grey pants, nothing unusual for her, except a more form-accentuating cut. I paused to give her a suspicious look.

"What?" she asked.

I shook my head. "Where are we going?"

She flashed me one of our usual Artorian jump points. Once there, we walked several blocks, during which my skin crawled and my mind replayed the first day I'd been on Artor with her, unarmored and under attack. Here I was unarmored again, only this time at her whim. At least she stuck right by me and no bullets erupted from the rooftops.

We walked in a silence neither of us seemed sure how to break. She stopped at a roadside terminal and signaled for a transport. When it arrived, she input the destination and sat across from me.

"So, where are we going?" I asked again.

Rather than tell me, she opened her link and showed me a tall, plaz spire building surrounded by a garden courtyard. I knew that place. It stood near the center of the city where I'd grown up. At the top of it was the most expensive restaurant around. I'd never even dreamed of eating there, but apparently, I was about to.

Once we got there, the lift took ten minutes to reach the top and when the door opened, I had the overwhelming feeling that we didn't belong. Maybe it was the stares from the crowd of other patrons waiting to be seated or the haughty once over the attendant gave us as we stepped out.

I definitely should have changed my pants. Then again, I didn't even own the sort of attire that would have allowed me to fit in here.

Kazan ignored everyone but the attendant, to whom she spoke quietly for a moment. His back went ramrod straight and apologies dripped from his lips as he scrambled to lead us to a small table against the nearest wall of windows. A row of empty tables around us formed a barricade of privacy.

"What are the odds of us keeping this space to ourselves?" I asked, laughing at the idea while so many people were still waiting for a table, but it would have helped put me more at ease. I sorely missed the weight of my coat. Knowing Anastassia was just as vulnerable, I kept myself on guard and one hand resting on the pants pocket that concealed a small gun.

Kazan cleared her throat and picked up her menu. "The odds are pretty good. I may have made reservations."

"Anastassia." Her head remained hidden behind her menu. Why did I suddenly feel utterly manipulated? "Anastassia."

She laid the menu on the table. "Can't we at least be friends? Is that too much to ask?"

"No, but don't play me or it will." Jey and Marin screwing with me were one thing, but her joining their ranks would be much harder to swallow.

Her gaze dropped to the crisp, white table cloth. "What happened before...after we... I didn't mean to be so angry with you. But that bond thing..." When she met my eyes, the mask was gone. "I know what that can do to you, to us, and I don't want it. We spend so much time together as it is and after that, I thought that if I put distance between us—"

"You thought you could prevent me from bonding with you."

She nodded. Her fingers writhed where she kept her hands clasped together on the tabletop. I let her steep in her discomfort for a minute, amused at the revelation that the woman who could shrug off an impending war with Fragia was so disconcerted when it came to relationships.

"For the record, I have no intention of forming a bond with

you. I don't know what rumors you've heard, but bonds don't just happen by association like our links syncing up. They have to be allowed to form. It takes a conscious effort. Which means I'd have to want to form a bond with you, and trust me, I don't."

"I see," she said quietly.

She stared out the window where sunlight glinted off the distant sky traffic. The soft music coming from the ceiling speakers, clinks of silverware against dinnerware, and muffled conversations couldn't mask the ensuing hush that settled over our table.

I didn't feel inclined to further ease her fears by revealing that even when I'd thought I'd wanted to form a bond with Sonia, it hadn't happened. Maybe I was defective. That was just as well in this case.

Anastassia didn't turn back until an impeccably dressed waiter came to take our order. When we were again alone, an unfamiliar waver hid just behind her trivial tone.

"What a relief. Chesser was unclear about it, and I don't usually keep Artorian men close to me. I didn't know the specifics of the process."

So she'd leapt to conclusions and treated me like shit because of them? I tried to keep my tone civil, but couldn't muster the effort to harness much else. "Yeah, I've heard all about your preference for Jalvians."

Her face flushed. "Where did you hear that?"

"Not from a particular Jalvian we live with, if that makes you any less uncomfortable."

Not that I expected him to brag about his conquests to me. Gemmen had made her preferences clear enough, and it was obvious she'd been quite close to Kess. I'd heard plenty of whispers about her personal life since I'd hired on to back up who she liked in her bed beyond Marin.

"This isn't going how I envisioned it," she said.

"Sorry to deviate from your unshared plans. What did you expect me to be doing right now?"

Anastassia sat back as the wine was poured and our first course served. When the waiter left, she gulped down half of her wine. "Enjoying dinner, laughing, telling me about the latest thing Jey's done to annoy you. I don't know."

In an effort to be nice, I tried the wine. It was rich and complex and sorely wasted in her gulping. The bread melted in my mouth and the salad reminded me of the crisp greens my mother had grown in her garden.

'Jey hasn't been the one annoying me lately', didn't seem the right way to proceed. If she wanted a conversation, maybe it was best to steer it somewhere less personal before I ended up more pissed off and back on her sleep shift.

"Gemmen has been having luck with my scouting patterns that you approved," I said.

"Oh?" She took a smaller gulp of wine and warily picked at her salad.

"I have a few other ideas I'd like to try if you wouldn't mind."

"What kind of ideas?" she asked.

"With a little restructuring, we could cut costs and make the whole operation more efficient."

"We?" Her eyebrows rose. "Gemmen put you up to this, didn't he?"

While Gemmen had encouraged my efforts to improve Cragtek, he didn't deserve to suffer her wrath. "No, I meant you and me, but you're busy. We both know that. I haven't seen you do a single new thing with the company since I signed on. As it stands, it's a mostly wasted resource. Let me help you make it more useful."

"You all want to control Cragtek." She put her fork down with enough force to send a tremor through the table. "But you know what? You won't be happy with just that. Next, you'll want half the fucking Narvan and the High Council's ear. None of you are ever happy."

I kept my voice level and held her gaze. "I know Cragtek is important to you and the Narvan as a whole because of the tech they acquire, but have you actually tried handing control of it to anyone?"

"No, of course not. I just told you—"

"Did giving your past partners nothing make them happy? Seems to me it makes them want you dead. How about trying something different?"

Anastassia's mouth dropped open for a second before snapping shut. She stared at her salad. Without her coat to hide behind, her stiff posture was plain to see. She emptied her glass and took her time swallowing it down.

When she did speak, her voice was as tight as the rest of her. "Just what other plans did you have in mind?"

"Further changing the raiding routes into Fragian space,

branching out into a few other nearby systems, that sort of thing. More stolen tech would yield more credits, which would finance a new medical clinic that Gemmen has been asking for. Also, setting up a front business, selling low-grade versions of the tech we find and alter, would offer employment for the extraneous population of Cragtek, reducing the need for family leave and providing additional income for you and the men."

"You seem to have put some thought into this." She exhaled loudly.

Our salads were cleared away and small bowls of soup took their place. We both stirred the steaming brown liquid. I tried to keep my focus on the bowl to give her some space, but I could feel her gaze homing in on me. My bowl had cooled enough to enjoy and was half empty before she finally replied.

"I'll tell you what; I'll give you two weeks off to see what you can do with the company. If we're both happy with the results, it's yours."

While I'd hoped she'd at least think about it, her degree of acquiescence stunned me. "Seriously?"

Anastassia looked at me for a long moment and then smiled. "Yes, seriously."

I couldn't help but grin back.

"Now, that's the face I was hoping to see tonight."

I laughed.

Dinner passed in a blur of expounding on my ideas for Cragtek, excellent food and two bottles of very potent wine. Anastassia paid the bill, which had come close to a weeks's wages for an average Artorian by the time we were through, without even the slightest deviation from her new-found smile.

"I was thinking," she said as we took the lift down to the street, "that in light of our level of celebration, it might be wise to Jump to one of the other houses and spend the night there."

She might not have been full out drunk, but Jey and Merkief would likely be back by now and notice that she'd been drinking more than her usual restrained public limit.

"How about we just go back to Merchess and get some sleep?" I suggested. "If you go right to your room, neither of them will know we've been out drinking together. Or, since you are the boss, you could just tell them the truth. We had dinner to discuss Cragtek business."

"I suppose that's true." She left that hanging in the air until the lift reached street level.

"If you're waiting for me to change my mind, it's not going to happen."

"Sleep it is then," she said. Yet she slipped her hand around my arm and led me into a darkened hallway that led to one of the currently closed businesses on the ground floor.

Once we were out of sight, I gently removed her hand and stepped aside. "We can Jump separately from here. Thank you for dinner and the chance at Cragtek."

"Thanks for agreeing to come." She eyed the space between us. "I suppose you'll want to head off as soon as possible."

"Not necessarily. I can work on more planning until you can get by without me."

"I've gotten by without you before. It's only two weeks, right?" Her smile made a forced appearance just before she Jumped.

Chapter Ten

Gemmen walked into the office that he'd told me had been Kazan's when she'd spent more time there. "Enjoying your last few days of freedom?"

I nodded. The furniture in the corner reminded me of Kazan every time I looked up from the vid, but I tried not to do that too often. I'd spent a good deal of the last eleven days supervising changes on Cragtek property to keep my time in her office minimal.

"So you're not missing her at all then?" He took the seat on the other side of the desk.

I sat back and scowled at his grinning face. "You're not funny. She's been checking in constantly, and I'm guessing, not just with me."

Gemmen chuckled. He might have been amused by her frequent presence in his head, but I wasn't. Her version of getting by without me wasn't what I'd had in mind. It was like she was standing right over my shoulder even though I'd been submitting in-depth daily reports to her. The only consolation was that she was mostly quiet, observing more than anything else.

"You can't really blame her," he said. "She's given you something huge. It's a big step for her, even if it doesn't seem big enough for you. She certainly hasn't made that sort of effort for anyone else."

He tapped his chin. "You're sure you're not missing her?"

"Good Geva, no, not in that way. What is it with everyone

thinking I'm stupid enough to form a bond with her?"

"No offence. I was just looking to explain her indulgence on your part," he said.

"We're not together. Not like that, on any level."

"If you say so." His face scrunched up and he shook his head. "Whatever you've been doing, keep it up, I guess. Like I said, she doesn't normally yield anything to anyone."

Unless she liked that I refused to get involved with her, I doubted there was much on the favorable side for me at the moment. The most non-direct work related conversation we'd shared since my interview had been at that last dinner. We did seem to work well together when coordination was necessary, but that was about the extent of it.

"It's just business. Speaking of which, did that last raid yield any significant new acquisitions?" I asked.

He launched into an animated report, after which we returned to expanding on our plans for Cragtek's future. I enjoyed my brainstorming sessions with Gemmen to the degree that our races fell away and it almost seemed possible that we were indeed one people of a common mind.

It was a couple of hours later, just as Gemmen was leaving, that Kazan's flustered voice in my head took me by surprise. *"Where are you?"* she asked.

"In your office."

"I'll be right there."

"Hold on a moment," I said to Gemmen. "She's coming."

He sat back down and gave me a questioning look.

"No idea." But she didn't fluster easily and that had me concerned. If she was going to go off about something I'd done here, I hoped Gemmen would back me up.

She walked in three minutes later. "A job came up. I need you back." Her tone didn't allow for argument and neither did the tension on her face.

"Let me get my things out of your office, and I'll be ready to go." I stood to reach for my pack. Its previous contents lay in the corner beside the couch on which I'd been spending my nights so I could devote as much time as possible implementing my plans.

Her gaze darted around the room. "Keep the office. I don't have time to use it anyway."

Gemmen chuckled in my head, though his face remained perfectly composed.

She stepped towards me. "You've done an excellent job here. Gemmen seems happy with your changes, and I'm happy with your projected profits. However, I do need you back beside me. Do you think you can handle both responsibilities?"

I managed to restrain my urge for enthusiastic blurting to a more composed, "Yes."

She turned to Gemmen. "You will now report directly to Vayen."

He grinned, but only after she'd turned away from him.

"I expect you to report any major changes or issues. I'm sure you grasp how important Cragtek is. Don't fuck it up."

I nodded. While I wondered if she would have put up more resistance had there not been some sort of emergency job, I was relieved that she hadn't. After getting my feet wet here, I wasn't about to back off without a good deal of resistance of my own.

She flashed me a jump point and we stepped into the void. I looked up from the cluttered alleyway in which we'd arrived to the metal dome sky of Thirteen. The dim artificial light indicated the night cycle, but I heard plenty of activity around us; transports humming down the streets, thumping music, men yelling and a burst of laughter.

"What are we doing here?" I asked.

"Hunting Kess."

"Mind filling me in?"

Her body tensed just before she rushed into a shadowed doorway at the end of the alley. I joined her there and made out Merkief's shape in the deep shadows of the building ahead of us.

"Jey picked up a sighting tip here two hours ago. He managed to get inside the building by posing as backup for the business group. They're signing a contract with Kess as we speak. Merkief is riding along on Jey's link to keep tabs on what's going on. I'm getting your ass and mine over there, so we can kill this bastard once and for all."

"Why can't Jey off him? He's right there." I wasn't sure if I should be worried that she was resorting to Kess's methods of interfering with contracts, or hopeful. After all, he'd been nearly successful both times. Maybe we'd finally be the lucky ones.

"The group hiring him is distantly associated with Marin. If we off him right now, it's going to cause Marin problems. We've not been getting along very well lately, and I don't want to give him further reason to be pissed at me."

Kazan and Marin not getting along sounded more like a cause for celebration. That viscu didn't even know who she really was. She deserved more than that.

"So we're going to follow Kess, let him complete the contract and then kill him?" I asked.

"Eventually, yes. I need information from him. Keep him alive and his head intact."

We dashed across the street to meet Merkief.

Merkief regarded us with a distracted nod. "Jey has the contract information. Timeframe is short. If we trail the target, we'll find Kess."

Kazan nodded. "Merkief, wait for Jey and then join us. Vayen and I will locate the target."

She shared the location she'd received from Jey and we Jumped.

"There he is." I nodded toward the white-haired man stalking the Jalvian target across the street. We followed, keeping out of sight and giving him plenty of space. If he meant to chase his target to a more out of the way place to kill him, all the better for us.

Within minutes, Merkief joined us. It took me a moment to spot Jey as he was still in disguise and wearing worn armor with far less weapon bulk beneath it than usual. They split away to cover Kess from the other side of the street. The noise of the marketplace faded away and traffic thinned, forcing us to scamper between doorways and building corners to remain unseen.

The target seemed to realize he was being followed and sprinted down the street. He ducked into a litter-filled back alley. Kess followed him in. The target spun around and held out his empty hands, offering credits in return for his life. Kess didn't let him finish. He pulled the trigger. The target dropped to the ground near a haphazard stack of scrap metal.

With Marin's contract safely completed, Kazan gave the go ahead to aim for Kess. We stepped into the open and fired.

Kess spun around, surprise plain on his face. Scrambling for cover he fired at me. It felt damn good to have the upper hand for once.

Jey and Merkief popped into the alley from the opposite end.

With a wall between us and Kess, I glanced over my shoulder to make sure Kazan was safe behind me. "He seems determined to blast through me today. Usually he saves his ammo for you."

"Seems he's all about changing up his attacks lately. Let's use it to our advantage. Keep him busy, I'm going to find a clear shot." Before I could stop her, Kazan edged her way down the alley, ducking in and out of my view. I was so occupied with keeping an eye on her that when a pulse wave rocked the alley behind where I'd last seen Kess, I had to bite my tongue to keep from swearing out loud.

Debris flew through the air. When it was clear enough to see again, I spotted Jey on the ground.

"Jey's down hard." Merkief's voice shook. *"Get Kazan down. Now!"*

She wasn't anywhere near me. Shit.

Her safety outweighed her orders to avoid a headshot on Kess. Two more shots whizzed mere inches from my head. If he noticed we were separated, he could easily fire a pulse in my direction too. If he took me out, Merkief would never reach her in time.

I ducked back around the corner I'd been hiding behind and fingered the pulse pistol inside my coat, but Merkief stood in the line of the wave. I also wasn't sure Jey would survive a second pulse even if I aimed a high. As much as I didn't like Jey, I didn't actually want him dead. He was good at his job.

The exchange of gunfire changed, revealing a sudden emptiness. Merkief had vanished.

I burst from my cover and rocketed toward Kazan.

Stone chips pelted my hands and face as the wall beside me shook with the impact of a pulse wave. The fringe of the wave almost knocked my feet out from under me. I scrambled forward.

The ground exploded, showering me with pebbles, garbage, and shards of wood. I leapt over the hole, and upon finally reaching Kazan, knocked her to the ground and spread myself over her. I waited for the next blast to come as I tried to focus on Jumping both of us to safety.

The blast didn't come.

"Get off." Kazan shoved me, disrupting my concentration.

Looking up, I expected to see a gun in my face. Instead, Kess held a battered Merkief in front of him. It seemed he wanted Kazan alive. At least, for the moment.

I got up but remained between her and Kess as I gauged the distance between us and how much warning he would have to fire the gun he held to Merkief's head.

"If I make a sudden move, can you hit him?" I asked.

She put her hand on my shoulder, peering over at Kess.

"Not with a clear shot. Not yet anyway."

Opening my link to Jey, I didn't get any response beyond a sense of his still being alive, but that fact seemed tenuous at best.

"Can we hurry this up? We're losing Jey," I said.

"I'm trying." She craned around behind me. "Merkief makes a damn good shield."

I hoped I did too.

Kess jammed the gun barrel deeper into Merkief's temple. "How about we even the odds?"

Merkief's desperate gaze lit upon me. *"Please tell me you have a plan?"*

"I'm working on it."

I reached behind me and halted Kazan's search for a shot by pulling her against me to keep her from Kess's sight.

"Stay back. If he wanted to kill Merkief, he'd have done it. He wants you. Did you see where Jey went down?"

She strained against my grasp. "Generally, yes."

"Jump to him, and get him to the tank. If you go quickly, Kess won't see you."

She strained against my hold. "I'm not running. He runs. I don't."

"And he's still alive after all his running. I'd rather you were too. Go. You can play this out again another day."

After the disaster with the Karinian Premier, I wasn't about to let her take unnecessary risks because of her bullheaded nature again. She paid me to protect her and I would, even if it was from herself.

"Since when do you tell me what to do?"

I clamped down on her arm, her armor stiff under my fingers, protecting her from anything more than pressure.

"Get out of here. Now."

She sent a blast of seething anger over her link. I let go. Seconds later the space behind me was empty. With Kazan and Jey safely away, I was determined to eradicate the pesky bastard.

Kess's eyes narrowed. He pulled the pulse pistol from Merkief's head and fired at me. I dodged but the edge of the wave hit me hard. It tore through my armor and into my shoulder. Pain shot through my entire body, flooding my senses.

Kess swore as I staggered sideways, revealing his true target had vanished.

With the gun no longer aimed at him and his captor distracted,

Merkief went limp, throwing Kess off balance until he let go. I held my wounded arm close to my chest, pulled my own pulse pistol from my coat and fired at Kess' head. I hoped that if I kept the blast high enough, Merkief's armor would protect him.

The wave blew apart several crates and threw Kess backward into a pile of garbage. He rolled toward the ground but I couldn't see where he landed.

"Merkief, get out of here!" I yelled. He vanished seconds later.

I ran toward Kess, intent on planting a bullet in his head the moment I got a clear shot, but when I saw the ground below the garbage heap, it was empty. The resourceful bastard had managed to Jump. The blast must not have stunned him as much as I'd hoped.

With my shoulder a tattered mess and a gaping hole in my armor, I sought out a more secure spot in the alley before contacting Merkief.

"Did Jey make it to the tank?" I asked.

"Kazan got him in, but he's going to be in there for a long while. How's your shoulder?"

I made myself look at the bloody mess littered with dirt, rock fragments and abrasive slivers from my armor. *"Not so good and the rest of me isn't far behind."*

"Find a medical facility for now."

"Why don't I just Jump there? You could patch it up for me."

Hesitation edged Merkief's voice, *"That's not good idea."*

My heart sank. *"Kazan?"*

"While I thank you for what you did back there, she's not in such a grateful mood. You've been fired going on eight times and called every name I know."

"Great."

While I didn't think she'd actually fire me, I did know her well enough by now to know she didn't forgive quickly, if at all. How many months of sleep shifts would that moment of authority cost me? She'd better not consider taking Cragtek back.

Merkief interrupted my pain-induced fuming. *"Get your shoulder looked at and lay low. I'll let you know when it's safe to show your face long enough to use the tank."*

If I sought help at a medical facility, I would be required to answer questions as to how I came to be injured. Refusing to answer questions would only encourage nosy and well-meaning medical staff to contact the enforcers. People who, even before

I'd come to work for Kazan, I preferred to avoid. That meant I needed to hole up somewhere until the tank became available.

Home sounded damn good. It had been months since I'd been there, not since dropping the few things I'd wanted to keep from the company-provided house. I Jumped into the kitchen to find the pile I'd brought still sitting right where I'd left it. The house was still in a general disarray from my haphazard packing when I'd moved out, empty and half-filled boxes were scattered across the floor, a stack of dishes on the counter I'd decided not to take, and clothing strewn across the table and chairs. I had even less inclination to deal with it now than I had when I'd been moving.

Judging by the thick layer of dust that blanketed the memories of my childhood and the family I'd lost, the cleaning bot had broken down soon after I'd moved out.

I avoided the frozen gaze of my parents in the still frames on the wall and went into the bathroom in search of a med kit. After much grimacing, swearing and several lightheaded moments, I emerged with a rough bandage shoved through the hole in my coat. Taking off my armor had proven too painful. That wasn't going to get me very far given the damage. It hurt like all nine hells, and the one stim I had with me took its sweet time taking the edge off.

I rummaged through the cupboards, but I'd taken all the food with me when I'd moved to my other house. More annoying, the liquor was also gone.

If my home was under surveillance, I didn't see any sign of it. A quick check of the city network confirmed it was still in my name, and a multitude of searches for me related to the address but there were no confirmed sightings of me here.

Feeling safe enough for the moment, I heaved a sigh, unfolded the blanket on the back of the couch and spread it out. Easing myself onto it, I willed the stim to work faster.

The throbbing of my shoulder kept me from any semblance of sleep and the stim made me restless. I looked around the room, my gaze falling on the empty spot on the wall where the glass case of family medals had once hung.

Did I want to put it back up? And if so, where? I didn't belong here anymore, but this place was mine. It didn't belong to Kazan to give or take away depending on her mood. Yet, as I lay there, surrounded by all the things my family had owned, I no longer felt comforted by it. Instead, there was a heavy sensation of judgment. I would never put a medal in our case. There was nothing honorable or valiant about what I'd chosen to do with my life.

The bot sat on the floor near the couch. I reached down and picked it up, imagining my mother's chiding voice at the mess her house had become. I took a long look at her smiling face, gazing at me from the still frame next to Chesser's bedroom door.

He'd hung it there after our parents had died and he often touched it when he'd entered or left his room. If any sign of his prints remained, they were buried under dust.

I got up and went in search of a toolbox.

Hours later, the bot whirred to life. I snapped its casing shut and set it on the floor. It spun in circles as if it didn't know where to start. After a few moments, it emitted a loud click and sucked up dust at a slow but steady pace.

The hum of the bot calmed me. I returned to the couch and watched its progress as my eyelids grew heavy.

Shuffling footsteps on the front doorstep jolted me awake. I jumped up and swore as I jarred my shoulder in the process. Yanking a gun from my ruined coat, I made my way to the door.

A glimpse out of the kitchen window revealed a familiar coat and pair of boots. Kazan. I sent Merkief a burst of annoyance for not warning me of her visit.

I opened the door and pulled her inside. "Get off the damn street." If my house was safe, I wanted to keep it that way.

She shook off my grip. "Hello to you too." Her lip curled and her eyebrows rose as she looked around. "I know you prefer living in a state of chaos, but this is a little extreme, don't you think?"

While I'd been blissfully sleeping, the effects of the lone stim had come and gone. I was relieved to see she'd gone from enraged to mildly peeved in record time, but the pain in my shoulder and aches everywhere had me on edge.

"The bot broke down. Is the tank open?"

She nodded, watching the bot meander across the floor, leaving semi-clean streaks in its wake. "Merkief said you'd been hit. I figured if it was bad, you'd have come to the ship hours ago."

"Where you were lying in wait to yell at me? That would have made things easier for you, wouldn't it?"

Kazan scowled.

"How'd you find me here?" I asked.

She plopped down in what had once been my father's favorite chair. A plume of dust rose. She coughed and waved it away. "Merkief offered his top five guesses. This was number two."

He knew me pretty well. I made a mental note to keep my mouth shut more often in order to keep some of my personal spots truly private. Not that she wouldn't have found me here on her own.

We stared at each other for a moment before she said, "Don't ever try to take over my fight again."

"Sure. Next time you want to do something stupid and get us all killed, I'll step aside."

Her nostrils flared. "I take it Kess got away?"

"I'm fairly sure I did pulse him pretty good, but he's damn fast with a Jump."

She fell silent, taking in the boxes, the layer of dust, and eventually, my half-assed bandaging job. "Do you want to stay here?"

And do what, watch the bot fight an overwhelming battle before it died a slow death? "Not really, but I thought I was fired?"

Kazan shot me a disgusted look as she stood. "You want back in or not?"

"I wasn't out until you fired me." She could be mad at me all she wanted. We both knew getting her out of there and saving Jey had been the right move.

"Have I mentioned that you're damn difficult?"

"If difficult keeps you alive...."

I couldn't be sure, but I swore she almost smiled. She covered whatever it had been by rubbing her hands up her face and smoothing her hair back.

"Go take a dip in the tank. Then meet us at the house on Jal," she said.

"My coat will need some work before I'm going anywhere."

Kazan held out her hand. "I'll see that it's repaired before you get back."

I winced my way through shrugging off my coat. She made a semi-successful effort not to notice my discomfort or look at the blood that had seeped through my bandage. Knowing that was the extent of an apology I would get, I handed her my coat and Jumped to take my much anticipated dip in the tank.

Chapter Eleven

Kazan walked into my room a mere ten minutes after I'd arrived at the house. "I see you finally decided to join us."

After her earlier tirade had cost me hours of enduring my shoulder in agony, I figured she owed me time enough for a long shower and a good meal before I returned to work. I hadn't exactly hurried back.

I continued to go through the bags I'd brought with me from my house. Jal was the last house I planned to leave anything important, but it gave me something to do while attempting to gauge her current mood.

She pointed to my coat where it hung on the wall. "It's only a temporary patch, but it should hold until the weave heals. We don't have time for you to break in a whole new coat. Speaking of which, you'll need that one in half an hour. I've lined up a job for the four of us on Armin."

That announcement was enough to make me drop the clothes I'd been shuffling around and face her. We didn't do much work in the Verian Cluster, home of zealous Verians and trade-crazy Arminites. It seemed the High Council had other hands to manage the Cluster, or perhaps it just didn't need much managing. Thank Geva, Kazan didn't seem to show interest in taking it on. She had her hands plenty full already.

"I'll be out shortly."

She nodded and left my room.

I reloaded my coat, armed myself and joined the others in the foyer to get our jump point. The four of us stepped out of the void onto a metal floor in a narrow hallway. Scuffs and dings told of age and a good deal of traffic. I took a deep breath of filtered air.

"Where are we?" I asked.

Kazan led the way. "The station over Veria Prime."

I glanced at Merkief and Jey behind me. They shrugged.

"You said the job was on Armin." Not that I minded the side trip. I'd always wanted to see the station where Chesser had first met Kazan. He'd been stranded there for a short while during the Jalvian occupation.

"I thought it best to put some distance between us and the job."

Since we could Jump from Armin back to the Narvan in less than a minute, her reasoning sounded damn weak to me. Nevertheless, I followed her past rows of doors set at regular intervals until she came to a stop. She entered a sequence on the keypad. The door slid open.

Kazan beckoned us inside. "I've rented this suite indefinitely. Note it as a safe jump point."

Just what I needed, another place to spread my belongings throughout the known universe. We went in to find three bedrooms, a small kitchen, a tiny bathroom and a common room in the middle.

Kazan called us together. "No one goes out unless you're with me. No interacting with anyone on this station unless I clear it."

The three of us nodded.

"Vayen, you're with me. It seems you owe Merkief and Jey a shift."

Despite the truth of that statement, neither of them looked happy to be left behind as we walked out the door. Her desire to keep us out of the public eye made me curious.

She went all of three paces before stopping to face me. "I'm unarmed, just so you know."

"Why?"

"We're going to meet with the Station Commander. It wouldn't look good if I went in armed. You, as my bodyguard, which is what you are here," she drilled the statement in with a serious look, "are permitted to be armed to the hilt."

"Good thing I am." What had gotten into the woman?

"I expected no less." She grinned and flounced off down the corridor.

I followed close behind, puzzling over what put the unfamiliar spring in her step. I understood angry, brusque, and stressed Kazan, but whatever this was, I was at a total loss.

In the ten minutes it took us to get from our quarters to those of the Commander, four people called out an excited greeting to Anastassia. She stopped to engage each one in lively conversation. I waited patiently behind her, doing my best to piece together this new situation. It seemed that along with the Verian population, her kind were prevalent here, making me feel like the odd one out, towering over everyone.

She came to a stop at our destination. Seconds later, a broad-shouldered human man appeared with a welcoming smile.

"Anastassia, it's been years! We've missed you." He ushered us inside, and the two of them flew into a fast paced dialogue about the happenings on the station.

I stood there, trying to be as unobtrusive as possible. This wasn't the reception I'd envisioned when she announced her intention to inform the Commander of our presence on his station. Kazan held no sway in the Verian Cluster. No one owed her any allegiance or tolerance. We were the kind of people you wanted off your station as soon as possible.

As the initial bout of conversation slowed, Anastassia glanced in my direction. "Oh sorry. Vayen, this is Nickoli Parishnev, the Station Commander."

We exchanged nods. I'd known she'd lived on the station, but I'd never envisioned her time there as anything but a place to be while spying for the Verian army until she met Chesser. It seemed I was sorely mistaken. This was Anastassia's home.

Parishnev turned back to Anastassia. "The twins will be happy to see you." He mumbled into what appeared to be some sort of com device on his collar and then resumed their conversation.

Moments later, the door opened to reveal two adolescents with wide smiles. Anastassia sprang to her feet. The three of them met in the middle of the room in a tangle of arms as they hugged each other. My eyebrows rose. Kazan, kids, and hugging did not exist on the same plane of reality.

She spared no thought for introductions this time around. The four of them sat talking for over an hour. From snatches of their conversation, I deduced that the brother and sister were around fifteen and had known Anastassia for most of their lives. I held up the wall, taking in the sight of her looking relaxed to a level I'd never witnessed.

Anastassia stood. "Vayen must be bored to death by now, and I should go visit Peter." They shared another round of hugs and then she led me through the corridors with her bizarre, bouncy step in full swing.

"Sorry, that kind of went on. It's been a long while since I dared come back here."

"Why dare now?" I asked using her unexpected choice of words.

"I didn't want Kess here. It never felt right, even when things were good between us. If you pulsed him like you say you did, he'll be recovering for at least a little while. With the three of you around, I figure we can quietly handle it if anyone else gets it in their head to cause trouble."

"Got it."

"Good. Now quit looking so damn menacing. You're scaring people."

I did my best to be shorter, smaller, and slightly more friendly. The last one was about as successful as the first two because I couldn't help but wonder who the hells Peter was and why her face lit up when she said his name. If she was involved with someone to that giddy of a degree, she wouldn't have dropped him for a couple of years, would she? Maybe her people viewed relationships far differently than mine.

Anastassia stopped at a doorway marked as a medical clinic. After taking a moment to straighten her shirt and smooth down any hairs that might have escaped her braid, she went in.

We walked through the mostly unoccupied treatment center to an office. A pale human man, who appeared to be around the same age as Kazan, was entranced with the vid on his desk.

"Hello, Peter."

He jumped in his seat and his large brown eyes widened.

"Anastassia?" A big grin ripped his face in half as he stood and wrapped his spindly frame around her.

She turned to me with a bright smile. "Vayen, this is Peter Strauss, the Chief Medical Officer."

My scowl deepened as I nodded toward him. The ease I shared with Anastassia was hard won, but what she had with Peter and these others made us seem like mere acquaintances in a distant but mutually beneficial partnership. Though we'd been working together for over a year, I didn't really know her at all.

Maybe Marin and I had more in common than I wanted to

admit.

Anastassia turned her back to me and resumed her conversation with the doctor. He cast worried glances in my direction. I enjoyed giving him cause to worry.

"Do you have a few moments, Peter? It's been a long time. Perhaps we could go to the back lab for a bit?"

I heard the hope in her voice and gritted my teeth. Strauss eyed me openly.

Kazan followed his gaze. "Vayen, the lab is secure. Would you mind waiting for me here?" *"Stop trying to intimidate the poor man! We all know you could beat the life out of him in three seconds. Peter is not like us, none of these people are. As a matter of fact, they're all harmless, so save the dark looks for later when we have actual work to do."*

"Sure." I didn't make much of an effort to ease up.

She followed Strauss toward the back of the clinic. *"Peter is a good friend of mine, could you please be nice?"*

Did she say please? Where did I lose the real Kazan?

She returned half an hour later with Strauss trailing behind. I got up from the chair I'd planted myself in during her absence. Her fingers fidgeted with the clasps on her open coat and her gaze refused to meet mine.

After a subdued farewell, she led the way back to our quarters. Kazan excused herself to her room for a couple hours. When she reemerged with her business face back in place, we Jumped to Armin and began to set up the job.

≈

Late in the afternoon on our second day, Kazan approached me. "You're the only one that's been in the public eye here. I'd like to keep it that way. Would you mind taking Merkief's shift?"

"Sure, I'm free."

Watching Kazan reveal her true self was better than being caged up in our quarters with Merkief and Jey's jealousy. I had a feeling it would be a long while before they came to terms with me controlling Cragtek. Kazan and I may have been partners, but this was the first time she'd granted me a benefit that blatantly separated me from them.

"I don't need you right this minute. I'm going down to Prime to visit someone. I just wanted you to know where I was. He's safe."

"Are you sure? You said you haven't been here in years. Allegiances change."

She sucked on her lower lip for a moment. "Vayen, he's a Seeker."

"You're going to see a Verian priest?" I stopped myself before 'whatever for?' popped out of my mouth. If I still tossed prayers, useless as they may be, toward Geva, I couldn't fault Kazan for seeking whatever spiritual solace she'd grown up with.

Kazan nodded. "This is where I will be." She flashed me the image of a small round room with pale orange walls and worn furnishings. "Give me two hours and not a word of this to Merkief or Jey." She took off her coat and handed it to me.

"All right." I watched Anastassia, unarmed and unarmored, disappear. And I didn't like that one bit.

I spent the next two hours at a table on the outskirts of the station market zone so I didn't have to explain her absence to Jey or Merkeif. Going over Cragtek reports through my link ate up the time while I waited for a distress call that never came. She returned on time, relaxed and smiling. After putting her coat back on, she again led me out into the station. We passed by two restaurants, a few shops, and then entered a bustling bar. The sign over the door proclaimed it The Sphinx. Kazan proceeded to the bar and struck up a conversation with a black-skinned, black-toothed creature behind the counter. He reminded me of meat left over a fire too long.

I recalled Chesser mentioning The Sphinx when he talked about being here during the Jalvian occupation. His voice spilled into my head, accosting me with images of his grinning face as he described meeting a female human spy that happened to be telepathically compatible with Artorian sex.

In the three days it took for Chesser's men to get him off the station, he'd convinced Anastassia to leave her life behind and join the fight against the Jalvian forces on Artor. The Verians had lost their fight against Jal but the fight over Artor had still been going strong. I didn't want to dwell on how he'd convinced her or speculate as to which one was using the other more. Perhaps they'd honestly been attracted to one another from the start as Chesser had claimed. I stared at a small table against the wall and imagined my brother sitting there. Chesser winked at me and faded away.

While Kazan and the black creature reminisced about the

Jalvian war, the occupation, and all the excitement—mostly the bad kind—that had followed, I occupied myself with watching the other occupants of the bar.

The station served as a major hub of activity within the Cluster as well as a place for travelers to await their outgoing vessels. Arminites chattered back and forth in their native tongue, trading only Geva knows what. Near translucent-skinned Verians, most standing two heads shorter than me, watched me warily with their close-set eyes on their flattened faces as they sipped their drinks.

The Cluster seemed so much more peaceful than the Narvan, sedate and hushed. Perhaps it was the general lack of Jalvians, with their military aims and ambitions. Or even much of an Artorian presence. I supposed we offered our own sense of chaos.

Kazan elbowed me. "Are you done gawking? I need to see Peter before we leave."

After the last time he'd appeared to have upset her, I didn't think she needed to see him ever again, but I didn't think it would be in my best interest to say so. Since he didn't seem to offer any sort of physical threat, I shrugged and followed her out of the bar.

Kazan met Strauss in his office. I took a seat in the waiting area. The two of them talked and then went to the back lab. When Kazan returned, she looked upset again. Strauss also appeared unsettled. He watched us leave with sorrow-filled eyes.

We walked down the corridor in silence. I slowed to match her lagging pace. "Everything all right?"

She dropped out of the main flow of traffic. Lingering by the wall, she stood there for a moment before saying, "We were just talking."

I tried to keep my tone neutral. "Did things not go well between you?"

"Not exactly." Kazan's gaze drifted away. She stepped closer, her coat rustled against mine. "He wanted answers to difficult questions." Her voice dropped to a whisper. "I didn't have any answers."

I couldn't imagine what sort of questions the scrawny doctor could ask that would have such an effect on Kazan.

"I don't know if I ever will." She turned toward me and rested her forehead on my shoulder.

I took that as an invitation to do what everyone else on the station did without a second thought. I hugged her. She pushed my coat aside and her arms wrapped around me. She smelled of disinfectant and a faint lingering of Strauss's cologne, but at that particular moment, I didn't mind. It had been too long since I'd enjoyed physical contact that didn't involve bruising, a training mat, or unwelcome sexual advances.

A perturbed voice cut through my peaceful moment.

"Anastassia Kazan, I will have a word with you."

Kazan stiffened and pushed herself away from me to face a Verian woman with short yellow hair and an annoyed-as-all-hells twist to her flat face.

"Who is this?" I asked Kazan.

"Hello, Arita. What can I do for you?" Kazan straightened her coat. *"Arita Palaz, the station's Second in Command."*

The little Second planted her hands on her hips. "You will explain why you are on this station."

"I'm visiting friends."

Palaz stepped closer. "There's been some trouble on Armin. You and your men," she glared in my direction, "wouldn't have anything to do with the extermination of Delchecka Combine's executive board or the sudden plummeting stocks that are sending the other trade organizations into a frenzy would you?"

"Why would I cause trouble on Armin?" Kazan asked.

While her face remained composed, her distress over whatever had happened with Strauss still bellowed off her in waves. It was a testament to just how shaken she was to broadcast herself like that.

"Do you want her gone?" I asked.

"In the worst way, but no, stay out of this." Yet, she moved back against me.

The Second's face tightened and her eyes filled with a zealous light. "Because you're evil. Your Seeker cast you out. There's no other reason why he would have let you leave." She advanced on us. "Your presence is bad enough, but then you have the nerve to bring this hulking, evil lout with you? I can see the taint of violence on you both. It follows you like a malevolent cloud."

In an effort to put her more at ease, I chuckled in Kazan's head. *"I'm hulking and evil?"*

"Jey is hulking, you're just evil," she said betraying a hint of amusement.

"You know I'd never do anything to harm this station or anyone on it, Arita."

If I had any doubts that this station was her home and that she cared deeply about it, they were gone now. That statement had been delivered with an adamant decree of truth.

"I know no such thing. You're not one of us. You never were." Palaz spun around and left.

Kazan watched her leave, visibly shaken even further than when we'd left the doctor. It bothered me greatly to see her mask so shattered, especially in public. People were staring.

Without question, I took her arm and guided her back to our suite. Her hand brushed over mine for just a second as she conveyed her silent thanks in my head before going inside. She cleared her throat and her mask slipped back into place upon facing Jey and Merkief.

"The timeline has been accelerated. Everyone is on for a double shift tonight. Rest up and pack. We'll be leaving in the morning."

When we rejoined for the job, she was back to her usual self. Once Armin was suitably shaken up to the High Council's specifications, she sent Jey and Merkief back to the Jalvian house while the two of us returned to the station. After a quick friendly conversation with Parishnev where she managed to work in some damage control on Palaz, we followed them.

ಎ

I'd hoped for a few days of normal rotation so I could get back to my Cragtek projects but Kazan dragged us all off on a five day Kryon contract that turned into a nine day nightmare on the Jalvian world of Syless.

The storms of orange sand that had raged against the doomed outpost left a perpetual howling in my head. It competed with the echoes of the screams of those that we'd lured inside what should have been a protective shelter during a storm. Jey's explosives had turned it into a massive graveyard. I didn't know if I'd ever forget Merkief's arguing or the pleading look Jey had given Kazan as he held the detonator or the fact that she'd taken the controls from him and pushed the button herself. It was only her cold shaking hand that had covertly sought out mine a second later that convinced me that she did in fact have a conscience.

As we'd done on Armin, killing a few people to spur a change wasn't new for us, but an entire colony, no matter if they were Jalvian or not, had been eating at me since the second day when she'd divulged the full contract specifications. The excuse that I did what the High Council demanded in order to keep Kazan in control of the Narvan didn't come close to assuaging my guilt this time.

I'd already donated my share of the Kryon payout to a charity on Artor under one of my many aliases. I didn't want any part of it. Even a long, hot shower hadn't removed the gritty, dirty feeling that clung to every inch of my skin and conscience.

From the lack of restraint when Jey placed a bottle of sour and strong liquor we'd nicknamed Hewr's piss in the middle of the table at the Merchessian house, I gathered I wasn't the only one having trouble coping. The liquor went down fast, and after so many stim-filled days and nights and scant meals, it didn't take long before the effects were in full swing.

Merkief only tore his accusing glower from Kazan to rip into Jey for the way he'd rigged the explosives to not allow for any survivors. Jey was clearly hoping for backup from Kazan for following the contract stipulations but she was barely keeping her eyes open.

"Merkief, enough," I said. "Both of you, go." I pointed them toward the stairs. Merkief stormed off. Jey gave me a surprisingly grateful glance before stumbling toward the stairs. Once both of them were safely out of sight, I turned to Kazan.

"I'll talk to them in the morning," she said before I could even phrase my question.

"I'd love to say that I'll take the watch shift, but I've got about five minutes of life left in me. Get to bed. I'll set the systems to auto."

She collected the glasses and the empty bottle and put them on the counter before heading up the stairs. Her slow, plodding steps exposed the exhaustion we all felt.

I activated the ground floor internal and external systems. Even then, I was uneasy about leaving the security station unmanned. Though I went up to my room, I kept my coat on and only removed the bulkiest of weapons. My eyes closed the moment my back hit the bed. Half an hour into an exhausted but restless sleep, my door opened.

I shot to my feet with a surge of adrenaline rushing through my exhausted, piss-soaked veins. A gun was somehow in my hand and aimed at the body standing in the doorway.

Kazan's haggard face came into focus. "I couldn't sleep.

There's no one on watch."

Realizing it was her and not an attack, my legs trembled. I put the gun away and sat down before I fell over. "I don't think I can stay awake. I'm sorry."

"I know." Her sunken eyes looked from me to my bed.

"You want to sleep here?"

"I don't want to cause any problems."

She was too tired to bug me in any sexual way, and I doubted even Jey could have risen to the occasion. I offered her one of my blankets. "Come on."

"You really don't mind?" Acceptance bled through courtesy.

"At least I'll know you're safe here."

With a faint smile, she draped her coat over my chair and took the blanket. She curled up next to me.

Listening to her soft breathing, my eyes closed and the restlessness that had haunted me before her arrival dissipated.

Something bumped into my arm. I snapped awake. My fingers moved of their own accord to weapons inside my coat, and I rolled out of bed onto my feet.

"Vayen, relax, it's just me."

"Right." I took a deep breath. The long disorienting sleep had left a haze on my mind. I got back into bed. My link revealed eleven hours had passed.

Anastassia reached over and brushed the hair from my face. Her hand lingered on my shoulder. "Thank you for letting me sleep here."

"Yeah, sure."

She donned her coat. "Merkief is up, and I smell food."

"Go eat. I'll wait here for a little bit."

Her eyes closed as she ran her hands over the weapons and supplies hidden in its inner pockets. When she opened them again, her gaze drifted over my bed and the blanket and then rested on me.

I sat up. "What?"

She took a deep breath and let it out. "I don't know what you've heard, and it's probably my own damn rumors coming back to haunt me, but you've got it wrong."

Her raised hand stopped the questions about to spring from

my lips.

"When you came back from your...leave of absence, you accused me of pulling Marin and numerous others into my bed. That's not true. I do have an ongoing relationship with Marin, I'll give you that one, but it's complicated and like the circulating rumors and intentional feints about my personal life, serves a purpose. Granted there have been others in the past, but since the three of you hired on, the only other person I've been with is you."

"Why are you telling me this?"

"Because I want you to know the truth." Anastassia turned and walked out the door.

Chapter Twelve

When I finally joined everyone, most of the food was gone. Anastassia paid no particular attention to me as I scraped together a meager meal. I had to admit, she was good at hiding what she really felt when she wanted to.

The three of them were chatting about some crop test Merkief was overseeing on Karin. Jey's eyes glazed when Merkief went into depth about the soil analysis and it caught me off guard that Anastassia kept right up with him. I looked to Jey. He shook his head.

That's when I realized something was off. We were all awake. After the Syless job right on the heels of the one on Armin, surely she couldn't be considering another big contract. Not right away. Could she?

"What's the occasion?" I waved my fork at everyone.

Anastassia stood and put her dishes on the counter. "We're going to Sere. I have a meeting to go over future Narvan contracts. You've all been active within Kryon. Your input was requested as well."

"Sounds like a great time, doesn't it?" Merkief said, still looking annoyed with all of us.

"Can't wait," I said.

The thought of sitting in a room filled with High Council puppets made my skin crawl. I'd been to Sere with Kazan on countless occasions, but the Council had never requested anything from me personally before.

Half an hour later, the four of us Jumped to Sere and made our way to the appointed meeting room. Four grey-suited High Council liaisons sat waiting at the table, their faces slack, eyes unfocused. We sat across from them.

Within seconds, they came to life. Somewhere, out of sight, High Council members controlled these unfortunate, living puppets.

As they addressed Kazan, I wondered what had happened to the minds that had originally controlled these bodies. Who were these people and what had they done to deserve this existence? Kazan's admonition to not ask questions where the High Council was concerned crashed through my wandering thoughts.

One of the puppets turned to me. "Mr. Ta'set, we have some individually focused questions regarding recent contracts. Please report to this room." The location of a room further down the hall flashed into my head.

Kazan planted her hands on the table. "I can answer your questions."

"That is not necessary. We shall proceed." The liaisons plowed on with their plans and inquiries.

I didn't know why they were singling me out. Maybe they too were finally acknowledging my partner status. I felt Kazan, Merkief and Jey watching me as I left the room.

The hallway was empty as I made my way to the room to which I'd been directed. The door was closed.

I stood there a moment. No voices, no noise. The hairs on the back of my neck urged me to draw a gun before opening the door, but I knew that would only get me in trouble. One didn't draw weapons on Sere unless one wished to be fired upon. I took a deep breath and opened the door.

An Artorian woman wearing plain clothing, but not grey, stood before me. From the faint lines around her eyes and mouth, I guessed her to be in her middle years and yet, she was quite stunning.

Artorians seemed in low numbers among Kryon. Seeing her offered me a small measure of comfort that I wasn't alone.

She smiled warmly. "Welcome, Mr. Ta'set. Have a seat."

I stepped into the room. The door clicked shut behind me. We were alone, but it sure felt like there were others watching. I took the one seat in the otherwise empty room.

"You had questions about my contract work?"

"Not exactly," she said. Then she asked, "Are you involved with Anastassia Kazan?"

"Excuse me?" Nosy bastards.

"Are you in a relationship with Anastassia Kazan beyond your Kryon partnership?"

Flashes of memory accosted me, her sleeping in my bed, our previous encounter, and the private dinner where she'd given me a chance with Cragtek. We were in some sort of relationship, but not the type she seemed to be implying.

"No."

"I see."

I wasn't sure if she believed me or if I'd answered incorrectly. Had they questioned Kazan? Had she said yes? Why did they care anyway? I put on my work face and forced it to stay in place.

"I'm testing a drug, and I require your assistance," she said. "It won't interfere with your obligations to Kazan."

"If you offered me a drink, I wouldn't turn it down, but I'm not into drugs."

"Lucky for you, this is a liquid." She pulled a golden bottle from a pocket in her pants. It fit neatly in the palm of her hand. "You've been chosen. I'm afraid I must insist."

"Chosen by whom? Why?"

My legs wanted to bounce and my skin itched. I needed to be out of the chair and on my feet. She was alone and from all appearances, she wasn't someone who should intimidate me, at least not in the way that she currently was — but I couldn't shake the feeling that I was in deep trouble. How did Kazan deal with these people on such a regular basis?

Her brows lowered a fraction. "If you would see your partner retain her position, you will cooperate."

I willed myself to remain still and to keep my link from seeking out Kazan's. I could handle this. It was one woman. One request. They wanted Kazan to remain in her position as much as I did. They wouldn't ask anything of me to jeopardize that.

"You can trust me." Her smile resumed its place as if no threat had just been uttered between us.

"Open up." She spun the top on the bottle and removed it to reveal a dropper beneath. A single golden droplet clung to the tip. "Quickly. We don't want to waste this." She came closer. "Just one drop and you can get back to Kazan's side."

What could one drop hurt? Besides, it wasn't as if I had much of a choice. I opened my mouth.

The drop landed on my tongue. Within seconds, a rush of pleasant heat washed over me, followed by an overwhelming feeling of well-being. I closed my eyes, reveling in the momentary bliss.

"See, that wasn't so bad." The woman ran her fingers down the side of my face, trailing down my neck to the collar of my coat. Her fingertips left swirling eddies of pleasure in their wake.

"Not at all." I opened my eyes as the initially powerful sensations faded to a dull glow deep within me.

"One drop every six hours for the next week. Then I need you to come in for an evaluation. Ask for me at the contract office. My name is Chandi."

"Sure." Going through an entire week feeling like I could endure anything, like nothing could ruin my mood, wasn't exactly a hardship.

"To clarify, this experiment is between you and me. Kazan is not to be involved."

"I understand."

Kazan held back information from me all the time. It felt good to have something important of my own for once. Maybe if the Council was pleased with my performance, I'd get a step further from Kazan's shadow, another step toward becoming a true partner beside her.

Chandi handed me the bottle, her hand brushing against mine. I marveled at the swirls of pleasure working their way up my arm.

"You can go."

I didn't particularly want to go, and I let that be known by seeking out a natural connection with her. She smiled but didn't reciprocate.

"That's not what you want." Chandi leaned in close enough to brush her lips over my cheek as she spoke, sending shivers throughout my body.

She was right, but when I reached for her, she stepped away, shaking her head.

I clutched the warm golden bottle, but it didn't hold the same magic as Chandi's fingertips. After slipping it into a pocket inside my coat and getting my aroused mind under control, I made my way back to Kazan.

I passed other Kryon along the way. My gaze drifted to the

female operatives, gauging interest and viability. While I guessed I could get a couple of them to touch me, bringing back the eddies of pleasure Chandi had introduced me to, a small voice of reason informed me that unless they were Artorian, there wouldn't be any more to it than that. Maybe that would be enough for the moment. I started to approach one of them, but that damned reasonable voice also told me that Kryon weren't safe to get close to in any manner. Look at what we did for a living, for Geva's sake. Frustrated, I returned to Kazan's side.

The meeting ended soon after my return with an insignificant amount of input on my part. For a moment, I was annoyed, but the glow assured me the meeting hadn't really mattered anyway. The Council was just making Kazan feel important, like she had some real choice in what they would ask of her, but we were all their puppets in one way or another. It was just that some of us wore grey suits while others wore armored coats.

On our way out, we stopped at the contract office. Kazan selected a quick job on Rok for the two of us and sent Jey and Merkief on their way.

"They still need some down time to make up for your absence," she said.

"Fine with me."

"Nice to see you so agreeable." She flashed me our jump point.

We located the target in short order and followed him to a quiet corner of a park to extract the required information. I held him up against a tree while Kazan did the questioning. The energy of the golden drop pulsed through me, more solid and steady than a stim, allowing for complete control of thought and action. I felt like I could hold him there, dangling and thrashing, for hours.

His pleading fell on ears intent with purpose. The only compassion I could offer was a bullet to the head the second Kazan gave the slight dip of her chin.

"What do we have next?" I asked.

"A meeting on Frique. One of the boring but necessary ones."

"I'll take care of the body if you want to file the completion. The sooner we get to Frique, the sooner we can leave."

She shook her head at my open dislike for the tiny planet. "Meet you there in twenty minutes." She flashed me the meeting location.

Right on time, I stood in the conference room wishing the

gasping air cooling units would explode so the government would be forced to buy more efficient ones. Men and women milled about in their calf-length tunics, looking perfectly comfortable. Only their decorated sashes of office set them apart from the farmers in the fields.

When Kazan arrived and took her seat at the long, wooden table, everyone else made their way to a chair. I stood behind her. The man to her right opened the meeting. It quickly devolved into discussions over farming techniques, during which Kazan tried to persuade them to use some of Artor's advanced equipment and processes. They wanted no part of it. Disgusted, I tuned them out, paying only attention to their body language. As if the pathetic Friquen people offered any sort of threat.

Two hours later and due for my next golden drop, I happily agreed when Kazan said she'd had enough for the day. We Jumped to the Jalvian house. The sharp corners and bold colors didn't annoy me half as much as they usually did. Even Jey's presence as I grabbed a meal bar from the kitchen didn't bother me.

I went to my room, closed the door, hung up my coat, and disarmed. Comfortable and alone, I realized the bar didn't have what I was hungry for. I set it on my desk and pulled the golden bottle from my pocket. The top spun off smoothly. A quick squeeze of the dropper landed a bliss-ridden droplet on my awaiting tongue. I closed my eyes and fell back into the embrace of my bed. Although the silken caress of the blankets sent a shiver over me, they didn't have the same allure as Chandi's touch. Even the memory of that brief contact made my mind buzz with pleasure. I wanted it again. No, I needed it.

Anastassia would be in her room by now. On the heels of her sharing the truth about her bed status and what sure as all hells seemed like interest since our dinner together, I doubted she'd turn me away.

Merkief or Jey wouldn't have any reason to go into her bedroom and she'd killed all vid feed in her rooms despite our reservations. They'd never know.

I palmed my door control and held my breath as it slid open. The hallway was empty. I dashed to her door and waved my hand over the controls. Nothing happened. Dammit. I hadn't considered that the ultra paranoid woman might lock her bedroom door even in her own locked house with bodyguards on duty.

I rested my forehead on the hard metal door. "Anastassia?"

"Is something wrong?" she asked from the other side. Footsteps came closer.

Couldn't I just want to talk to her? Or touch her or, more importantly at the moment, have her touch me?

"Nothing's wrong. May I come in?"

"Give me a moment."

Was she undressing? What would touching her do to me? I needed to find out. Now.

The door slid open. "What's going on?"

She stood her ground, not yielding even a fraction of her personal space to me. She was also annoyingly fully clothed.

My pulse raged with anticipation. Her arms spanned the door frame, blocking my access.

"I just wanted to talk to you for a minute. Privately."

"You're telepathic, idiot." She thwacked my forehead with two fingers. It wasn't the pleasurable sensation I'd come looking for.

"In person."

Suspicion couldn't have been any clearer on her face if it had been written in ink. "I don't think that's a good idea."

"I do." Taking her hands in mine, I gently pried them from the doorframe and walked her into the room far enough that the door closed. The hard metal against my back was a definite improvement.

"You need to leave." Her voice remained calm and full of her usual control, but I could feel the blood racing through her veins where my fingers rested against the warm, soft skin of her wrists.

"Not yet." I had no plans to do anything completely against her will, but she'd been hardly subtle about wanting my attention.

I closed my eyes, blocking the part of her that stood in the way of what I'd come for. My mind sought out hers, sliding along the natural connection we shared. When I found her, I heard a faint gasp.

"Vayen." Her mind opened to mine in much the same tone as her voice, trembling and protesting without much conviction. "Please don't make this harder than it already is. We can't do this. Not here and not with Jey and Merkief around." Her hands slipped from my grasp.

"Why not? There isn't any feed in your room."

Her fingers ran along both sides of my face, pulling my head down to hers. It stopped inches short of where I wanted to be when her forehead met with mine. While her fingertips elicited sparks of pleasure far beyond Chandi's touch, I couldn't help but wonder what kissing Anastassia would feel like. I adjusted my stance to make up for our height difference, shook off her hands and moved in to find out.

My lips met with her cheek for the briefest moment before she spun away, putting far more distance between us than I wanted. The drug inside me clamored for more contact, promising pleasures beyond my wildest dreams.

The connection between us swelled with energy, surrounding me with glimpses of her desires, all of which included us together and most of which vividly illustrated things I was fully capable of doing right that instant. Then it slammed shut.

"This isn't like you." She backed away.

She wanted me, but now that I was willing, she didn't? What damned game was she playing?

"How would you know? Last time I was drunk out of my mind thanks to you. Maybe you'd rather be drunk too so you can pretend I'm my brother."

Her face flushed to a deep red, but she looked me right in the eye. "He's gone, and you're not him. I've never considered pretending such a thing."

Staring someone down was a game I was good at. "Then what was all the supposed honesty for this morning if this isn't what you wanted?"

"I did but..." Her tight-lipped mask wavered a fraction before regaining control. "That was a mistake."

"I don't believe that and Geva knows you don't either."

"It was," she said adamantly.

The effects of the drug surged, but even the sense of well-being it provided paled when it came to the wave of frustration and anger that enveloped me, sucking me down to the place I'd sworn to leave behind.

Anastassia retreated farther. "Go to Cragtek. Leave. I don't want to see you for a week."

"Merkief and Jey aren't going to like that."

"They'll get over it," she said.

"Me leaving, is that what you really want?"

"Yes." Her gaze dropped and she turned away.

I punched the door control. The second it was open far enough for me to squeeze through, I stalked across the hall. While my hands thrust clothing into an empty pack, I contacted Merkief.

"Keep both eyes on Kazan. I don't know if she's told you, but Kess has a connection on Sere, somehow, somewhere."

"Where are you going?"

"Cragtek. I'll be out for a week."

He sighed in my head. *"I don't know how I'm supposed to get all this shit done when I'm constantly having to watch her back. You're not the only one with side projects. We'd like a week off duty too, you know."*

"Sorry. I'll make it up to you."

I wanted to tell him to blame Kazan, but that would have only made him ask why, and I didn't know how to explain what just happened. I doubted that she did either.

৵

I spent half of the first day seething in my office. The golden bottle stayed in my coat pocket despite a lingering headache. I didn't want to feel good, and I certainly didn't want to deal with the fact that any pleasure that came from the drug would be one-sided.

The headache eased on the second day and while I had vastly enjoyed the sensations the drug had offered, I had no interest in going through that level of frustration again. To fill the rest of the days of my banishment, I dove into Cragtek, tightening local security, exploring new profit areas and meeting with the scouts. Their reports were always thorough, but dry. I got a better read of what they saw and the possible value versus risk by talking to them.

By day four, I'd resolved myself to the fact that Anastassia had issues beyond the obvious. Without the drug in my system, I didn't crave her touch. I also didn't quite blame her for sending me away. My desires had been all encompassing. Having opened my mind to her, I guessed she'd seen that too.

It occurred to me that I should possibly apologize, but Anastassia would want to know why I'd had the sudden change of heart. Chandi had made it quite clear that I wasn't supposed to share that information. I'd have to make it up to Anastassia another way.

Hunting down Kess came to mind.

I Jumped to Sere to see if I could find anything on a possible information leak. Fa'yet had looked into it, but I knew Kryon a lot better now than I had then. I hoped I could find something he'd missed.

I'd barely been on the base ten minutes when Chandi's voice intruded on my link's Council connection. I knew Kazan suffered such intrusions from Kryon and Council members, but they'd left me alone. Until now.

"Checking in early? Need to resupply?" she asked.

"No. I'm here to see someone."

"Report to the room where we last met. I think we have something to discuss."

"Now?"

"Immediately," she said before cutting contact.

Chandi was directly linked to the High Council, if not one of them herself. If she was so intent on using me, perhaps I could return the favor. I headed to the appointed room.

This time, we weren't alone and there were no chairs. A broad, hooded and cloaked figure stood beside Chandi.

"You're not following directions. How many doses have you missed?" A scowl tainted her beautiful face.

Kazan had told me to never lie to the High and Mighties, but she hadn't mentioned being polite. While that was probably common sense, I wasn't in a sensible mood.

"I don't know. I've been busy."

"Is that so?" She cocked her head and nodded to the cloaked figure. "You haven't been by Kazan's side in days."

How did the nosy bastards know I hadn't been at her side? Did they have contacts at Cragtek? I cursed inwardly. Only Geva knew how many eyes they had at their disposal.

Chandi said, "What exactly have you been busy with that would excuse your disregard for my orders?"

"There's a leak within Kryon. Someone is delivering information to a former member who is out to kill Kazan. I'm here to investigate."

Her brows rose to the fringe of dark hair across her forehead. "Kryon acting against Kryon? I hardly think so. That's punishable by death."

"Then someone deserves to die. How about you help me figure out who that would be instead of pumping me full of some drug?"

"You don't find the drug enjoyable?"

"It's great. I'm sure whomever you want to sell it to will be happy to buy it, but I have more important things to attend to."

The hooded figure stepped forward, taller than Chandi and three times as wide. Whatever was under that cloak, it had shoulders even wider than Jey's.

A male voice emanated from the thick brown cloth. "Perhaps you don't fully understand your situation, Mr. Ta'set. You work for us. What's important is that you follow our orders."

Did he think he could intimidate me? That was my job. "My orders are to protect Kazan. Anything beyond that is secondary."

Shoulders shook his head. "That's where you're wrong. She brought you into our circle. Offered you up. You are ours now. She has become secondary, whether she wishes to admit it or not."

"What do you mean she offered me up?" The shadow of betrayal perched on my shoulder, feeding my paranoia with whispers.

"It's not your place to question us. Now, show me the bottle," said Chandi.

What difference did some stupid pleasure drug make to the High Council? I knew they used drugs to control some of their targets, but I worked for them. I couldn't be a target. We didn't act against one another. Chandi had said so herself. What had I done to elect myself as their prized lab viscu?

"I don't have time for this. Find someone else."

My hand wrapped around the cursed cold glass in my pocket. I tried to crush it, but the glass was too thick and its shape too compact.

"There's a damned information leak within Kryon and it's putting one of your lead operatives in danger. Isn't maintaining the orderly control of the Narvan a bigger concern for you?"

A bullet tore into my calf. Pain penetrated my shock and shot up my leg. I glanced from the wound to Chandi, who held a gun in her hand.

"What the fuck?"

She put the gun away. "Our concern is that you're not following orders. Operatives who don't follow orders get hurt. Do you understand, Mr. Ta'set?"

I yanked the golden bottle from my pocket and hurled it at her head. She dodged aside with surprising agility. The bottle hit the wall behind her and bounced onto the carpet, unharmed.

"Kryon doesn't act against Kryon, huh?" I shifted my weight off my bleeding and throbbing leg.

Chandi retrieved the bottle and started towards me. "We're not Kryon, Mr. Ta'set. The High Council has its own set of rules."

The man shoved me to the floor and pinned me down. His expansive heavy bulk atop me made it hard to breathe. "Give him the drug, enough to make up for the gap in the testing cycle."

Chandi spun the top off the bottle and filled the dropper. Shoulders grabbed my face in his meaty, pale-skinned hands and wrenched my mouth open. Liquid splashed off my tongue and coated the inside of my mouth with sticky sweetness.

"Remember, Mr. Taset," she said. "This drug is a gift. It can take all of your pain away. Take two drops every five hours for the next week. I have a feeling you'll need it."

The room began to spin. I pinched my eyes shut and breathed deep through my nose. My thick tongue fought to form words. "You gave me too much."

"We don't make mistakes." The weight on my chest eased and then was gone.

The room and the voices in it grew distant. The pain in my leg slowly turned from a throbbing agony into a faint tickle. I knew it should hurt, but it didn't. There were too many swirling, beautiful lights behind my eyelids, blazing sparkling, lazy trails of pleasure, like Anastassia's fingertips running up and down my body. I didn't care about anything else.

Chandi said, "He can't stay here."

"I'll take care of it."

A foreign tingle, like a light electrical shock, snaked into my brain. It didn't hurt; it merely distracted me from the lights. Someone grabbed my arms, intensifying the pressure of Anastassia's fingertips taunting me. For a disorienting moment, I felt like I was floating and then the hands deserted me, leaving me in the solid embrace of something that offered no stimulation. I gave myself over to the warm, sparkling glow.

I woke to find myself in my office at Cragtek, sprawled across my newly arrived prantha hide couch. My arms shook as I pushed myself up. The drug hadn't left me so weak when I'd used it before.

Groggy memories of my visit to Sere knocked on my brain's thick door. I swung my legs over the edge.

Pain burst through the haze when my boot hit the floor. I'd been shot. Holy hells, how long had I been out? Dried blood stained the other half of the couch. I shook my head, but it refused to clear.

Blood loss, idiot. Anastassia's imagined figure stood in front of me, shaking her head.

I needed to get to the tank. When I tried to stand, dizziness threatened to hand me over to gravity. I sat down on the floor instead. At least then I wouldn't fall over the instant I arrived on Kazan's ship. The low, woven carpet of my office morphed into unforgiving metal.

Merkief ran to my side. "Vayen, what are you doing here?"

I would have thought the bloody leg would have been an obvious clue, but my blurry vision informed me that my coat covered the wound because I was sitting down. "I got shot. What are you doing here?"

He glanced up at the tank and then back at me. "You're going to have to wait."

Kazan's limp, naked body floated in the clear healing gel.

"What happened?" I asked over the sound of the pounding that had suddenly erupted in my head.

"Kryon job. I told her to wait for you, but she insisted the three of us could handle it."

"Kess?"

"No. Fragians," Merkief said.

It was all too much at the moment. I lay back on the cool floor and blinked a few times. I hoped that if I could concentrate on something other than the pulsing noise in my brain, Merkief and Kazan would disappear so I could haul myself over to the controls, pull up my profile and drag myself up onto the platform. When I woke, I would have a clear head and be better equipped to deal with what had happened between Anastassia and I, Kess and his spy, and the Council's demands.

"Vayen?" Merkief's worried voice broke through my effort to make him vanish.

"Yeah?"

"Can you wait? You look awfully pale."

Since Merkief refused to disappear, I focused my inward attention on my leg. I could move it. Nothing seemed broken. Nothing horribly vital was hit, just a bullet lodged in muscle. Chandi had given me a warning, not certain death. Not that the loss of blood or the aftereffects of the large dose they'd administered were doing me any favors.

"I'll be all right. How long will she be in there?"

"She'll be out shortly. It's Jey you're waiting for. He took a pulse blast for her."

I picked up my head and stared until he came into full focus. "Just what in the nine hells were the three of you doing?"

"Infiltrating a Fragian outpost." He looked away. "We did get the information that the High Council wanted."

"Well, that's just great. I'm sure they're pleased."

Had Chandi and her friend known what Kazan was slated for when they'd drugged me? If she'd truly been in danger, would I have even been able to help her if she'd contacted me? Hells, had any of them tried to contact me while I'd been useless? If I was supposed to keep taking this stuff, I needed to make sure I stayed alert.

Merkief grabbed my arm. "Come on, let's at least get you in bed while you wait. It will be far more comfortable than the floor."

I let him help me up. He made a pretty good crutch as he helped me to my room.

"Why, with all the available Kryon, would they send Kazan out to infiltrate a damned Fragian outpost? She's too important to the High Council for such a reckless mission," I said.

"It wasn't exactly reckless. Jey and I were with her." He brought me up alongside my bed.

"That's not what I meant." I let go of him and sat down.

Merkief straightened his coat. "The outpost is too damned close to Merchess. She wanted to evaluate it firsthand. You know how she is."

"Stubborn and trying to get herself killed?"

He chuckled. "Something like that. You can take it up with her later. Get some rest."

"Thanks."

He turned to the door but then spun back around. "While I have you here, we should have a few drinks on our next off shift. I haven't seen much of you lately."

I couldn't chance hanging out with Merkief. He was too good at picking up on even the slightest hint and running with it. My best defense was avoiding him until Chandi's little experiment was over.

"I've been busy, and I don't see that changing anytime soon."

"I see."

It hurt to see his confusion and disappointment and know that I was the cause of it. "I'm sorry."

He nodded. "I'll let you know when the tank is open."

I waited until he'd closed the narrow door before pulling the bottle from my coat pocket. If I had to wait, I figured I could be somewhat comfortable. Two drops weren't near as intense as the large dose, but it was enough to allow me to drift off into pleasant dreams of fulfilling what I'd seen in Anastassia's mind.

⁂

"You're finally awake?" Anastassia's face loomed over me.

"Maybe."

I rubbed the tank gel from my eyes. Without the drug in my system, the lights were too bright. The sheets scratched against my skin. Why was she standing so damned close?

"I didn't know there was a rush. You wanted me gone, remember?"

She sat back in the chair beside my bed and studied her hands in her lap. "I know you had to wait, but Merkief said the wound wasn't fresh when you got here. The tank can only do so much. The longer you put off using it, the less effective the gel is. I can't afford to have you hindered by permanent damage."

"I wasn't delaying on purpose."

Anastassia studied me. "You need to take better care of yourself."

I snorted. "And you need to not take insane contracts."

She cleared her throat. "If you can keep your mind to yourself, I could use you on rotation."

She could use me? I was already being used. How many puppet masters could I handle?

Chapter Thirteen

Since Chandi could find me on Sere, it seemed safer to meet with Fa'yet at his house on Karin to continue my search for the Kryon spy. He welcomed me into his common room and offered me a glass of Friquen red. I sat across from him and sipped, taking in the opulent furnishings in the warm glow of his artificial fireplace.

Fa'yet gave me a questioning glance. "So?"

"Kazan had asked you to check into the possibility of a spy on Sere. Did you ever find anything?"

"I would have told her if I had."

"Nothing? No clue, no hint, not even a whispered rumor?" I asked.

"There were a few rumors about Kazan, but nothing to do with a spy." He swirled the wine in his glass and took a sip.

Rumors seemed to follow her. Or she enjoyed creating them. I didn't know what to believe anymore.

"Well?"

Chandi's prescribed dose of the drug beat through my veins, convincing me that nothing could stand in the way of me solving this problem.

"I can't tell you everything. I want to, but I can't," he said.

"Quit being so damned cryptic and just spill it."

Fa'yet set his glass down on the low, square table between us. "You don't understand."

"No, I don't. You won't tell me." Good thing I was on the drug and not a stim, otherwise I would have been inclined to shove him up against a wall and hold him there until he started making sense.

He took a deep breath and held up an empty hand. As if that would calm me down. "This might be easier if Kazan were here. She'd understand."

"She doesn't know I'm here."

And I much preferred it that way. The damned drug made it nearly impossible to listen to the calm voice that kept trying to explain why I didn't want to get involved with that mercurial, Jalvian-loving woman. Logic tried to tell me I should focus on work, that it would help me get through this test, or challenge, or whatever game Chandi was playing at. Over the past week I'd been trying to stretch my doses out as much as I could while still managing to avoid the aftereffects. But even then, the shifts working beside her were distracting as all hells.

He grimaced. "Sorry. I just invited her."

Kazan arrived in the midst of our awkward silence. She took in our near empty glasses, our faces, and the open wine bottle on the table.

"Care to enlighten me as to why I'm here?"

Fa'yet waved her to the empty chair beside me. "Vayen asked about that spy search you sent me on awhile back."

"You said you never found anything." She took the filled glass he offered her and set it down on the table.

"Not on a spy. I did, however, hear a few things you should probably know."

"And you're just telling me now?"

I was glad he was the one on the other end of her utterly peeved look. "Let him talk. He wouldn't say anything without you here."

"This came from within the inner circle," Fa'yet said.

I glanced between them but neither seemed to feel the urge to explain. "Which is?"

Kazan turned her look on me. "Not now."

"You've done wonders with the Narvan," Fa'yet said.

"I've not had any complaints."

His voice took on an unfamiliar bristly tone. "Not formally."

"What the fuck does that mean?" she asked.

"The resources of the Narvan are staying in the Narvan."

"That's how I want it. We need further repairs and stability to make up for the setbacks caused by the intersystem war. I've explained this to the circle and to the Council."

"Other systems have their own needs as well, but their advisers are complying with the Council's wishes to expand. You've got the Fragians on your doorstep."

"Our doorstep," she said firmly.

Was I going to have to separate them? I set my glass aside and shifted forward in my chair.

"Of course." He held up his hand again. It seemed to have as much effect on Kazan as it had on me.

"You brought this up. Now you're telling me that the understanding I had within the circle meant nothing? They're jealous of me standing up to the High Council's demands and now they're making some half-assed effort to get rid of me by feeding information to Kess?"

His jaw tightened as he shook his head. "Not the circle. This goes higher."

"They wouldn't," she said, shaking her head, "not after all I've done for them."

Fa'yet slammed his fist down on the arm of his chair. "We've all done a lot for them. You're not the only damned one to make sacrifices."

I stood, hoping to break the direct line of tension between them before this got ugly. "What exactly do the Fragians have to do with this?"

Fa'yet gave me a slight nod. He took a moment to refill his glass and then turned his attention back to Kazan. "They bring a similar level of technology, more established outposts, and a drive to conquer. They've moved from being the enemy to your competition."

"They can't do this."

"Think, Anastassia. If the entire High Council wanted you gone, you'd be dead."

"But I've explained my safety net to them. They wouldn't take that risk."

"You know we'd all follow your wishes—" Fa'yet said.

I did a quick mental inventory of her standing orders and came up short. "Which wishes exactly?"

Kazan scowled. "For Fa'yet, I'll allow calling them wishes. To everyone else, they are demands or orders. Should I die or disappear, the Narvan will become a very unruly holding for my would-be successor."

"And what's my role in this safety net?" I asked.

"You don't have one." She captured me in a hard stare. "If you're as loyal as you say you are, you'll be dead before me. If you're not, you'll be the one trying to take my place."

"Oh." I sat back down.

"The majority of the High Council might value your threats, but this faction..."Fa'yet shook his head slowly. "They seem to have other plans beyond you or your position."

"But if a faction is willing to disregard me entirely and offer my system to the Fragians, the High Council would lose the Narvan and all its assets. The Fragians would lay waste to it and move on."

"Not if the Narvan were neatly handed to them," Fa'yet said.

This couldn't be true. It just couldn't.

"Don't the High and Mighties realize that even if they retain the natural resources of the Narvan, its people would be enslaved or exterminated?" I asked.

Kazan's head dropped into her hands. "They wouldn't need the people. They'd have the Fragians."

My people. Gone. All on the whim of a council who hid behind grey-suited zombies and hooded cloaks. Kryon didn't act against Kryon, but the High Council had its own rules.

Chandi hadn't hesitated to shoot me. "Why use Kess?"

"From what I've heard, there's only a small faction who are backing the Fragian proposal," Fa'yet said. "At least, so far."

"And they don't want to expose themselves just yet," I mused.

Hope lit Kazan's face. "Then we have time to change their minds."

Hope was just an inch away from desperation.

"What are you thinking?" I asked hesitantly.

She downed her wine and set the empty glass on the table with a loud clink. "We're going to attack the Fragians."

◦≥

Three bullet-free weekly reports to Chandi later, I stood beside Kazan in the command center of the Jalvian cruiser that she'd appointed as our flagship. The projection map next to us flickered to life. An array of various-sized blue blips hovered in loose formation in the vast space between the spheres marked as Merchess and the first of the Fragian controlled outposts scattered throughout the Rakon Nebula. Four red blips, each double the size of our largest vessels, crept closer. Ten smaller ships trailed behind them. With the entire Jalvian fleet advancing and active Fragian scouting patrols, a surprise attack was too much to hope for.

"They'll be within range in a matter of minutes," the Jalvian captain informed Kazan.

"Good thing we're ready." She leaned in to study the map and then stepped back. "I'll be monitoring all reports. Keep them frequent and brief."

She turned to the three of us. "Jey, you'll go with the Sylessian ships. Merkief, take the division from Rok. I expect you to keep me updated. Vayen, you're with me."

The ship shook. Static filled the vids for a second before returning to the external view. No Fragian ship revealed itself. Ear-splitting blasts ran from one end of the expansive hull to the other.

"What the hell was that?" Kazan squinted at the nearest external vid.

The captain consulted with his crew. "The scans don't show anything."

Kazan turned to Merkief and Jey. "Go. Now."

They Jumped.

She sat down at an empty post and closed her eyes, sinking deep into the fleet's network. I stood behind her, one hand on a gun and the other on her shoulder in case we needed to Jump quickly.

The captain glanced between us and then focused on me. "All the ships on the front line have reported damage with no visible targets."

Kazan's eyes fluttered open. "Recall all fighters. Fire the ship's weapons whether you see anything or not."

She activated the terminal in front of her and scanned through the external feeds transmitted by ships throughout the Jalvian fleet. In the painstaking minutes it took for the dispatched fighters to return to their carriers, bright shots of energy ripped from the nothingness of space, blasting apart the retreating vessels. Fragments of our fallen drifted away.

"They've got to be firing from somewhere," Kazan said.

The feeds flipped by at a manic rate and then froze. "There!" She pointed at a narrow black ship with a pointed tip floating lifelessly amongst the remains of our fighters.

My gaze drifted from the small, dead ship to the six distant but approaching Fragian cruisers. Kazan swore as beams of deadly light pelted the hulls of our fleet.

White light filled the vids.

A long, high shriek registered in my ears. Fire burst from the command post. White lightning arced from the terminals along the far wall, sending crewmembers hurling through the air. A woman standing near me screamed. Her gaze locked onto the other side of the room.

I turned to see a fist-sized hole open to the blackness of space. Cracks ran up the wall, expanding with each second. She began to pray loudly. Others around her joined in. I spared two breaths toward their effort while simultaneously cursing the Fragians before forming a Jump for Kazan and I to our preordained fallback ship near the rear.

When we came out of the Jump, Kazan fell to the floor from her seated position as there was no chair to catch her. She floundered there, her mind still caught deep in the network. I brought her to her feet and led her distracted body to the command center.

She shook off the link trance for a moment, walking into the room of her own accord.

I turned to the nearest crewman. "Seal these doors. I don't want anyone else in here until we leave."

For all I knew, the faction had agents planted throughout the fleet. Keeping an eye on the twenty-three men and women in the room was enough of a challenge with the battle going on around us.

The Fragian lines formed up, matching ours.

Reports revealed that six of our frontline ships, including our previous post, now served as nothing more than hazardous obstacles. I didn't need a closer view to know the tiny specks drifting in the debris were uniformed bodies of the crew who, moments before had been busy working beside us. The fading effects of my last dose did nothing to outweigh the guilt of not being able to save any of them.

One of the crewmen vacated his seat, offering Anastassia his terminal. I cringed at the manic pace with which she flipped through the feeds. She came to a stop on the nearest Fragian vessel. The hatch doors opened. I held my breath and waited for fighters to emerge.

Instead, long, narrow beams of bright light blinded us all.

My eyes refused to open. Tears ran down my face. "What the fuck was that?"

Kazan's voice wavered as she whispered, "They just vaporized everything small between us and them, including the four ships we had closest to them."

"How many lives is that?" I asked.

"We can't think about that right now," she said, her voice still far from steady.

I touched Merkief and Jey's links to verify they were still alive. Both of them were just as shaken as Kazan was.

Reports and questions began to bombard her terminal. I leaned in close to try to skim them as fast as she did. A request to retreat was followed by several more. I'd never thought to see the day when a Jalvian force would ask to back down from a fight.

I resorted to link speech to keep our conversation private. *"Are we staying or going?"*

Kazan stared at the terminal and the display of visible ships in range. *"You know the gamble I took here. If we leave, we lose everything."*

I distantly wondered if it had been the drug keeping me calm and collected, because its effects had vanished and so had my confidence that we would live through this. The more I considered the reality of what Artor would look like once the Fragians had slagged the cities and decimated my people, the more fear seeped into every thought. I placed my hand on Kazan's shoulder as much for my own comfort as hers.

"If you call on the Artorian fleet to fill in the gaps here, can you make them all work together?"

She rubbed her temples. *"That would leave the Narvan unguarded. Can you imagine what that array could do to a city?"*

"Yes, that's why I'm asking. Let the Artorian fleet guard the Narvan from here while we still have a chance of defending ourselves."

Another of our ships vented its air and crew into the battlefield before imploding seconds later. I felt her wince through her coat.

"I'll summon the Artorian fleet," she said, her fingers dancing over the terminal.

Kazan allowed the Jalvian fleet a degree of retreat in order to give my people time to get through the jump gates to join us.

Her muscles stiffened and relaxed in a maddening cycle as she alternated between using the terminal and her link to convey orders. I kept my link open to Jey and Merkief in case there was anything I could convey to them so she could focus on her other linked contacts.

From my level of dry mouth and headache, I ascertained I'd far exceeded my dosage timeframe. As much as I disliked chancing a dose around Kazan, it couldn't be helped. Ducking out of the room, as had been my prior alternative, wasn't an option. I couldn't leave her unguarded here. I also couldn't afford to be hindered by the withdrawal. She needed me in top form.

Getting the bottle open single-handedly inside my pocket was easy enough, but the dropper would draw attention from the crew. Instead, I removed the dropper and tipped the bottle until a line of wetness ran down my finger. From there it surprised and concerned me how simple it was to rub my hand across my mouth and get a quick dose without anyone taking a bit of notice.

A much needed sense of wellbeing flooded through me. I closed the bottle and let it fall back into the depths of my pocket.

The Fragians weren't giving us much space to fall back. Jey and Merkief followed Kazan's instruction, taking their divisions of the Jalvian fleet to target the Fragian vaporizing array in the hopes we could prevent another mass slaughter.

The rest of our fleet still suffered from the harassing shots from Fragian ships that seemed to be invisible. While our Jalvian ships made the best of the upgrades the Artorian University had garnered from stolen Fragian tech, their weapons would have been much more effective if we had a solid target. A few of their half-destroyed fighters floated amongst the wreckage but not near enough to account for the destruction they'd wrought on our fleet.

Kazan approved the request to deploy a small number of Jalvian fighters. They scattered, darting erratically toward the Fragian ships. It seemed like hours before they were in firing range.

Sweat lined the palm of my hand on Anastassia's armor. My skin tingled with the promise of so much more. She was right there in reach and the urge to let my hand wander was hitting me hard. I had to keep reminding myself that she was busy supervising a damned war to keep the Fragians off my homeworld.

I speculated on the drop equivalent of the dose I'd taken as I again buckled down my very distracted thoughts that had nothing to do with what was going on around us. She didn't want me in her head or her bed. She'd said so. I didn't either. But it was all I could think about with every fresh dose.

One of the Fragian cruisers drifted away from the others, explosions rippling across its exterior. A burst of cheering filled the command center when it blew apart moments later. One of the large red blips on the projection map near the captain winked out.

Anastassia grabbed my hand and squeezed it. I could feel her elation though our linked connection. We still had so much farther to go before I could even consider distracting her with the pleasure-filled thoughts that her momentary touch elicited. It hurt to do so, but I forced myself to let go of her and step back.

The arrival of the first of the Artorian fleet, rocketing from the nearest jump gate, sent a burst of pride through me.

"Tell them to pick up a few of those dead Fragian fighters," I said.

"Already on it." Fixated on relaying orders through linked contacts, her fingers again stilled on the controls.

In an effort to stay focused, I tried to watch the other crew members, but everyone was giving us a wide berth and was focused on their jobs. I looked to the projection map.

Another of the large Fragian vessels fell back in the formation. I waited for signs of stress or destruction, but instead, it flickered and then disappeared.

Kazan's fingers snapped back into action, pausing on one of the front line feeds as a fiery ball shot debris into the Fragian ship in front of it. Orange fissures scrabbled across the second ship's hull.

The feed switched, offering a disorienting view from one of the Artorian ships somewhere above us. The foremost Fragian ship again raised its hatch doors, spilling its vaporizing light into the field of wreckage.

Kazan yelled for the live feeds to be cut.

The vids went black.

The room went black. Shit. I grabbed her with both hands, not knowing if the ship was about to implode or if the power had simply been disrupted.

The captain swore. "Report!"

A voice called out, "We've lost power. We're checking into it, sir."

The captain shouted orders. Crewmen called out status reports. Footsteps shuffled and bodies banged into terminals.

Someone said, "I can't get the backup systems online."

Throughout the room, fingers pounded on dead terminals, as if sheer force could bring them to life. I brushed over Jey and Merkief's links in case I needed an alternate jump point. Both of them were busy dealing with their own situations and didn't acknowledge me.

An explosion sounded from the doorway.

I leaned in close to Kazan. "We need to leave. Where?"

A pulsewave burst through the room, shattering terminals and unarmored bodies in its path. I threw myself over Anastassia. We slammed down on the unforgiving terminal as the wave blasted into us. My coat protected me well enough, but the force of the pulse took my breath away and left me feeling as though I'd just gone ten rounds with Jey and lost every damn one of them.

"Vayen?"

"I'll live. Stay down." I gasped as I slowly disentangled myself from her and the destroyed terminal to get to my knees.

Emergency lights flashed from the corridor outside the blasted open doorway. A haze of smoke filled the room and it stunk of burnt wiring. Moaning and whispered prayers assured me that some of the crew had survived.

I couldn't see who had fired the pulse or where they were now, or if they were alone. I swallowed hard and tried to calm my ragged breathing as I listened to where everyone was in the room.

A woman whimpered, two sets of footsteps shuffled near where I'd last seen the captain. Whispers. Soft clicks of standard issue stunners being charged.

I kept one hand on Kazan's back and drew a gun with the other.

A scuffle. Grunts. A gunshot. The thud of a body falling to the floor.

I tensed, my hand fisting the collar of Kazan's armor as I strained for the slightest sound in the smoky blackness.

Another gunshot, this time it thwacked hard into my chest. For a long moment, I couldn't breathe. They were close, too close. Another shot or two like that in the same spot and my armor would give.

I wouldn't be of any use to Anastassia in the tank. Not to mention, I hated how loud and stark everything was now when I woke from a tank visit. Leaving these people to their fate didn't set well with me, but Kazan needed to be safe and as much as the drug assured me I was fine, the deep pain in many of my ribs said otherwise. I said a prayer to Geva that our attacker would leave when we did and tried Merkief again.

He must had sensed my urgency this time. He flashed me a jump point immediately. Seconds later, we arrived in the command center of a Rokish ship. I managed to make it to my feet through the black spots that taunted my vision and pulled Anastassia up with me. She held one arm awkwardly and her face was bloody.

The lights were glaring after the blackness. Merkief ran over to us.

He took one look at her face and turned to me. He grimaced. I must not have looked any better.

"What happened?" he asked.

Kazan shook off my hold on her coat. "Pulse wave, Vayen on my back, and terminal meets face." She wiped at the blood dripping from her swelling nose, smearing it into the blood from her split lip.

"Our feeds went dead." She glanced at the nearest screen. "What's happening out there?"

Merkief led us to the projection map. "They vaporized their wreckage. Seems they don't want us picking up any more of their tech."

The remains of the Fragian forces retreated to their own space. Our sensors lost them. The red blips fizzled out one by one.

Merkief waved to someone at the rear of the room and pointed to Kazan.

A medic rushed over and interposed herself between Kazan and the projection map. "Let me take a look at that for you." She dabbed a wad of gauze on the blood dripping from Kazan's nose.

"I'm fine." Kazan snatched the gauze from her, pressed it to her nose and waved the medic away.

The medic didn't move. Kazan shot her a look, made quite fearsome by all the blood on her face, and strode to the other side of the map. Her steps were not as sure as usual and she wasn't using one of her hands.

"Why don't you sit down for a minute?" I asked, thinking I could do with a seat myself.

She turned her glare on me. "I'm kind of in the middle of a

battle here?"

I took a good look at the feeds. "Unless they have a second wave lying in wait, which I doubt because they would have used it by now—"

"Or they're hoping we'll chase them down and land in a trap they've set," Merkief said.

Kazan shook her head, wiping at the blood now trailing down to drip from her chin. "If that was their plan, they would have fallen back earlier when we were clearly losing. They could have easily wiped us out."

I let the two of them argue tactics and glanced between her swelling face and the map. The last of the red ships blinked out, leaving only a sea of blue behind. I opened my link to Anastassia.

"You've made your point. Let's just hope the faction reads your reports and takes note. Now, you've got ten minutes to pass on any further orders and then you're going to the tank."

She cocked her head. *"Is that so?"*

I nodded, but instantly regretted even that much movement. *"It would look good if you're injury free when you turn that report in. And you should do that before the Fragians get a chance to put their twist on how it went down."*

Merkief's brows rose as he looked between us. "Jey and I can keep you updated, Kazan, if you have something you need to attend to elsewhere."

Her puffy lips drew down into a scowl. For all her bluster, exhaustion from maintaining her deep link trance further tinted the bruising now appearing around her eyes. I knew I had her when she turned to Merkief and started spouting off orders.

When she finished, we Jumped to the ship. I slowly readied the tank while she undressed. Though I tried not watch her directly, I couldn't help but notice the swollen spots on her arms and chest from where she'd hit the terminal.

"I didn't mean to hurt you."

"I know. I'd rather be bruised and bloody than dead." She eased herself onto the tank's platform. "You better be getting in after me."

"As long as you promise not to go to Sere alone."

"Good point." She turned to look at me. "How many operatives does the faction have at their discreet disposal?

I was having a hard time keeping my hand off the nearly empty bottle in my pocket which would ease my aches if I took the rest of it. Keeping my mind to myself while she was naked just a few steps away, wasn't any easier. I took a deep breath and let it out slowly.

"The faction has access to all of our Kryon contract work," I said. "That's a given. I'm sure they have spies within the planetary governments and their own scattered contacts, just as you have yours. They wouldn't resort to Kryon against Kryon, but that doesn't mean they can't send anyone else after you. Not to mention, all the Jalvian worlds knew we were going to battle. Their faction might be feeding the Fragians information too. For all we know, they warned the Fragians of the impending arrival of the Artorian fleet. At least one of their ships left as soon as the fleet arrived."

She paled and started to sit up. "I can't default on Kryon contracts; that would give the faction more leverage against me. How am I supposed to defend my position with the Fragians with every credit-hungry street-corner assassin after me?"

"Merkief and Jey are watching over the fleet. I'm watching over you. Get healed up, and we'll figure it out later." I activated the platform before she tempted me any further.

She muttered something about 'bossy Artorian men', and then went silent as the tank closed and the healing gel put her into an instant deep sleep.

While she was out and safe on the ship and Merkief and Jey were busy, I figured it would be a good time to check in with Chandi. If nothing else, I could get a feel as to whether she was part of the faction or she and Shoulders were their own brand of evil.

I took a few minutes to clean up and take a couple extra drops to dull the pain. Then I Jumped. Sere greeted me with its usual indifference which thinly masked the bone-chilling feeling of a hundred eyes watching my every breath. Without waiting for an invitation, I proceeded directly to our usual room. Chandi didn't disappoint me.

"I don't stand in this room all day everyday on the off chance you'll drop in, you know."

"Never thought you did." This time there was a chair. I gingerly settled into it. "I figured you'd know the second I arrived and summon me here. Thought I'd save you the trouble."

Shoulders arrived and closed the door behind him. He came over to stand right next to me. "What's the meaning of this?"

"He's being agreeable." Chandi's tight smile confirmed that I'd managed to annoy her. "How's the battle going?"

"Well enough. Seems to be over for the moment."

"Is that so?" A muscle along her jawline twitched. "And your partner, she out celebrating?"

"Resting."

"Losses?" she asked.

No point in lying. She'd know soon enough if she didn't already. "Heavy."

"Interesting."

The twitch told me she was in the faction but her indifferent response made me wonder. Was she on the sidelines or in the middle of it all? Then again, maybe she was good at hiding behind her own mask.

"The drug is fine. I'm sticking to your doses. What exactly do you want from me in these reports, and how much longer am I expected to do them?"

"You're a slow learner, Mr. Ta'set." Shoulders punched me in the gut with his massive fist. "No questions. Just do."

Black spots did another dance over my eyes. Even shallow breaths elicited an impossible to hide wince. "I am doing. I'm just asking what the point is." If I could get a lead on their motivation, I'd better know if they were for or against Kazan.

Chandi pursed her full lips. "You will double your dose."

"I need to be able to work."

She smiled and handed me another bottle. The weight of the cool glass offered me comfort, the promise that everything would be fine.

"Yes, you do. You should see the contract clerk before you leave. We'd like to observe your solo abilities. We may have a special job for you in the near future," she said.

"I already have a job." The last time I'd said those words, I'd swapped a normal life with Sonia for Kazan's blood and bullet-filled world. Trading Kazan for Chandi and her High Council schemes wasn't a move I was willing to make.

"How's your leg?" she asked.

I glared at her as I dropped the bottle into my pocket. It clinked against the almost empty one.

"Why am I bothering with these reports? You don't even ask about the effects of the drug."

"We don't need to ask. We can see everything we need to know."

Did they have me under some kind of surveillance, was someone reporting on me? If they did, I needed to keep them off my back so I could keep Kazan safe from Kess and the faction.

I did my best to hide my limping gait and went to see the contract clerk. If they wanted to see what I could do on my own, they'd get their chance after I took a trip to the tank. This was what I'd been training for, wasn't it? To step out from her shadow and be noticed for my own abilities? This was my chance.

Chapter Fourteen

Kazan's face hovered over me as I woke in my bed on the ship. "Job go bad?"

"A little. I'm fine."

But I wasn't. She was too damn close again and the air was too dry to breathe. The sheets felt like they were lined with pins. I hated that damned tank.

"You're fine now, but you've been out of the tank for six hours. Yeah, I checked the records. What if I needed you while you were off getting killed on a solo job way over your head?"

"You, of all people, can't be seriously asking me that."

"I take back up." Her brows furrowed. "Whatever you were doing, you shouldn't have been doing it alone. If you need help, all you have to do is ask."

But I couldn't ask. Chandi had made it clear that the job was to be mine alone. Sure, hunting down and eliminating a newly decreed ex-Kryon operative wouldn't have been my choice of solo job, but here I was, alive and ready to take my shift with Kazan. This was the fourth solo job I'd taken in the past month. Each contract was more difficult than the last, but it seemed I was better than I gave myself credit for. I didn't need Kazan overshadowing me on every damn job.

"I said I'm fine. The job was fine. What's on the schedule for today?"

She ran her hand over her hair and down her braid. "You've been, I don't know," she shrugged, "reckless lately. If you're attempting to prove something to me, stop it. It's not necessary."

"Reckless? You don't have any right to call me out on that front either." I yanked the blanket back. "I need to take a shower so we can get to work."

"Vayen."

Why wouldn't she just leave me alone so I could get a dose in my system and get back to myself again? "What?"

"Your hand."

I glanced down to where my fist still clenched the edge of the blanket. It was shaking. Why hadn't I noticed?

"I'm hungry, all right? I might have skipped a meal or two."

"A few more than that, I'd say. You've been losing weight."

Since I'd started taking Chandi's drug, food had lost its appeal. I didn't need it. But this shaking, I didn't like that one bit. I needed steady hands to work. I'd have to tell Chandi about this new development.

"I've been busy, that's all," I said.

She nodded. "If you say so. Clean up, get a good meal in you, and wait for me on the Verian Station. I'm going to visit Marin."

Marin. My hand shook more, but this time, it was because the rest of me was too. "I'd rather you didn't."

"You both get that same clenched teeth scowl when I mention one to the other. Clearly something happened between the two of you, but he won't say a word. Would you care to enlighten me?"

What was I supposed to tell her? Marin worked with Jey to get rid of me and both of them let you worry for weeks while they knew the truth? Then again, he also helped me when I wanted to leave you and gave me a place to stay.

I might have a gut feeling about him, but that hardly served as concrete evidence against a man she'd known far longer than me. Not to mention, I'd be sowing doubt in her already ultra suspicious mind about Jey, who, while not my favorite person in the known universe, was just as devoted to protecting her as I was. He didn't deserve to be on her bad side.

"No," I said.

"All right then, I need to see him. It's important."

Picturing Anastassia with Marin, doing the things she'd shown me in the glimpse into her desires, did nothing to improve my mood.

"Then go," I said with far more venom that I'd intended to share.

She stepped back. I couldn't tell if she wanted to punch me in the face or cry, but I was glad she Jumped before doing either. I didn't care if it was time for my next dose or not. If I was going to wait alone for a few hours, I deserved to enjoy myself. I took my four drops and then two more for good measure. After a shower and change of clothes, I grabbed my coat and weapons and Jumped to the Verian Station.

∞

"Vayen, wake up," Anastassia whispered in my ear.

I didn't remember falling asleep. And I certainly didn't remember falling asleep with Anastassia beside me. Her fingers gripped my shoulder through my shirt.

"Vayen."

Though it wasn't skin to skin, she was right there, touching me just on the other side of the barrier of cloth. Each fingertip sent a pulse of dull warmth down my arm and across my chest.

"What the hell is wrong with you?"

I opened my eyes to see her glaring at me. What was she so pissed about? "Nothing's wrong with me."

She crossed her arms over her chest. "I don't smell alcohol, so what are you on?"

Nothing she could know about. "I'm not on anything."

I stood and put on my coat, running my hands over it to make sure everything was in place. "How was your visit with Marin?"

"Not good, but don't change the subject. At first I thought you were just in a better mood, but it's more than that. Not eating isn't like you. And have you looked at yourself in a mirror lately?"

I knew the pressure of being Chandi's puppet had brought a level of gauntness to my face, but it wasn't like Kazan had a private market on showing stress. The dark circles under her eyes weren't doing her any favors either.

"I'm just working a lot."

"I noticed. You've been taking solo Kryon contracts, but you haven't been using the tank much," she said. "I haven't needed to."

Did she assume I ended up in there after every solo job? I was better than that, and she should know it.

"I don't expect you to use it for every ache or scratch, but come on, you came on your last shift limping. That shouldn't happen.

You're hardly in top condition. When was the last time you went a few rounds with Jey?"

"I wasn't limping, and I haven't needed to waste time keeping in shape for sitting in front of a wall of vids. I've been working."

"About that, Merkief mentioned that two of you haven't gone out or actually talked in a couple months. I'm glad you're settling into all this so well, but you do need to take a break now and then."

Damned Merkief. I was beginning to see why Kazan kept her friends at a distance. I hoped he was still speaking to me when this experiment was over.

"I'll cut back on contracts if it will make you happy." Chandi would have to understand.

Anastassia ran her hands over her face. "You're not even getting mad."

"Would you like me to?"

"Yes. Something. Anything but that stupid smile that's been planted on your face too often lately."

"I thought you liked it when I smiled."

"Not like that." She shook her head. "Get something to eat. You look like you're going to fall over. We'll talk about this later."

"So what did happen with Marin? He still after you to retire and live the peaceful assassin's life?"

"And you're blissing your mind away. Both of you seem to forget that the Narvan is on the verge of being handed over to the Fragians. I'm not sure which is more aggravating."

"My bet is on Marin. He doesn't even know about the faction or the Fragian proposal, and you can't tell him. That's got to be frustrating."

Her fists clenched. "And you know, but you don't care."

"Of course I care."

"Then show it, dammit! Clean yourself up and stay on watch while I get a few hours of sleep. When I wake up, I'm going to visit my friend on Prime to get some quality counsel."

"This friend knows the situation?"

"No, of course not, and he won't. I need an outside perspective to help me find a solution."

I was supposed to be finding a solution. Not her.

The drug embraced me in its warm glow, soothing my ire. There would be plenty of time to defeat the faction and Kess once Chandi's experiment was over. I patted the bottle nestled safely in my pocket.

∾

Five hours of flipping through news feeds from Veria Prime and the colonies on Veria Minor left me hungering for a few drops from the golden bottle, but with Kazan onto me, I figured it best to lay off until my shift was over. A knock at the door provided a much-needed distraction.

I waved my hand over the door control. A solemn Verian man in scarlet robes edged with unfamiliar golden geometric-shaped patterns waited for me to acknowledge his existence.

"Can I help you?" I asked.

He bobbed his shaved head covered with vibrant swirling tattoos. "I was told Anastassia Kazan is in residence. I have an important message for her."

I made a note to discuss with Anastassia the fact that some-one on the station was freely giving out her residence status. She might not see these people as a threat, but I didn't discount any-one, especially with the faction after her.

"She doesn't want to be disturbed at the moment."

"I am Seeker Tomias, and I have direct orders to report to her if certain events should come to pass. One has, and so here I am."

Uncertainty niggled at me. Perhaps, like everyone else on the station, this man was from her past and she'd want to see him. Better to play it safe since she was already annoyed with me.

"I'll let her know you're here."

I stepped aside to let him in and then kept an eye on him while I went to Kazan's door and opened it. "There's a Seeker Tomias here to see you."

Kazan jumped out of bed, tossed her unbound hair behind her shoulders and tugged on her clothes. She dashed past me.

Standing beside her door, I watched the two of them greet each other in the fashion of familiar Verian's, their hands on each other's shoulders as they touched foreheads.

"It is with great sadness that I am here. Our friend and father has passed on."

Kazan's hand flew to her mouth. Tears welled in her eyes. The short man reached over to pat her arm. She took a deep breath and composed herself.

"Tomias, how?"

Her gaze brushed over me. I kept my attention elsewhere to

offer her a semblance of privacy. In fact, I was busy searching for any past mention of her on Veria Prime and doing a little research on Verian seekers.

"Peacefully, I suppose. Our father was old. His heart was weak, and it finally failed him."

"When?"

"A few hours ago." Tomias took her hand in his. "I know this is sudden, but it's not unexpected. I assure you, I saw to the body myself as you instructed. Everything is as it should be."

Kazan nodded. "I need to be alone for awhile. I'm sorry to rush you off, but it's been a long day and now this."

She walked Tomias to the door. "Thank you for coming to tell me yourself."

"Of course, Anastassia. Our father didn't have much in the way of possessions, but he indicated a few items he wished you to have in the event of his death. Come see me whenever you're ready."

"I will. Thank you."

The door closed. Anastassia walked blindly to her room.

I went to her. "Anastassia?"

She dodged out of my intended embrace. "Not right now, all right?"

I let her by so she could slip into her room before the tears welling in her eyes escaped. Anastassia Kazan didn't cry with an audience.

҂

She emerged from her room early in the evening and came to my doorway with her gaze stuck on the floor. "I need to visit Veria Prime to see Tomias. I want to get this taken care of before we get to work."

"You want me to come along?"

"It would be better if you didn't, but yes." Anastassia smoothed her shirt, a long, plain blue one that masked any hint of curves beneath it. Without a weapon in sight, and her hair loose, she didn't look at all herself.

I wanted to go with her, but it had been so long since I'd had a taste from the golden bottle. My mouth was dry. My entire body ached, but my head, it was killing me. Even a single drop would help, but I didn't dare, not with her going to Prime unarmed and so distracted by emotion.

"Why shouldn't I come along?"

Free from its usual braid, her hair fell around her shoulders. She pushed it back from her face. "Verians abhor violence. Think Palaz, but on a city-wide scale."

"But your Seeker didn't hate you. Neither does Tomias, from what I've seen."

"I can hide who I am. I've done it for years. You," she shook her head, "you exude who you are."

A drop would help with that too. My hand snuck into my pocket and cradled the bottle. "So why chance it?"

"The faction. Kess. Fragians." She sighed deeply.

Seeing her so vulnerable, I couldn't help but get up and wrap my arms around her even without the promise of pleasure from the drug. I ran a hand over her back and didn't encounter a single holster or weapon, just soft, pliable Anastassia pressed tight against me. Despite the pain in my head, my mind started to tingle. Great Geva, I wanted a drop. I'd been imagining the sensation of her body pressed against mine with the soft, warm lights intertwining, binding us together since that night I'd gone to her room.

She stiffened and pulled away, not far, but enough to remind me that this wasn't the time for such things. I let her have her space.

My search for this Seeker she called both friend and father had come up empty. "Who was this man to you?"

"I lived on the station for years with my own father and older brother while we did our research. When they became casualties of the war with Jal, Res came to see me. He'd heard I had a telepathic gift and offered to train me. Verians consider it god-touched."

Anastassia slumped against the wall. "But I wasn't Verian so he could only teach me portions of the Seeker training. Tomias, who had come to Res at the same time, got it all."

"Wait." I held up my hand before my mouth hit the floor. "You were training to be a Verian Seeker?"

"I'd lost everyone important to me. I was young. It seemed like a way to do some good."

I tried to envision Anastassia in the gilded robes of a Seeker, her shaved head decorated with swirling tattoos. The image refused to form.

"But it wasn't?" I asked.

"I wasn't *good* enough." Her voice grew quieter. "Res said he saw it in me. I also wasn't one of them. He gave me what training he could, but I wasn't content to be half of something. I left with his blessing and joined the army."

"So does Palaz hate you because you're not hiding who you are as well as you think, or because you spurned what she considers your god-given gift?"

"I don't know." She sighed. "Tomias knows I'm important elsewhere, but he's never concerned himself with anything bigger than the people in his care. Res was the same way." Her hands twisted together. "I can't deal with the Palaz's of the world right now."

"I'll deal with them for you."

Anastassia smiled, her hands falling to her sides. A wonderful wave of warmth washed through me, like the drug but different. It did nothing to quell the pulsing in my head, but for a few moments, I didn't care about the pain quite as much.

"Let's hope it doesn't come to that. But thanks." Her smile faltered. "You'll need to leave your coat and any visible weapons behind."

"Right." I shed the offending coat and deadly items. If the little, peace-loving Verians decided to give us a problem, I figured I could do a suitable amount of damage with my bare hands. If it came to the faction's agents, we'd have to Jump rather than fight.

She looked me over and reached up to run her hand over my cheek. The warmth came again. I closed my eyes to savor the sensation.

"You really do look like all nine of your hells, you know. Don't let this job destroy you," she said.

"I'm trying not to."

I'd tried to turn Chandi down. If I wanted Anastassia to keep her position and my body to remain bullet-free, I needed to finish this damned experiment. Hopefully before my head exploded.

"Are you all right?"

"Just a bad headache. I'll be fine."

Anastassia reached into my coat before I could stop her. Her fingers explored the shapes in my pocket. It was with great relief that when she pulled it out, she held my tin of stims.

"Take one of these. Just one. I don't need you bouncing off the walls."

I took the tin from her hand, smiling for a moment as her fingers slipped into mine. Then, as if she realized what she was doing, she pulled her hand away and stepped back further. I popped the stim into my mouth and slid the tin safely back into the pocket beside the bottle.

She flashed me a Jump point, the same place she'd shown me when she'd first gone to see her Seeker. There was no one around to notice our sudden arrival in front of the red, wooden door engraved with patterns similar to the ones that lined Tomias's robes. The door was set into a dome-shaped building. A rectangular building stood behind the dome, looking much like a renovation afterthought.

Anastassia knocked and then followed my gaze. "Housing for the acolytes. This," she pointed at the dome, "was Res's home."

"An odd mix." The curves against the hard angles didn't fit what I considered peaceful surroundings.

"Facades aren't a big priority here," Anastassia said as footsteps thudded toward the door. "They are much more concerned with what's inside."

The door opened to reveal a Verian girl, likely no more than ten years old. A long, copper-tinged blond braid hung over her bare shoulder. Her shirt, two sizes too big, hung from her petite frame. Her yellow-green eyes darted between us.

Anastassia introduced herself and asked for Tomias.

"I'll get the Seeker." Her tiny hand indicated a bench inside the door. She scampered down the narrow hall.

The girl returned moments later. "Seeker Tomias will be with you shortly. He asks that you await him in the garden." She led us through a door at the back of the dome that opened into a walled garden. The girl bowed and left.

Kazan took one of two benches set a conversational distance apart. Dense, trimmed bushes lined the garden filled with overflowing plots of plants. A sea of orange, spice-scented flowers were in bloom. She closed her eyes and breathed deeply.

I gave her shoulder a squeeze and wandered off to an unobtrusive spot against one of the dormitory buildings.

Tomias arrived with a cloth-wrapped bundle in his hands. "I'm glad you came so soon." He sat across from Anastassia. "In the years since you left your training, our father often spoke of you. He always wished you'd return to us. You still can."

She shook her head. "This isn't my place."

"I could use your help. My acolytes are few and the needs of our people are great. Etara, the girl you met, is the eldest and most promising, but she is far from being ready to assume her full duties. It is a big city, Anastassia. I am but one man."

A shadow passed over her face. "I'm not one of you, Tomias. Res made that quite clear by limiting my training."

"Yes, but you can do so much here with the training you did receive. Think of all the people you can help."

"I help them in my own way." Anastassia shook her head. "I tried, Tomias. This life isn't for me."

He cracked a guilty smile. "So you have said, but you can't blame me for asking one last time."

"I'm sorry."

"Never mind that." He unwrapped the cloth from the bundle.

A tinkling voice invaded my natural paths without invitation. *"You can hear me, yes?"*

I glanced around the courtyard. Etara entered through the doorway we'd come through and came to stand next to me.

Dammit, I really didn't need a curious little girl in my head. Not to mention, how in the hells did she just barge in there? I had defenses for Geva's sake. I should have felt some measure of pressure indicating a new presence awaiting my approval, but there'd been nothing. I looked to Kazan, hoping for some guidance, but she and Tomias were deep in conversation.

"It's rude to barge into someone's head like this," I said.

"I've never seen an Artorian before. Tomias says all Artorians have the gift. An entire planet of Seekers must be very peaceful."

"Not exactly."

The stim took the edge off my headache, but it didn't do near as much as it should have. The adrenaline it forced into my system made me shaky. And edgy. I needed to get out of there, to get away from the overwhelming spice of the flowers and the high walls of the garden that threatened to close in on me.

My bottle. I'd left it in my coat back on the station. My hands clenched and unclenched, seeking the comfort of the glass bottle. My mouth was dry and my tongue too large to be contained. My stomach heaved. Nothing of consequence came out. I covered a second round with a few muffled coughs. My watering eyes made out Etara staring at me.

I walked away, circling around to the other side of the garden where I could still clearly see Anastassia. Verian telepathy required being in a close vicinity, that detail I had been aware of. However, the blatant disregard for my initial defenses worried me.

Anastassia accepted a book from Tomias. She thumbed through the pages and asked something of him.

Etara tapped my arm. I jumped. Either the headache was playing with my senses or the girl had an amazing gift for stealth. I scowled, hoping she'd get the hint.

"How can your homeworld not be peaceful? With the sharing of thoughts, there would be no reason for sadness and everyone can share joy."

"Just because we have mind speech, doesn't make us like you. Now, go away."

Etara's voice grew louder in my head, swirling around as if gathering power. *"You've hurt people."*

The girl's abilities were stronger than any Artorian I'd encountered. Her will battered my deepest mental defenses, and her intent to dive into a full probe was clear as the sky above me. I threw up every mental block I knew of.

"I have to protect her, it's my job."

The same scorn-filled light I'd seen in Palaz's eyes took hold in Etara's. *"She's hurt people, too. I can feel it from you. You are both evil, yet Seeker Tomias talks to you without judgment. It's not right."*

Strangling children wasn't something I was comfortable with, but I didn't know how long I could hold off the probe-like missiles she hurled at my defenses.

"Anastassia, we need to go."

She looked up from the folded russet robe in her hand. *"Is the formidable Vayen Ta'set afraid of little girls?"*

I glared at her. *"Ones that are about to see things they shouldn't see, yes."*

The pressure increased. Sweat beaded on my forehead. My stomach threatened to heave again. I held onto the rough wall in an attempt to keep the worst of my shaking masked from Anastassia's gaze.

Etara stood right in front of me as if to block my escape. *"You're warning her, aren't you?"*

Tomias sped over to us, a frown on his face. Anastassia followed close behind with her brow furrowed and questions pelting my mind. I was too busy fending off the tiny demon to answer her.

If Etara was this strong as a child, I didn't want to stick around to see what Tomias could do. We needed to leave.

The girl raised her hand, jabbing an accusing finger into my stomach. "Killer!"

Anastassia blanched, clutching the stack of items to her chest.

Tomias pulled Etara away, holding her against him. "What is the meaning of this, Anastassia?"

"He's my bodyguard. He's had to do things to keep me safe."

Tomias turned Etara to face him. "They are not of us. We'll talk about this later." He gave her a gentle push toward the door we'd come through.

The pressure in my head eased as Etara disappeared from view.

The Seeker brushed his mind against mine, confirming my worst fears. He was indeed far more powerful than the girl or any probe I'd encountered before. My defenses held together by mere threads and those were quickly unraveling.

Anastassia put her hand on Tomias's arm and said in her very Kazan voice, "Please don't do that."

Tomias stepped away as if her touch burned. "You're right. This is not your place. You should go."

Anastassia's shoulders slumped. Her head bowed over the gifts Res had left for her.

Tomias held the door to the domed house open for us. "Our father always wished for you to find peace. I hope that one day, Anastassia, you will."

When we had passed through, he did not follow. The door closed.

Anastassia turned to me, resting her forehead against my shoulder. Res's gifts pressed against my chest.

"Take us somewhere else. Not the station. Somewhere I can be alone for a little while," she said.

I formed a Jump to the ship for both of us. The effort burned, like sharp nails scraping against shredded flesh. I clenched my teeth together, refusing to let any evidence of my agony reach Anastassia's ears. It seemed suitable punishment for the pain I'd caused her.

The house on Frique would probably have suited her better, but in my condition, I felt safer here. Besides, I was due to check in with Chandi.

She rested her cheek against mine. "You should use the tank while we're here."

"I will." Eventually. A visit to Sere without any of the drug in my system would lead to more of Chandi's bullets.

"You will right now." She pulled back far enough to look me over. "If your defenses are low enough for a little girl to crack them—"

"She may have been young, but come on. Why didn't you warn me about how strong they are?"

She stared at me blankly. "I don't know what excuse you're attempting to make, but I'm not buying it. You're a huge liability to me and the High Council. Whatever you're going through, we'll deal with it, but first, I need you healthy. Go." She gave me a gentle push toward the tank room.

If she hadn't been following right behind me, I would have lied right to her face and promised I would go to the tank later.

"Anastassia, I can't. Not right now."

"Do I need to make it an order?"

I'd rather thought we were beyond orders between us, but apparently she didn't. "I need to go do something."

"You're on duty for another hour. You can go do whatever you need to on your own time. After you get out of the tank."

I spun around. "I can't use it."

"Vayen, you're going in the tank. It's for the best, really."

Aside from Jumping directly to Sere that moment, which would really piss Anastassia off, or divulging the truth about Chandi's experiment, which would have the High and Mighties on my ass, I didn't have many options.

"I thought we had a contract?"

"You're not working, not like this. Quit stalling and get undressed." She went to the terminal and set down the bundle she'd received from Tomias. Her fingers danced over the controls.

I undressed and laid on the cold platform. It began to rise.

"When you're done in there, we're going to dinner and we're having a long talk. No arguments."

The gel hit my back as the platform lowered, bringing its own form of soothing warmth. A faint tingle enveloped me as the numbness set in. Seconds later, I knew nothing.

◈

I woke to darkness and the faint hiss of the ship's air scrubbers. When I sat up, the lights came on. Not wanting to let Anastassia know I was awake yet, but wondering where she was, I chanced a touch with Merkief's link.

"What's wrong with you?" his accusing voice thundered into my head.

Pressing my pillow over my face did nothing to soften his volume. *"I'm fine."* For the moment anyway.

"Hardly. You better pull it together or Jey's going to take your place."

Of course he would. He'd try, anyway. Anastassia didn't need a new partner to deal with while in the middle of this faction mess. She needed me beside her. I had to call Chandi off for now and if that meant taking another bullet, so be it.

"We'll be done in a few hours. Meet us at the house on Artor. We need to talk," he said.

"Get in line."

Like more talking about things I couldn't talk about would be of any help. I cut contact.

A quick shower, a meal bar and a Jump later, I made my way to Chandi's meeting room. It was empty.

And then it wasn't. Six grey-suits plowed through the open doorway.

One said, "Remove your armor."

The rest aimed guns at me. I took off my coat and set it on the floor. The speaker nodded toward the lone chair. I sat.

Taking a bullet to prove my point was one thing, but my odds against living through five in the head weren't very good. Chandi, Shoulders and three other cloaked figures strode through a door at the other end of the room.

The muscles along her jawline looked like a blood-crazed firing squad. "Why is there no trace of the drug in your system?"

"I need to stop this experiment, at least for now."

Shoulders nodded to one of the men standing near me. The zombie snapped to life and punched me in the gut.

"You're a very slow learner. How did you make it into Kryon again?" Shoulders asked.

One of these days, I was going to even the score with him. Preferably when we were alone and I was in better shape. The tank may have removed Chandi's drug from my system, but it couldn't repair the months of neglect my body had suffered while I'd been feeling great.

The group of three cloaked figures conferred and then one

said something to Chandi. She turned to me.

"This regeneration tank Kazan has hidden away, you've used it?"

I nodded.

"She never shared knowledge of it with her previous partners. Where is it?" she asked.

"I can't tell you that." If the High and Mighties didn't know from Kazan, they sure as all hells weren't finding out from me.

"I recommend that you do."

She nodded to Shoulders. As he plowed his way through the grey-suits, I braced for another round of meaty-fist-to-gut action.

"What's going on here?" A deep male voice asked. "Where is your cloak?"

Shoulders froze. I looked past him to see yet another cloaked figure stride into the room. Chandi spun around. The three others backed away from her. The zombies maintained their positions.

"Just a check on Mr. Ta'set's progress," Chandi said.

"You and your followers were given a deadline. You haven't met it."

"We're making good progress. We only need a little more time."

Deep Voice shook his hooded head. "No. You were given ample time and resources to make your Fragian proposal a reality. You lost. He's ours now. As discussed, we have further uses for him."

I was glad I was sitting down. Not only was Chandi part of the faction against Kazan, she was leading it. But now she was shut down. Relief flooded through me.

Was her drug supposed to keep me from protecting Anastassia so her faction would have an easier time of taking her out? I wanted to point out the fact that even with me drugged, her plan had sorely failed. However, in light of Deep Voice declaring new ownership of my puppet strings, I kept my gloating to myself.

Chandi smiled sweetly. "I didn't exactly lose. Were you aware that Mr. Ta'set has access to Kazan's regeneration tank?"

I felt Deep Voice's gaze land on me. "Is this true?"

Just when I thought I'd found some help. I sighed. "Yes."

"It would be in your interest to provide the location of this tank. We have been asking Kazan for quite some time, but she's been rather uncooperative."

"She's like that," I said.

"Your assistance would be greatly appreciated."

"I'm afraid I'm like that too."

"You've been cooperative with Chandi," said Deep Voice. "So I doubt that's the case. Perhaps you're just loyal, and we value loyalty. Would it ease your conscience to provide a general location and let us fill in the blanks?"

With the damned robes and hoods, I couldn't get a good read on anyone in the room but Chandi, and she didn't appear near as defeated as I would have liked. Deep Voice strode forward. The gunmen lowered their weapons and backed away. Shoulders stayed beside me.

"I don't think so," I said.

"That's unfortunate." His gloved hands emerged from the long sleeves. They grasped a thin metal rod with a pointed tip.

Shoulder's hands kept me in my seat as Deep Voice jabbed the tip of the rod into the back of my neck. A sharp pain ran down my spine.

He pulled the rod out. "The tracer won't bleed enough to send him to the tank, and I'm guessing, given his current lack of assistance, he's going to hold out going as long as he can." He turned to Chandi. "To make up for your violation of protocol—"

"I thought dealing with him face to face would make him more cooperative."

"You were wrong and now he knows you."

"Yes, thank you for pointing that out." Her jaw started to twitch again.

"He's an addict," said Deep Voice. "I suggest you give Kazan a good reason to bring him to that tank."

Chandi nodded to Shoulders. I swear, even through the hood, I could see him grin.

❧

I came to in an alley. It was dark, but there were voices in the distance. The drug pulsed through my veins, converting the pain from the beating Shoulders had given me into a mild tingle. I'd fought back, but that only earned me a few broken knuckles. Whatever Shoulders had on under his cloak, it was solid. Geva only knew what race he might be.

Dried blood caked the side of my face, pulling my skin taut. I imagined I was bleeding in quite a few other places as well. Shoulders had fully enjoyed himself. Only after I'd lost the ability to fight back had they mercifully poured a massive dose down my throat.

I consulted my link for the time. My mind recoiled as a spike of pain drove through it. Whether it was an effect of the drug or something they'd done to me, I wasn't sure.

Using the wall behind me, I got to my feet. A cool breeze sent a pleasant wave of goosebumps over my skin. I wasn't wearing my armor. Rapid blinking brought enough focus to my one good eye to locate my coat lying at my feet.

When I reached down to pick it up, I lost my breath. The already dark alley dimmed. Even through the pleasure-filled embrace of the drug, the pain of several broken ribs was clear. There was no way I could mask that from Anastassia. She'd order me back into the tank, no matter how much I protested. I needed to find somewhere to get help, somewhere she couldn't get to me.

Cragtek had a good medical staff. If I could make it through the pain in my head, they'd take care of me. I could claim some emergency situation there and stick around until I healed enough to work without wincing. I wouldn't need the damned tank.

I sat down, and with my coat held firmly in the hand that wasn't a bloody swollen mess, formed the Jump to Rok. Another spike drove through my head, bringing me to my knees and sending tears streaming down my face. I let the Jump go. The pain eased, handing me back to the warm embrace of the drug, which even though it had only been minutes since I'd awoken, didn't seem as strong as it had at first. I was coming down. Though without access to my link, and not having any way of knowing how much they'd actually given me, I still had no idea how long I'd been out.

Where in Geva's name had they left me? I had to be somewhere easy to find if they expected Kazan to locate me when I couldn't contact her.

I carefully made my way to my feet and groaned my way through pulling my coat on. Maybe if I had another drop or two, the pain wouldn't get to me quite as much. I reached into my coat. No bottle. I let out a string of profanity that would have made even my military-hardened brother gape.

The alley opened onto a street devoid of land transports. The dome overhead was of high quality, smooth and clean behind its faint night cycle glow. This had to be an Artorian world, either Karin or Moriek.

Lights and loud music came from one of the doorways as I walked down the street. Someone had dropped a bar in the middle of a daytime commercial district. I wasn't thirsty and anyone left there at this late hour would more than likely steal my weapons and finish what Shoulders had started rather than help me. I kept walking. With each step, I felt worse.

I finally came to a main cross street that offered a land transport call station. I pushed the button and leaned against the post to wait. Within five minutes, an automated transport rolled up to the curb. The door slid open. I grunted and groaned my way in and sat down with a loud hiss. Being in pain was one thing, but knowing it wasn't going to end anytime soon made it far worse. And the drug still masked a good deal of what Shoulders had dealt.

The transport display offered the names of the streets. Nothing looked familiar. I expanded the view and located a restaurant name I recognized. Near it was a park with a grove of dense trees, one with an intricate carving at head height that marked it as a jump point. Karin. There was help on Karin. Fa'yet. I punched in his address and winced my way through the endless ride.

There wasn't room to lie down in the transport, though that didn't stop me from trying. By the time the door opened, I was hot and cold, clammy and dry and beyond desperate for even a single drop from the missing golden bottle. Fa'yet's door stood farther from the street than I remembered.

I knocked. He didn't answer. How could he not be home? The one time I really needed him and he wasn't there. My head hurt too bad to try the link or even natural speech.

The few windows at ground level were locked. He had to have good security if this was his main public residence. I didn't need to actually get in, I just needed to set off his alarm. I poked around the first lock. The lights came on inside. If his system was anything like Kazan's, he'd be notified immediately.

A bullet pierced my leg just above my boot, proving to be the final straw in my quest to remain standing. I fell to the ground.

"Don't shoot." I spread out my empty hands, praying he could see that in the dim light.

"Roll over, slowly."

"Fa'yet, it's me." Rolling over proved more excruciating than I'd expected. I lay on my back, trying to catch my breath.

"Why are you tampering with my locks? Someone send you for something? You should have known better." He still held the gun in his hands and it was still aimed at me.

I hadn't taken into account that he'd be just as paranoid as Kazan. "I needed you here, to let me in. My link is down."

Pressure hit my link, but nothing came through. At least other people trying to contact me didn't hurt.

He lowered his gun. "What happened?"

"Can we go inside, please?"

Fa'yet glanced around and put the gun away. "Yes, of course. Come on." He reached down to help me up. "Sorry about your leg."

"Least of my worries right now." My vision faded in and out as I lurched to my feet and limped to the door with his help. "Before I pass out, I need you to promise me you won't let Kazan remove me from your house."

"I hardly think you're going to pass out from a single bullet. Anastassia's standards are a bit higher than that." He held the door open for me.

I grabbed his arm. "Promise me, no matter what she insists, that you will not let her or anyone else take me from your house."

The lights came on as we went inside. Fa'yet grimaced and reached out to steady me with both hands. "Who did this to you?"

"Promise me. No one." I knew I sounded like a raving lunatic, but I was losing touch with my hands and feet and the floor looked very inviting.

"I promise. Now why don't you lie down before you pass out?"

His efforts did little more than slow my fall as blessed darkness carried me down to the floor.

❧

"What do you mean, you won't?" Kazan's angry voice roused me.

"Keep your voice down, the man needs to rest."

I opened my eyes, though only one obeyed. The other side of my face throbbed. I ran my good hand over the swollen mess.

Rich brown walls rose to the high ceiling lit by a single point. I looked away, but the glowing orb of light danced in front of the wooden chest of drawers against the wall and over the thick tan blanket that covered me. Like Kazan's homes, this room was furnished comfortably, but with nothing overly distinctive to offer itself as a jump point.

Kazan and Fa'yet both stared at me. Neither of them looked happy.

"Give us a few minutes, will you?" Kazan asked.

Fa'yet glanced between us. I shook my head. Even that small movement made me dizzy. He went to the door, five steps away, and stood there.

"We don't need a chaperone, Isnar. Get out."

His first name was Isnar? I'd never known. He'd never shared it with me and I'd never asked. If she was breaking out the private name card, we were both in for it.

"I'm sorry, but I made Vayen a promise. I'm not letting you Jump him out of here."

"Of course I'm Jumping him out of here. Look at him. He's a fucking mess."

I'd disappointed her. Whether she wanted to toss me in the tank out of compassion or disgust, I wasn't sure.

"I can't go to the tank," I said.

"You will." Her gaze bored into me. "And you will stop using whatever you've been frying your brain with, deal with your problem, and get back to work. Dammit, Vayen, I really don't need this right now. You know that. You know what's at stake. If this is how you choose to deal with the strain of our job, you're not the man I thought you were."

"Ana!"

His single word had the effect of a slap in the face. Her seething attention snapped to him. I'd never witnessed anyone else outright chastise her before.

Fa'yet returned to my side, interjecting himself between us. "I'll look after him. You well know I'm qualified, though why you both picked me for this cursed duty, only Geva knows."

"Clean him up. I'll be back tomorrow."

He returned her glare. "I don't take orders from you."

"Damn shame. You're the only dependable man I know."

Anastassia may have been speaking to Fa'yet but her words cut deep. I wanted to tell her the truth about the faction and my part in it all, but Chandi knew too much and I didn't know how she got her information. If I exposed the faction, I'd lose whatever saving grace Deep Voice had to offer and have Chandi and Shoulders on my ass more than they already were. Then there was the Narvan. It needed to remain in Anastassia's hands. I had to keep my mouth shut. Which was somewhat a relief, as swollen and bruised as it was.

"You should go." Fa'yet said with an unfamiliar note of open hostility.

She Jumped. I'd chosen my protector wisely, not that I'd had much choice.

"Thanks."

"Shut up. She's right. She doesn't need to deal with your weaknesses right now, not with the High Council splintering."

"I didn't ask to be beaten."

He pointed at me. "That's not entirely the issue here and you know it."

Deep Voice had called Chandi off. I could toss the golden bottle aside without Shoulders coming after me. My aching body cried out in protest, pleading for the comforting bliss of the drug's embrace. I could go back to Sere and ask for more. Chandi would give it to me. She'd be happy to. But this time, I would control the doses. There'd be no required reporting back, not with Deep Voice watching her. I just needed to heal enough to be able to form a Jump.

"Vayen, you're getting clean, with or without Anastassia's help. She needs you, but right now, you're nothing but a liability." He shook his head. "I'll get my doctor in here. I did what I could, but you're pretty messed up. Get some sleep."

He shut the door behind him. A lock clicked into place.

Prisoner or patient? Perhaps both, but it was worth it to keep Kazan's tank out of the High Council's manipulating hands. If they truly wanted her to offer up the Narvan's forces and resources for their expansion efforts, holding the secret to her seeming invincibility over her head would be the perfect ploy. The Narvan would be back in the business of war and everything I'd done in the name of maintaining peace would be for nothing. For the sake of my brother's dream and my own sanity, I couldn't let that happen.

Chapter Fifteen

Ribs bound, hand and leg bandaged and a good deal of me coated with healing salve, I took a good look at Anastassia.

She'd ducked in an hour ago to look me over, hadn't said a word, and left the room. She'd come back in five minutes ago but maintained her silence. The hostility of yesterday had vanished.

I wished Fa'yet were in the room, but after the doctor had left, he'd assured me that he meant to stick to his promise. Anastassia hadn't even attempted to lay a hand on me, so he must have impressed his intent upon her too.

"You look miserable," she said.

"I am."

"Good." She came around to sit on the edge of the bed beside my feet. "Why don't you just go to the tank? I could really use you right now."

"I can't. You have Jey and Merkief. They can help you just as much as I can."

"If they weren't both fried from our Fragian attack, I'd agree with you, but they need some downtime and now they have to cover your shifts. I'm trying to go easy on them, but there is so much I need to do."

She tilted her head to gaze up at the ceiling. One hand fiddled with the latch on her open coat. "This isn't all just some martyrish stunt over a crazy surge of jealousy is it?"

I winced as I sat up and considered throwing something at her, but nothing lent itself to my cause. "This is serious, Anastassia."

She nodded and refocused her gaze on the bed cover.

"I'm sorry I can't be there. You have two perfectly able-bodied men who will do anything for you. Let them."

"I am," she glanced at me and away again. "But they're not you."

Did she actually care or did she just miss using me to her benefit? I'd lost track of which column was in the lead.

"I'm doing all I can right now," I said.

Silence stretched between us. Her fingertips made a faint rasp as she rubbed them over the metal latch. The bed creaked as she shifted to face me more.

"Are you hungry?" she asked.

"Fa'yet's taking good care of me."

At least here, I could count on food I was familiar with, none of Jey's surprise burning spices of Jalvian fare or Kazan's bland Friquen or Verian whims.

She nodded. "He's good at that."

What the hells was up with the awkward small talk? "I noticed. So what did he do for you?"

"He better be right about this," she muttered.

I sat up a little more. The salve took the edge off, but it didn't do near the job Chandi's drug would have, or even a stim for that matter. Fa'yet's doctor had cautioned against giving me anything beyond the salve in the fear that it would impede my effort at overcoming addiction.

"Right about what?"

"My first partner, Zsmed, he thought he'd get even with me for not sharing my position with him." Anastassia took a deep breath and let it out. "I'd been keeping tabs on several young men on Jal and Artor, scouting the upcoming talent, you could say. And yes, you were one of them."

I'd known she'd scoured my records when she'd hired me, but I'd had no idea she'd been stalking me for years.

"One night I made an offhanded comment about some of you over dinner. Little did I know, Zsmed had met with a Fragian delegation in the hopes of working out a trade. He'd run the Narvan for them in return for whatever resources they asked for. But like me, Zsmed didn't want the Narvan tossed into war. He figured if he could get me to hand control over to him quietly, the High Council and everyone else would be happy."

"Except you," I said.

"He wasn't all that concerned with me in that regard." She frowned. "He took it upon himself to procure two of the men I'd mentioned. He handed them to the Fragians. He..."

Anastassia slid off the bed and went to the door. She stood there with her hand hovering over the panel. It was trembling.

Gemmen's warning about the then nameless Zsmed hurting her through someone else came to mind. I shuddered. One of those men could have been me.

"I'm sure you made Zsmed pay for what he did."

Her head bowed and her shoulders drooped. "It wasn't enough. Nothing could ever be enough. They were innocent, and I couldn't save them. I couldn't hand the Narvan to the Fragians. They'd have killed millions and enslaved the rest to strip the resources until they were no longer needed.

I wanted to get up and go to her, but the doctor had demanded that I stay put and Fa'yet had backed him. "Come over here, before I get myself into more trouble by getting up."

She turned back toward me, but she didn't budge. "This job can be hard beyond imagining, harder than you think you can deal with."

Our natural connection opened. At least whatever was wrong with my link didn't hinder that. I was also happy to discover that this connection didn't make my barely tolerable headache any worse either.

She allowed me into her memory like she had when she'd once shared Chesser with me. I became Anastassia.

I sat in a room littered with half-eaten meals in disposable containers. Clothing was strewn about the floor. I looked down at my hands, turning them palm-side up and back again. Bruised skin stretched tight over the bones. Cuts streaked my forearms. Dirty fingertips traced both the fresh cuts and the scabs. My abdomen hurt. I lifted my torn black shirt, stiff with blood and smelling of old sweat. A long shallow cut ran from one side to the other.

I couldn't remember where I'd been or the faces of the men who had attacked me. They'd taken a credit chip and my gun, but those things didn't matter, I had more.

One hand flew to my neck. Despair filled me when my fingers met with bare skin. The comforting cold metal of my neckband was gone. The last reminder of a future that might have been. Chesser's face blurred in my mind.

Common street thugs had stolen the one precious thing I had on me. Tears ran down my face as I curled up on the thin mattress and cried until there was nothing left.

Chesser's gift was lost. Everything was lost.

After a while, I rifled around until I found a ragged armored coat, not the far more expensive self-healing kind she wore now. Judging by the pile of clothes on top of it, it hadn't been worn in quite some time. Reaching inside one of the pockets, my fingers wrapped around a sealed package. I pulled it out and tore open the paper. A stack of blue patches spilled onto the floor. My heart pounded. I picked one up, exposed the adhesive and slapped it on the inside of my forearm. Mindless well-being flooded through me. My heart rate slowed and my eyes drifted shut.

Anastassia's memory let me go, her awareness retreating into her own mind. "Escaping isn't the answer."

I stared at her, unable to form words. She could be broken just like anyone else. We weren't so different after all.

Just when I felt closest to her, I recalled her initial response.

"You weren't going to tell me about this until Fa'yet made you. You were perfectly fine with judging me, with making me think I'd failed your lofty standards when you couldn't even maintain them yourself."

"I didn't want you to think less of me," she said.

"But it's fine if you think less of me?"

She came to my side and perched on the very edge of the bed. "I'm sorry. For what it's worth, I do admire your devotion to overcoming this addiction on your own rather than using the tank as an easy way to clean out your system. Though I wish you would. I hate to see you like this, but Fa'yet assures me there should be no lingering damage."

"Well, I'm sure you did the same thing. Wouldn't want to let you down and all that."

Anastassia's hand sought out my less swollen one, grasping it tightly as she kissed my salve-free cheek. "Actually no, I used the tank."

Warmth rushed through my veins, the heat far more intense and headier than the drug had ever been. My anger melted away.

"I came to Isnar after I'd lost the necklace your brother had given me. He helped me a great deal. Recovery is not an easy road, but we're both here for you."

She grew distant for a second. "Duty calls."

I didn't want her to leave, to take the warmth and calm with her. Releasing her hand wasn't easy, but I made myself let go.

"Stay safe," I said.

"You too."

The room seemed terribly empty once she disappeared.

Three days later, Fa'yet's doctor gave me permission to leave the bed. The bruises, minor cuts, and the majority of the swelling had vanished thanks to the healing salve. My ribs ached and my leg and knuckles throbbed, but using the walking stick he'd left for me allowed me to get out of the bedroom I'd been stuck in for four days.

While I hadn't minded the first day of downtime, the extended inactivity and not being able to use my link drove me crazy. There were only so many hours I could stomach the inane local vid feed. Merkief's daily bitching about my shitty behavior over our natural connection was almost a welcome break.

Fa'yet sat at a small table in the kitchen. He smiled as I came down the hallway toward him. "Feel good to be up and about?"

"I'm not as up and about as I'd like to be, but yes."

"How's your link?" he asked.

Pressure came and went in my head as it had since I'd come to Fa'yet's house. I didn't know who was trying to contact me or why. That only added to my agitation.

"Still not working."

"If you need to go to the University to have the LEs check it out, I can take you."

"We'll see."

If Chandi knew the drug would fry my link, she might be waiting for me on Artor. If I could see her alone, I might get another bottle. Paranoia whispered in my ear. Or she might have an agent there to kill me for failing to deliver the tank's location.

I sat in the only other chair. The two plates filled the small table. The man was outfitted for living alone. I'd seen no hint of anyone else in the house, no stray piece of clothing or bit of décor that screamed anything but Fa'yet. There was no secret companion hidden away behind the locked doors of his common room. At least Kazan had the three of us to keep her company.

"Keep eating like you've been and you'll be back on your feet in no time," he remarked as we both started on the fish he'd grilled for us.

"It's been a long time since I've had food this good." Real food, freshly imported from Artor, the kind I'd grown up with rather than the median Artorian fare Merkief and I picked up with Jey and Kazan in mind. And it wasn't out of a box, wrapper, or off a menu.

How did Kazan go so long between meals of what she truly wanted, the kind she'd been used to on the station? Then again, I couldn't imagine her cooking her own food or allowing the security risk of visiting favorite or familiar food markets every few days. The very thought of Anastassia, bristling with weapons and armor, tending to a prantha steak as it sizzled and dripped juices made me laugh out loud.

"Something funny?"

"Just thinking." About Anastassia. She hadn't been back to visit me. "Have you heard from Kazan?"

"Not today."

"Yesterday?" I asked, suddenly not at all amused.

"Yes, she's been checking up on you. She's fine."

But he hadn't heard from her today. I set my fork down. My appetite had vanished. The faction might have attacked her directly. Kess may have taken another run at her. I wasn't there. I needed to be there, wherever she was.

"You all right?" he asked.

I forced a nod.

"You look a bit pale all of a sudden. Do you need to lie down?"

"I'll be fine." I picked up my fork and poked it aimlessly into the fish.

Inspiration smacked me on the head. Our natural connection still worked. However, it was less subtle than the communication through our links, like the difference between gazing at someone across the room and getting thrown into a conversation. Merkief had only been harassing me on his off shifts. I didn't know what she was doing and I didn't want to distract her with such sudden contact, but I needed to know she was all right.

I reached my mind out to hers, seeking the familiar path strung between us. *"Anastassia?"*

"While I'm happy to hear your voice, I'm kind of in the middle of something. I'll drop by later, all right?"

"Sure." I wanted more than that, to know what she was in the

middle of and to be in the middle of it with her.

She'd closed off our connection, but she was alive and happy to hear from me. She would be here later. The elation I'd felt when she'd visited three days before returned. Who needed Chandi's drug when I had this heady rush at my disposal?

"Vayen?"

I snapped out of my thoughts to see Fa'yet watching me. "What?"

"What's going on in there?"

"Just checking in with Kazan. I'd forgotten about our natural connection."

"You got all," he twirled a hand in the air, "giddy-looking there for a second. Is there something you'd like to tell me?"

"No? Why? About what?"

"You know exactly what. I've seen that look before, though never on you." He thumped my shoulder and got up to clear his plate. "This explains things."

"It does?"

"Being bound to Kazan? Hells yes. That would drive any man to seek an escape. I can't believe she agreed to that."

"She didn't. I didn't...how..."

I forgot how to swallow, how to breathe, how to fight my way through the blackness at the edges of my vision. A bond.

"Of course she doesn't understand it," he said. "She's probably keeping you at an extreme distance, knowing how she avoids attachment."

I didn't even remember initiating the bonding process. I'd tried so hard with Sonia, and nothing had come of it, but now it just happened? And of all the screwed up women in the known universe, with Anastassia?

"What was it," he asked, rubbing his chin, "some twisted dare to prove your loyalty? I mean she had to choose you, an Artorian, for a reason. It would stand to reason that if you were bonded together, you wouldn't turn on her like Kess did. No offence, but I can't see any other reason why she'd agree to this."

I nodded for lack of a better answer. Agree? Hells, she was going to kill me.

Bonded to the same woman my brother had been? If Geva hadn't already turned her back on me, this depraved act would surely do it. I hadn't wanted this. She surely didn't. We'd both said so.

Fa'yet paced back and forth through the black fog floating before me. "No wonder you've been trying to dilute the effects with another drug. Not the best solution, but effective."

The fucking golden bottle. Chandi was to blame, I was sure of it.

"I think I need to lie down now."

"Of course, here." He handed me the walking stick and held my chair steady until I got my balance.

"Promise me you won't say anything to her about this," I said.

"Oh no, that's all on you." He shook his head. "Just make sure you deal with that particular issue elsewhere. I like my house how it is, whole and standing."

⌇

Anastassia and I sat in Fa'yet's common room. He seemed more comfortable having us there than in his personal space. It gave us all a little privacy.

"I only have a few minutes. I just wanted to see how you were doing," she said.

"Better." I tapped her leg with the end of my walking stick.

She grinned. "And in a better mood too, I see."

A sense of rightness came over me. This was where I was supposed to be, beside her. Though perhaps, it was a good thing that she couldn't stay long. The more time we spent together, the faster the bond would solidify and the harder it would be to hide.

"I'll be ready to get back to work soon," I said.

"How's your link?"

I sagged into the chair. "Still not working, but not quite as painful when I try to use it."

"So it is improving then, even if slowly. How about the other problem?"

"Are you asking if I'm still clean?"

She nodded. "I always hated when Isnar would ask me that."

"Still get the shakes here and there, but I'm eating and sleeping better."

"You look much better." She reached down next to her chair and handed me a pack. "I brought some extra clothes for you."

"Thanks."

"Don't thank me, it was Merkief's idea. He grabbed them after he was done searching your room."

My grip on the stick sitting across my lap tightened.

"He was intent on making sure you didn't have any hidden stashes. In any of your rooms, actually," she said.

Violated didn't cover it. Betrayed. "And just what did he find?"

Her sympathetic smile eased my aggravation. "Nothing but your usual chaos. Would it kill you to pick up after yourself now and then?"

"It might."

She laughed but quickly sobered. "I have to warn you, Jey isn't taking this well. He's asked to speak to you alone."

Merkief had warned me about Jey's threats. I wasn't surprised, but neither was I excited about the prospect of facing him.

"What did you tell him?" I asked.

"That he'd have to wait until you're out of Fa'yet's house. I'll not have anything damaged here."

"But you're going to let him have at me."

She gave me a long look. "If you were Jey, what would you be feeling right now?"

I sighed. "Like I'd want to beat some sense into him for putting you at risk."

"You can talk your way out of it. I have faith in you."

My brows rose. "Really. Well, that's comforting. I'll remember your sentiments when hulking Jey is pounding on me. You could just order him to back off."

"I could, but that wouldn't solve anything between you, now would it? He'd see me favoring you despite an obvious failing, and he'd also see you hiding behind me. I have a feeling that wouldn't agree with you."

I pushed my loose hair out of my face. It felt odd to have had it down for so long, but lifting my arms high enough to bind it back was too painful, and I wasn't about to ask Fa'yet to do it for me.

"All right then. Can you Jump me to my office on Rok? I'll attempt to talk to Jey and, if I'm not back in Fa'yet's bed for a week, I can get some work done."

"You're not staying at Cragtek. Not on your own. The temptation would be too great. It's too soon."

"I'm sick of doing nothing here. I can't even use my link for Geva's sake. Gemmen can be my jailer for the day and Fa'yet can take night duty. I'm sure he has work he should be attending to."

Uncertainty played over her face. "I'll be checking in on you too. Not that I don't trust Gemmen, but he's got an entire company to oversee."

"Sounds fair."

"We should get going then. I need to get back to Marin."

The calm her presence brought me evaporated. "No."

"What do you mean no? I thought you wanted to get out of here?"

"You're not going back to Marin." Not now or ever. Geva be damned, Anastassia was mine and I wasn't about to share.

Her eyes narrowed as she stood. "That's not for you to decree one way or the other."

"There's something off about him. I don't trust him."

"Of course there's something off, he kills people for a living."

I shook my head. "So do we."

"We're not like him. He's about the credits and the highest bidder," she said.

"And we're just following orders?"

Her gaze dropped. "We're doing what we have to so the Narvan can remain at peace."

I found myself on my feet and yelling. "So that's the kind of man you choose to be with, the killer for hire?"

Anastassia backed away. "Aren't you supposed to stay off your leg?"

"Answer the damned question."

The door leading to the rest of the house burst open. "I've got this, Ana." Fa'yet rushed over, placing himself firmly between us. "He's had terrible mood shifts the last few days. Don't take it personally."

He grabbed my arm and yanked hard. "You should go lie down."

I knew he was protecting me and the bond that had reared its possessive head, but the bond was stronger than I could have imagined. It pumped endorphins into my system to deal with the threat standing between us and more than enough to deal with the one named Marin.

Anastassia stood there, staring. I'd never seen fear in her eyes, not like this, not aimed at me.

"Vayen." Fa'yet snapped his fingers in my face. "Close your eyes and take a deep breath."

I didn't have time for stupid breathing exercises. Marin needed to be eliminated. Even if it wasn't about the bond, he posed a threat to Anastassia. I formed a Jump to Twelve. The spike in my head had dulled over the past few days and with the energy the bond lent me, I was able to hold my destination long enough to step into the void. I was going to kill that viscu and nothing could stop me.

I stepped out of the blackness into a small room lined with brown walls. Fa'yet shoved me backward onto the bed I'd been in for the past several days.

"What the fuck are you thinking?" he asked.

Stunned, I shook my aching head and slid my way to the edge. "What did you do?"

"Hijacked your Jump, you brainless fool. You come in here, demanding I help you. You eat my food, take up my spare bedroom, rack up my medical tab and expect me to stand by while you storm off to kill some unlucky bastard, unarmored, and apparently doing the deed with nothing but your bare hands?"

I looked down. Damn, he was right: no coat, no weapons.

Fa'yet slumped down beside me. "The bond turns us into Jalvians, I swear, all these urges swinging from one extreme to the other and no filter in between to allow you to stop and think things through."

"You were bonded?"

He nodded. "Once, a long time ago." He sunk into silence.

Since he didn't offer any more information, I considered his past off limits. "If these bonds are so troublesome, why haven't the geneticists bred them out of us by now?"

"Most of us aren't trained and equipped to leap to violence. It's not normally that troublesome," he said.

As my head cleared, it occurred to me that we'd left Kazan standing in the common room. "Did she leave?"

"I thought it best under the circumstances." He studied his hands on his lap. "You're going to need to learn to control those urges if you want to have any chance of making this work with Ana. She doesn't know what sets us off or calms us down, and she certainly had no idea what she was getting into when she agreed to this. You'll need to stick to small doses of her until you find a balance that works for both of you."

"Maybe I should go talk to her."

"Sure. It seems you can Jump if you really want to. Go tell her all about how you're now obsessed with her. She'll love that." He exhaled loudly. "You do realize that if you screw this up and she spurns you, you're stuck with it until one of you dies?"

I cursed Chandi again. "What should I do?"

"Small doses of Ana, small doses of information. If you can work it so she comes to a full understanding of the bond on her own, all the better."

"But she's with Marin. How am I supposed to pretend that doesn't bother me?"

His brow furrowed. "Well, I would have advised to never form a bond with Ana to begin with. She's not one of us and she's going to bother the hells out of you." He rubbed a hand over his face. "But neither of you asked my opinion on the matter before plunging into this and it's too late now."

It was. I held onto the sensations Anastassia unintentionally offered when she was near and prayed they were worth the lifetime of aggravation I was about to embark on.

Great Geva, Gemmen was going to give me so much shit when he learned about this. Everyone was. I fought the urge to put my head in my hands.

"Do your best to not know when she's with him. Stay busy, elsewhere if you can. For all you know, she's working for him, or fighting with him. They've not been getting along for quite some time now, if that makes you feel any better."

Just the thought of them talking to one another was enough to make my teeth grind together. "If they're not getting along, why does she want to be with him?"

"I'm sure she has her reasons. Let me show you something. I'll be right back." He left and returned a few minutes later with an envelope in his hands.

"I've had this for awhile and showing it to you violates our agreement, but now that I don't have to worry about you running off after her, you deserve to see it." He held out the blank envelope.

I took it and lifted the flap. Paper. These were the sorts of messages that were meant to be destroyed upon reading. Yet, the precious secret words were in my hands. Inside was a short note, written in Sonia's hand. Most of it was blacked out beyond retrieval. He'd kept her location and most of the details safe. I made out enough to understand that she was thanking Fa'yet for his help and that she'd joined and recently had a child. She wished me peace and hoped I'd find a life I was content with. Her words formed a soothing balm over the wound that had been our abrupt reunion and parting.

"You wanted her to be happy and she is. What you did for

Sonia couldn't have been easy, but you did it. Is it any less to ask of you to endure a little discomfort on Ana's behalf? After all, it could be you writing to me with the same news some day." He grinned.

"I highly doubt that, but thanks."

He got up and went to the door. "You owe me a few promises. Stay in this room."

"I will." Until I got myself under control, there was no safer place to be.

❧

After another two days under Fa'yet's care, I'd managed to bring my mental defenses back up to a level both of us felt comfortable with. No Verian priests would be able to ransack my brain without warning. Not that I planned on visiting any Verian planet or colony ever again if I could help it.

Jumps became tolerable, though two in close succession sent me back to bed with a pounding headache. The doctor had checked me over, declared I was fit for light duty, took back his walking stick and left. Fa'yet and I agreed that it was time I move on with recovery, both from the drug and the revelation of the bond. I thanked him profusely, left a credit chip on the bed to cover the medical tab and packed my things. My Cragtek office was only a thought away.

Rok greeted me with familiar surroundings and Gemmen's scarred, smiling face. "There you are. I've been trying to reach you. I take it that partner of yours has been keeping you too busy as usual?"

"Something like that."

"Yeah, yeah, keep your secrets to yourself then. Look at these." He held out several sheets of still films. "Scouts captured these a few days ago."

I shuffled through the images, holding them up to the light to discern the black Fragian needle ships from the blackness of space. "New ships?"

"Same basic models on the outside. Don't know about inside. We've been seeing increased numbers on our end of the nebula."

"Are they planning another attack?"

"We haven't been able to intercept much chatter. What we have has been heavily scrambled."

I searched the films for evidence of recognizable modifications. "Have you been able to capture one of these?"

"Not yet."

"Keep trying and let me know if anything changes. If they are planning an attack, they'll hit Merchess and Twelve first. We need to keep them as far from the Narvan as possible."

"Agreed. You might also be interested to know that we've finally been able to isolate the compounds the Fragians use to wipe the minds of their pilots."

"Impressive. How about neutralizing the effects?" If we were able to effectively interrogate Fragian prisoners we'd have a much better understanding of everything we stripped from their ships.

"No, the mind wipe is permanent. However, if we were able to replicate the drug, our own crews would be able to use it should they be captured."

"Our men are doomed once they're captured anyway. Losing a month or a year of their memories for the safety of the rest of us isn't too much to ask. Do it."

"Understood. Will I be able to reach you if the Fragians move?"

Link contact was still uncomfortable, but if everything else was improving, I had confidence that would too. "Yes, and I'll be here on and off for at least a couple days."

"Good." He took the films from me.

I left him to his work and went down the hall to my office. I figured I might as well get the conversation with Jey out of the way while a little evidence of my encounter with Shoulders remained. Maybe it would earn me some sympathy. I sat down at my desk.

Jey arrived within minutes of my invitation, fully armed and armored. "About time you show your face. You look fine to me."

"I'll let Fa'yet's doctor know you approve of his skills."

He put his hands on my desk and leaned forward. "Your weak and reckless behavior put Kazan at risk. You're supposed to be protecting her. You're her partner for Geva's sake! What the fuck were you thinking?"

Jalvian's didn't bond, but they did seem to develop a single-minded devotion to a chosen focus. Having experienced the bond, I had a new appreciation of just how devoted Jey was to Anastassia.

"I *was* protecting her."

"By losing touch with reality? You were supposed to be watching her back!" The vein on his forehead pulsed.

"It's not what you think." There, let him chew on that Kazan-like answer.

"I don't know what to think!"

He slammed his fists on my Moriekian marble-topped desk. That had to hurt.

"And I don't know what more to tell you without getting someone killed, which would probably be me, and as much as you might like that, I'd prefer to remain pain-free for a while."

He spun away, stalking back and forth across my narrow office. "Does Kazan know this?"

"No, and I'd appreciate it if she never found out."

"So now you want me to do you a favor?"

Any more truth and Merkief would have put the pieces together, but thankfully I was dealing with Jey. I hoped handing him a tidbit to hold over me and Kazan-ish vagueness would keep his fists at his sides.

"Consider it doing Kazan a favor," I said.

"You're done then? Clean? Because I swear, if I ever catch a hint that you've gone off the deep end again, I'll make sure you never return to duty."

"Yes."

His pacing stalled. "You owe me and Merkief two week's worth of shifts. The second you're officially back, forget about sleep."

"Got it."

"Good." He Jumped.

I sank into my chair and considered calling him back. Two solid weeks with Anastassia was sure to end up far worse than ten minutes with Jey's fists.

How long could I keep my distance from her? It had been days since I'd seen her, and knowing our last conversation had ended with her upset with me and running off to Marin, nagged at my conscience no matter how many of Fa'yet's prescribed breathing exercises I did.

Small doses. I could do this.

I needed an excuse to see her that would force all thought of Marin from her mind so that I wouldn't have any reason to be the man who had frightened her last time. I rubbed my hands over my face. I really needed to make up for that too.

What did she like? My wrongs with Sonia were made right with rare shells and an expensive dinner. Anastassia avoided personalizing her spaces. She didn't collect anything but weapons, and that hardly seemed an appropriate apologetic gesture. She ate from anywhere she wanted at any time. I sighed.

But she'd lost something precious, and she'd shown me how much that loss had meant to her. She could never replace Chesser's gift, but I could. I knew the jeweler he'd used. The receipt was still in his room.

Since I'd managed to bond myself to the one woman I shouldn't have, the odds of me using my gift chit on anyone else were minuscule. I could redeem my one-time use DNA coded chit and attempt to redeem myself at the same time, both with Chesser and Anastassia.

I Jumped to Artor to make arrangements for a reproduction of the neckband she'd lost. The jeweler had just finished pulling up the detailed file and giving me a lecture on the inappropriateness of copying my brother's design when an insistent contact burst through the buzzing fog in my link. I handed the old man a credit chip loaded with enough motivation to overlook my inappropriate behavior and left.

Safely out of immediate public view, I opened contact. Deep Voice thundered into my head. *"Report to Sere immediately or your life will be forfeited."*

I made sure no one was watching me and Jumped to Sere. A pair of grey-suits were waiting for me. While they weren't openly armed, I had little doubt that they would have guns in their hands in an instant if needed. They led me through the corridors to a different room than I'd previously used with Chandi. One of them opened the door and gestured for me to go inside.

Deep Voice stood waiting. We were alone.

"Ignoring my contact isn't the wisest move. I'm the one that's on your side, if you'll remember."

"I wasn't ignoring anyone. You and your friends screwed with my link with your last overdose. It's still not working quite right."

"That's unfortunate." He widened his stance. "The tracer has gone dead. You've failed your task."

"That depends on which side of the task you're on. I'd say I succeeded."

"I'd advise you to keep your petty attempts at humor to yourself, Mr. Ta'set. Another period of silence like that and a few witty quips will be all your friends have left of you."

For supposedly being on my side, and that was highly debatable, he was still an ass. "As I said, it wasn't intentional."

"What are your feelings toward Kazan?" he asked.

I wasn't sure what to make of his darting conversation, but I sensed wrong answers would end whatever remained of his goodwill, if one could call it that. "Could you be more specific?"

"Did the drug do its job? You're a bright man. I'm sure you've figured out Chandi's goal by now."

My heart sank. "The bond?"

"Of course. Lower your inhibitions enough to allow your Artorian bond to form. I can't tell you how pleased we were when Kazan picked one of you." His gloved hands emerged from his sleeves to clasp together.

My bond wasn't even real, not natural, not by my choice. It formed from wanting her touch, to be near her so she could touch me. That's what I had wanted thanks to Chandi, but now I was stuck with this bond for the rest of my life. Or Anastassia's. Did they expect me to kill her to get rid of it? My hands clenched.

"It's unfortunate that you have so much Jalvian physical resilience remaining in your bloodline. I'd hoped to remain above Chandi's level, but you've left me little choice. Since you have so little care for your own body, we'll have to find another way to motivate you."

I wanted to wrap my hands around his neck, to crush his throat, to rip the damned cloak from his body and see what I was really dealing with. I almost got to my feet twice, but thought better of it. "If you harm her—"

His hood shook. "Any harm that comes to your dear Kazan will be because of you. You will convince her to comply with our wishes, to stop hoarding the resources of the Narvan and advance outward. Conquer the Fragians if you don't want them on your homeworld. Take the Rakon Nebula and beyond. Explore the universe, spread your beloved Artorian advancements and gather new knowledge. Give your Jalvian cousins new worlds to conquer. Grow, expand, go forth and explore. It's what your people were meant to do."

Put that way, his requests didn't seem near as insidious as I'd expected. The High and Mighties wanted control over new territories, my people wanted more worlds to populate. We could help so many others with our advancements, our wealth of knowledge. Our ability to engineer climate controls and high-quality domes could improve the lives of entire planetary populations and allow for new colonization opportunities.

But my people were at peace. They were flourishing. Expansion meant moving to other territories and most people didn't take kindly to our friendly invasion, some not at first and others not at all. Our history was full of failed expeditions that had set off with the best of intentions.

War would only slow that down or halt our own advancement all together as it had before. Everything Kazan and I did was to keep the Narvan at peace, serving its own people. The Narvan didn't want to serve the High Council. And if expanding the Council's hold regardless of the cost was their true goal, neither did I.

"And what if I don't convince her?"

"Do you really want to ask that question, Mr. Ta'set? I wouldn't disappoint us a second time."

Deep Voice vanished. High Council members had the ability to Jump? I'd not considered that before. I began to wonder if sharing the link technology with the Council had been Anastassia's buy-in to Kryon. She'd been there at the beginning of the program and it would explain how she'd risen to system advisor so quickly.

I'd been around Sere enough to have a general idea of its layout. With quarters available to all Kryon members and the staff of grey-suits along with the general facility space, my mental map ran into walls before it located where the High Council members were housed. Being linked would allow them to live elsewhere. For that matter, there could be more than one Kryon base.

Given those few I had met, I guessed the the High and Mighties were more diverse than the Kryon members I'd encountered on Sere. How big was this inner circle Fa'yet and Kazan had talked about, and how much of the known universe did the Council already control? The room blurred as my mind tried to cope with the fact that my entire existence, my focal point in the universe, could be nothing more than an insolent, stubborn blip on their map. I was merely a pawn and Kazan an irritation, stubbornly wedged into her position with her threat of disaster should she plucked from it. How could I hope to stand against them?

Chapter Sixteen

With Cragtek business wrapped up on Rok and a week of hard physical training to get back on track to where I had been before Chandi's drug had its way with me, I felt ready to return to work. The tracer was dead so I didn't have to worry about avoiding the tank and my Jump tolerance was improving. Fa'yet's advice about small doses of Anastassia didn't fit into my schedule of keeping Jey's fists out of my face and avoiding Deep Voice's threats.

Technically I now owed Merkief and Jey three weeks of extra shifts, but when I arrived at Kazan's house on Jal, Jey held up two fingers, glared at me and went to pack. Maybe he couldn't count or maybe he was being considerate. Either way, I didn't argue.

Anastassia looked up from the datapad she was studying while she ate. "Where is he going?"

"Merkief and Jey are leaving for two weeks. Seems I owe them some time off."

"But they can't both leave at once." Her brows drew together. "You're still recovering. You can't be expected to be on all day and night. And certainly not for days on end."

I wasn't sure how I was going to manage that myself. However, my stim tin was full and the assurance that neither of them would be around to notice if I slipped with hiding the bond, made me confident I could manage.

"We'll work something out."

"Like hell you will." She stood and started toward Merkief's room.

I grabbed her arm. "Let them go. They're wiped out."

"And tomorrow, you'll be the same. Don't get me wrong, I'm glad you're back, but I wouldn't have expected more than a couple days out of you when you were in top form. And let's be honest, you're not."

"I know, but still, let them go. I had a deal with Jey."

She pulled her arm away and rubbed it as if she could erase my touch. Her gaze darted up and down, back and forth, never quite meeting my eyes.

Her unease seeped through our natural connection.

The bond had strengthened that too. We'd never be able to totally shut the other out. I could already imagine her ranting about this weakness I'd cursed her with.

"This is how you talked your way out of a trip to the tank?"

"Yes."

"Well, then, I hope you're up to the task." She sat back down and picked up the datapad.

I hoped I was too. Having her that nervous around me bothered me to no end. Crowding her would only make things worse.

I let her go about her business. The rest of the afternoon was spent examining what Merkief's search had done to my room—which seemed to have left it neater than I kept it—and then sitting at the security station, waiting for her to announce that she was hungry.

"You've been out of the food loop lately, what are you hungry for?" she called from her office.

While 'you' was the truthful answer, I was certain it wouldn't assist with my goal of not posing a threat to her. "I kind of had something planned, if you don't mind."

"Oh really?" Her voice was hesitant as she peered out of the office doorway. "And what might that be?"

"Get your coat and I'll show you."

"An armor required dinner?"

"Not exactly, but I'm not as reckless as you are with spontaneous dinner plans."

She finally broke out a smile and her stance relaxed. "Why do I get the idea that this dinner plan of yours isn't all that spontaneous?"

"Neither was yours, I as I recall."

I couldn't help but grin. I'd been too many weeks without her banter and laughter. Check-ins over the link or our natural connection didn't compare to the warmth an calm of being next to her in person.

This damned bond made it hard to keep my emotions in check when she so close. It was going to be a weakness. For both of us.

"I'm glad you don't do that more often," she said.

"Do what?"

"Smile like that."

"What is it with you and policing my face?"

"Sorry, but that one is going to get you into trouble. Or me." She cleared her throat and went to get her armor.

This winning her over thing was going better than I'd expected. I prayed I could keep my hands to myself and my emotions under control for the rest of the evening. And the two weeks afterward.

How the hells was I going to manage this?

"Are you all right?" she asked as she came back into the room.

"Yeah, why?"

"You looked worried. I know you've set yourself up for a daunting task. If you're too tired, I'm sure there's something in the kitchen."

Daunting was right, but I wasn't about to suffer through a meal bar when I'd spent most of the day before planning this. I'd bought supplies and prepared the house. We would be alone. The only thing that could possibly ruin the night was a Fragian attack.

"I'm fine." I held out my hand.

"Where are we going?"

"It's a surprise."

Her smile vanished. "You know I don't like surprises."

"I'm not Jumping you into an ambush, Anastassia. It's just dinner."

She slowly slipped her hand into mine. "Fine, but if I end up dead over this, I'm haunting you for all eternity."

The thought of having her gone forever threw me into a panic. Fa'yet's calming voice told me to close my eyes and breathe deep. I was not going to screw this up, dammit.

"Are you sure you're up to this?"

I nodded and formed the Jump to Frique for both of us. I would have preferred the Verian station, except it contained Verians and that spineless Strauss. So I'd opted for scorching Frique. I'd planned ahead for that too, knowing it would be midday there when we arrived.

Anastassia stepped out of the void and headed straight for the house control panel. "Why is it so cold in here?"

"Because it's so hot out there. Don't touch that." I pulled her away from the panel and brought her to the table that sat against the half wall of the open kitchen.

"Sit."

She arched an eyebrow. "Can I breathe, or do I need to wait until you tell me to?"

"Sorry, it's just—"

"You're nervous. I can feel it." She studied me. "Why can I feel it? I thought you said your link was secure now?"

"It is." I scrambled to muffle our natural connection as much as I could.

"Here," I pulled out a chilled bottle of her favorite Friquen red and poured her a glass. I needed her a little less perceptive or I was going to inadvertently reveal too much.

"You were prepared." She took an appreciative sip. "Why here? I thought you didn't like Frique. Loathed comes to mind, actually."

"You're right, but you do."

"Ah." She swirled the wine in her glass as she watched me reach into the cold storage to pull the rest of the food that I'd brought earlier.

I would have liked to recreate some of the meals Fa'yet had made for me, but my cooking skills were more rudimentary. I stuck with one of my favorites.

When I pulled raw peppers from the bag and began to slice them, Anastassia's mouth dropped open. "You're making dinner? You cook? Since when?"

"Since my mother dragged me away from playing 'Crush the Jalvians' out in the yard and into the kitchen. She told me that I'd need to feed myself someday, and I'd want to know how. As it turned out, she was right."

"That was thoughtful of her."

It was more like my mother wanted to make sure I could feed myself when everyone else was called to duty, but I let Anastassia think so. Thoughts of my mother did not help keep me at ease. Both of her sons had bonded to the same non-Artorian woman. I doubted that she'd be at all pleased about that. I tried to focus on the knife in my hand instead.

"It's nothing fancy. Fa'yet's a much better cook."

"He is? Why don't I know this? I've known him a lot longer and he's never cooked for me."

"Maybe I'm just lucky." The room filled with the tangy aroma of the peppers as they cooked.

"I think he likes you more," she said.

"Did the two of you work together at some point?" I asked, trying to make it sound more like a snarky comment than the serious question that it was.

She smirked. "I wanted to when I first came into Kryon, but he's a solo kind of guy."

"So you were never together?" Why was I jealous of Fa'yet? I concentrated on slicing a couple bread pockets and filling them with thick cream.

"No, just friends, as if it matters to you."

It did and I was relieved to hear it. I stuffed the bread with thin slices of cured prantha meat, spiced cheese and the still steaming peppers.

"That smells wonderful." She took the plate I handed her and eyed her near empty glass.

With her drink refilled and one of my own, I sat down next to her, picked up my bread pocket. It tasted just as a good as I remembered. Better than my own enjoyment was feeling hers seeping through our connection.

"This tastes even better than it smells," she said.

Anastassia devoured her dinner as we talked about inane things.

When we'd finished, I put the dishes on the counter for the bots to attend to and led Anastassia into the window-lined, wooden common room that she loved so much. She sipped on her third glass of wine and sat back on the couch with a relaxed smile.

"This is nice. We've been so busy working while you were gone, there hasn't been much downtime. I deserve a night off, right?"

"Yes, you do." I sat on the other end of the couch, making sure to keep plenty of space between us, though I wanted none.

"Do you want to know why I like it here even though it's hot and backward compared to the rest of the Narvan?"

"Beyond enjoying hot and backward?"

She snickered and shook her head. "Before Jal attacked Veria Prime, my family often came here. My father was exploring the connections between the farming processes on Prime and Frique, how they both chose primitive methods in the midst of so much available agri-tech."

"Farming in the middle of a forest?"

"No, observing from afar. The Friquen government wouldn't give him permission. They were afraid we were stealing their secrets to give to the Verians."

"You stayed in this house?"

"We had a portable lab and my father's research ship."

"If you were only observing, what did you need a lab for?"

"Soil analysis. We needed to know what made Frique so fertile so we could help the Verians."

"You *were* stealing their secrets."

She grinned. "Maybe a little."

This was going so well, the conversation, the smiling, her being at ease with me. My heart raced. I could make this work.

"So you had the house built?" I asked.

"Yes, to hide what lies under it from any scans."

I didn't need our natural connection to sense her hesitation.

"What's under it?"

"My father's ship." She chewed on her lower lip and gazed out the window at the trees. "Where the tank is."

As touched as I was that she dared share her secret with me, I wanted to scream at her. It was one thing to keep a jump point to the tank hidden from Deep Voice, but now I had the exact location. I had that general hint he'd asked for. I'd have to make sure to give Deep Voice no reason to dig into my head.

"I always thought you had it parked on an asteroid somewhere," I said.

"Too risky." She shook her head. "We'd just returned from a stay on Frique when he and my brother were killed. The ship contained the memories of our last days together, and I wanted to preserve it in a place where no one could take it from me, where we had been trying to do something good. It's peaceful here, away from all the noise of Artor and Jal and the High Council's demands."

"I suppose it is."

Not that I appreciated the climate, but having seen what sort of pressure the High Council could apply, I did understand the value in having a place to step away from it all. She'd tried to show me that once, but I'd been too new to her world to see it.

"You finally get it, don't you?" She smiled sadly. "I'm not sure if I should be sorry or glad."

"You can be glad because you're not alone anymore."

"I suppose I'm not, am I? I don't know if that's good or bad either."

"It's good. Wait here a minute."

Before the wine made her more melancholy, I needed to cheer her up or I was going to give into my urge to hold her tight and make her happy in other ways.

I went to the bedroom I used during our infrequent stays on Frique. There wasn't much there so I'd hid the jeweler's box under the mattress in case Merkief got it in his head to do another search of my things.

With the thin, square box in my hands, I returned to the couch. "I got something for you."

The words felt wrong. It wasn't what the rite stated I should say, but this wasn't a gifting ceremony. It was a re-gifting. And there was no written ceremony for that. Probably because it was fucking forbidden. I tried to shove my anxiety back down my throat and keep my voice casual so as not to alarm her.

Anastassia set her wine glass aside and sat up. "For me? We don't do that. I mean, we haven't done that. It's—"

"New?" That sounded better than what was in her eyes: fear of yet another level of intimacy breached. I wasn't giving her an official declaration of my intent to join with her, I was merely replacing something she'd lost. That's all. There was nothing official about it.

"Despite everything that I did...and with what you shared with me... Well, I wanted to say thank you."

I placed the box in her hand and sat before my legs gave out. Why was I so damned nervous? She wasn't going to say the things I wanted to hear. I'd not said the correct words to begin with. Not one of them, actually. Even if she'd remembered the details of the ritual Chesser had performed in Artorian, which she hadn't even known much of at the time, she wouldn't have accepted my proposal. No way in all nine hells. She hadn't technically accepted his proposal either.

This wasn't real. I repeated those words to myself a hundred times in the span it took her to remove the lid from the box and peel back the paper to reveal the silver neckband. Her eyes went wide and instantly filled with tears.

"You found it?" Her voice shook as much as her hands.

"No, but I had an exact reproduction made by the same jeweler. He had all the specifications on file."

The Friquen sunlight caught on the etching. Tears spilled down her cheeks. "It's perfect."

Warmth filled me, and I couldn't help but grin despite her tears and the fact that neither of us had said the right things.

"Put it on."

Her shaking fingers fumbled with the clasp.

"Here." I took the band from her hands and placed it around her neck. The clasp snapped shut with a quiet snick. I hoped to never hear that sound again. She should wear it always.

Anastassia ran her hands over the band. I came around in front of her and was caught up in the most peaceful smile on her face. This was the woman I'd seen on the Verian station, the one I'd caught only glimpses of when her work mask faltered. This was the face I wanted to see every day, the true one, the one that could be touched and loved, especially if it was only in the privacy of our off hours.

She wrapped her arms around me. "Thank you," she breathed in my ear.

I held her there, not wanting to lose the tranquility that surrounded me when she was so close. Maybe that made me selfish, knowing she didn't want this. I might not have wanted it either, but the peace her presence brought was a giant consolation that I found myself already quite attached to.

Her mind opened to mine, stronger than before, thanks to the bond. Her presence fluttered about, touching here, caressing there. I basked in her gratitude.

The gifting period of the courtship ritual finally made sense to me. I'd always thought other men had lost their minds when they spent countless credits to fulfill their prospective mate's wishes. Now I couldn't stop wondering what else I could get for her so we could return to this closeness again very soon.

"Maybe we should sit down," she said.

Reluctantly, I let her go and returned to my spot on the other end of the couch. She took off her coat and laid it beside me. Her presence in my head intensified.

Lost in a myriad of pleasure-filled sensations, I almost forgot Fa'yet's warnings. If she got too close, she'd see the bond for herself. She couldn't get much closer than she was at that moment. I reluctantly muffled our connection again.

"Stassia, I think we should—"

"We've both been dancing around this for months, what's the matter?"

"Nothing, it's just..." My mind was too jumbled from her attention to work through any elaborate reasoning to keep her at a distance. "Every time one of us attempts to start this, you end up pissed at me and that's going to make the next two weeks miserable for both of us."

"I've been pissed at me, not you. Now shut up before you ruin a wonderful evening."

She straddled me on the couch, pressing her body against mine. Her racing heart reverberated between us. Fingers slipped into my hair seconds before her lips crushed mine.

While I'd certainly kissed women before, Anastassia had never been one of them. I reveled in the intense sensations passing between us and felt her doing the same.

The physical aspects became a distraction to the familiar ones in my head. Wonderful, exciting and intoxicating as they were, I didn't know what to do with everything all at once. There was a reason for the gifting period of the bonding ritual. It would allow both of us time to acclimate ourselves to the new emotions and sensations while working up to physical sex.

My hold on my mental efforts went off kilter. It was as if this was my first time all over again. Oh Geva this was embarrassing. This was the sort of relationship she wanted, the one I'd seen in her mind. I certainly wasn't opposed to it, but could I do all of this at once?

Before I embarrassed myself too badly, I decided to focus on this new experience that she offered. Surely she'd understand if I was lacking elsewhere just this one time. And if I could keep her main focus out of my head, the bond might remain hidden.

My hands drifted down to her narrow waist. I pulled her closer. Her thighs slid alongside mine. One hand served to hold her while the other wandered upward, snaking over her silken shirt and the hard muscle it concealed beneath. I met with several holster straps along the way to the bare flesh at her neck. My fingers brushed over the hard metal to the smooth skin of her throat. Her pulse pounded beneath my touch.

The connection between us flared as she sought out my wavering mental efforts. I'd just made my way to her breast when her hand clamped down on mine. Our connection faltered.

"You've never done this before," she whispered.

I froze. "Did I do something wrong?"

I'd seen what she wanted me to do, and I swore I was following along pretty damn well. She closed off her mind enough that I couldn't tell if she was disappointed or angry.

Anastassia sat back a little. "No, you didn't do anything wrong. I'd just assumed, you know, that you'd—"

"Been with other non-Artorian women?"

She nodded.

"I'm not Jey."

"But you're both from the same promiscuous root of a race for goodness sake. I've seen how women look at you. Don't tell me you've never pursued a single one that wasn't Artorian."

"I haven't really had time to consider it."

Living with Anastassia didn't exactly yield a lot of free time to connect with people outside of our line of work. I didn't trust those within it enough to let them in my head for fun.

"No. This isn't good, Vayen. Don't you see?" She raked her hands through her braid, making a mess of it all. "You can't fixate on me. That leads to that crazy bonding trait your people cursed yourselves with, and that would be a disaster."

"I don't know as I'd go so far as to call it a disaster."

"I would." Anastassia slid off me and moved her coat over to sit. She pinched the bridge of her nose and sighed. "I know this is probably a horrible thing to say, and I'm sorry." She turned to me. "This, just now, reminded me of the first time I was with Chesser, like this."

Guilt pulled me down and kicked me a few times for good measure. As much as I hated to admit it, she was right. This was a disaster. I started to get up, but she grabbed my hand and held on tight.

"I don't want things to go as badly for us as they did for Chesser and me. I'd liked what we had, what you and I have, but when he started talking bonding and joining..."

She let go of me and waved her hand in the air. "It all went to hell."

"What do you mean?" Other than the couple arguments I'd witnessed, Chesser had given me no indication that things weren't right between the two of them.

She rolled her eyes. "We enjoyed working together. We were having fun when free time allowed for it. Next thing I know, he announces he bonded to me and presents me with this necklace.

"Then he started acting like he owned me and talking about starting a family and when I would be relieved from duty so I could start a household. Good God, Vayen, I didn't want any of that."

"He actually expected you to step down once you were joined?"

She nodded. "No matter what I said, he was hell-bent on starting a family, and he wasn't about to have me in harm's way at any stage of the process."

Having experienced the bond myself, I understood what had driven him to his stupidity, but still, he should have known her better.

"He only wanted to protect you," I said.

"Look at me, Vayen, do I really need protecting?"

"I wouldn't be here if you didn't."

She let out an exasperated sigh. "True, but back then? I'm not some delicate treasure to be hidden away. I can take care of myself. After all Chesser and I faced together, he should have known that."

"Yes, he should have."

She smiled.

"The bond turned him into an idiot and all we did was argue. It was miserable."

Would we be any different? I prayed for a little mercy from Geva. I hadn't asked for this, but dammit, I was going to attempt to make the best of the mess Chandi had lulled me into.

"You were miserable, but you planned to join with him anyway?" I asked.

Anastassia cringed. "The way he explained it, once he had bonded himself to me, there wasn't a damned thing I could do about it. I was stuck with him for the rest of my life and he'd be miserable without me."

Stuck. That wasn't a word I wanted her to live with either. Maybe I could bury the damned bond and pretend it didn't exist. But the more I tried to convince myself that denial was possible, the more I recalled that warm peaceful rush she offered. In the wake of Chandi's drug, I sorely needed that. We were both stuck.

"It wasn't like it was all bad," she said quickly. "I did love him. But we had such different ideas about our future together that I couldn't see either of us ending up happy."

Having seen the two of them fight, and understanding the

bond better now, I couldn't argue with that.

"I wanted to make the best of it, but everything was so complicated. We never got a chance to figure it out," she said.

"I don't know as you would have. Either of you, I mean."

While the calm she'd brought my brother had made a dramatic difference on him, it hadn't been one I'd appreciated at the time. She didn't understand our culture enough, nor did she want to slip into the role that would have made the two of them work.

Anastassia had her own life then and she sure as all hells did now. And Chesser had been worried about her safety then? I rubbed my forehead and tried to contain the heavy sigh that threatened to burst forth.

She eyed her empty glass on the table beside her. "Your brother's death complicated my life in ways I still haven't been able to deal with."

Anastassia opened her mouth and then closed it. With a slight shake of her head, she picked up her coat and stood.

"I don't want to get caught up in arguments over what this is or isn't, and I don't want to bond, or join, or anything else your people might have hidden away in your genetic or social codes, but tonight, the earlier part, was good. If you can promise that there are no strings attached, I wouldn't be opposed to doing it again. Assuming you take some time to go enjoy other women too and we're away from the prying eyes of your ever observant co-workers."

"Got it."

The night wasn't a total loss after all. A few more dates like this and I might convince her that I was more open-minded than my brother when it came to expectations of our future together. I just had to figure out a way to make the High and Mighties happy so there would be a future.

Chapter Seventeen

Anastassia sat in her tiny office on the ship. As I entered I noticed, with extreme dismay, that the neckband was gone.

"I'll be fine here," she said. "I swear I won't leave until you get back. Just promise me you'll go find someone."

"This is weird. You realize that, don't you?"

"If you want to repeat last week's date, it's necessary. I don't care if she's Artorian or not, just find a woman and have a good time with her."

It was far too late for that. I had no interest in other women, even if Geva herself had handed me the opportunity. That was part of the bond's purpose and its urges were deeply ingrained.

My efforts at keeping distance between us over the past week were mostly fruitless. With Jey and Merkief gone, we shared every meal together. We worked side by side except when I could convince her to work remotely from her house office under the guise of allowing me to get some Cragtek work done from there as well. We even slept at the same time to maximize working hours. Thank Geva, she'd had the idea of coming to the ship to sleep securely and separately so we didn't have to share a bed in one of the houses.

Arguing about her line of logic would only make her suspicious so I did my best Jey impression and tried to look excited at the prospect of having sex with someone else.

"I'll be back in a few hours then," I said.

"Take your time."

I'd expected her to smile and wave me off, but for getting her way, she looked awfully perturbed.

"I'm only doing this because you're asking me too."

"Go on then." Her tight-lipped attention returned to one of the datapads on her desk.

My office on Rok seemed like the perfect place to avoid having sex. I Jumped there and settled in. Rather than put Gemmen in the position of keeping secrets, I contacted him through my link.

"Any further progress on the Fragian front?"

"Nothing worth reporting as of yet," he said.

"Keep me posted."

"Will do."

Why couldn't the Fragians pick now to make a move? Defending my people wasn't a problem, but driving them into a war to placate Deep Voice clawed at my gut, especially after the losses we'd suffered the last time.

The Fragians would strike back soon. I was sure of it. When they did, we'd wipe them out once and for all.

Anastassia's voice slipped into my head. *"Vayen?"*

"No, I haven't found anyone yet. It's only been fifteen minutes."

Her voice was as tight as her face had been. *"It's not that."*

"What's going on? I'll be right there."

I stood and did a quick once over of the weapons I had on me.

"No. Your office at Cragtek, is that secure?" she asked.

"Not as much as the ship, but yes."

"Go there and stay, no matter what."

"Stassia, what in the nine hells is going on?"

"I'm not sure, but I don't like it. I have a contract I have to take care of. Alone."

Alone? Not if she was as concerned as she sounded. I Jumped back to the ship.

Her head snapped up from where she'd been holding it. The hair around her temples appeared disordered.

"What are you doing here? Are you deaf?" she asked.

"You're not going anywhere alone."

"Well, you're not coming with me. That was specified."

"I don't like this at all," I said.

If the High Council wanted us apart, they had a reason. Chandi sending me into drugged oblivion while ordering Kazan off to antagonize the Fragians came to mind. Had Deep Voice grown impatient already?

"I don't either." Her eyes narrowed. "Why don't you smell like a bar?"

"Why should I?"

"Picking up women? Seems a logical place to start."

"There are other alternatives. Can we focus here?"

She rubbed her face. "I need to go."

"If you won't take me, then take Jey."

"Thanks to you, he's on leave."

Jey was dependable to a fault when it came to Kazan. Having him close to her without me around didn't set well, but I knew he would protect her. He'd ended up in the tank for her many times before.

"If you tell him you need him, he'll be here."

"Fine. Keep Merkief with you then."

"Why? If you're going to call them both back, you keep them."

"Just do it." She stood and closed up her coat. "Whatever you hear, promise me you'll stay put. Got it?"

Open-minded about her facing danger was one thing, but allowing her to walk into what screamed High Council trap was quite another. I grabbed her arm.

"You're not going."

She shook me off. "I don't have a choice."

So that's how they were playing this. I swallowed hard.

"You tell Jey that if anything happens to you, I'm holding him responsible."

Anastassia kissed my cheek. "Stay safe."

I basked in a few seconds of peace before she stepped away.

"You too," I managed to say when what I wanted to do was grab her and demand that she not leave.

She bowed her head and Jumped.

Whatever she was doing, the Narvan needed her. The alternative was death and destruction.

The bond flooded me with anxiety, urging me to go after her. I told it to shut up and Jumped back to my office. Anastassia didn't want any part of the damned bond and I wasn't thrilled to be a slave to it either. These things were designed for mundane individuals who worked in offices, factories, and labs on Artor. Their mates probably did the same thing. Anyone's biggest concern was staying focused on each other for the benefit of their offspring. Maybe the soldiers who'd fought in the Jalvian war knew my aggravation, but like my parents, many of them went off to serve together.

A knock sounded on my door. Merkief's presence touched my link. I let him in.

"Nice." Merkief glanced around as he approached my desk. "So this is where you hide out."

"I'm not hiding out."

He shrugged. "Didn't mean anything by it."

After all that had happened lately, I wasn't sure where exactly we stood. I decided to stick to safe topics for now.

"What did Kazan tell you?" I asked.

He held up three fingers and ticked them off as he went.

"Not to give you any shit, to watch your back, and to physically hold you down if it looked like you might leave this room by any means."

"Any hint as to what she's doing?"

"She and Jey left the ship with enough equipment to blow Thirteen off the charts."

The bond screamed for me to go to her. I took a deep breath.

Kazan could take care of herself and if there was any doubt about that fact, she had Jey for backup. Jey. It should have been me. He could stand beside her just as well as I could. Probably better, considering I wasn't in top form. But he wasn't bonded to her, I was. It was my job. My duty.

Merkief cocked his head and looked me over. "You all right?"

"I'm fine," I snapped. "Sit down before you wear a hole in my rug."

"I'm just standing here. I don't think—"

"I said, sit."

"From as worked up as you are, you must know what's going on. Is it serious?"

Damn right it was serious. How could it not be? My mind raced, searching for any leverage I might have to use with Deep Voice. But unless I wanted to hand him the regen tank or launch the Narvan into another war against whichever newly encountered race took issue with our overtures of assistance and trade, I had nothing.

"I'm not worked up," I said as calmly as I could manage. "And no, I don't know what's going on."

He snorted. "For the record, this is where I'd be giving you shit."

"Duly noted." I pointed him to the couch. "You should be with her, not me."

"Just following orders."

Anastassia kept a tight hold on our linked connection, but her tension seeped through our natural one thanks to the fledgling bond. Knowing she was distracted, I allowed it to open a little more. I waited for any hint of what she was doing or how it was going.

Merkief sat in silence, looking around the room. "So, you look more rested than I expected after being on duty for a week."

"Can we do the small talk another time?" He was distracting me from the lack of anything helpful over my connection with Anastassia.

"Look, I'm sorry about going through your rooms. I was trying to help."

"I know. It's fine." I did my best to put on a more friendly facade.

"Right. Sorry."

In light of all the uncertainty going around, I let Gemmen know I was on site and to increase security. With all of Cragtek's armed men and ships on alert around me, I could concentrate on Anastassia.

Merkief's eyes went wide and his hands tensed on his lap.

"What?"

"Someone fired shots into the building where Kazan and Jey were setting charges. Jey assures me she wasn't hurt badly."

Badly? Dammit. I clutched the arms of my chair.

A man materialized just inside my door. He raised his gun.

I dove for the floor behind the desk. A bullet shot through my chair and sank into the wall. Merkief fired and the man dropped. Merkief fired several more times before I could stop him.

Running over to the body, I was dismayed to find him very dead. Was Deep Voice growing impatient or had Chandi's faction ramped up their efforts despite being called off?

"If there's a next time, try to give me a chance to beat some information out of them first," I said.

"Sorry." Merkief put his gun away. "I thought this room was secure?"

Gemmen raced in. "I heard shots." He took in the man bleeding all over my expensive rug. "I didn't leak anything, I swear."

"I know you didn't."

I brushed a few stray hairs back behind my ears. Shoulders had probed me when they'd implanted the tracer. While he hadn't found the ship in my head, he'd found this room and he'd dropped me here. How many of my jump points had been compromised?

I slammed my fist down on the desktop. It didn't matter if I had a thousand men on guard outside my door when assassins could Jump directly in.

Gemmen grimaced. "I'll get the body. Need anything else?"

"Send a couple men in."

"Is that wise?" Gemmen asked.

"My security measures have already gone to shit, a few more eyes in here aren't going to make things any worse."

Gemmen nodded and left. Moments later, two armed employees walked in. I repeated my order to keep any attackers alive for questioning and then pointed Merkief toward the door.

"We're waiting outside."

"You sure?"

"If Kazan needs either of us, we need to be ready and able. They can handle it now that we know to be ready."

We stood in the hall, watching men and women go about their business as if Shoulder's buddies weren't Jumping into my private refuge, riddling my personal belongings with bullets and trying to kill me.

Merkief leaned against the wall. "I take it you know who is behind this?"

"Generally, yes."

"You're not going to tell me, are you?"

"No."

"You sound more like Kazan every damn day." He pulled out a gun, checked it, and kept it in his hand.

An explosion rocked the wall behind me. Silence followed. I gave it two full minutes before sending Merkief in.

He came right back out and shook his head. "Dead. All of them. They've moved up to suicide attacks with grenades."

This had to be Chandi's people. Deep Voice had indicated that he wanted me alive. Or maybe he'd written me off.

I hazarded a glance inside. The weaving on the wall behind my desk hung in tatters. The blackened remains of my chair sat behind the toppled marble desktop and shattered wooden remains of the desk. Only my couch remained mostly untouched by the attack.

What remained of three bodies lay near the door. Trying to kill me was one thing, but spreading out the casualties was not acceptable, especially not when they weren't even given a chance.

I spun around to find myself face to face with Gemmen. "Take care of your men. The mess in there has obliterated any details they've been using as a jump point. They won't bother us here anymore."

Merkief came up beside Gemmen. "I have to go. Jey's hit badly."

"Tank-bad?"

"He-doesn't-think-he-can-Jump-bad. Kazan is under fire. Six men left. I have to go."

"What about Jey?"

"You'll have to Jump him."

I shook my head. "She made it very clear I couldn't be there. No matter what."

But Merkief couldn't Jump Jey. That would leave Kazan unaided and under fire. Dammit. She couldn't Jump Jey while under attack.

"He has to do it himself. I don't want Anastassia left alone," I said.

Merkief paused in his protest to raise an eyebrow.

Shit. We never called her anything but Kazan. If either of them used another name, I'd never heard it.

He said, "What if he can't do it?"

Then Jey dies. Merkief would never forgive me, and Anastassia would be irate if I defied her orders to save him and equally irate to lose him. I had to admit, I didn't want him dead either.

"He has to."

Merkief looked ready to punch something.

"Go." I didn't make a habit of ordering Merkief around, and my assertiveness didn't ease his forming snarl. He Jumped without another word.

I stood aside as Gemmen directed his men to carry out my orders.

Merkief's frantic voice cut into my head. *"Jey made it to the ship, but I lost contact. Did you get anything from him?"*

Going to the ship wouldn't compromise her contract. *"I'll go check on him."*

Jey was sprawled face down on the floor when I arrived in the tank room. Removing his coat revealed a blood-soaked shirt. By some miracle, his mangled chest still rose and fell.

Once I had him stripped down, I lifted him onto the platform and started the cycle. The initial scan estimated nine hours of tank time. I hoped none of us would need it before then.

Fa'yet's breathing exercises did little to keep my mind off of what Anastassia and Merkief were doing. Brushing over their natural connections was enough to tell me it wasn't anything I'd approve of. I decided that if I wasn't allowed to be beside her, maybe there was something a little higher up I could do to help.

I tried my connection with Chandi but got nothing. She'd cut me off. It took an hour before I worked up the nerve to try Deep Voice himself. He didn't acknowledge me. At least he hadn't also shut me out or I'd have been hesitant to leave the ship ever again. The image of the shattered bodies in my office kept vibrantly intruding on my thoughts.

Chandi had killed two of my people who were just doing their job. She'd destroyed the one room I had made my own in the entire damned universe. She'd tricked me into bonding with Anastassia and now Chandi was trying her damndest to take me out.

I knew how the Council's threats worked. No doubt they'd told Anastassia that her position was at stake if she didn't complete the contract without me, making her earn it all over again on her own. I sat there for hours, riding along on the faint hint of a natural connection Merkief allowed me as long as I didn't distract him. The entire time my stomach was in knots and the urge to Jump to Sere and hunt Chandi down regardless of the consequences grew hard to resist.

Anastassia's distracted voice flitted into my head. *"There are riots on Merchess."*

Finally, something constructive I could do. *"I'm on it."*

"Be careful."

"I will."

I cut contact with Anastassia and Jumped to one of the reported trouble spots on Merchess.

A man slammed into me and shouted as he ran past, "Fire! The Keefe slaves are revolting!"

That sounded like a good place to start. I headed for the billowing smoke. The Keefe family's territory writhed with squads of armed family guards and hordes of less equipped slaves.

I located the familiar face of one of the Keefe cousins. "Get these people under control."

The uniformed man looked me over for a second and then recognition lit in his eyes. He snapped to attention.

"We're trying, sir."

"Tell Vikorus, if he wishes to maintain his place as the Keefe head, he'll keep his slaves safe and maintain some order here."

"Yes, sir."

"I'll be checking up on you." I gave him a good hard look before departing.

A glimpse at the local network revealed several other hot spots. I Jumped to the Ka'opul city. Looters dashed past me, arms laden with stolen goods. Three Ka'opul guards scrambled after them. I grabbed one by the arm.

"Where is everyone?" The Ka'opul's held the largest city on Merchess, and consequently, a large, well-trained enforcement staff.

"Four blocks over. Buildings are exploding!"

Angry shouting reached my ears. A lone man stood before a storefront raging at the crowd surrounding him. I shoved the guard in his direction. "We better help before they tear the place apart."

We pushed our way through the mob. I fired a shot in the air. All attention focused on me. "Go home. Anyone caught on this street in two minutes will be shot."

Uncertainty murmured through the crowd. I fired into the air again.

A high powered bullet thwacked into my armor, knocking the air from my lungs for a second. I stumbled into the guard beside me. Another shot sounded. Blood blossomed on the guard's forehead. He toppled over. The crowd scattered. My would-be assassin stood on the rooftop across the street. I recognized her. Kryon.

Chandi wasn't using her own agents anymore. This effort was officially from the High Council, and I'd been on the other side of it. Had Anastassia failed her contract? Were we all marked?

I drew my pulse pistol and sent a heavy wave her way. The windows on the store beneath her shattered, spewing plaz shards into the air. I fired again before she could recover. The trembling front wall sent out a warning rumble. I ran toward the building and fired the last remaining full charge. The wall tipped inward and collapsed upon itself, sucking the roof down. Her body fell with it.

After taking a moment to make sure she was dead, I Jumped to a known point nearest the next hotspot. My chest throbbed. I reached up to discover a hole, almost two fingers wide, in the front of my coat. Whatever she fired hadn't made it through, but I had a feeling she'd managed to pass the mark along to the next bastard willing to try.

Placing myself in the middle of a mass of Ka'opul guards, I set about organizing them to deal with the chaos. Their presence didn't stop a bullet from digging a trench along my right temple. I ducked down, working my way out of the crowd who were busy spinning around in search of the gunman. A spray of bullets sounded behind me.

Bolting across the street, I broke through the nearest door and slammed it shut. Immediately, I noticed an odd smell and turned back to the door. A blast of heated air hit me from behind. Shit.

I dove out the window. Plaz shards cut my face and hands as my body careened onto the street. A snap below my shoulder sent knives of pain through my arm.

An orange cloud filled the air. Intense heat washed over me. Brick fragments rained down. I coughed to clear the thick smoke from my lungs.

Three guards ran towards me. I couldn't make out what they were saying over the ringing in my ears, but two of them yanked me to my feet. The third watched the surrounding buildings, a gun ready.

I caught sight of the new attacker. A man stood across the street with a gun in his hands. I slipped out from the grip of the men beside me.

"Get away!" I yelled.

In an effort to mask the hole in my armor, I held my broken arm against my chest.

Two shots rang out. A bullet hit my sleeve and beside me, one of the helpful guards toppled to the ground. The other two ran.

The Kryon agent sped off. Was the High Council really willing to set off her safety net or were they just deadset on taking me out while Anastassia was occupied?

I had every intention of following the fast-disappearing man, but a round of rib-wracking coughs ended my chase before it began. After popping a stim, I made my way off the street to find a safer place to stand for the defenseless seconds it took to perform a Jump. I wasn't in any shape to face another Kryon. I arrived on the ship and monitored the remaining hotspots through my link, passing orders to linked contacts on-site.

Jey's progress in the tank didn't promise an end to my pain anytime soon. I swallowed a second stim. Once I felt up to it, I bandaged my shoulder and head, and then picked the plaz from my face, neck, and hands. Somewhat more comfortable and alert, I sat down to check for updates on Merchess.

The slave riots in the Keefe city were quelled. The Ka'opuls seemed to have things in hand, but the Nikera family, who ran the least prosperous city, had left a message requesting Kazan's direct attention with a hostage issue. I gathered what energy I had left and Jumped.

I made my way to my linked, yet deficient guard contact.

"Why hasn't this situation been resolved?" I asked.

His gazed darted over me, surely taking in the bandages, cuts and bruises. "They've taken five of the Nikera family, including the family head, Asmed."

"Damn." Getting past the family's personal security hinted the involvement of yet another Kryon member. "Where are they?"

He pointed to a plascrete bunker surrounded by a scant row of guards.

"How many are holding them?"

"We don't know."

"Do you have a confirmed jump point inside that building?"

"Sir, if you go inside, they'll kill Asmed," he said.

I wasn't all that thrilled with Asmed's performance or his choice of security. Saving the other innocent family members took priority.

"I'll deal with that when I get inside."

He glanced at the bunker and flashed me the jump point.

I stepped out of the void into a ransacked building. Five figures cowered in the corner on the far side of the room.

A lone Kryon stood between us with a pulse pistol in his hand and a scowl on his face.

"I wondered when you'd show up," he said as he fired.

A light pulse wave knocked me to the ground. The room spun. I blinked several times, but my vision refused to clear.

His footsteps drew closer. I pushed myself back to my feet and tried to make sense of the doubled images swimming before me.

"Tell me where the tank is, and I'll make this quick," he said.

Wavering on my feet, I fought to aim at one of him. "Is that why everyone is trying so hard not to kill me outright?"

"Nothing personal, just following orders."

"Whose orders?" I asked.

"The High Council. So you might as well tell me before more people get hurt."

I fired. He stood there unharmed.

"Dammit, I don't want to do this," he said.

He fired at Asmed's head. The man fell to his knees and collapsed face first onto the ground.

Wails rose from the remaining Nikeras. They pressed into the corner, nearly crushing one another in their efforts to disappear. The youngest, an adolescent girl, found herself shoved to the forefront. She reached a trembling hand out to the dead man. Tears ran down her face. Her lips mouthed a single word over and over. Father.

I couldn't allow the Council access to the tank. Not even for the price of innocent lives. Many more would die if that happened. I prayed for a lucky shot and fired again.

His head remained whole. He squeezed the trigger.

A bullet found the hole in my coat. Pain erupted between my neck and shoulder.

He twisted and fired a shot into the corner.

"Don't!"

But I was too late.

The girl cried out, clutching her side.

He turned back to me. "Just tell me where the fucking tank is!"

I had to protect Anastassia. The haze lifted from my eyes and my target came into focus. I shot again. This time I didn't miss.

The moment the man hit the floor, the three Nikeras bolted for the door. I staggered over to the girl they'd left behind.

"Come on," I said, holding out one hand, while attempting to contain the blood running down my chest with the other.

Her terrified gaze rose to meet mine. Blood seeped through the fingers clamped on her side. "It hurts."

"I know." I scooped her up and stumbled out the door.

She clung to me. "Am I going to die, too?"

"Not today."

Her trembling, bloody hand squeezed my arm.

Two Nikera guards rushed toward us. I handed her off while I figured out where to Jump with what little energy I had left.

A medical facility would be a wise choice, but I'd be an easy target there and only endanger more innocent people. From what I could tell, he'd missed anything vital, but there was a lot of blood and it wasn't showing signs of stopping. I took my chances with waiting and Jumped to the ship.

The blessedly blurry sight of Jey's naked body floating in bubbling fluid faded in and out. I let Merkief know I'd been hit and where I was. The next thing I knew, the hard floor rushed up to greet me.

*

Merkief's face came into focus. "Welcome back to the living. I wasn't sure you'd make it."

I sat up, running a reassuring hand over my whole and healthy chest. "Where's Kazan?"

"Asleep. I just got her out of the tank."

"Jey?"

His voice boomed from the hall. "Alive and well. Thanks."

We'd all made it. Thank Geva for that.

By the time Anastassia woke, the rest of us had showered and eaten. She sat down across from me at the table where we'd all been waiting, her wet hair still dripping down her shoulder.

"You've certainly been busy," she said.

"I didn't have much choice in the matter."

"The Nikeras send their thanks for the rescue of Asmed's daughter."

Gratitude from people willing to leave a wounded kid behind didn't mean much to me. "I gather you've been busy too."

Her gaze dropped. "You could say that."

"What did you do?" I looked to Merkief and Jey. Neither of them would meet my gaze either.

"It doesn't matter now. It's done," she said.

"Then you better tell me before I'm inclined to beat it out of all three of you."

She sighed. "We blew a couple Fragian bases."

"How far into their territory?" I asked, getting a very bad feeling.

"Deep."

"With only the two of you?"

"Seems that it doesn't take more than that when the charges are well placed," Jey said.

"Yes, you've proven your proficiency with placing charges." I said. "I take it you were provided with information on where to place them?"

Anastassia nodded.

Had Deep Voice tried to give her an edge over the Fragians or was something else entirely going on within the Council? Trying to untangle the plans of the High and Mighties made my head hurt. Why couldn't they just let us be?

"How long do you think it will be before the Fragians retaliate?" I asked.

"Too soon, I'm sure. We should all prepare," Anastassia stood. "Jey, oversee the preparation of the Jalvian forces. Merkief, take the Artorian fleets. Vayen, we'll need every available Cragtek ship you've got. I want everyone ready to go at a moment's notice."

Merkief and Jey Jumped to their assignments. I stayed in my seat.

"We're going to do this?" I asked.

"It's fight for the Narvan or lose it."

"I don't want to lose you in the process."

She smiled sadly as she stood. "I don't want to lose you either."

"You almost did yesterday. They openly used Kryon. At least three of them. I didn't recognize the others."

She dropped back into her seat and stammered. "Kryon? Are you sure? Merkief said he didn't recognize anyone during the attacks at Cragtek. We assumed you'd been injured in the riots."

"I was, by Kryon. I saw them and spoke to them, Anastassia. They wanted the tank and then they wanted me dead."

Anastassia shook her head. "But... she promised. We had a deal!"

"She who? What was the deal?"

"I don't know, they're always cloaked. A woman. She said if I complied, you'd be safe."

"Did she have someone with her? A big man? Wider than Jey?"

Her eyes widened and she paled. "You've dealt with her? With them directly? Why didn't you tell me?"

"I was keeping you and the tank safe." I swore. "Her name is Chandi. She's Artorian and she's leading the faction against you."

I didn't think it was possible, but she grew several shades whiter. "You've actually seen her and she told you her name?

What else have you been up to that you've kept from me?"

She sprang from her chair. It scraped across the metal floor with a piercing shriek. She loomed there, fists pressed into the tabletop. "Are you working with them? Did they promise you my position?"

"Of course not! I didn't want any of this, and I certainly didn't enjoy our meetings. You do recall my condition when I was at Fa'yets?"

"The Council did that?" she all but whispered.

I wanted to get up and hold her, to get to her calm down long enough that we could work through this next Fragian attack together, but she was far to tense for that.

"Please tell me you didn't send the Narvan to war over some nebulous threat to me," I said.

"Not exactly, but your safety was on the table." She started to pace. "They have someone else ready to fill my position. Someone that they feel could easily nullify my safety net. I've lost my leverage."

She made three passes along her side of the table before she came to a sudden halt. Her gaze locked onto me.

"What if they killed Res?" she asked. "If they want me gone, they'd try subtle jabs first, try to knock me down, make me more vulnerable without having to play their full hand."

"Tomias said his death wasn't a surprise."

"Perfect cover, wouldn't you say?" she asked.

"I'd say you're being overly paranoid."

"And the Council openly sending three Kryon after you, after promising to leave you alone, that's my paranoia too?"

"No. That was real." Too real.

She nodded. "And if they're willing to go after you to get to me, they're willing to go further." She turned away and headed down the corridor. "I can't let them kill anyone on the station. Attacks on us are one thing, but I will not allow her to harm him." She sprinted toward the armory.

I ran after her. "Him who?"

While I gathered there were people she cared about on the station, I didn't consider any of them important with the sort of emphasis she put on the word. If she was putting that pathetic doctor on a pedestal above me or even herself, I'd kill him and save the High and Mighties the effort.

She got the armory door open and ducked inside. It shut with a heavy clank just before I could catch her. I punched in the code, but the door wouldn't open. I didn't have a jump point inside the room so I settled for pounding on the heavy door with my fists. The thunderous racket filled the ship, reverberating along the walls.

"What are you doing? We're about to have Fragians marching on our doorstep!"

"I'm taking care of Chandi and her faction once and for all."

Dread filled me. The bond screamed for the door to melt into slag that very instant. "You can't harm them. Anastassia, if you touch them—"

Her muffled voice said, "I plan on doing a lot more than touching."

"They'll kill you!"

"Maybe. But he'll be safe." Her thoughts were edged with whispers of revenge and weapon choices.

"Where are you going? They're not on Sere, not all the time." If I could get her to show me, I could Jump with her.

"I know where they live. They bring the inner circle there to meet with all the Council members. You'll be safe here. Goodbye, Vayen." Her link and our connection slammed shut.

My heart leapt into my throat. She shouldn't have been able to close our connection, not with the bond in place. But just like that, she was gone, leaving a vast emptiness inside me.

As much as I wanted to hope that she was standing behind the door, reconsidering her plan, my gut told me she was gone. I rested my forehead on the cold metal and prayed for a miracle.

Chapter Eighteen

In the wake of Anastassia's abrupt departure and the terrifying vacuum it created where my bond was concerned, I took a few moments to get my shit together before contacting Jey for a jump point. If I couldn't talk reason into her, maybe he could.

Jey left the Jalvian officers he'd been talking to and waved me over to an empty corner of the room.

"Where's Kazan?" he asked.

"Can you reach her?"

"No." His brow furrowed." Why can't I? What's going on? We're all preparing to fight the war she started. Where is she?"

"I don't know." The words came out as a strangled hiss. "She failed to share her jump point when she locked me out of the armory and left on a suicide mission."

His jaw tightened and the vein on his forehead rose. "How could you let this happen?"

"Me? I don't control her. You think you could have stopped her?"

Jey grumbled and exhaled loudly. "So what are we supposed to do?"

My hands clenched and unclenched at my sides, helpless. I hated helpless. Whether she was here or not, the Fragians were going to retaliate.

"Continue with preparing the fleets. If she makes it back, we'll be ready."

"And if she doesn't?" he asked.

The High and Mighties had someone else to plunk in her position with an unknown agenda and Geva knew what allegiances. They wouldn't need the tank to hold over Kazan's head if it was already removed from her shoulders. The three of us would become loose ends in need of snipping.

"Then we're screwed," I said.

"You seem awfully sure of that." He glanced around the room. "Is there something you're not telling me?"

"A lot of things, and none of them bode well. Do you have the Jalvian fleet under control?"

Jey straightened his shoulders and stood tall. "Of course."

"Then I'm going to check on Merkief and then head to Rok. If you hear anything on any front, let me know."

"I will." He headed back to the waiting officers, but his concern leaked through our linked connection, revealing just how unsettled he was beneath his commanding facade.

I Jumped to Merkief's location and was heartened to see that he was also fulfilling his orders with great efficiency. Kazan had chosen them well and had honed them to suit her needs. Where that put me, I could only wonder. When danger arose, Kazan handed them entire fleets. I had twenty-six mismatched ships. Most of which were suitable for crews of ten rather than hundreds and were outfitted for quick attacks on one or two ships, not outright war. I'd send them in because the Narvan needed a full show of force, but I also knew that I'd be sending most of my men to their deaths and that truth didn't sit well with my already jumbled nerves.

Merkief had little to say to me and even less after learning Kazan wouldn't be making an appearance to appreciate his efforts on her behalf. Coupled with the fact that it felt as if he could see right through my work face to the stricken and writhing bond, I didn't stay long. Those who had needed to see that Merkief had my backing and thereby, Kazan's, had seen me. I Jumped to the semi-familiar comfort of the temporary office Gemmen had set up for me.

My ships were always outfitted with the latest upgrades and waiting for new targets so I didn't have any of the rush Merkief and Jey did. I informed Gemmen of our plans and made a short speech to the crews who were present. With the ships already in space redirected to patrol Merchess, there wasn't much more to do than wait.

The bond wanted to wallow in my private space, perhaps punch a few things and certainly curse everything and everyone who had filled Anastassia with the urge to leave my side, but none of that would keep the Fragians from our doorstep. I settled for five minutes to pull myself together. No wallowing, punching or swearing, just breathing, in and out, steady and calming like my mother had shown me as a child and like Fa'yet had expanded on. The bond could twist all the knots it wanted in my stomach as long as it left my head clear and my hands steady. I wasn't Jalvian; I could control my urges.

I took advantage of the meditative state to sink deep into my link. Preparations for the upcoming battle were taking shape. My contacts within both fleets had left me detailed reports so I could monitor progress on various levels rather than just taking Merkief and Jey's word. Kazan had often done the same, though in less dire circumstances. I'd considered it distrustful of her, but now, alone and without her guidance at such a critical time, I adopted her practices with only minor thoughts of hypocrisy.

Something cold and hard registered against my forehead. My concentration shattered.

"About time you woke up," Kess said. "Hands on the desk."

"And if I prefer to keep them on a gun?"

"I'd say you're a little late on the draw. Which is surprising really." He shoved the gun deeper. "Put them on the table."

I kept them where they were. "How did you get in here?"

"Not all your men are immune to bribes." He rolled his eyes. "Don't worry, it wasn't Anastassia's pet, Gemmen. He's as loyal as ever and mostly unharmed. Can't say the same for the two nosy men in the hallway, though. How about you get up slowly and move to that battered couch so I can keep my word that you won't get hurt."

"After all the times you've tried to kill me, now you're suddenly concerned about my safety?"

"Let's cut the crap, shall we? They've got Anastassia."

Despite my best meditation efforts, my heart missed a beat. "The Council?"

He nodded. "I also hear you're bonded to her. Poor bastard."

"Where is she? How do you know they have her?" I had to get there. She needed me.

"We have a deal to make first."

"I don't have time for deals!"

"She's not going anywhere," he said. "Relax."

"Are you insane?"

He laughed. "Only because she drove me to it." He backed up a step and nodded me toward the couch. "You two must be pretty damn tight if she gave you this place. She wouldn't budge and inch for me."

"If you think I'm going to sit here and have a chat..." I flew from my seat and pulled a jump point from memory. A bullet slammed into my coat from only inches away, disrupting my already tenuous hold on the Jump and sending a wave of pain down my left side.

I rushed Kess and knocked him to the ground. The bond flooded my system with energy. I held him down. "Show me where she is. Now."

"Our deal doesn't work that way."

I didn't care if his brain went to mush. I dove into his mind. And slammed into a wall. For a Jalvian, he had excellent mental defenses.

Kess twisted violently, sending me rolling in the opposite direction. "That was rude."

"So was shooting me." I got to my feet.

"Please. I went for your armor, even considering all the shit the two of you have done to me. I don't have one of those mag-ic-heal-your-ass-in-a-few-hours tanks. I have private doctors, weeks of down time and more scars than I can count."

"Not exactly sorry about that. You were trying to kill us."

"If I was trying to kill either of you, you'd both be dead. That was never the plan."

"Could have fooled me."

"All right, I might have tried to off *you* a few times after you turned Marin down. But Marin only wanted her scared enough to retire to his complex. She'd be safe there."

Though he stood across the room, he might as well have punched me in the head.

His words rang in my ears. I went to the couch and sat down. "You're working for Marin?"

"Not recently, but yes, I had been. You were supposed to join me, but Marin was worried Kazan was on to him and stalled too long in making his proposal to you. Then you screwed every-thing up by going back to her. We could have made a great team, you know."

"Hadn't really crossed my mind."

"We still could," he said.

I stared at him blankly. "Why in all the nine hells would I want to work with you?"

"I've kept her alive just like you have. I'm not the bad guy here."

"You deserted her. You've been attacking her for years! You've come damn close to killing her more than once. Don't you dare compare yourself to me."

"That time on Syless was an accident." He shifted on his feet. "Marin's got a gift for persuasion and Kazan can be a self-centered bitch. You know what I mean, and you deserted her too. Don't get all righteous."

"I went back."

"You're a more tolerant man than I am. I'll grant you that." He relaxed his stance, but still kept the gun aimed in my direction. "Just because I left, doesn't mean I don't appreciate the important role she plays in keeping our people safe. I've been trying to do the same."

I laughed. "By working for Marin and harassing Kazan?"

"I needed credits and he had an excellent medical staff, but after you and the other two came on, the credits no longer out-weighed the risks. You nearly got me twice. I know Kazan's moves. She's predictable, but you..." He shook his head. "I wanted back in Kryon, and Chandi cut me a deal."

"Let me guess, get Kazan out of the picture and you could have her position."

Kess snorted. "You have loftier goals than I do. I just wanted the Council's damned oppressive observers off my ass and a way back into Kryon so I could do something more meaningful than chase Kazan around until you offed me."

"But she still had you chasing Kazan around," I said.

"No, she wanted me to kill you, or the other two. She wasn't all that particular as long as Kazan was left vulnerable. She had other agents willing to take Kazan out." His knuckles turned white. "But my deal just turned to shit. Kazan just killed Chandi."

Anastassia had taken her revenge and she was alive. But for how long?

"And what do you want me to do about it? I need to get to her! Give me a damned jump point."

"And I need a partnership to prove myself in order to get back in good favor with Kryon now that my other way in has fallen through. We can watch over the Narvan together. What do you say?"

"No fucking way. I have a partner."

"You won't. Not when they're done with her." He lowered his gun a few degrees. "Come on, I can see how much you want the jump point. You'll have a few minutes in her cell before security reaches you. All you have to do is say yes."

As if Anastassia would ever forgive me for bargaining with Kess. Merkief and Jey would never understand; they'd be against me in an instant. There had to be another way to get to her, a way with a less vile string attached.

"What makes you think the High and Mighties will want me to stick around now that Kazan has acted against them?" I asked.

"You didn't act against them. She did."

"I doubt they'll make that distinction."

"Really? Why are you still here while she's in a cell?"

"Because..." The Fragians were going to attack. While Chandi's faction might have wanted them to succeed, not everyone in the High Council was in agreement. They needed someone to head the war and with Kazan out of the picture, that fell to me. If they wanted me to lead their damned war, they owed me something.

"I have to go," I said.

"What about our deal?"

"There won't be one."

"That's unfortunate." He raised his gun and fired.

The impact of the bullet hit the edge of the collar of my coat as I Jumped to Sere. The grey-suits took note of me as I staggered out of the void. I reached up to rub my neck, assuring myself that Kess hadn't been lucky and headed for the room where I'd last met with Deep Voice.

The halls were mostly empty, lending an unusual level of silence to the hushed Kryon base. Did they all know what Anastassia had done? Were they making an example of her somewhere?

"Vayen," Jey's voice popped into my head, *"Long range scouts have confirmed that the Fragians are on the move."*

"Head to the jump gate and get your fleet through. The Cragtek ships will meet you just beyond Merchess."

"Got it. And the Artorian fleet?"

Did I want Merkief and Jey to also gain credit or would that make me weak in the eyes of the Council? If I planned to bargain, I needed to be in charge.

"I'll take care of Merkief and the Artorian fleet."

"Any word on Kazan?"

"I'm working on it," I said, wishing he would shut up and let me do just that. The empty halls were making my skin crawl.

"Then perhaps you should focus on her and leave this war to me."

"Not that I doubt you could handle it, but I can't do that. Not yet anyway. If I need someone to assume control, you're my first choice."

War was what his people did best after all.

I cut contact with Jey and contacted Merkief, relaying the meet up point. I gave up on roaming for a moment so I could concentrate on reaching the rest of my own contacts throughout the fleets one by one, passing orders and gathering reports.

A grey-suit tapped me on the shoulder, breaking my concentration. "Mr. Ta'set, come with me."

"Where are we going?"

"A meeting. A very important one," he said.

"I'm not going anywhere until you can assure me that Kazan is here and alive."

The man's lips twisted in a mockery of an obliging smile. "I'll take you to her now."

"You do that."

He headed off down the hall the way I'd come.

I wanted to run, but I didn't know where we were going. The damned grey-suit took what seemed like hours to lead me to the room Fa'yet had once informed me was where Kryon trials were held.

A female liaison turned to me as we entered. "Ah, Mr. Ta'set, kind of you to join us."

Not one of the damned robed bastards had dared attend in person. Instead, a host of armed zombies lined both of the longer side walls of the room. No wonder the halls had seemed empty. Nine Kryon sat at the back of the room, silent. Fa'yet was among them. He avoided my gaze, staring forward with sorrow etched deeply on his face.

Anastassia sat alone, bound to a metal chair at the front of the room. Blood oozed from a gash on her lip. The left side of her face was swollen. She glared at everyone in the room from under the disarray that had been her neat braid only a short while before.

Despite my best efforts, our natural connection remained

sealed and her link closed. My tongue forgot how to work. All I could do was stand and stare while my mind sought out any possible way of freeing her from a room flooded with armed High Council members.

I scanned the grey-suits, searching for anyone familiar, but they all had the same level of emotional vacancy, uniform, and bland faces, as if all hint of personality had been sucked from them. Other than being male and female and a variety of familiar races, nothing set them apart from one another. Deep Voice had always appeared in person. I had no way of knowing which one was my loosely-termed ally, but from the vast number of Council members in attendance, I knew he was there.

The High Council continued with their proceedings. One liaison spoke after another as if they were holding a private conversation elsewhere that we were only privy to half of.

"She invaded our private space!"

"Drove her to it, I say."

"You've placed too much trust in your circle."

"Kill her now. Make an example to the rest."

"We've suffered a great loss of lives. Make her pay!"

While the zombies along the walls bickered, the one beside me went slack and then reanimated. He whispered, "Shouldn't you be running a war right now?"

"We need her," I said.

"She's only one woman, proficient surely, but you'll do well enough."

"This isn't a *well enough* situation. My homeworld, an entire system full of innocent lives hangs in the balance. You pushed her to this, now let her follow through."

"That was our consensus, but then she pushed *us* to this." He grabbed my arm and guided me toward the door. "You should leave now. What is to come will only distract you from the war you must win."

"I won't fight your war if you don't let her go."

The zombie's brows rose in an uneven manner. "You'd willingly let Fragians overrun the Narvan?" He chuckled dryly. "We both know that's not true. Now go."

He was right. Perhaps the bond hadn't left my head as clear as I'd thought. If I couldn't bargain for her freedom and I couldn't fight the High Council off, what in the nine hells could I do?

"You make it sound like I have the choice of leaving her, but I don't. You and your damned faction saw to that."

"The bond is unfortunate given the circumstances. This out-come was not in our projections." The zombie's face scowled. "I'll see that she's granted a quick death. The bond we forced upon you will be severed."

"Killing her quickly is your version of doing me a favor?" I shoved him away. "That's the best you can come up with? Your faction set the Fragians upon us. They sent Kryon out to kill me, and if Kazan is to be believed, others close to her as well. You've had deals with her and deals with me but you don't seem intent on following through with any of them!"

The Council bickering came to a sudden halt. The room full of grey-suits turned their attention on me. So did Anastassia.

"Forcing my hand is most unwise, Mr. Ta'set," Deep Voice said. "You may feel we don't follow through on our deals but be assured, we do follow through on our threats."

He left me and walked into the center of the room where he cleared his throat and spoke loudly. "Most of you are aware of the varying opinions on what to do with the non-compliant Narvan. As we mourn the loss of four of our revered members, let us not also forget that one of them took matters into her own hands, dis-regarding our processes and arguments. She has been served her justice. Now, let us give this wayward Kryon hers so that we may focus on containing the chaos that recent actions have brought upon us."

The room went quiet and the majority of the liaisons went blank-eyed. Those that remained kept a close watch on the rest of us.

"I knew you had your own deal with them," Anastassia said. "You were always so adamant in your professions of not want-ing to kill me. I should have guessed that you were just waiting and pushing for someone else to do the dirty work. I suppose you tipped them off about Res?" She banged the back of her head against the chair. "You play innocent too well. I should have stuck to Jalvian partners, at least they never fucked with my head."

"Anastassia, I didn't...I never—"

"Enough," one of the grey-suits yelled. Three of them rushed me, backing me toward the door and into the midst of a crowd of vacant liaisons. "You will remain silent or you will be removed from the room."

The three zombie men, two of them broad Jalvians, formed

a wall between me and Anastassia, offering me only glimpses of her bowed head.

The rest of the liaisons sprang to life. A woman went to stand beside Deep Voice.

"Anastassia Kazan," she said.

Anastassia picked up her head enough to look at them. I would have given anything to suffer her piercing glare rather than witness the defeat on her face.

"Your murder of four High Council members and the violation of the trust we held with you is inexcusable. Many of us wish for your immediate execution. Some recognize that it was internal discord that brought these deaths upon us. A few argue that an execution does not set enough of an example for the rest of the inner circle."

The female liaison turned to stare at the nine Kryon at the back of the room and then turned back to Anastassia. "We have come to an agreeable sentence."

Deep Voice said, "You will spend the next two years with our security developers. This breach will not occur again."

I forgot to breathe for a moment. My body defaulted to auto-pilot while my head tried to wrap itself around this lenient and horrifying sentence.

Two years with a development team didn't sound so bad considering the alternative. Still, being without her for that long would seem like forever thanks to the bond. And there was the war to deal with. And her safety net. And explaining to Merkief and Jey why she wasn't there or why they couldn't communicate with her. All that, while also having to deal with whomever the Council had in the wings to take on the Narvan's advisory position.

I might be dead long before she came back to attack me with spiteful allegations of aligning myself with the High Council—if she didn't shoot first and question my corpse later.

"In the meantime," Deep Voice said. "Mr. Ta'set will hold the Narvan as was agreed."

My mouth fell open. It wasn't bad enough that she'd come to that conclusion, now the bastard was outright confirming it.

I started towards him. "We never agreed on anything!"

One of my guards punched me in the gut. As I gasped for breath, I couldn't help but wonder if Shoulders was controlling the man.

The woman waved to two other guards. They made quick

work of extracting Anastassia from the chair. As they led her away, I saw she was limping and holding one arm close to her chest. They'd been none too gentle about bringing her down. There would be no dip in the tank before she joined the development team. She'd have to live with whatever damage they'd done.

I threw everything I had into one last attempt to break through the wall she'd constructed between us but received nothing more than a splitting headache for my efforts. She was gone.

Deep Voice and the others turned to me. My three guards slipped around behind, giving me a full view of the barrage of attention.

"Bring her back," I demanded.

Deep Voice's liaison shook his head. "You will advise the Narvan in Kazan's stead. We trust this will not be a problem for you?"

I stared at the door they had taken her through. My stomach lurched.

"A problem? More like a thousand of them! You know she's set up a safety net, right? Death threats, assassination attempts, upheaval throughout the system?"

One of the others said, "You are used to these things. We voted for you because you knew her contacts. You can harness or prevent the chaos her threats contain."

"But I don't know—"

Deep Voice held up his hand. "Are you saying you'd prefer if we passed this position on to someone else? We've been settled on you for quite some time, but there are plenty of other qualified candidates to choose from."

It hadn't been Kess or some random unknown they'd threatened Anastassia with. It was me. The weight of the Narvan slammed onto my shoulders. I swallowed hard.

"No, I'll do it."

"Good." He nodded to one of the other grey-suits.

The other man went to the back of the room and returned with a black bundle in his arms. He handed it to me and stepped away.

Deep Voice said, "She won't need that anymore."

Anastassia's coat weighed almost as much as she did. She must have taken a good portion of the armory with her.

"We'll be watching you," he said.

Of that, I had no doubt.

"You are dismissed."

I made my way out of the room with blurry eyes and uncertain feet. How long would it take for her contacts to get restless? Damn the High Council. Anastassia had never shared her private contacts with me. Why would she? She'd expected this day to come from the start.

Hollow, as if someone had shoved me into a vacuum chamber and slammed the door, I Jumped to the ship. I tried Anastassia one more time. Still nothing. Why couldn't she have been Artorian? Everything I'd ever heard about bonds was unreliable thanks to her. There was a reason we didn't often join outside our own race and now it was smacking me in the face.

I went to her room and stood in the doorway as I had so many times before. This was her place, and as I slipped inside, I expected her to burst in and scream at me for invading it. I rather hoped she would, but the only screaming was in my head.

I clutched her coat, wishing she was in it. The armor was hard and cold, smelling of guns and oils. I hung it on the hook beside her door.

The neckband I'd given her sat on the table beside her bed. I picked it up, tracing the patterns engraved on its surface. No hint of her body's warmth lingered within the metal. I put the band down. She wasn't here. If I wanted to be alive when she was released, I needed to make it through this war the High and Mighties had thrust upon us.

I contacted Jey for a jump point. He looked mildly annoyed when I arrived a minute later.

"No Kazan?"

My voice seemed distant and amazingly in control. "We'll discuss it later. Where are we?"

Jey led me to a projected display floating above a table in the middle of the room. "See those red spots?"

Three glowing circles floated between the fourth and sixth Fragian worlds.

"They're half the size of a damned planet. What are they?"

He slapped a still frame film on the lighted table. "Shipyards."

We had regular scouting runs, both Jalvian and Cragtek. "How did we overlook these?"

Jey and the Jalvian commander exchanged guilty glances. Jey pitched his voice low. "We don't know exactly, but trust me, I'm looking into it."

"What are they producing?"

"Fighters mostly. All smaller craft. Their usual models. The scouts reported seeing hundreds of ships detach and head deeper into Fragian space," Jey said. "There are a thousand more still docked there. Looks like they are planning to stuff their base ships full and come after us."

"Has Merkief seen these?" I asked.

"Yeah," Merkief tapped me on the shoulder. "You're late to the party. We're looking at taking them out now. If they get all those ships deployed, they'll grind us into the ground."

"The fleets are in position for this?"

Merkief and Jey nodded. "You'll need to inform your company ships, but everyone else is ready to go."

"If you don't mind, I'll have them take out any strays. They're not built for all out attacks of this magnitude. Have the Fragians noted our presence?"

"We've shot down four scouts and we're praying we didn't miss any. Beyond that, we haven't seen any major signs of action. Once we move in, all bets are off," Jey said.

"Right. Carry on then." I left them to their plans and stared at the projection, wishing Anastassia stood beside me.

Merkief Jumped back to his Artorian ship. Jey conferred with the commander, and from the concentrated look on his face, several others via his link.

"They're ready to launch the first wave at the shipyards in two minutes. Weapons are powering up now," said Jey.

"We're close enough for that?"

He shook his head. "This is why I'm in charge of the Jalvian fleet. You're too busy being out of commission for weeks at a time to keep up with the latest specs."

"Good thing I have people to keep track of that for me, like you." He could think he was in charge all he wanted, but he had damn well better acknowledge that I was standing in for Kazan for now.

The ship rocked. People shouted orders back and forth. Jey strode to the display beside the commander. After a moment of pointing and deep debate, Jey returned.

"What was that?" I asked.

"A reaction wave from the explosion that took out one of the shipyards. Seems the weapon hadn't been truly field tested and the reaction was much stronger than anticipated. Two of our front line ships were damaged as was the second shipyard."

"Acceptable, given the end result."

"I would agree, except the third shipyard was alerted by the wave and has launched the majority of their ships. We're about to get swarmed."

"We've lost communication with the Rokish ships. It seems to be jammed," called out one of the crew members.

"That's nearly half of your fleet." I examined the display. The Jalvian ships that had been dispatched from Rok were scattered along the front lines. "Is it their proximity to the wave, the ship-yards, or a technical issue?"

Jey mumbled, "They have older communication equipment. The Fragians may have been able to block it. They captured a few Rokish scouts recently."

"You'll have to relay orders through linked crewmembers."

"There are only a few I have contact with, and I don't have time to play messenger."

I watched the interplay of blue and red as our fighters engaged the swarm of sleek black Fragian ships. Around us, orders were relayed with precision. The commander retained control of his ship, consulting Jey from time to time.

The Rokish ships were acting independently, even of each other, and suffering sorely. "Do you have a jump point within the Rokish fleet?"

"I established emergency points within all three fleets before we arrived," he said as he flashed me a location.

"Good. I'll take care of them. Give me what contacts you have and let me know what you need us to do."

He cocked his head. "You're letting me call the shots?"

"For the moment. Don't make me regret it."

I might disagree with a few smaller points of his planning, but overall, I had to trust Anastassia. She'd put Jey in charge of the Jalvian fleet for a reason.

Jey grinned, but his excitement vanished a second later, replaced with the same solemn sternness worn by the com-mander. "Be careful over there. I don't want to be the one to have to give Kazan any bad news."

"I will."

I Jumped. The void spit me out into an empty bunkroom. It took me a minute to get my bearings, but I found my way to the control room in short order. The commander's eyes widened when he spotted me.

The ship lurched. I grabbed the nearest console to keep my footing.

A crewmen shouted, "Sir, we've been hit!"

A shudder passed through the entire ship, accompanied by a deep groan.

"Jey, another jump point. Now."

Jey flashed me a location and was gone.

I took in the doomed men around me, wishing I could Jump them all to safety. But then, which to choose? There wasn't enough time and I wouldn't have had enough energy for more than three double Jumps in such close succession even on my best of days. I closed my eyes and Jumped, praying Jey had the foresight to verify the next ship was still intact.

Metal walls encased me as I again stepped out of the void. Offering a quick prayer of thanks, I sprinted for the control room.

Swift efficiency filled the command center. The crisp uniforms of the Rokish men showed no sign of sweat and their faces no hint of worry, only concentration. I made note of the commander's name so that he and his men might be commended later—assuming they fared better than the last ship.

I set about getting the Rokish ships in coordination with the rest of the Jalvian fleet and passed information along to Jey. From here, some of the Fragian ships were visible in the external views, though they were doing a fine job of moving just enough to evade our larger weaponry. They shuffled around, moving in and out of sight.

Since they still had our sensors blocked along with communications, I had to ride along on Jey's link enough to see his map while also conveying positions to the crew and passing along that information to my contacts and those Jey had given me. Cragtek ships darted in and out of range of the visible Fragian fleet, doing what damage they could against targets much larger than they were used to taking on. They also offered additional eyes for me and took some of the Rokish fighters into their formations, so I didn't have to keep track of them as well.

Hours dragged on, but with my help, we went from being picked off to making good strides at evening the numbers. The attacks were silent inside the heavy-hulled ships. Each bright orange fireball lifted my spirits, until the next glance Jey took at the projection map revealed a mass of red creeping onto the edge of the display. I swore. We'd only been fighting their front line.

The bulk of their fleet wasn't even here yet.

We expanded outward, redoubling our efforts to destroy every possible Fragian vessel before the new threat arrived. Most of Jey's and all of Merkief's ships lagged behind to deal with the remaining shipyard. Being surrounded by the enemy was not the image I wished to portray to the High Council.

A bright flash of light was our only warning that the first of the next wave of Fragian ships was within range. My stomach sank to my feet as another of the Rokish ships fell victim to it.

"Take those damned ships out!" I relayed my order to everyone I was connected to through my link.

My head swam with a host of voices reporting from their posts. I tried to follow each one and convey orders as quickly as possible using the doubled vision of Jey's projection map and the external views in front of me. Time became irrelevant as minutes fragmented into seconds, each one with a direct purpose and cost in lives.

On a ship on the front lines, surrounded by a crew full of Jalvians, I lost touch with my body, giving myself entirely over to the voices that needed me.

Each time the external view went white, the crew's reports took on a frantic urgency. The dodging game the Fragians had played earlier brought a new level of terror now that their numbers had swelled.

Any ship of a design that even hinted that it might be armed with an array became a top priority. I tried not to think about how many of our own fighters were being sacrificed in our efforts to take those ships down.

The commander shouted his orders just over my shoulder. Several other Rokish ships drew too close to us. "Spread out. Get us away from this sitting target."

I reinforced this message through my channels, ordering everyone to maintain as much distance as possible in all directions. Losing one ship here and there was an acceptable loss, but if they managed to take a large number of us out at once, they'd be able to surge through the hole and we'd lose everything we'd slowly gained.

The Jalvian and Sylessian ships began to catch up, filling in the gaps around us. Jey launched his fighters. They swarmed around the nearest Fragian vessels, intent with purpose. I brushed over Merkief's link to find the Artorian fleet also coming up behind us.

I began to entertain the thought that we might actually win this war.

My concentration shattered when the external view flooded with intense light. The ship shook violently, throwing my dazed body out of my seat to land heavily against the station next to me. Fire erupted from the floor as something on the levels below exploded with a force that made my ears ring. I scrambled away from the gaping hole in the floor filled with searing heat and got to my feet. Sirens wailed and automated systems issued warnings about structural damage and failing life support.

The commander paused in his tirade of orders to shake my shoulder. His voice was strangely muted through the ringing in my ears. "You need to leave."

I searched for something to say to the man who was about to die.

The commander shouted in my face, "Go!"

I didn't have time or the wits to get another jump point. I defaulted to Jey's ship, hoping he wasn't on the verge of imploding too.

Arriving in the command center on shaky legs, I found Jey barking orders at four officers who were relaying them to the rest of the fleet. Three ships exploded on our front line. Rokish ships. I wondered which one had contained the men I'd just been working beside.

I rubbed my eyes and after settling into a seat someone offered me, set about reestablishing the chain of contacts I'd dropped, including Jey who was in the same room. I needed to know what he was thinking so that we were acting with one mind.

"Keep at them!" I said. "We can't afford to lose this. They'll be at our doorstep next."

Jey nodded. Staring at the display, I searched for any advantage but found none. This was going to come down to numbers, luck, and prayers. I didn't know if the Fragians even had a god. If they did, I hoped it was deaf.

The Jalvian crew around me worked efficiently, relaying orders with even tones and focusing on their jobs rather than the devastation outside. There were no pleas for retreat. Maybe they'd gotten a stern talking to after the last Fragian encounter.

The display offered little assurance of our victory one way or the other. Fragians were dying. We were dying. If nothing else, I hoped that we were able to keep the losses even. Maybe then the

High Council would give me the benefit of the doubt and keep the Fragians in their own space.

Minutes stretched onward as information hurled into my head and the cacophony of voices threatened to overwhelm me. The deep link trance slowly sucked me back in as a rhythm settled into my mind. Merkief and Jey argued in my head, both forming different plans about where they wanted to proceed. Though it bothered me, knowing I'd further be pushing Merkief away, I sided with Jey. We needed aggression, not caution.

Someone shook my shoulder. Jey came into focus. "Get out of your head for five minutes and eat something."

He shoved a meal bar into my hand. I dutifully ate and then drank the water someone else handed me and sunk back into my link.

"They're falling back," Merkief reported.

"Don't ease up. Take out as many as you can. I don't want enough survivors left to put up this level of resistance again anytime soon."

"That will mean more losses. The Fragians are getting desperate out here."

"Better losses now while we have them on the run than what we'd sustain if caught off guard in the future," I said.

Merkief wielded his aggravation openly as he spoke, *"Our fighters have been out there for ten hours. They're getting tired and sloppy. Are you sure you want them to give chase?"*

"Just do it."

"The losses are on your head," he said, cutting contact.

He was definitely going to be a problem later. But I had more pressing emergencies to deal with at the moment.

My Cragtek ships eagerly joined the Artorian chase efforts. I had little doubt they'd return to Rok full of salvage. I dismissed what remained of the broken Rokish fleet. They'd suffered the heaviest casualties.

I made a note to talk with Jey about more evenly upgrading the entire Jalvian fleet. Jal didn't deserve the best of everything just because it was his homeworld.

The lull offered a break from the flurry of battle reports as they switched gears into losses in both ships and lives, ships in need of repairs, two that would need towing home, and complaints about the initial disorganization in the Rokish fleet. A list of commendations started trickling in, mostly from within the main Jalvian fleet—they reveled in medals and recognition.

Jey sent his ships after Merkief's, determined not to be out-shone by Artorians. I didn't stop him.

I searched ahead on the charts and decreed a cut off line. We couldn't chase them all the way to Fragia. It was too risky given our losses. As we passed one of the smaller planetoids in the nebula, one of the lead ships reported a line of enemy vessels waiting on the other side. The enemy had formed a cutoff point of their own.

Reports of more of their damned energy arrays, came roaring into my head. Seconds later, the planetoid burst. Fragments pelted our fleet, overwhelming shields, damaging external weaponry and sensors, and puncturing already weakened hulls. One of my contacts broke off his report with a scream and went silent.

Damage reports flooded my mind with an unending buzz of numbers and pleas for assistance. The voices grew in volume until they became a deafening roar. The information trails blurred until they turned as white as the beam of the Fragian array.

My eyes flew open as my hold on the link fragmented. I gasped as if there suddenly wasn't enough air on the ship to sustain me.

"Vayen?" Jey's face loomed in front of mine. "Let it all go. Breathe."

I tried to push him back but my strength was gone, like I was stuck in slow motion. I needed air. I needed space.

He grabbed my shoulders and shoved me back in the chair.

"Get a medic over here. Now!" Jey shouted orders at the ship's commander and several others, holding me down all the while.

His hands on my shoulders became a lifeline, a solid grip of the reality around me. The networks and all the chaos had vanished. The flood of numbers and voices had gone silent. The chair and his hands were real. I blinked. Nothing floated behind my eyelids but blackness.

A red-suited medic pressed her fingers to my neck. I looked up at her face and blinked. Nothing focused right. The edges of the room had a funny glow to them, golden and pulsing.

She flashed a bright light into my eyes. I swatted her away. Her light clattered on the metal decking and rolled under my chair.

"He's in shock. We need to get him out of here."

My tongue was thick and my words halting. "Have to stay."

Jey got right in my face. The edges of his hair glowed. "Don't worry. You're not going anywhere without me and I'm kind of busy here. Just sit tight, all right?"

When I nodded, he let go. He pulled the medic aside.

My head started to throb, a bright light pulsing behind my eyelids. When had I closed my eyes and why couldn't I open them again? They were so heavy.

The pulsing light grew brighter and the throbbing turned to pounding. Pressure formed in my link, and I cringed, waiting for it to burst, but it slowly subsided. The pounding didn't, it kept growing, like someone was driving a molten spike into my brain. It was every bit as bad as when I'd gone off Chandi's drug.

The sounds of the crew around me wavered distantly like I was underwater. Jey's muffled voice echoed in my ears but most of what he said didn't make sense.

We were at war, suffering major losses, deep in enemy territory and I couldn't even control my own damn body. If we lost this, the faction would win the Council over. The Narvan would go to the Fragians. Entire planetary populations would be wiped out. I had to get back on my feet. I forced my eyes to open.

The medic jumped back. "How is he still awake?"

"I told you he would be an unruly patient." Jey got in my face again. "Don't fight it. Sleep. You overloaded your link."

"We have to win."

"We will." He gave me the most sincere smile I'd ever seen on his annoyingly perfect Jalvian face. "And if you promise to sleep now, I might even let you take some of the credit."

Chapter Nineteen

"Wake up, damn you!" Merkief slapped me across the face. I told my eyelids to open but they resisted. Merkief's voice grew distant. I became dimly aware that my face hurt. My tongue was stuck to the roof of my mouth. Where was I and why was Merkief so angry? I tried my eyes again. This time they obeyed, but the light was so bright I closed them again.

"Wake up!" He grabbed my shirt and shook me, but the muscles in my neck refused to do much about it. I opened my eyes enough to see the room jangle around in a disorienting blur.

"Come on!" His voice took on a hysterical edge as he dropped me back onto the pillows. "Jey's missing and I still can't contact Kazan. Stocks are plummeting throughout the Narvan, there's chaos in the streets, the governments are demanding Kazan speak to them. The Jalvian military is demanding to speak to Jey. Gemmen is demanding to talk to you. The High Council wanted a report on the war and the Narvan two days ago. The only people who will listen to me are the research teams I've been working with and they're crying foul because all their funding disappeared. What the fuck do I do?"

"Water," I managed to say.

"I don't have time to play your nurse. Get out of that damned bed and help me."

"What happened?" How long had I been out and how far had Kazan's safety net unfurled?

Merkief raked his fingers through his hair and grimaced.

"This is a waste of time. You're fucking useless." He vanished.

I tried to get up, but it was as if my body was in slow motion and weighted down. The door opened and a uniformed person came to my bedside. After a moment, recognition kicked in. An LE. I focused on the room, beating the fog from my vision and mind. The University. Jey had said something about my link being screwed up.

"Can you hear me?" he asked.

"Yeah."

"Good." He tapped notes into the datapad he carried.

A second uniformed man came in. He gave me water and helped me sit up.

"Do you know where you are?" the LE asked.

"Artorian University. What's wrong with my link. What happened?"

"You," the LE pointed a finger at me and scowled, "nearly fried your implant. We had to put you into a coma and inject nanites to repair it." His scowl deepened. "Ideally we would have replaced your implant, but we were informed your recovery needed to be swift and all efforts should be taken to assure no data was lost or recorded in any manner."

That sounded like Jey's sort of informing.

"That was for your own safety," I said.

I would have hated to clean up security breaches here. We needed the link experts and all their knowledge for emergencies such as this.

"We were told that also." He tucked the datapad under his arm. "The nanites have been flushed from your system. As soon as the medication wears off, you'll be free to go. I do hope you properly appreciate the efforts we have taken on your behalf."

"I do. Thank you." I made a note to make a sizeable donation to the University.

He nodded. "Rest for now and don't even think of taking off without my clearance. You can be reckless again once you are discharged but not before. Is that clear?"

"Yes." I would have chuckled at his motherly chastising if I'd had more energy.

The LE left. His assistant remained, running his datapad over me and nodding at whatever it displayed.

"Where did my friend go?" Now that I was more awake, I had a hundred questions for Merkief and the ability to coherently ask them.

"I believe he left," he said, stepping back and tucking his data-pad into the pocket of his uniform.

Merkief's description of the mess the Narvan had become sunk in with brighter clarity. Jey was missing. What had happened with the Fragians?

"How long until this all wears off?"

"Four hours, maybe five." His eyes narrowed. "Don't even consider taking off after three. I don't need Kazan firing my ass or worse when you keel over on the job."

I sank back into the pillows. "That's the one thing you don't have to worry about at the moment, but yes, I'll wait here."

This was all her fault. If she hadn't left, she'd have been the one leading the war. She'd be beside me. Her cursed safety net wouldn't have gone off and Jey wouldn't be missing.

Over the next four hours, control of my body slowly returned and my link abilities began to come back. Jey had left reports on the end of the war. I skimmed them enough to understand that our losses had been heavy after the last attack, but we'd destroyed the remaining Fragian vessels. That had to have at least bought me some leverage with the High Council.

As to where Jey had gone, I could only guess that he'd attempted to quell the beginnings of Kazan's unfolding mess. When, at last, my link had recovered enough to reach out to him, all I got back was a sense that he was alive but unresponsive. I tried Merkief and got the same thing. I hoped that was a glitch in my link, but my gut told me it wasn't.

On a mad whim, I reached for Anastassia, but there was nothing there. The only assurance that they hadn't killed her was that the bond was still in place. The more I thought about her, the worse the ache within me grew. Fa'yet had said I needed to distract myself with work to keep my mind off the bond. Well hells, I had an entire system full of work crying out to me, as well as a summons from Deep Voice.

"Get me out of here," I demanded of the next LE assistant who came to check on me.

She came running back with the LE I'd spoken to before. He waved his monitoring equipment over my head, tapped a few things into his datapad and nodded.

"You're clear to go. Please take care of yourself a little better, will you? I can't guarantee we'll be able to fix it so quickly or at all next time no matter how big a gun barrel is waved in my face."

"Sorry about that."

He shook his head, sighed, and shooed me out of the bed.

It took me a few minutes to get my vertical bearings and get dressed. As I put my coat on, I considered where I might find Jey or Merkief. With chaos springing up everywhere, where would they have gone first? The options were overwhelming. Merchess was a mess. I decided to start there.

Siro, the head of the Ka'opul family had to be on Kazan's contact list. He sat at his desk with four armed guards behind him and two at the door I'd just come through. He didn't waste time with pleasantries.

"Why can't I contact Kazan?" he more demanded than asked.

"She's indisposed. You're stuck with me for now."

Siro cocked his head and smirked. "Nice try. She'd have let me know if that were the case. It would be in your best interest to turn her over immediately."

"I don't have her, nor have I harmed her." My words sounded reasonable to my own ears, but no one was going to buy them. Not when they were following her orders.

The men behind Siro drew their guns and aimed them at me. I kept my hands empty and at my sides.

"If you'd like to continue doing business as usual, I suggest you put those away before someone gets hurt," I said, doing my best to remain calm.

Siro held up his hand. The men put their guns down. "I've had many prosperous years under Kazan. If I find any evidence that you had a hand in getting rid of her, or you cut into my profits, I'll make life quite unpleasant for you."

"And if Kazan's cut of your profits drops or is not in the proper account on time, I'll make life unpleasant for *you*."

Siro nodded. "Then let us both aim to remain pleasant."

"Indeed."

I Jumped to the point nearest the Keefe family and made my way to their stronghold. One of the guards at the door of the family compound left his post and followed me as I entered.

Vikorus met me in the hallway before I could reach his office. He looked just as happy to see me as he would have to see a dozen Fragians on his doorstep.

"If you think I'm going to roll over like Siro, you're mistaken."

Often in states of rivalry, the family heads rarely shared information. It appeared my news transcended their competitiveness.

Two guards rushed in behind him and I had little doubt more were on the way.

"Let's save some time, shall we? I know you're following Kazan's orders." I tried the same calm tone I'd used on Siro.

The slightest inclination of his head was all the warning I had before bullets flew.

Without any backup, I had little choice but to keep my shoulders up and my head down as I returned their fire. There would be no playing nice until this whole mess got sorted out. I couldn't afford to be considerate or lenient.

Thankfully his house guards were good, but not top notch. The three of them were on floor in short order. I shoved Vikorus against the wall and held him there.

"Close the doors and call off your guards or you'll be hiring a lot of new help tomorrow."

He bucked and kicked, but he wasn't a large man or very strong. Another guard rushed into the hall. I took him out before he had a chance to assess the situation.

Vikorus grimaced and then went silent for a moment. The doorways along the hall slid shut. "I expect full reimbursement for the help you've killed and the damage the other one did."

There was a welcome glimmer of hope. "Which other one?"

"The Jalvian. I was following orders. Kazan can't fault me for that."

I wished I could. From what I could tell, Merchess was where the problems had first bloomed. I let him down but kept my hands around his neck.

"I want the trade routes re-opened immediately. Drop the embargo on your space port and call off the blood-feud with the Nikeras. I highly doubt Kazan endorsed that move."

He shrugged. "Seemed like the perfect opportunity."

"It wasn't. I don't suppose you happen to have contained the troublesome Jalvian?"

"He took seven of my men down before we managed, but yes."

I let him know my displeasure with a great deal of added force around his neck.

"Where might I find him?"

"Cell. Lower level," he said with effort.

"Have him brought here and we'll do a nice, friendly exchange. Got it?"

Vikorus nodded. His face turned red. I let up enough that he wouldn't pass out.

A knock sounded on the door a few minutes later. I dragged Vikorus over to it. "Open it."

He palmed the lock and the door slid open to reveal Jey slung between two straining guards. He was unconscious.

"You're lucky you didn't kill him. Kazan would have been very angry. So would I."

Vikorus rubbed his neck. "We thought as much so we held him until we could verify the situation."

"Too bad you didn't exhibit the same forethought with your other actions. There will be no reimbursement."

I propelled Vikorus toward his guards, slapped a hand on Jey, and formed a Jump for the two of us.

When we arrived on the ship, I half hoped to find Merkief floating in the tank, but it was empty. Bruises covered Jey's chest. Whether they were from Vikorus's men or elsewhere, I'd have to wait to find out.

I hoisted him up on the platform and loaded his profile. Whatever they'd used to incapacitate him, it hadn't caused any major damage. The tank estimated he'd be in for two hours, which meant at least that long to recover after he came out. I felt better about my odds of locating Merkief and surviving the rest of the day with Jey at my back.

With four hours to waste, I considered the few contacts I knew Anastassia and I shared that could help contain her safety net. Though using my link would have set better with me, I knew I'd have to go with in-person confrontations in the hopes of proving my honest intentions. I made a quick list of the obvious choices and decided to start with Gemmen. He'd be safe enough to meet without backup.

The company base emitted an odd vibe the moment I stepped out of my office. Rather than a guard standing near my door or posted in the middle of the hallway of main offices, one stood, armed and waiting, facing me.

"Gemmen is waiting for you." He inclined his head in the direction of Gemmen's office.

I couldn't help but note the missing 'sir' I'd grown accustomed to. "I know the way."

The man squirmed under my gaze but held his ground. When I started down the hall, he followed.

Gemmen didn't smile when I opened his door, but he wasn't holding a weapon either. He nodded to the empty chair across from him.

"I rather hoped you'd be dead," he said.

"Hello to you too."

That's when I realized I'd been so focused on Gemmen and his reaction that I'd missed the guard entering behind me, whose weapon I became keenly aware of at the back of my head as I sat.

"I expected more from you." Gemmen sure as all hells looked Jalvian now.

"I could say the same. I thought you worked for me."

"I worked for her first." His hands were clenched on the desktop. "What did you do?"

"Everything I could. She's not dead, so can we dispense with the weapons and hostility? I could use a little help here."

"You're here and she's not. So either you tell me exactly why that is, or I'm inclined to let Xander put a bullet in your head."

"You know what? If I could explain the reasoning behind Kazan's suicidal behavior, I would. I've been too busy trying to fend off Fragians, locate my friends, and halt the havoc you and all her contacts have wrought on the entire Narvan and beyond to figure it out on my own. So I suggest Xander puts his gun away before this mess get's any uglier than it already is."

Gemmen glanced at Xander and then looked me over long and hard. "You said she wasn't dead."

"She's serving a sentence."

His mouth dropped open. "Someone had the gall to imprison Kazan?"

"There are bigger fish in the known universe. She fucked with one of them."

Gemmen sat back, chewing on his thoughts like a tough steak. "All right then. Xander, tell the others that the project is off and see what you can do to facilitate the cleanup."

I heard Xander's gun slide into a holster as he left. Once the door closed I asked Gemmen about Merkief.

"Haven't seen him."

The friendly face I longed to see and confer with didn't make an appearance. He might have sent his gunman away, but suspicion remained in his gaze.

"I could really use your help in keeping order on Rok."

"Watch your back." His dire tone sent shivers down my spine.

I had the urge to turn and make sure Xander had left but I kept my gaze locked on Gemmen. "I plan on it."

"I'll do what I can with the locals."

"Thank you." After his warning, I deemed it safest to Jump directly to the ship. Merkief would have to hold on. If I couldn't even expect a halfway warm welcome from someone I considered a friend, I didn't want to contemplate what kind of reception I'd get from the Jalvian government.

While I waited for the tank to finish with Jey, I formulated a report on the Fragian conflict for the High and Mighties. Once he was out and moved to his bed to rest, I spent more time with his and Merkief's reports.

True to his word, Jey had done a surprisingly impressive job of assigning credit where it was due. There were no standout heroes, only a lengthy list of those who had done their part well, including some of the Artorian crews. He'd also neatly outlined how all our efforts had worked together to achieve the end result. This wasn't the work of the Jey I'd first met, but it was clear that this was what he was meant to do. Kazan had seen it in him.

I wondered what she had seen in me. Maybe I excelled at filing reports. Or was I merely the idiot that she was so fond of calling me, bumbling about on my quest to find my point of greatness. For all I knew, I'd blinked and walked right past it.

Sighing, I attached both of their reports to my own and sent the whole thing off to Deep Voice. If anyone would call the faction off once and for all, it would be him.

Jey found me sitting at Kazan's desk in her tiny office aboard the ship. I hadn't found anything helpful in my search of her terminal, no hint at her full contact list or secret instructions for contacting her. Having given up, I'd closed my eyes and tried to seek out some peace in this space that was hers. When Jey cleared his throat, I was dismayed to discover I hadn't found that either.

"I guess this makes us even," he said as he pulled his wet hair out from under the collar of his coat and shifted his shoulders until the armor fell into place.

"I suppose so. Thanks for that, by the way."

He nodded. "So where is our missing boss and why do you still look like shit even after your spa vacation at the University?"

I wished I didn't have to keep answering that question. Every time I had to acknowledge that she was gone, it felt like I was stabbing myself. I cursed the bond and the ancestors that had plagued me with it.

At least I could tell Jey the truth and not care quite as much that my voice was as unsteady as the rest of me. "The Council has her. She killed four of the High and Mighties."

He sank into the nearest chair. "She did what? Why?"

Jey stared at me like I had answers and was keeping them from him. If I lost him now, I highly doubted I'd ever regain his trust, not without Kazan to mediate.

"She got it in her head that they were going to kill someone, a man that I got the impression she cares about very much. That's all I know. Any idea who that might be?"

"Marin, maybe?"

He wasn't on the Verian Station. I took a little comfort in knowing she hadn't gotten into this mess on his behalf. "I don't think so."

"And you knew this when?" he asked.

"Just before we hit the shipyards. I barged in on her trial on Sere, caught the tail end of it, and came to you."

"So you knew where she was and that she wasn't coming to help us."

"I didn't think it would help to share that just then," I said.

I took a chance and opened my link to him enough that he could see the truth of what I was saying. I showed him a painfully defeated-looking Kazan in the trial chair.

He seemed to visibly shrink, as if someone had let some of the air out of his body. I wondered if I done the same at the time. If so, that would explain why I felt like I was short of breath.

"She's serving two years. I don't know where. I can't reach her. I haven't been able to since she left. Can you?" The words tumbled from me.

Jey killed what little hope I had with a single shake of his head. The intensity of his gaze diminished and wandered around the room. I didn't dare attempt to relax.

"Two years for four lives?" he asked.

Two years seemed liked forever at the moment, but deep inside, I knew he was right. I scrambled for a logical reason. "She does a lot of work for them and has the Narvan to run. Maybe they're taking that into account."

"Maybe."

My gut was telling me that Deep Voice had decided on me taking her place for a while now. If they'd been working on taming or deposing Anastassia since I'd come to be her partner or longer, why would they throw away the chance when they had a prime opportunity? What if they didn't really intend to bring her back?"

Jey interrupted the onset of a panic attack to ask, "Did you find Merkief?"

"Not yet. I was waiting for you."

He nodded. "Things are crazy out there. It's like all nine hells broke loose the moment the fleet hit Narvan space."

"Blame Kazan for that." I explained about her safety net.

"Well, that's just fucking great. Why didn't she call off the madness when she'd received her sentencing?"

Because she thought her safety net was doing just what she'd intended, making life miserable for the bastard who took the Narvan from her.

"Maybe she couldn't or her mind was elsewhere. I don't know. She wasn't talking to me."

"What about us then? With the Council?" he asked. "Who's advising the Narvan?"

As long as I could keep his anger and suspicion channeled elsewhere, I'd have a chance at keeping him beside me. That meant I was going to have to make some concessions.

I held my breath for a moment and let it out in a long hiss. "Me, according to the High and Mighties. The three of us according to me. If Kazan needed help, I sure as all hells do. You up for it?"

"You?" He snorted. "I don't have much choice, do I? You couldn't even stay awake in the middle of a damned war."

"Oh come on, it was toward the end. And I read your report. You had everything as well in hand as could be expected. I wouldn't have done it any differently."

He looked me in the eye and smiled. "Thank you."

"So where do you think Merkief would have gone? He came to see me before he went missing." I tried to remember which specific things he'd been ranting about. "He mentioned stocks, the planetary governments, looking for you, and the Jalvian military."

"If you hadn't found me on Merchess, what would be your next bet?" Jey asked.

"The planetary government heads."

"Then let's start there. Which planet?"

Home. Our home. I wanted to smack myself. Of course, that's where he'd go. "Artor."

Chapter Twenty

Kazan kept a jump point right in the central government building, but that seemed like asking for assassination now. Jey and I opted for one of our seldom-used jump points. From there, we stuck to public land transports.

The transport dropped us in the lower level of the adjoining building. Overhead, sky transports landed and departed. A horde of chanting protestors surrounded the building, drowning out the sounds of the street and air traffic. From what I could make out from vocal mayhem, there were several groups here. One marching up and down the street, others waving signs and shaking fists. Another sat chanting on the stairs, creating a bottleneck in the foot traffic.

We fell in with a crowd of officials dressed in civil regalia. Our armored coats stuck out in the midst of fine, pressed shirts and glinting chains of office, but I figured if there were Artorians who wanted us dead, they'd be less likely to risk a shot with us surrounded by their beloved elected officials.

As we made our way through the towering, columned-flanked doors, my gaze darted over the faces of visitors, interns, aides, and the officials they served and revered. The room swelled with the deafening din of arguments and protests. We wove through the throng to one of the Premier's aides. I demanded a meeting with the Premier, named a room and headed there with Jey beside me.

The Artorian Premier, a thin man with grey threaded through his shoulder-length, black hair, marched into the room just as we took our places at the long oval table. A single aide entered behind him. She set her datapad on the table and glanced from me to her leader, who remained standing.

He leaned forward, fingers splayed on the glossy tabletop. "What in Geva's name is going on?"

"Kazan is out for awhile. You'll be answering to me in the meantime."

"A while? That is not acceptable!" He stepped away from the table. "I am the public face of Artor's leadership. Kazan's absence is creating a cascade of problems, and dammit, I'm the one our people hold responsible!"

"I'm working on taking care of things."

"How?" He shook his fist at me. "You're sitting here, wasting my time, wasting our people's time. If you entertain any hopes of stepping into Kazan's place, I'd suggest you get to work."

I drew on my very limited patience. "I thought you'd want to know why she's not answering your messages personally."

"Assuming you didn't kill her, in which case, I hope you know what the hells you're doing, or we're all in for more of a nightmare—" He sucked in his lips so hard it looked as if his face might cave in, then lowered his voice. "Look, I don't care if she answers my messages personally or not, as long as one of you takes care of the mess out there."

I crossed him off my list of contacts to be concerned about and stood. "Did anyone else come to see you today?"

"Yes, the polite one, the other bodyguard. He said he'd do something about the mess too, but unless you're deaf, you can hear the shouting, so I hope you plan on doing more than he did."

"Did he say where he was going when he left?"

The aide cleared her throat. "Sir, we need to get back to the meeting, the councilors need your guidance in these trying times."

I glared at the aide. She glared back. Audacity from the Premier was to be expected, but aides served for a living, they were not known for spine or courage.

"Perhaps you remember if the polite bodyguard mentioned where he was going next?" I asked.

"I'm afraid I don't remember." Her hands crept toward her back.

Jey's gun snapped into his hand and aimed at the woman. "Don't."

She dashed around the table, heading for the door. Jey fired.

With no armor to protect her, the bullet caught her in the thigh and sent her spilling onto the floor. Still, she scrambled for the door.

I grabbed her with one hand and ran the other over her back, locating a stunner and yanking it from its holster. I tossed it on the table.

The Premier gaped and held up his hands. "I had no part in this!"

"Get back to your meeting." I pointed him toward the door the aide had tried so hard to reach.

He shot for the exit so fast, it was a wonder he didn't run into the door before it had opened wide enough for him to escape through.

Keeping her arms pinned at her sides, I spun her around. "I know you were just following orders, but I suggest you tell me where Merkief went."

She spit on me.

Disgusted, I scowled at the glob of spittle sliding down my shoulder. "Have it your way then."

Merkief was in trouble and I didn't have time for this. Violating our common morals, I forced my way into the woman's mind.

Faces, words, and plans sped past me. A glimpse of Merkief's harried face. I pulled back enough to focus on the surrounding memory. She'd been working in tandem with another agent on Jal, not knowing which planet we'd visit first. She'd asked Merkief to go there next, plying him with fears of Jal rising up against Artor, and had notified her partner when Merkief had Jumped.

I cut the probe and thrust the stunned and mentally battered woman from me. "She sent him into a trap on Jal."

Jey fired again. Her body fell to the floor.

"You have a safe jump point?" I asked.

Jey nodded and flashed me the location.

We arrived in a smooth archway of black stone threaded with thin lines of greens and blues, one of the rare bits of pleasing architecture amidst the stark lines and angles of the Jalvian city. I recognized one of Jey's rough carvings at hip height, lightly knifed into the hard surface.

"Where are we?"

"We're a twenty-minute walk away from the Capitol building."

"Then we should hurry." I followed his loping lead. "Do you think he would have Jumped directly there?"

"Doubt it. He would have used Kazan's point, that restaurant storeroom."

"Let's head there."

"It's on the way," Jey said.

I wished Jal sported similar public transportation to Artor. Other than the people-clogged transparent plaz tunnels suspended high above us to link the towering buildings together, walking on the street was our best option. Most of the population tended to remain in their homeplex if they weren't off conquering someone, or, now that Kazan was in charge, defending the Narvan.

A second of humming was all the warning we had before a wave of electricity hit. Damn stunners. I gritted my teeth and fought the momentary paralysis. With two targets to absorb the wave, the effect was lessened. Jey recovered a second before I did, bowling over a young Jalvian in a military uniform.

Jey hit him once in the jaw, which proved to be enough to daze him. "Who sent you?"

"No one," he said while blinking his eyes rapidly.

"Good, then you won't mind taking us to this no one." Jey put his hand on the man's shoulder and jammed a gun into his ribs. "Start walking."

The towering plex looming in front of us looked like most of the rest of them. Some were taller and others shorter. Most were the blue-grey of stone commonly used for plascrete on Jal. They all shared the same general bulbous shape, rather like a giant rounded shrub on a thick trunk. A few, like this one, had cleaner exteriors with more windows on the living levels. I couldn't imagine how many people lived inside that thing.

Lacking the skills to properly alter their planet as a whole, Jalvians concentrated their efforts on individual structures. Each plex acted as a town of its own.

"Please tell me we're not going in one of those," I said. The thought of being surrounded by so many strangers at once turned my already tight shoulder muscles to stone.

"No," said the young man.

Jey kept a tight hold on the man's shoulder, crushing the blue cloth between his fingers. "How many more watchers?"

"Enough. They'll know you're coming before we get there and I don't even have to be a mindfreak like him to make that happen."

Lucky for this watcher, Jey had him. I let the familiar insult go in light of everything else we were dealing with.

As we turned a corner beyond the shadow of the plex, the restaurant Kazan used for a jump point came into view. Six armed soldiers stood outside. I crossed that off as another compromised jump point.

"We've been expecting you, " said a general decorated with so many medals that he sounded like a chime as he walked out the front door.

I wasn't in the mood to play any diplomatic games in front of bystanders. "Yeah, yeah. You have guns. We have guns. You want something. We want something. Let's go inside before anyone gets hurt, shall we?"

He scowled through his neatly trimmed grey-blond beard. "We would prefer to speak with Kazan."

"So would we, but she's not available right now."

Jey shoved our guide at the line of soldiers as we bore down on the man in the doorway. The soldiers turned to face us as we entered their midst but none of them seemed inclined to fire. They merely watched warily as we went inside. Two of them followed us.

Half-eaten meals and scattered personal belongings attested to the quick evacuation that had recently occurred. The general, in his pale blue uniform, stepped forward. Four additional men rushed to his side, all with their guns aimed at us.

I wondered how many of those medals he'd earned attacking my homeworld. My fingers twitched, aching to tear the shining display off his chest. I saw no sign of Merkief.

"Where is he?" I asked.

"Subdued. Where is Kazan?" From the deeply etched scowl on his face, it appeared he'd never smiled a day in his life.

I recited the same lines I'd given everyone else. The ache within me grew. What was she doing and was she all right?

"Vayen." Jey jabbed me in the side.

I realized the general had said something. Fucking bond. If someone else didn't kill me, the distraction of the damned thing would.

"You're not the first partner to try and usurp Kazan's position. There is a protocol for this, and I'm afraid you're not going to live through it." He signaled for the men to fire.

Jey stepped in front of me. "Wait!"

Bullets pelted his coat, knocking him backward into me as he raised his arms to protect his head. I staggered, trying to keep us both on our feet.

The firing halted.

The general's voice boomed in the sudden silence. "You would protect this Artorian? Stand aside and return Kazan to us. We'll leave your reprimand in her hands."

Jey cast a sideways glance at me. "He's telling the truth. Vayen is only holding her place until she returns. Isn't that right, Vayen?"

"Yes," I said.

While I appreciated his endorsement, the underlying threat he conveyed came through much clearer than I would have liked in front of our audience.

The general motioned for his men to put their weapons away. "I would speak to you for a moment," he said to Jey rather than me.

Jey said, *"You mind? This will probably go much smoother if you let me handle them."*

As much as it pissed me off to lose face in front of a room full of Jalvians, I knew he was right. *"Go ahead."*

Jey followed the officer to the other side of the room where they delved deep into conversation. The soldiers milled about, most of them looking at me like they wished they still had their guns in their hands.

Merkief's voice crept into my head. *"Don't go to Jal."*

"Little late for that. We're already here."

"You found Jey?" he asked.

"And now I found you. Guess I'm not so fucking useless after all."

Merkief grunted.

"You all right?" I asked.

"I think so. They gassed me as soon as I Jumped in."

Good thing they'd realized it was him and not me or they would have happily filled him full of bullets.

"You're not going to like this and I don't have time to explain what little I do know right now, but Kazan screwed with the Council and they put her away for a couple years."

Merkief went so silent I had to nudge his link to make sure I hadn't lost our connection. *"They put me in charge. I'm going to need you if we hope to hold this together until she gets out, so please don't go as berserk as the rest of the Narvan right now."*

I waited for an answer, but all I got was anger and confusion and then he cut contact.

Jey returned. Two of the Jalvian soldiers left through the kitchen doors at the back of the restaurant.

"They went to get Merkief," Jey said.

The general and the rest of his men left through the front door. I prayed Merkief waited to pitch any protests until we were out of Jalvian sight.

"And just what were the two of you talking about?" I asked Jey.

"You might want to be in charge here—"

"It's not a matter of want. The High Council ordered me to be in charge."

He glanced at the door the Jalvians had left through. "Then they won't mind if I'm your emissary to the Jalvian worlds."

This wasn't going at all as I had planned. Then again, what did?

Jey took half a step back but otherwise held his ground. "My people didn't mind Kazan because she's not one of us, neither Artorian or Jalvian. She brought opportunities for challenges and victories. You are the enemy."

"I hardly think so. Didn't we just fight a war together?"

He cocked his head and raised an eyebrow. "Would Artor's Premier bow before me?"

"Point taken. I hope the High and Mighties understand."

"They can't want the Narvan in an uproar anymore than we do. It's not productive."

Merkief, pale and bleary-eyed, stumbled through the kitchen doors. I grabbed his arm to steady him. The soldiers didn't return.

"Get to the ship and sleep that off. Don't use the tank. Jey and I are going to continue putting out fires, and if this day keeps going the way it has, one of us will need the tank far worse than you do."

Merkief gave me a tight nod and Jumped.

Jey and I spent the next sixteen hours diffusing riots on Karin, hunting down six men who were poisoning crops on Artor, and removing three obstinate Sylessians who had managed to shut down the planet's only spaceport. During that, we were shot at four separate times, someone hit us with a pulse blast and ran, a building we'd just met in blew up seconds after we walked out the door, and a smuggler we'd just convinced to return to his more subdued ways on Karin was shot in the head before we could finish our meeting.

Singed, limping, and covered in bruises under our armor, Jey and I Jumped to the ship. Merkief, looking much more himself, met us in the tank room.

"Which one of you goes first?"

Jey pointed at me.

"I'll live. I just need to sleep."

"No, you need to be in top form. We have a lot more days like this one ahead. Get in the tank."

When did Jey become the rational one? I got undressed and laid on the platform. As it began to rise, I looked at the two of them standing there. Either of them could easily kill me in my sleep. What if Kazan had left orders with them? She'd always insisted that I'd turn on her. Surely she'd have planned for that. Who better and closer to leave private orders with?

I tried to sit up but I'd already reached the top of the tank and only had enough space to lift my head. As the platform slid inward over the healing gel, the curved tank wall distorted their faces. Were they talking to one another, plotting against me? Merkief would opt for a pillow over my gel-crusted face. Jey, probably a bullet to the head. Then again, Merkief and I hadn't been on the best of terms lately. I could feel his hands around my throat. I started to yell for them to stop the cycle but thick, warm gel flooded into my mouth. My body grew distant and my eyes drifted closed.

Chapter Twenty-One

As my eyes opened I realized that the conversation Anastassia and I had been having as she lay beside me had been a dream. It wasn't her sitting in the chair beside my bed either. It was Jey.

"What are you doing in here?" I asked.

"I could leave and let you take your chances with Merkief standing over you like I caught him doing twice since we took you out of the tank."

So it was Merkief. I hadn't expected Kazan to ask that of him, but I supposed that made him the best choice. But I was still breathing.

I sat up. "What was he doing?"

"Mumbling to himself, maybe to you, I don't know for sure. He hasn't had much to say in your favor lately. I didn't feel comfortable with him in here while you were lazing about all defenseless."

Jey looked silly sitting in the chair where Anastassia had often sat. The seat was in size with the room, small, and it all but vanished under Jey's armored bulk. It fit her perfectly, probably being original to the time her family had used the ship.

Jey snapped his fingers. "Hey, focus here. I know you have a lot on your mind, but if you go drifting off like you did back on Jal, you're going to get yourself killed."

"When did you become my bodyguard?" I reached for some clean clothes.

"I was thinking more of a partner, actually."

"I—"

"Put your eyeballs back in your head." He chuckled. "Come on, we made a halfway decent team when we were fighting Fragians. Merkief doesn't trust you at the moment, but he trusts me. If I stand by you, he'll have no choice, and we need him."

I couldn't argue with that even though, on some level, I really wanted to. What would my father or Chesser say to know I was seriously considering working side by side with a Jalvian? Not just working with him, we'd been doing that, but trusting him like I trusted Anastassia. And look where that had gotten me. I shook my head. Could partnering with Jey go any worse?

Jey must have taken my shaking head as a signal that I needed more convincing. "Merkief has a bunch of projects going on Artor and Moriek that Kazan had him looking into for the High Council. That's where I sent him off to, by the way. I'm sure they'll want those continued if they haven't already been on your ass about it. Not to mention, I'm the one keeping the Jalvian worlds in line for you."

"Won't this just alienate Merkief further?"

"I like how you didn't say no." He stood. "Go take a shower. We've got work to do."

Somewhere, Anastassia was laughing her head off. She'd wanted us to get along, but partners? Before I made any decisions, I needed to talk to Merkief.

Clean and dressed, I strode out of the bathroom. Jey was waiting right outside the door with his arms crossed.

"No, you're not running off to chat Merkief, we've got bigger problems," he said.

"Who said I was going to Merkief?"

"Contrary to what either of us would like to admit, I do know you." He shook his head. "Let him simmer. Once he sees how hard you're trying to keep the Narvan together, he'll come around. Talking is just going to end up with one of you in the tank. We can't afford that right now."

He had been hanging out with Merkief far more than I had over the past few months. If I was going to work with Jey, I was going to have to start trusting that he also knew what he was talking about outside of battle situations.

"All right then, what's on fire?"

"Marin just doubled the already astronomical price on your head."

I slipped into my usual web of holsters. "That was sloppy

of him."

"I did have to do some digging to get to the source of the increase. He wasn't that sloppy."

"Oh, so you're just that good?"

He grinned. "Exactly."

"Your armor in good shape?"

"Yeah, why?"

"Because Marin and I weren't even on speaking terms when Kazan was around." I slid into my coat and adjusted the slits to line up with the weaponry beneath.

"Something tells me you're just a little bit happy she's not around at this particular moment."

Despite my relief at a valid excuse to get rid of Marin while Anastassia wasn't around to dissuade me, I was pretty sure my work face was firmly in place. "Why would you say that?"

"Kazan made it no secret that you and Marin didn't get along. Why do you think she did his work and visited him on my shift and not yours?"

She'd been with him more frequently than I'd known? She'd been hiding it from me? I wanted to hit something.

"Then there's that little vacation you took at his urging. I'm guessing that's what started it all."

"You still friends with him?" I asked.

"Never was. Just happened that our goals aligned that one time."

"Good." I flashed him the jump point to Marin's office and stepped into the void.

Marin's door was closed. I waved my hand over the sensor. It didn't open. I shot the controls and kicked the door. Another kick loosened it enough to shove it aside on its track. With a gun ready, I burst inside. The room was empty.

Jey arrived just in time to follow me down the hall. He had a gun in his hand and his mouth shut. We made our way to the opposite end of the compound from where our quarters were. I figured if Marin had private rooms, he'd want them as far from his employees as possible.

Electronic eyes slowed our progress.

"There's another one," Jey said as he ducked back around the corner. "If we keep looping around, we'll never get there."

I consulted the snippets of maps of Marin's compound that I'd dug up on in dark corners of various networks.

"There's a security station three turns back and down a level."

"Take out the source?" Jey asked.

"It would beat sneaking around."

"He might have a secondary station somewhere."

"I'll take that chance," I said.

We skirted two bots that went about their business without sounding any audible alarms. When we got to the narrow, grated stairway, another waited at the bottom, its sensors blinking blue and yellow. Without any visible tasks and no actual movement, sentry duty seemed the most logical deduction. I pulled out my pulse pistol and hit it with a light wave. The bot slammed against the wall. Its sensors went dark and the metal shell fell to the floor with a hollow thump.

We'd made it halfway down the stairs when one of Marin's house guards burst from the control room doorway. Bullets sped towards us. I ducked and spun away from Jey, nearly losing my footing on stairs that were clearly designed for shorter feet. Jey turned sideways, ducking low in his coat as he took three stairs at a time. While the guard concentrated his fire on fast-approaching Jey, I shoved the pulse pistol back inside my coat and pulled out a standard one. Seconds later, my bullet sank into the guard's forehead.

Jey whipped around. "I had him."

I shrugged. "Check the room."

He pressed himself against the wall and poked his head inside for a split second before glancing back at me. "Empty."

"Only one guard? I'd expected Marin to be a little more paranoid."

Jey smirked. "Maybe he expected you to be a little less audacious."

"Like no one else has ever considered going after him here?"

I ducked into the room and fired several rounds into the vid system. No one else needed to see what I was about to do.

Jey followed me down the corridor. Now that we didn't have to worry about someone watching the feed and sounding an alarm, our path to Marin's private quarters was far more direct.

"He does have quite a reputation," Jey whispered.

"So do we."

At the next turn, I halted and signaled for Jey to stay back. Two female slaves strode past, laughing quietly. We waited until we couldn't hear them before trying the corridor again. This time it was empty.

There weren't any maps of this section of the compound, but I had a fairly good idea that one of the three rooms at the end of the corridor contained Marin. The slaves had to have come from one of them and I doubted Marin let people, even his, roam about in his personal spaces without supervision.

Jey nodded toward the doors. "Which one?"

"Middle." If I was wrong and set something off, Marin would likely come running and that would make killing him even easier.

We stepped into the main corridor. Nothing sprang from the ceiling, no flashing lights, or blaring sirens. I couldn't detect anything on the wall that might indicate sensor beams. The women hadn't appeared to walk in any particular pattern. The floor stayed solid beneath us. I took each step slowly, just waiting for a spray of bullets or a face full of gas.

I turned to Jey. "Go back to the corner and wait there."

He scowled. "Why?"

"If he's got some sort of trap in there, I'd rather you weren't stuck in it too."

"I don't like it, but all right." He dropped back. "Yell when you need me to march in and save your ass."

I left him behind and hoped I wouldn't need exactly that. I'd never hear the end of it.

The door in the middle opened like any other. No blades swooped down from the ceiling. No guards stood waiting. Instead, I was greeted with clean air and one of Marin's shirts draped over a chair beside a small table. An assortment of weaponry hung on the wall to my left, all rather artfully displayed and some behind clear plaz cases. A couch, two chairs, the table, a pair of boots in the corner, it looked like any other common room. Three closed doors, one on each wall, offered more options. I caught the sound of running water. A bathroom?

Flat against the wall, I waited.

The door opened with a muffled snick. A boot. The bottom corner of a long armored coat. A hand. An arm. A chest. I aimed above the shoulders. A nose. A jaw. I fired.

The body crumpled to the burgundy carpet. Blood flowed from the bullet hole just behind his ear. Then I got a good look at his face.

It wasn't Marin. I recognized the man as one of the Guild Assassins. Dammit!

Heavy footsteps pounded with my pulse. The door beside the bathroom opened. Hoping to get information from whoever it was if I was wrong again, I aimed for the chest and fired.

Wearing only a pair of pants, Marin stood staring at me, his mouth hanging open. Blood oozed from the hole in his chest. He sagged against the doorframe of the bedroom and slid down the molding to sit on the carpet.

"How did you get in here?" he asked between heaving breaths.

The same way anyone could get into one of our homes or the ship. I'd simply Jumped and walked and shot. All it took was one compromised jump point and someone could take me out as I left the bathroom or walked into the common room. Even a fully trained assassin could be caught unaware in an environment he considered safe.

I fired again. Blood dripped from the corner of his mouth as he gasped, coughing.

Kess knew my office on Rok. Geva knows what jump points I might have inadvertently revealed to Deep Voice's tracer or when Shoulders had probed my drugged mind. I'd been so intent on not revealing the ship and tank that I'd not considered that they might glean other points from me. They could have Fa'yet's house, all of ours, my family home, my favorite spots, any of our work jump points. Every damn one of them could be compromised.

Unless I planned to hole up on the ship for the next two years, the moment I lost favor with the High and Mighties, I could be Marin, dying on the floor of his own common room, wearing only a pair of pants.

Sweat ran down my forehead. I lowered the gun.

Marin's head hung forward, his chin propped on his bloody chest, cocked at an angle so his one eye watched me walk toward him. He coughed again. A horrible, wet, racking cough. Pink, bubbly spittle dripped from his lips to his shoulder. We stared at each other for a long moment. I had nothing to say, and it seemed he wasn't up to speaking. His body heaved twice and then went limp.

Not wanting to take any chances, I knelt down and checked his pulse.

Dead.

I counted to a hundred and checked again.

Still dead. No tricks. No medical miracles would save him. I'd expected this to be harder, that he'd have more defenses, that there would be some impressive showdown between us, a match of equal skills. But he was flesh and bone like everyone else. And so was I.

I shoved the gun back in the holster. There were several large contracts for Marin's link or proof of his death. Looking down at him, I realized the bigger insult would be not to cash him in at all. Let his death pass unmentioned. I didn't need his credits, nor did I want to advertise that I'd just killed Anastassia's lover. Deep Voice probably wouldn't like that huge roadblock in his plans to keep Anastassia and I bound together.

I contacted Jey. "It's done."

"That was easy."

I shivered. Would someone say the same thing about me?

"We're going to the ship to wait for Merkief. I want the three of us to stick together from now on." I Jumped before he could say a word.

Kazan's office sat just outside the door to the tank room. I stepped in and locked the door.

Killing Marin may have protected Anastassia, but would she forgive me? Telling her what Kess had confided could either help my case or turn her away if she didn't believe me. Did I want to take the chance of her never speaking to me again? That is, if learning I'd killed Marin didn't do the job already.

There should have been a feeling of relief. He was gone. He'd never manipulate her again. Yet, my skin crawled and my hands shook.

I reached into my coat and sought out the silver flask I'd not touched in a long time. The top unscrewed with the twist of a finger.

Anastassia's chair offered little comfort as I settled into it. With Jey close by and secure in my only safe-haven, I dared take a drink of the potent, foul smelling liquor. Heat streamed down my throat.

My hands shook a bit less when I raised the flask a second time. By the time it was empty, I didn't notice my hands at all. Or much of anything else. My eyes drifted closed.

My bedroom was too far away. The desktop looked comfortable enough. I shoved the terminal aside and rested my head on my arms.

Behind my eyelids, Marin looked up at me from the floor. Dried blood around his mouth cracked and flaked onto his chest as he grinned.

"Be careful," he said, and then he laughed.

The sound went on and on, rolling down the empty halls as I ran, repeating through the mirrored bots that whirred around my head, echoing into a thunderous roar that I couldn't escape. I woke in a cold sweat to find the lights had gone out and the door was still locked.

My link assured me of Merkief and Jey's presence nearby. My nerves needed to settle before I was ready to face either of them. The only way I could think of to find some measure of solid footing was to make sure I remained in the Council's favor. I sank deep into my link, contacting anyone I could that I even considered might be able to assist me. Working through them, I subdued a small portion of the chaos Kazan had unleashed upon the Narvan.

❧

I'd been at the helm for two months and yet the Narvan remained only half under control. Too many small pockets of mischief and destruction plagued the populace. Kazan's safety net had certainly lived up to her expectations.

Running the Narvan, even without her mess, wasn't easy. Anastassia's perpetual pinched and distracted demeanor made complete sense now. However, she'd brought the Narvan together in layers, building up her juggling routine over a matter of years. The Council had thrown all her balls at me in a day and now they were also on fire and covered in spikes. I needed more help before I ended up damaging my implant again.

I'd been avoiding Fa'yet. Nothing that had sprung up seemed incited by him. He'd been at Kazan's trial. He knew I could never do what Deep Voice had insinuated. But he'd also not stood up to defend me, or her, nor had he offered to help me after the fact. Maybe he was waiting for me to come to him.

I cautiously opened my link to him. *"Can we talk?"*

"Not a good time."

"I could really use your help."

"I'm not working against you. Leave me alone." He cut contact.

I put my head in my hands. Anastassia had said he was the most dependable man she knew. After all he'd done for me, I'd thought so too. But it seemed we were both wrong. Gemmen,

Merkief, and now Fa'yet. When I needed friends, Geva laughed in my face and gave me Jey.

Just when I thought my day couldn't get any worse, I got a summons from the High and Mighties. I let Jey know I'd be on Sere and to get some rest while I was gone. If trouble meant to find me there, having him around wouldn't do a damn bit of good.

When I arrived at the jump point, one of the grey-suits detached himself from his post to escort me to a meeting room I'd not visited before. Not that the venue made much of a difference. The contents were much as I expected—a single chair, three cloaked figures and two more grey-suits, one of which closed the door behind me.

An unfamiliar voice said, "You've done well. We are pleased with your progress."

"Glad to hear it, but I doubt you brought me in for compliments."

Deep Voice made himself known. "Are you enjoying your promotion?"

"Enjoying is not the word that comes to mind. And it's more of a temporary position, isn't it?"

"That depends," he said.

A chill ran up my spine. "On what?"

The third cloaked figured snarled, "Whether she cooperates."

Why did the woman have to be so obstinate? Geva only knew what she would sink to just to cause the High Council grief.

Deep Voice said, "We require your assistance with Kazan."

I could see her or maybe talk to her? The bond surged with energy. "Of course."

"Your willingness to cooperate will go on record."

I'd barely comprehended his words before a sharp prick on the back of my neck registered. The room went black.

When I woke, I was alone. Dark walls blurred in and out of focus. My stomach heaved. The High and Mighties were fortunate that I'd been too busy lately to eat anything beyond Anastassia's stock of meal bars or my gift would have been more significant. My legs trembled as I got to my feet. What the hells had they done to me? I racked my foggy mind for any clues but came up empty. The room spun. I grabbed the chair to keep my balance.

Jey's frantic voice infiltrated my foggy head. *"Where are you?*

Are you all right?"

"Kryon business. Sorry, I didn't expect to drop off the radar. I'm fine."

"Great Geva, man, don't do that."

It may have been the residual effects of whatever the Council had done to me, but I found his blatant concern amusing. *"I'm going to need to sleep."*

"Whatever you need, just let me know."

I wished Anastassia was there to witness Jey being worried over me, to see us working together and how surprisingly well that was going. Maybe she'd have some insight on how to pull Merkief back in.

I Jumped back to the ship and dropped into bed fully armed and in my coat. Like every other night, I forced myself to focus on work until my mind gave up and surrendered to sleep. It wasn't working. Anastassia permeated every thought, no matter how hard I tried. Exhausted and still feeling ill, I fell into a restless sleep.

Chapter Twenty-Two

Anastassia called my name, sometimes far away, sometimes near, but I couldn't find her. I ran through the fog, passing shadowed corners of buildings and faces of people I'd known throughout my life. No one would help me no matter how desperately I begged. Her pain flooded my mind. I had to find her. I had to get her to the tank.

"Anastassia!" I shouted her name over and over, not caring who heard me or what they might think.

The fog cleared just enough to reveal her silhouette lying on the ground. Her back was to me. She started to roll over.

"Vayen?" Her voice was all wrong.

I froze, afraid to step closer.

"Vayen, wake up."

Then I saw her face. Blank. Empty. A featureless plain.

A gagging shriek came from my mouth.

Her hand stretched out, her arm grew impossibly long, distorted and thin. She shook my shoulder.

"Vayen!"

My eyes flew open, and I jerked upright. Merkief scrambled backward. The lights came on, blinding me for a moment. My heart threatened to burst through my chest. I slid off the bed and grabbed a gun from inside my coat.

The last time he'd been caught in my room, Jey had made it sound like Merkief was considering offing me. He'd been helping us, but maintaining an awkward distance since Anastassia's sentencing. I'd been keeping Jey beside me and delegating other tasks to Merkief to attend to in person where we felt it was safe or by link. With all of us working long shifts, I'd resorted to sleeping on the ship as I had when I'd been alone with Anastassia before all nine hells had broken loose.

But now, after two months of the unspoken alliance we'd settled into, Merkief was again lurking in my room. Had he just been biding his time, working up his nerve?

"Where's Jey? What are you doing in here?"

Merkief held out his empty hands. "Jey's asleep. You've been working the man to near death. You must not be far behind. You've been out for a couple shifts."

I couldn't afford to miss an entire day of work, there was too much to do. What had Deep Voice and his friends done to me to sap that much energy?

"Why were you in here?"

"You were making a lot of noise. I came in to make sure you were all right."

"If you just came in, why were the lights off?"

His gaze dropped to the floor.

I slid off the bed and kept the gun on him. "What did she order you to do to me?"

Merkief's shoulders sagged. "Something I couldn't bring myself to do."

"Not even after three chances? I find that hard to believe. You've always followed her orders before, even when they were unpleasant."

"Would you rather I killed you in your sleep? She figured that would be the easiest route. No talking me out of it that way."

"Seems I didn't have to do any talking."

He glared. "Did you kill her?"

"No. I told you the truth."

"Not all of it. You're hiding something. You were avoiding me before she disappeared. That was plenty of time to plan her demise and devise your convincing cover story," he said.

"I'm glad you think it's convincing. It's real. Not that the damned High and fucking Mighties did me any favors with it. She'll likely be right with you and reaming your ass for not killing me."

He straightened himself and dropped his hands to his sides. "Why would she want to do that if what you said is true?"

I didn't like the way his hand lingered next to the slit in his coat that allowed instant access to his pulse pistol. "Because they lied to her."

He shook his head slowly. "You've told the lie so many times, you believe it yourself."

He stared right at me, daring me to shoot him as he pulled out his pulse pistol.

"Dammit, I didn't hurt her. I wouldn't."

"Not even for the Narvan?" His finger slid along the trigger.

"I didn't ask for this!"

"But you just happened to end up with her position anyway," he said.

I didn't want to shoot him, but I didn't really want to take a pulse blast either. The only thing that would convince him was the one truth I didn't want to admit. Not out loud. Not to anyone. I'd been doing a fine job of burying it with work.

"I'm bonded to her, you idiot. Put the damn gun down."

His mouth hung open. "And you have the nerve to call me an idiot?"

"Yes, well." I nodded at his gun.

He put it away. "That explains why you're turning into Jey."

"I most certainly am not!"

He raised a single brow and nodded. "So why were you avoiding me?"

"Because, you stupid jealous woman, you know me too damn well. I knew you'd pick up on the bond before I was ready to talk to Kazan about it."

"Talk about it, surely she knows if you allowed the bond to form?"

"She left before we had a chance to discuss it." I sat down on the edge of the bed. "Not a word of this to Jey."

Merkief shook his head. "You bonded to her without her concent? That was..." He waved his hands in the air and shook his head again. "I don't envy you in the least."

"Thanks." Now that that was out in the open, maybe our friendship had a hope of recovering. "You up for some work?"

He made a passing attempt at a friendly smile. "I suppose we could give Jey a day off. If you don't mind me at your back instead?"

"Yeah, we're good." At least I hoped we were. I needed them both and we had a long way to go before Anastassia's return.

❦

Jey strode into the office of the Artor house. He stood there with his arms crossed over his chest.

I finished going over a list of recommendations regarding the new Premier of Moriek before putting the datapad down. "What?"

"Look, I know you're busy. Managing the Jalvian worlds has kept me overwhelmed in addition to all the bullet dodging, tank time and keeping up on our Kryon work. How Kazan managed all this on her own is beyond me."

"She had reliable contacts and the planetary leaders in her pockets, I, we, don't have that luxury." I raked my fingers through my unbound hair. "And if you hadn't heard yet, Kess was so kind as to take credit for killing Marin."

Jey dropped into the chair across from my desk. "We took Marin out over a year ago. How's he angling that?"

"From what I can tell, he's been quietly building the business, and he's only now up and openly running again." I wanted to slap myself for leaving Marin to rot and destroying the security records. "He's taken over the complex, which also means he's got a solid hold on Twelve."

"Is he threatening us?"

"Not yet."

But lording over a gaggle of assassins was a far cry from Kryon work. I doubted Kess would be satisfied for long.

"Then don't worry about him right now," said Jey. For sounding like blowing Kess off, he still looked concerned. "You're going to burn your implant out again if you keep up this pace. The Narvan and the Council can do without you for a couple days."

"Days? Are you insane? Karin and Syless are in a major dispute over the price of fleet upgrades. There's some damned crop blight on Frique that Merkief is covertly trying to solve with a team of Artorian scientists but if they're discovered, that will blow up in our faces. We've got two ongoing Kryon contracts, and I have a meeting on Sere in six hours. Then I've got Artor's—"

Jey held up a hand and shook his head. "When was the last time you had a meal that wasn't in bar form or took a shower that lasted more than two minutes?"

"I don't know," I shooed him away. "Get out of here. I have work to do."

"Vayen, we've got the Narvan under control and the Fragians are quietly licking their wounds. Those couple small colonization groups we've sent out haven't reported any major mishaps and you said that has the Council pacified for now. We've completed enough Kryon contracts in the past year to put even Kazan in awe. Put the damned Council meeting off for a couple days and get cleaned up. Enjoy some real food. Find some pretty little Artorian and have a good mind fuck or whatever it is that you do. But for Geva's sake, sleep. You look half dead."

Sleep wasn't an option, not beyond the few hours it took to overcome exhaustion, unless there was a suitable amount of mind-numbing alcohol involved. Every time I closed my eyes, Anastassia was there, whispering. I couldn't hear what she was saying. I couldn't touch her. All I knew was that she was in pain and that there wasn't a damn thing I could do about it.

Sleep left me angry, frustrated, and surging with energy that wanted nothing more than to destroy whatever or whoever was hurting her. But I couldn't, so I burned that energy doing contracts and turning demands back on generals, premiers, officials, board members, primes, councils and any other self-serving fuck who wanted something from me. Concentrating on work kept the bond buried deep inside where it couldn't be a distraction.

"No." I picked up the datapad.

He slammed his hands on the desktop and stood, leaning low to put his face right in front of mine. "We need a break. All of us. Even Kazan took breaks now and then."

She did. She went to see Marin. And they argued or they... I thrust the thought away. He was dead and she would learn that when she returned. And I'd have to live with her reaction. Hopefully live with it.

I took a deep breath and let it out. She spent time on Frique, remembering her family, basking in the sun and the shadows of the trees. But her family was gone and the sun was hot and trees were just trees without her to smile up at them.

She also visited the Verian station. The bond sent a jolt through me. The one to blame for this fucking mess, he was on that station. He'd taken her away from me. I could find him and make sure he never drove her to insane behavior again.

"Two days. Verian station. We're leaving now."

Jey stepped back and laughed uneasily. "See that wasn't so hard. You do plan on resting, right?" He retreated to the doorway.

"You don't look like you're thinking about resting."

"Have all the fun you want on the station, just remember that it's Kazan's home, so don't fuck it up for her by causing any trouble."

I took a moment to access the station through my link. "You now both have your own quarters. Enjoy them and leave me alone."

"I'll let Merkief know." Jey stood there a second longer as if he were about to say something more but then gave me a quick nod and left.

❧

Anastassia's room on the station greeted me with sterile coolness. The station's cleaning bots had done their work. Not a single hair, fingerprint or faint scent of her lingered. Her clothes, clean and pressed, hung in the closet. A few trinkets and a couple uncut Artorian firestones sat on the table beside her bed. Everything in its place. Everything but her. I closed the door and headed out.

The station's occupants cast curious glances as I wandered the corridors. I didn't even know who I was looking for. After half an hour, every man became a target of suspicion. Maybe Strauss had an answer. I made my way to the medical clinic.

A woman in a green uniform met me just inside the door. "How can I help you?"

I strode past her to Strauss's office. It was empty. How did he manage to be in every time Anastassia popped in, but the one time I did, he was out?

Spinning around, I addressed the woman, "Where's Strauss?"

Her gaze darted around as if searching for help. "He's not in at the moment."

"No shit. Where is he?"

"You'll have to come back later, sir."

It occurred to me to check the station network to locate his quarters. Why hadn't I thought of checking his schedule beforehand? Fucking distracting bond. I stormed out of the facility and down the corridor.

The doctor's quarters were two levels up, but only minutes away thanks to the lift system. By the time I reached his door, a local member of station security was striding down the hall toward me. That damned meddling woman must have summoned him.

Strauss opened his door before company arrived. He peered around me.

"She's not here," I said. "Can I come in?"

The doctor caught sight of security coming up behind me. "Is there a problem?" he asked the uniformed man.

The guard glanced from Strauss to me. "I don't know, is there?"

I stood a good two feet over the little Verian, glaring down at him. "There might be if you don't get lost."

"He's the friend of a friend. I'm sure he'll behave." Strauss gave me a pointed look. "Won't you?"

The station network revealed that two more men were on their way. Talking my way out of killing Marin and maybe even Strauss was one thing, but causing a scene and the danger of possible witnesses was really pushing my luck.

"Of course."

"Good, then come in," Strauss said.

He stepped back and closed the door once I was inside. The retreating footsteps I expected to hear outside didn't happen.

"He's still out there." Damn witnesses restricting my actions.

"I don't doubt it." Strauss smiled weakly. "So to what do I owe this unexpected visit?"

"Anastassia has been busy lately but she didn't want anyone to worry about her long absence. I know she frequently visits you. Is there anyone else I should notify?"

"Why couldn't she tell me herself? She's always sent personal messages before. Is she all right?"

"Yes."

Though she hadn't been the last time I'd seen her and the Council said she hadn't been cooperating, so it only stood to reason, she'd be even less all right after that. My teeth ground together.

Strauss frowned and his eyes narrowed. "If you're one of her bodyguards, and she's so busy, why aren't you with her?"

"She's safe enough for now." At least I hoped she was. "The three of us are taking a short break, a vacation of sorts."

"I see," he said, though he didn't look all that convinced.

I hoped he'd lunge at me or something so I'd have a valid excuse to snap his stick-like back. Instead he remained like a small frightened animal, frozen in place.

"You might let the Commander know. His children are quite

attached to her. I don't know who else."

"No one else comes to mind? I wouldn't want anyone to worry," I said.

"No, sorry."

Dammit. Strauss wasn't concerned enough to convince me that it was his safety that compelled Anastassia to rush off. But I had been sure he was the one who could have led me to Anastassia's precious *him*. Now all I had to show for my efforts was security on my ass.

"Thank you. I'll let the Commander know." I gave him an obligatory nod and left.

As I made my way to the Commander's quarters with my not-so-discrete escort in tow, I dug into Strauss's files on the station network. Like my visit, my search gained me nothing. Whatever was between him and Anastassia, it was off the record.

The Station Commander gave me the same accusing look as everyone else upon hearing of Anastassia's absence. He swallowed my words with visible reserve, and even more aggravating, he offered no further clues as to anyone else I should talk to on her behalf.

I walked back to my quarters, glaring at any man who dared meet my gaze. Once inside, I heard my tail leave. As if the station were any safer just because my door was closed. Even if they had my door sensor flagged for activity, didn't they realize I could Jump to Strauss's quarters now that I'd been there and had a good look around? I could put a bullet in his head while he slept and no one would know for hours. Of course, they'd suspect me and maybe they'd have vid feed if he was paranoid enough to have surveillance. Was it worth it?

I rubbed my hands over my face. Maybe Jey was right. I needed sleep. That, at least, might help me think more clearly.

In order for sleep to have any hope of being restful, I reached for my flask. It came right out of my pocket, still empty from the last time. I swore and tossed it at the table.

Anastassia had to keep something on hand here. I rummaged through the tiny kitchen and came up with a couple bottles of her favorite Friquen red. I didn't bother with a glass. When the second bottle was empty, I fell into my bed and closed my eyes.

Sleep must have come because I woke to discover nine hours had passed. Though I didn't recall any dreams of Anastassia, I didn't feel rested. I sat up and rubbed my eyes. Throwing the blankets aside, I swung my legs over the edge of the bed and contemplated how I was going to get my exhausted ass through another day. As usual, nothing more viable than a stim came to mind. I opened my tin and popped one in my mouth. Sweet and chalky, it went down with a single swallow. Moments later the tingle of energy I'd come to associate with waking up, flooded through me.

I went about my usual routine, getting dressed, checking weapons and ammo and stocking my coat. Then I remembered I was supposed to be resting. How was I supposed to do that? I sighed and took off my coat and clothes and went to stand in the shower for twenty minutes. The hot water didn't make me feel any cleaner or make my neck and shoulders any less tense.

Unarmed and unarmored I went down a level to find something to eat. Sitting alone, I ate a plate of gummy noodles and bitter Verian vegetables that the woman at the food counter had recommended. The whole time I shoved food into my mouth, all I could think of was that Anastassia probably would have liked it and that I was an idiot for trying to fit in on the station like she did. Whether I had a gun and armor on or not, I didn't belong. Her people tolerated me when she was around, but without her shadow to mask me, they knew I was trouble and I could feel them all watching me. They knew she wasn't there and they blamed me. I couldn't take another two days of this.

With my coat and weapons back in hand, I Jumped to my new office on Rok. There was nothing there to remind me of Anastassia. Surrounded by my Cragtek staff I felt safe enough to get some work done while still allowing Jey and Merkief their time off.

The first day went well enough with me checking in periodically with Jey and concentrating on reports from my contacts, Cragtek business, and overseeing meditations between Karin and Syless through my link.

When my eyes begged to close, I stretched out on my couch and let them. That respite didn't last long and without my usual tight schedule to keep me on track and otherwise occupied, I couldn't escape my own mind.

How was I going to get Anastassia to forgive me for killing Marin? As long as I'd been working for her, I'd been told they were frequently fighting. If that was the case, why did she bother with him? The things I had glimpsed in her head the last time we'd had sex flashed through my mind. She desired physical contact of the sort I wasn't able to provide. Maybe she simply needed another option that she trusted. I could provide what she liked... if I got the procedure.

I'd already screwed myself with giving Anastassia my Joining gift. With her not being Artorian, we'd never secure proper clearance for reproduction, her rights as a full citizen, or an officially acknowledged joining. However, with the Artorian Premier currently in my pocket, pulling a few strings wasn't out of the question. I felt myself smiling for the first time since Anastassia's trial.

Two hours after telling the Premier how this was going to happen whether he and his all-interfering staff of genetic trackers liked it or not, and also after placing a generous sum of credits in the account of a certain member of the board of review for the genetic reproduction correction procedure, I arrived at the designated fortress-like clinic. My genetic code had made the green list.

The smiling receptionist blithely went over the required forms, verifying that everything was stamped, properly coded, and approved by the review board. She then led me to a room and informed me that I was to undress and someone would be with me shortly.

The damned procedure itself was kept under lock and key so all I knew was that I was about to be knocked out and would wake up with everything as it should have been if some long-dead geneticists hadn't fucked with my genes. The being unconscious part made my neck tense even further, but I'd left some heavy threats with the Premier, so I felt fairly assured that nothing untoward would happen to me while I was out.

Undressed and wearing only the thin, white robe they'd left for me, I sat on the bed in the middle of the room. I greeted the woman wearing green medical staff clothing when she entered but got nothing more than a standard reply. Her uninterested gaze attested to a lack of recognition. I tried to relax as she administered an anesthetic.

A cold numbness invaded my body as her smile loomed over my face. "See you in a few hours," she said in a deep, slow voice.

The room faded away.

❧

I woke to the same woman flipping through my file.

"Oh, good, you're awake," she said. "I'll be back in half an hour to sign off on your documents."

She left me alone in the room smelling of antiseptics. Her clicking footsteps faded down the hall. I lifted the sheet and parted the robe. Nothing looked different. Nothing felt different. I put the robe back in place and ran my fingertips over my scalp. Nothing. A search of my neck and face yielded the same. Frustrated, I got to my feet, pulled off the robe and ran my hands over my entire body. Not a cut, stitch, scrape, bruise or even sore spot.

"You won't find anything," she said from the doorway where she stood holding her shoes in her hands. She walked in and slipped her shoes back on. "Sorry, couldn't resist. You all do the search. It never gets old, though this view is more impressive than most." She winked as she removed my clothes from a cabinet on the other side the room and handed them to me.

Annoyed with her attention, I dressed in record time.

"You won't notice any results for the first thirty-six hours. After that, some swelling may occur." She smirked.

I glared at her.

She cleared her throat. "You will encounter new sensations, don't be alarmed. These are normal and not something to call your personal doctor about. Please be aware that you are now able to procreate and should take the necessary precautions if a child is not the desired outcome of your activities."

The woman picked up my file and checked it again. "Looks like everything is in order. I'll see that this gets filed for you. Go home and enjoy." She smiled and wandered out of the room.

Home. I Jumped to the house on Artor and let Merkief and Jey know where I was. Merkief arrived minutes later but I was already in my room. With Anastassia gone, any hope of enjoyment was still almost another year away, but at least I'd be prepared. Only Geva knew how I was going to make it that long with the distraction of the unacknowledged bond looming over my every breath. The heavy workload, daily stim use and drinking myself to sleep were already taking their toll. I didn't want to consider what the rest of my life would look like if she outright refused me.

Chapter Twenty-Three

A summons from the High Council hit my link with the force
of a hammer on my skull. I'd been waiting for this day, a tiny ray
of what I prayed would be light to lead me out of the tunnel I'd
walled myself into in order to survive. It was time to face Anastassia and her imminent accusations, to deal with the bond, and to
somehow avoid a war over who'd be advising the Narvan.

I contacted Merkief. *"I'm going to get her. I want both of you
to meet us on the ship."*

His elation hit me hard. I wasn't the only one who had been
waiting anxiously for this day.

*"I'll do my best to keep Jey back so you have some time with
her,"* he said.

"Thanks."

The ship was her safe place and I hoped it and having Merkief and Jey on hand would give me the chance to explain things
before she tried to kill me.

I Jumped to Sere and made my way to the room I'd been
assigned. Two cloaked High Council members. One guard, who
closed the door behind me. One chair. I sat and got comfortable,
quite used to this routine by now.

"Where is she?"

A female voice said, "You've done well with what you have
been given. We are pleased."

"Glad to hear it. Where is she?" I wanted a full night's sleep
and a morning without a stim. I needed Anastassia back working

beside me.

The second figure stepped forward. Deep Voice. "You have been quite cooperative. Some would say, far more so than your predecessor."

"You didn't really leave me much choice. And what do you mean, predecessor? She *is* coming back."

Deep Voice said, "We're satisfied with your performance."

"So you've said. Repeatedly. I'd be satisfied if you gave me Anastassia. Right now."

"You may want to reconsider," said the woman. "Would you truly be willing to hand over the Narvan after all you've done to gain control of it? We've noted the programs you've created, negotiations, the colonization efforts, your handling of the conflict with the Fragians, coordinating trade routes with other system advisors, and the contracts you've completed. The system has never run so efficiently. Your people are flourishing under your control. We would see them continue to do so."

I gripped the arms of my chair to keep from lunging at them. "You bonded me to her. You made me want her back. You have no idea of the torture you've put me through."

"There's a simple solution for that, Mr. Ta'set. Accept the Narvan permanently, and we'll see that you suffer no longer."

It was hard to speak past my heart beating madly in my throat. "You know I can't agree to that."

I had worked hard and I couldn't lie and say their compliments had fallen on deaf ears, not when I knew what they'd said was true. The results of what I'd accomplished were plain to see.

Did I really love her or was that the bond talking? The bond I hadn't wanted, but having tasted it, didn't want to give up? Was that the addict in me talking?

Maybe I had been deluding myself this whole time about the viability of working things out with Anastassia. Even if real feelings were involved, did it matter in the grand scope of things? My people were thriving, and Jey and I could continue to do so much more for them with the resources the Council allowed. Anastassia had her own ideas and plans for the future. She'd left me. She'd run off to defend some other man, leaving me with a nest of seething chaos.

"We fully endorse going forward with your current partnership. You've worked well together. Having both of you at the head of the Narvan has brought a unity the system has not seen

in centuries. All you need to do is stand up and walk out the door."
Deep Voice said.

The High Council had two years to build on the lies they'd
planted during her trial. If Anastassia already had decided to kill
me, she wouldn't give me a chance to explain. I knew how she
was when her mind was made up. She'd been the one to launch
the damned safety net in the first place. People had suffered and
died; the very same people she'd sworn to protect. For the sake of
the Narvan, would walking out of this meeting alone be the wiser
move?

She left the Narvan. I didn't take it from her. I earned this.

I stood. My entire body clenched not unlike being hit with a
stunner. I dropped back into the seat and cursed the idiot fore-
fathers that altered our genetics to include the fucking bond. I
wanted to rip the arms off the chair and beat the High and Mighties with them.

Even after all I'd done, all I'd been through in the past couple
years, I still wasn't strong enough.

"Give me Anastassia."

Deep Voice let out a loud sigh. "You're sure?"

"I am."

He raised his hand. A hidden door opened on the wall to
my right. Two grey-suits entered with a sagging figure strung
between them.

The clothes she'd worn when I'd last seen her had been
replaced by a grey suit, the same as worn by her escorts. Hair
hung in her face.

I sprang from my seat and ran to her. What had they done?

The Council's zombies let her go. She teetered on her feet. I
grabbed her before she fell.

Anastassia looked up, her hair parting to reveal sunken eyes.
Her face was lined anew, and the old lines deeper.

My breath caught in my throat. "Anastassia?"

Her voice was hoarse. "Am I dead, too?"

I shook my head and held on to her arms, hoping she'd regain
her balance while basking in the relief of having her in my hands.

Tears trickled down her gaunt cheeks. "But you are."

"I'm pretty sure I'm not."

Though, after seeing what had been done to her, I formed a
quick list of those who would be dead before the day was out. I'd
start with those in this room. I pulled Anastassia against me and

yanked a gun out of my coat with my free hand.

"Before you ruin everything you've done, you may want to Jump her to that tank of yours," Deep Voice said as if the fact I had a gun in his face didn't matter in the least.

If Anastassia knew where to find the damned High and Mighties, I'd get it from her. Then I'd make sure they all paid for what they'd done. I put the gun away. It took me a moment to formulate a Jump for both of us due to Anastassia's current state. It was a far cry from the image I'd held in my mind.

A bolt of pain threatened to rip my head in half. I gasped and covered my ears with my hands in a feeble effort to block the deafening wail in my head and the white hot rod that I swore protruded from my skull. On my knees and sapped of strength, I realized I'd dropped Anastassia. She sat next to me with her head in her hands, rocking back and forth.

After ten minutes, the pain subsided enough that I dared access my link. Dead. I tried reaching Merkief by our natural speech. Nothing.

A third cloaked Council member stood over me. "I wouldn't recommend trying to Jump again until I give you permission."

The cloak fell to the floor to reveal what lay underneath. "Do you understand?" The voice came from a small black box strapped to the upper end of a seven-foot tall blue-shelled creature.

"You have Kazan to thank for this demonstration. We felt it fitting that since she was the reason for the need, she should help with the development." The unveiled High and Mighty cocked a blue shelled protrusion that I guessed to be its head.

Though it walked on four legs and from its chest hung a pair of long, thin arms each bearing a single claw, it stood much the same as anyone else. I wondered what other unknown races the Council's cloaks hid. I got to my feet and stood between it and Anastassia.

It pointed a blue claw at me. "Should you Jump to our home to attempt to commit the murders I see behind your eyes, you will fall to the floor, writhing in pain. Our servants will scoop you up and deliver you to us so that we can cause more."

With a deafening snap, a pair of transparent wings edged with barbed tips sprang from its back. They arched forward, encasing me and drawing me toward its body. My face rammed against the hard shell, the rough surface scraping my cheek. A thick, yellow liquid oozed from the wings, burning where it touched the bare skin of my face, neck, and hands. The barbs pressed into my coat with a vice-like force, driving the armor into my flesh at each pinpoint tip.

Its voice vibrated through the shell pressed against my ear. "We will not tolerate another such incident as the one Kazan brought upon us. Should you think that you may be able to tolerate such pain, through whatever means, you will also be unable to Jump to freedom. Each attempt will only double what you felt just now. It is not a matter of pain, but a field that disables your link and anything other than standard brain function. Do you understand?"

I managed to hiss, "Yes," through clenched teeth.

The pressure of the barbs eased on my back. "You will do well to warn your employees of our security advancements should they also feel any urge for retaliation."

The wings opened, allowing fresh air into my lungs. The creature backed away, shaking out its wings, or jaws, whatever they were. Yellow ooze splattered onto the floor.

I stood, shuddering, dripping with burning slime, afraid to move for fear the thing would wrap me up, pulverize me with its barbs, digest me, and spit my bones upon the carpet.

"You have control of the Narvan. Do not let Kazan endanger your position." It flapped its wings once more before snapping them down and inward against its back. "You may go." The thing disappeared, and with it, the pressure in my head.

When the others had left, I wasn't sure, but Anastassia and I were alone. The burning sensation on my skin eased with each passing moment. I scooped Anastassia up and formed the Jump to the ship with no small amount of hesitation.

The welcome sight of the tank room's bright lights beckoned as I stepped from the void.

Jey ran to my side. "Kazan?"

Anastassia kept her face buried in my coat and her arms wrapped around her chest. Her entire body trembled.

I knocked him aside, dashed to the platform and laid her on it. As I made quick work of removing the suit, Jey attached himself to me again. So much for Merkief keeping him back.

"What in Geva's name did they do to her?" Jey asked.

"A long experiment. Now back off." I shoved him away.

On the platform, Anastassia curled into a tight ball with her back to me. Bones protruded where there had been muscle.

I nodded to Merkief who now sat at the controls. The platform carried Anastassia into the tank. Merkief left the control terminal and came to stand beside Jey, both of them gawking.

"I'll get her out of the tank. Get out."

Merkief nodded but his eyes narrowed. "What is that stench and that crap in your hair?"

"One of the Council members threatened to eat me."

I walked toward the door, driving the two of them before me. "We'll discuss it later. Right now, leave."

Merkief pulled Jey through the doorway. "There's nothing we can do in there right now. There will be plenty of time to talk to Kazan when she wakes up." He glanced at me. "After Vayen talks with her first, of course."

Jey gave the tank one last long look before stepping out and allowing the door to close.

With only the whirring of the tank fans and the occasional faint whoosh of filtered air from the ship's vents to keep me company, I watched the lines of her stats creep upward. The first of them flattened far below her previous profile's baseline. Two hours later, three of the other remaining seven lines also dropped off. The damage could only be undone so far. Whatever injuries she'd suffered, her body had healed naturally as best it was able. Her profile was far out of date.

The sour smell of my coat started to get on my nerves. The tank estimated another four hours to complete Anastassia's cycle. I decided to take a quick shower and get something to eat rather than sit and stare dismally at the screen.

As I walked past Merkief and Jey's rooms, they called out, asking how Kazan was doing. I broke the news of the long road to rehabilitation ahead of her, waving off their further questions with my need to get cleaned up.

The hot pelting water felt wonderful, rinsing the hardened slime away and some of the tension from my neck and shoulders. Anastassia was back and only a few rooms away. We could get back to working together, discuss the bond, and toss the concerns of the High Council back in their faces.

I stepped out of the shower. Or she could hold a grudge the size of Merchess, refuse to acknowledge the bond and start a fight that would knock us both from the High Council's good graces forever.

There was no way to know until she woke up.

Chapter Twenty-Four

After removing Anastassia from the tank, I spent ten hours cursing the High Council, casting worried glances in her direction and alternately sitting beside her and pacing the length of her room. I should have slept, but I didn't dare try. I couldn't even gather my thoughts together enough to get any work done.

"Stand still. You're making me dizzy." Her voice was quiet, a shadow of her usual annoyance and authority.

I came to a halt at the end of her bed and took in what the tank had done for her now that a spark of life lit her face. The lines had eased, giving her the effect of five years older instead of fifteen. The blanket didn't mask the gauntness. Food and exercise would make up for what the healing gel had been unable to cure. I hoped.

"How are you feeling?" I asked.

"Alive, I think." Her gaze drifted to me and tears welled in her eyes. "So what are you? A clone? A ghost? Another hallucination?"

"Anastassia, it's me." I went to her side and sat on the edge of the bed.

She scooted away, stabbing her temples with her fingers. "I saw you, touched your cold body."

"I don't see how that's possible. I've spent a lot of time in the tank, but I'm sure Merkief or Jey would have mentioned it if I'd died."

She sat up, her brows drawing together as she clutched handfuls of hair alongside her face. Her words came slowly as she stared at the bed. "They demanded I take part in their testing. That field. They kept me pumped full of some drug that drained me so I could barely manage a single Jump, but that was all they wanted, me to Jump into their damned test site. But I wouldn't do it. Not after the first time. But then this blue creature, he got in my head and forced my link to Jump."

"I think I met him."

Her hands dropped from her head to wrap around her sides. She began to rock. I reached out to her shoulder, but she shrank away before I could touch her.

"It hurt him to force the Jumps. He suffered a degree of the effects of the field along with me. I could feel him in my head. They yelled, threatened, and beat me. I let them keep forcing it."

So *that* was what the High Council considered uncooperative.

"I refused their demands. Then they resorted to promises, telling me they'd let me see you." Anastassia shook her head. "I didn't believe they would follow through. They started slipping me news of the Narvan. The havoc my safety net had caused, your scrambling to keep the Narvan together, and the attacks on you."

Her rocking ceased, but she still wouldn't look at me. "I thought I could give you advice, do something to help. So I went along with it, and the Jump hurt like all your nine hells. The blue bastard wasn't there to take the damage with me that time."

"The field hurts, I know." My head ached just thinking about the single encounter. I couldn't imagine enduring the driving pain over and over again.

"But then they brought you in. Dead. One of my contacts had been successful and taken you out. I got you killed. If I'd cooperated sooner, I could have saved you. A day earlier. An hour." Her voice shook. "But they kept their word, they ordered Merkief to hand your body over to them and they brought you in." She reached out to my arm, but stopped before making contact and returned it to her side.

"They promised to help Jey and Merkief hold the Narvan together for me if I would continue to cooperate. Neither of them was ready for that. I knew they'd need all the assistance the High Council could give them. I needed to know the Narvan was protected. I promised your brother I'd keep your people safe. I owed him." Her voice dropped to a ragged whisper. "And I'd killed you."

"I'm not dead." I pulled her close despite her wincing and wrapped my arms around her. "They knocked me out and drugged me with Geva knows what to pull off their charade. No wonder I felt like shit when I came to."

Her body sagged against my chest. "When I could sleep, when I could dream, I mean, when the pain wasn't so bad that I was just unconscious, I swore I could hear you. Faint whispers. Never enough to know for sure if I could really hear you or it if was my imagination."

With my cheek resting against her forehead, the bond deep within me settled into a soothing warmth. My body eased into a state of relaxation I hadn't enjoyed in years. I closed my eyes and breathed deeply. This was what I needed. Had I taken the High Council's offer, I would have never found this peace.

"I had similar dreams." I said. "Their drug must not have had as full of an effect on our natural connection."

Anastassia ran a tentative fingertip down the sleeve of my coat. When she came to my hand, her fingers slipped into mine. "The Narvan?"

"Is running just fine."

Everything was just fine. I took another deep breath and let it out slowly, marveling at how just having her close dulled the strain of the overwhelming workload that was getting more out of hand every moment I spent sitting there with Anastassia. A day ago, wasted minutes would have driven me mad, but now I ignored it all and smiled.

"Merkief and Jey?"

"Anxious to see you."

She pulled away enough to turn and look me in the eye. "So where are they?"

"They're giving me a few minutes to..." Oh Geva, how was I going to explain the bond to her? All my well thought out lines evaporated in a heartbeat.

Anastassia stiffened and yanked her hand from mine, taking the warmth and calm with her. Everything began to speed up again, crashing in all around me. Having tasted the reprieve she offered, I craved more. This was all too fast, too hard to explain when she was hurt and confused.

"Merkief says you won't let them in. Why not?" She scowled, looking more herself by the second. "Were you working with the Council?"

"No. Never like that. They lied to you."

"But you were. You said so before." She swung her legs over

the other side of the bed. "I suppose you're planning to wring some agreement over control of the Narvan from me? You'd never share it, not once you've had it in your hands."

Her gaze darted around the room, no doubt searching for a weapon. Luckily, they were all put away.

"Stassia, this isn't about the Narvan."

"Really?" She slid from the bed, pulling the blanket with her and wrapping it around herself. "Then why won't my bodyguards follow my orders?"

I didn't even want to think about what Merkief had told Jey to keep him from rushing in. Be it truth or fabrication, Jey wasn't going to be at all happy with me.

"Because I need to explain some things. In private." I swallowed hard and plodded onward for better or worse. "I know you don't want this, but I'm—"

She Jumped, leaving me to stand alone, declaring my bond to thin air.

Damned woman. I racked my brain for where she might have run off to that she'd consider a safe haven beyond the ship. Knowing she held Fa'yet in high regard, and might consider him able to defend her against me if she wasn't up to it, I steeled myself for another brusque dismissal and contacted him.

"Kazan is free. If you haven't already heard."

"I hadn't." He sent a wave of relief over the link, sounding much more like the friend I'd thought I'd lost. *"Is she with you?"*

"Not exactly. Is she with you?"

"No. Don't tell me you lost her?" he said.

I hoped not. *"Can you do me a favor and contact her? Tell her I'm not out to kill her."*

"Is she armed?"

"Probably by now."

"I'll see what I can do." He broke contact.

I contacted Gemmen with the same favor. Beyond the two of them, I couldn't think of anyone she'd count on to stand beside her after being out of contact for so long.

Kess's unexpected voice broke through my dismal thoughts. *"Kazan just walked into my office."*

Shit. I wanted to punch something. This was all going so wrong, so fast. *"Don't shoot her."*

"She looks like she's about ready to lose it, and she's got a gun."

I opened my link to Merkief. *"Standby with the tank. Kazan is acting erratically. She Jumped to visit Marin before I could stop her, and now she's threatening Kess."*

Merkief swore in my head. *"She's not in any shape to face him."*

"I know. I'm going to get her."

The pale blue walls and tan carpet of the Assassins complex greeted me with a sense of trepidation larger than I'd ever felt when Marin was alive. The office door was open. I ran in.

She must have stopped off in her rooms on the complex to dress and arm herself, but her armor still hung in her closet on the ship. It pained me to see her standing there so vulnerable, knowing that if Kess got a shot in, I might never get the chance to explain myself to her.

"Anastassia, put the gun down," I said.

She spun around and fired a bullet into my chest.

Thank Geva my armor held at such close range. It had seen a lot of wear lately and I hadn't set aside time to let it fully repair. Stumbling back, I fought to force air back into my lungs.

Kess stood. He held out one empty hand, the other rested on a still holstered gun at his side. "Anastassia, please, put the gun down."

Her head whipped around to face him. Anastassia fired, just catching the collar of his coat. I doubted she'd missed his head on purpose; she was just out of sorts.

Kess drew his gun.

I sprang forward, knocking Anastassia to the floor. She landed hard on her back. With the gun wrenched from her hand, I pinned her down.

"Stop it, before you get yourself killed."

Her body bucked beneath me. "Get off! He's got a gun!"

"Put it away," I said over my shoulder.

"If she shoots at me again, I will fire back, dammit." I heard his gun slip into its holster.

Wide-eyed, Anastassia glanced between us. "You're working together?" She slammed the back of her head into the carpet and grimaced. "I should have seen that coming."

"Anastassia, it's not like that," I said, wishing we were alone back on the ship, without Kess of all people.

"You've got Fa'yet playing on your team now too?" Her face went white and sweat broke out on her brow. "And Gemmen? Why didn't you just kill me when I got back? Do you need a fair fight to ease your conscience?"

Mindful of her smaller frame, I eased my hold. "None of us want to kill you. If you'd just listen—"

Her eyes widened further, giving her a crazed cast. "Where's Marin? What have you done to him?"

I couldn't tell if she was asking me or Kess. He and I exchanged worried glances.

One of her hands snaked free. She punched me in the face. "You have to corroborate your stories, and you think I'm going to trust a word you say?"

There was no time to put any finesse on the bare truth. "He's dead. You're better off without him. If you had half an inkling of what he did to—"

She squirmed free enough to land a knee in my back. I decided a few bruises from me holding her down were preferable to her possible escape.

"Marin was manipulating you, me, even Kess," I said.

"Prove it," she hissed, still fighting to get free even though I was using more pressure than I wanted to.

"Kess said—"

"You're listening to him now?" She let out a wild bark of laughter. "I liked you better when I thought you were dead."

Her words wounded deeply. I released her, not regretting the force with which I did so. "You know what? Go see Merkief and Jey. I'll be in my office on Rok when you're ready to listen to me."

Anastassia scrambled to her feet, her face distorted in a sneer. "Listen to you? Oh, I see how this goes. Plan to lord over me and the Narvan?" She stalked over, stopping mere inches away. "I'm sick of being the High Council's puppet, and I'll be damned if I'll stand for being yours."

"Have your Narvan if that's the only thing so fucking important to you." I regretted the words an instant later, but it was all I could think to say to defuse her anger.

Her mouth hung open. She gave me a long silent once over and then Jumped.

"Well, that didn't go very well," Kess said.

I shot him a look that caused him to shut up and avert his gaze as I Jumped. When I arrived in my office on Rok, the empty desktop was hard and cold and the chair not as comfortable as I recalled. The darkness of the room offered little solace, but I wasn't in the mood for light. I pressed my eyes shut and rested my head on my arms, replaying the past hour and wondering where I should have blurted out something about the bond. After further thought, I wondered if that would have only made things worse.

I heard a click in the darkness. The door made an awful screech as it was forced open. I sprang to my feet with a gun in my hands and activated the lights.

Jey stood there with a gun aimed at my head. "You have some explaining to do."

"Put the gun down."

"You sold out to Kess? That's why he's been leaving us alone?" He shook his head and walked in. "I stood by you. I backed you with my people. I took bullets for you!" The finger of Kazan's almighty protector trembled on the trigger. "How could you do that to her?"

"I didn't. You claimed you know me so don't get all crazy just because Kazan's back. Sit down so we can talk about this."

"Like you talked to her? I'd love to see you try."

Hoping that the last couple years of goodwill hadn't truly vanished in an instant, I put my gun away. "She was going to get herself killed. I kept that from happening. Isn't that what we've been paid to do all along?"

He took in my empty hands. "Are you working with Kess?"

"He did propose that at one time, but no, I am not working with Kess. As you'll recall, if you give yourself a few seconds of rational thought, I've been working with you."

"Then why did it sure as all hells sound like you two were—"

"Kess and I found a little common ground. That's all. If Kazan wants specifics, she'll have to come and get them. Alone."

If I ever had a chance of convincing Anastassia of Marin's motivations, I'd need to come clean about some things, but I doubted she'd want her mistakes paraded in front of an audience anymore than I did.

"I see." He lowered his gun and remained silent for a moment. "Merkief claims this bond you have will prevent you from harming Kazan. Is that true?"

So he knew. I sighed.

"For the most part, yes. Look, I harm people for a living just like you do. If I really wanted to hurt her, I could, but even without the bond, I don't want to. Does that answer your question?"

"I suspected he was glossing over that." He put his gun away. "But if I catch any whisper that you're lying about Kess, we will talk again." He Jumped.

The room filled with silence. I sat down at my desk, wondering if the two of them could convince Anastassia to see reason.

Half an hour later, her voice popped into my head. *"I'm waiting."* She flashed me her room on the ship.

As if I was supposed to know she'd been waiting for me to Jump there? I notified Gemmen of the damage to my door and stepped out of the void into Anastassia's room.

She stood with her hands on her hips and a scowl on her face. "You bonded with me? Vayen, what the hell?"

This was not at all how I'd wanted to broach the topic. I made a mental note to throttle Merkief and possibly Jey.

She closed the space between us with three swift steps and smacked my chest with her open palm. "You said you didn't want this either and you sounded pretty damn adamant at the time. I've done everything I could think of to make you not want this all along. Why, dammit? Why would you do this?"

"I didn't intend to."

"Don't lie to me. You said yourself that you have to want to bond with someone for it to happen."

"All right then, I tried very hard to not want to."

"Not hard enough, apparently." She spun away.

I doubted telling her that the High Council drugging me into it would make her any more accepting. "It's really not that bad."

"I'm not Artorian! I can't do this. We can't do this. The High Council will have a heyday holding any sort of relationship over our heads."

"Anastassia—"

She backed away and paced the small room. "They do that, you know. Twist you, hold things over your head. Anything to make you more cooperative."

Her hands clenched and unclenched at her sides in rapid-fire succession. "Why do you think I stayed with Marin for so long? If the High Council ever followed through on their threats to kill him, it wouldn't be that big of a deal. No one else liked him. He didn't have a family. He didn't hold a position that would leave a big vacuum if he should not be able to hold it or disappear. He was a suitable choice, there when I needed him but in the dark about Kryon and the High Council."

My jaw dropped and I found myself sputtering. "Convenience, that's all he was to you? Someone to hop in bed with when the urge struck?"

I acknowledged that I'd grown cold and likely more callous than I wanted to dwell on during my time in the High Council's spotlight, but I couldn't fathom such thoughts about a long time lover.

Anastassia froze mid-step and spun on her heel to face me. "He conveniently kept the Council's focus off of you, idiot. My focus too." She let out a loud rumbling groan. "Damn you and your stupid bond!"

She dropped down on the bed and put her face in her hands. "They know, don't they? The High Council?"

"Yes."

"They've got to be rubbing their hands together with glee about now."

Telling her the Council had been quite willing to terminate the bond she was so against by killing her also didn't seem the best way to diffuse her concerns.

"It's old news now. I'm sure they've got bigger things to focus on," I said.

She'd panicked when she couldn't reach Marin. I'd seen it. She couldn't be that heartless. "Didn't you care about Marin at all?"

"Marin? The High Council is doing a dance over your bond, and you want to talk about Marin?"

"I killed him." Maybe she'd care about that.

Anastassia studied me, her gaze lingering on my hands where they hung at my sides. "I'm not surprised. At least I wasn't here to see it."

"You don't care that I killed him?"

"Of course I do. A little. Maybe a lot. Hell, Vayen. I don't know. Marin and I hadn't been getting along very well since I hired you. He could sense my attention was elsewhere." She waved her hands in the air. "Until this morning, I thought you were dead. There's a lot for me to absorb and try to make sense of right now, all right?"

"Was it at least quick?" she asked quietly.

I nodded.

"There's something else you need to know." I sat down next to her on the bed. "When I left to relocate Sonia..."

She regarded me with silent curiosity.

I explained how Marin had talked me into walking away, how he'd done the same with Kess. I told her of Marin's obsession with her and the lengths he'd gone to in order to drive her to the supposed safety of his arms. As I went on, color leeched from her face. She fisted the blankets beside her in a white-knuckled stranglehold.

When I finished, she sat there, stammering, alternating between names, threats, and profanity.

"Kess contacted me when you Jumped into Marin's office. He didn't want to hurt you. Leave him be and he should leave us be. For now anyway. I don't imagine he'll be content there for long."

"I don't trust him."

I patted her hand. "Neither do I. So are you all right with this bond? I mean, you and me making a go of it?"

"No, but I don't have much of a choice, do I?"

I snatched my hand away. "We don't have to join or anything. I'm just letting you know that—"

"That you'll fly into a jealous rage every time another man touches me, looks at me, or happens to be in the same room?"

"I'm not like that."

She gave me a deadpan state. "That's not what Jey said."

"He's not even Artorian! What does he know?"

"He was in the room when you brought me back. He witnessed your behavior first hand."

"You'd been gone for years, for Geva's sake. I think I'm allowed to want a few minutes alone with you."

Why couldn't Anastassia be Artorian? From everything I heard, at the first hint of a man declaring his intent to bond, women's eyes grew wide, giddy grins broke out on their faces and hints for gift design patterns were dropped within minutes.

She stood and walked away. "We'll deal with this bond business later. Right now, I'm being summoned for a meeting on Sere. You?"

I opened up my link. No messages. Why wouldn't they summon me too? Did they know I'd hand the Narvan over uncontested, or was this meeting something else?

"No. Be careful."

Anastassia closed the distance between us once again, but this time without hitting me or angry words. "I will." She wrapped her arms around me. "I'm sorry for what I said before, about liking you dead. Between what the High Council had told me and—"

"It's all right."

I basked in the feeling of her in my arms, soft and warm.

Again, the bond eased within me, uncoiling with calm assurance that everything was as it should be. Pulling her tighter against me, I became acutely aware of her body pressed against mine and the stiffening reaction that ensued a second later.

Anastassia froze. Her hands pried my arms from her back. She stepped away and eyed my pants. "What the hell is that?"

I grinned. "I'm sure you're far more familiar with how this works than I am."

Her eyebrows shot up and so did her voice. "You had the procedure done? Oh, no." She shook her head, backing away. "You... but...of course, you'd pull strings. You're just like your damned brother."

"I'm not." I needed to make that clear right away after what she'd said he'd expected of her.

Her gaze darted back to my pants. I thought she might crack a smile, but the momentary upturn of her lips wavered and collapsed. "Do they know about this too? It's another nail in one of our coffins if they do. You realize that, don't you?"

"We'll be fine."

As long as we could work together, I'd show the High Council that having both of us around was in their best interest. Having Anastassia beside me wouldn't endanger my position, she would enhance it. We'd be like before, only better.

"I've only been awake for a few hours, and I've already shot you. Your 'fine' is damned weak. Beyond that, you're thinking with the wrong head. I'm not hopping in bed with you. This is bad enough already."

She just needed some time to calm down and get back into the swing of things, the bed and the bond would fall into place.

"Don't keep the High and Mighties waiting." I put a smile on my face. "When you get back, we can begin your briefing."

"You are talking about the Narvan, right?"

"Of course." I restrained my laughter until she'd Jumped.

❧

An hour later Anastassia returned to my doorway. "Let's go up to the house. I've been breathing filtered air for too long."

I let Merkief and Jey know we were leaving the safety of the ship and asked them to stay onboard. Anastassia and I had a lot of information to cover. I didn't need to be distracted by either of them hovering around her.

The two of us arrived in the clearing outside the house. With her beside me, the sweltering Friquen air wasn't quite as distasteful as I'd remembered. Even so, when we went inside, I activated the house cooling systems.

Anastassia glanced around. "Nothing's changed."

"Why would it? I haven't been here since you left."

She sank into a chair at the dining room table. "Why do I have the feeling you've been everywhere else?"

"Your safety net didn't leave me much choice." I sat down next to her. "Don't worry, I kept all your general directives. The Narvan is safe and prospering. Just like we both wanted. Your favorite Verian station is secure. The Merchessian family heads are behaving. Cragtek is making a nice profit and remains hidden. The couple colonization crews we sent out have been reporting back with favorable results. The Fragians have made a few forays into the Nebula but are generally sticking close to home since our little conflict." I shrugged. "It's business as usual, for the most part. No major changes."

"You don't get it. My contacts are out of the loop. I'm unable to reach well over twenty of them. I can only assume you had something to do with that. Marin is gone. Merkief and Jey are following your orders rather than mine. The High Council wanted to reiterate their threats about exacting revenge and spent the rest of the time questioning me about you instead of laying out their demands for the system and upcoming contracts. Two new planetary leaders have been appointed while I was gone. I don't even know these people. They only know you." Her voice wavered and her hands were at her temples again. "It's like I'm starting all over again and my competition is sitting right here."

"You haven't been gone that long." I nudged her shoulder gently. "It will just take a little while to get back up to speed. And we're not competing. We can run the Narvan together."

"Not according to the High Council. Seems you've made some new friends." Her voice dropped to a whisper. "You may have said you were giving the Narvan back, but they were pretty adamant about you being at the helm."

"They actually said that?"

"Several times. And since when is Jey your partner?"

"He's not. You are."

"Really? Because I just got an earful of the two of you working together, to a degree that I find highly unbelievable considering that the last I knew, a conversation between the two of you consisted of trading insults."

"We were working a lot."

"A whole damn lot, if what half of the Council said was true." She sighed. "I always assumed you'd fall back to Merkief."

"That would have been easier, but I needed Jey. You should have seen him when we were facing the Fragians. Even I was impressed."

"Sorry I missed it." Warmth lit her face as she smiled. "I hate to make your ego swell any further, but I have to say, I'm proud of you."

She squeezed my hand. Her link opened to mine, sharing a wealth of mixed emotions along with a faint hum, like distant static.

"Thanks. Are you tired?"

"A little. Sad isn't it?"

"You just need to get your strength back, that's all." I pulled her to her feet.

"Come on, I'll talk you to sleep."

Anastassia shook her head. "You're going to try anything to get in my bed, aren't you?"

"Probably."

She smacked me on the shoulder and headed toward her bedroom. "You are welcome to sit next to me and start your Narvan briefing until I can't keep my eyes open. However, if you ever do want a chance of something happening between us, I don't recommend trying anything while I'm asleep."

"Got it."

"Good." She sloughed off her coat, hung it up, and lay down on the bed. "So, I walked out of the trial two years ago, what happened next?"

Great Geva, it was going to be a long night.

Chapter Twenty-Five

I woke with Anastassia curled up next to me, her arm tossed over my chest and her head resting on my shoulder. The first thing I realized was that I'd actually slept and I felt rested. I wanted every morning onward to be like this one.

The second thing was that all of me was eager to start the day with Anastassia. I needed to put some space between us before the strong urges from below convinced me to disregard her warnings.

"Stassia, wake up."

She stirred, cracking open one eye.

"You need to eat. I'll get us something, and then we're going to work on getting you back in shape."

Anastassia sat up, looking indignant. "Something wrong with my shape?"

"No...it's just...I mean..."

She laughed. "I know what you mean."

I pulled on my coat and Jumped to a Friquen restaurant I knew she liked. Twenty minutes later, I returned with breakfast. We went over more Narvan business as we ate, and then, since the Friquen house didn't offer a room large enough to train in, we went outside. Anastassia turned her face up to the morning sun and took a deep breath.

The air smelled of the acidic spice of evergreens and moldering leaves to me, certainly nothing to inspire a peaceful smile like the one that graced her face. But I enjoyed watching her smile.

A clear patch of low grass twenty paces from the house offered enough space for us to move around. The oppressive heat made me glad to slip out of my web of holsters and armor. Anastassia wore her usual attire, a loose-fitting shirt and pants.

With a determined look, she came at me. I knocked her down. Too easy.

She sprawled onto the grass with a soft thud. When she didn't spring back to her feet with her usual ease, I reached down to help her up.

"Are you all right?" I thought I'd backed off enough. Then again, we'd not practiced together in awhile. Maybe I'd misjudged.

Anastassia nodded and went back to her starting position. With flying feet, she came at me again.

I knocked her down.

This time she lay flat on her back, gasping.

I dropped down beside her. "Stassia?"

She let out a shaky breath. "Maybe I should start with Merkief. He's always been the more sedate of you three."

"I'm sorry. Did I hurt you?" I checked her body for any sign of injury but found none.

"I'll live. What the hell have you been doing while I was gone, bench pressing Jey?"

"Working. A lot."

"I don't remember you being that quick before either." She slowly got to her feet. "Let's hold off on this for a bit, all right?"

"Sure." Next time I'd remember to hold back more. I'd become too accustomed to sparring with Jey.

We spent the rest of the morning going over Narvan business and then, after lunch, I called Merkief and Jey in. Jey hung back when Merkief and Anastassia went outside. We watched them out the window, spinning around each other. With each hit Merkief landed on her, I cringed.

"He's not hurting her."

Anastassia got back to her feet and went through the set of punches they were working on.

"I know."

The two of them finally dropped into a productive rhythm. Their blocks and strikes formed a beat that my ears couldn't hear, but my mind knew by heart. The two of us had run through this warm up routine, and various versions of it hundreds of times.

It should have been me out there. Every beat drove home the

fact that I stood inside while another man stood in my place. "Do you think they'll be all right for a bit? We have work to do."

Jey shook his head, chuckling. "When Merkief warned me of how overprotective you might be, I thought he was exaggerating. Vayen, how many times has Merkief been on duty? Have you ever had cause to be concerned about his abilities before. Shut up and quit being stupid with all your bonding shit."

"I'm not being stupid."

"Believe me, you are. Get a hold of yourself or I'm going to start berating you for being Artorian again."

"Fine."

I flashed him our jump point and let Merkief and Anastassia know that we were leaving. Dismay flooded from her link into mine. When she turned to the window where I stood, she looked lost. That twisted my stomach up even more than watching her with Merkief, but she needed this. I stood beside Jey and Jumped.

We spent the next two days apart. Anastassia worked intensely with Merkief while I dealt with snide demands from the Artorian Premier who was at odds with Syless and Rok over defense contracts and possible treaty breaches. When Jey and I returned, I found Anastassia sitting at the table, sharing a meal with Merkief.

He took one look at me, grabbed his plate and vacated the room. Jey's reprimand about my possessiveness hit home.

"You don't have to run just because I'm back. Sit down and finish eating."

"No way. Good luck." He cut contact.

"Anastassia?"

She slammed her fork down and stood to face me. "You ditched me. What happened to running the system together?"

"The negotiations ran on, as I expected they would. We've been dealing with various tensions between Artor and the Jalvian worlds since you've been gone. They're testing each other again. Things will settle down soon and we can all get back to business as usual."

"I'm perfectly capable of sitting through long meetings."

"I know that." I approached her cautiously. The fork was still in reach. "It's just that Jey and I have been working on this for awhile and getting you involved—"

"Would weaken the authority you've worked so hard to build up."

"Yes."

"And I don't have all the details or know the new Prime of Rok."

I felt her snare tightening as she stalked forward but it was too late to run.

"Yes."

"So you've replaced me with Jey and expect me to sit back and watch the Narvan go on while I wait for you to need the backup team? I suppose you expect me to be all smiles and play house when you deem it worthy to visit. Let me tell you, that's not going to happen."

I rested my hands on her shoulders. "I don't want that to happen. I want to work with you. Listen to me." I poured reassurance into our linked connection since she still had our natural one sealed off. "I only took Jey because he's been working on this with me. When something new comes up, you'll certainly be involved. I thought you needed to rest up anyway."

"Involved?" She twisted out of my grip. "I'm the one who put you in charge, remember? I handed this position to you for safe keeping and now you'll allow me to be *involved*?"

Despite the calm her presence offered, years worth of frustration surged to the forefront. "For the record, you didn't put me in charge."

I drove her backward. "You did everything you could to *not* put me in charge. And you didn't hand me anything, you disregarded all you'd worked for and the well-being of the Narvan to run off on a killing spree to protect some other man. I was left to pick up the pieces amidst the giant fucking mess you unleashed."

She was very fortunate that we did have the bond between us at that moment to keep me somewhat in check. Even so, the release of all my frustration on the person who caused it felt damn good.

"If the Council likes how I put the Narvan back together, I'm sorry, but the whole system is benefitting. I really can't see where you'd have an issue with that if you'd take a moment to look beyond what you did to your own damned self."

Jey cleared his throat. I glanced away from Anastassia's seething glare to see both he and Merkief watching us.

"Get out," Anastassia and I said in unison.

They looked to each other and back at us. Merkief nodded to Jey. They both Jumped.

Anastassia pushed me but I didn't move, which only seemed to infuriate her further. "What I did to myself? The Council killed people. Innocent people. If they killed someone close to you, what would you do? Just let them do it again and again until they got what they wanted?" She shook her head. "I did what I had to."

"To protect *him*." I needed to take care of whatever was between us so we could get back to making us work.

"Yes."

"Who is he?" I drove her back step by step until she bumped into the table. The still half-full plate clattered across the tabletop. The fork fell and her glass tipped, rolled off the table, and shattered on the floor.

She grabbed at the table to keep her balance. "He's no one you need to worry about. Really. It's not anything like what you're thinking."

"Where and who. Now."

"No." She dropped her hostility and switched to the utterly reasonable tone she used in delicate negotiations. "You were already bonded to me back when you stayed with Fa'yet, weren't you? You were ready to rip Marin apart with your bare hands after I set you off. I'd never seen you so angry before. Like now."

Anastassia closed her eyes and stood perfectly still. "Well, go ahead then and start ripping, because that's the only way you'll ever get to him."

My rage came up short and fizzled. "I won't hurt you."

She peeked at me and let out her breath. "Then drop this. Promise me." Her hands trembled where she held onto the table.

I nodded, unwilling to say the words. If letting this man who meant so much to her slip through my fingers helped bring us together, it was a concession I was willing to make. At least, for now. I needed her beside me like she'd been before. If we could work together, the rest would fall into place.

"Only if you'll promise to do a contract with me."

"Shouldn't you rest first? You just got back," she said.

"Resting and I don't get along much anymore. Unless you're not up to it?"

She stepped away from the table and sniffed. "Of course I am. Give me five minutes and don't you dare go easy on me."

This was the Anastassia I'd longed to see. "You got it."

❧

I sat in the tank room, watching Anastassia's still form in the tank. Again. She'd been back almost a month, but every contract sent her back here. And I sat there with bruises covering my chest and back and a burning line on my neck where some bastard had come too damn close to a lucky shot.

The static I kept picking up from her link plagued me every time we worked together, making it hard to concentrate. It didn't help that she still had our natural connection tightly shut and she refused to talk further about the bond or helping to ease my frustration in other areas. I didn't want to push her on any front or we'd be back at each other's throats.

It wasn't as if the Kryon contracts I'd chosen for us were too difficult. Our rhythm was off. I'd always known where she would move and what she'd expect of me, but now, we fumbled, never sure who was leading. We'd literally tripped over one another this last time. Even worse, our target had escaped. We'd never fucked up to that degree before.

It wasn't a huge surprise when the Council's summons hit me. Anastassia still had an hour to go. It would probably be for the best if she didn't come with me. I called Merkief in to get her out of the tank and stay with her since I didn't know how long they planned to reprimand me.

Deep Voice's cloaked form stood before me in our usual meeting room. "We find your performance lacking since Kazan's return."

"So do I. We're working on it. She needs time to recover from what you did to her."

I recognized the gait of the same female who had been with Deep Voice when they'd told me of Anastassia's release. She stepped away from the other four silent figures in the room.

"Anastassia Kazan is providing an unnecessary distraction. We warned you of this potential problem, yet you insisted on bringing her back into our midst."

"Like I said, we're working on it. The Narvan will be much better off with two strong advisers. She just needs a little time."

"Your system already has two strong advisers." Deep Voice said.

"But Jey was only filling in. The Narvan was hers before it was mine. You can't expect her to just step down, not after all she's done for you."

"Mr. Ta'set," said the woman. "We didn't expect her to come back at all. However, in light of your service record, we gave you a chance to make it work. You failed. Now we're telling you to clean up this mess and get back to work."

My stomach dropped to my feet. "You can't be asking what I think you're asking."

"Let me make this clear, this is a direct order," she said. "Eliminate her."

Rage coursed through me. I jumped to my feet. Three guards aimed their guns at my head. I froze but refused to sit.

"I most certainly will not!"

Deep Voice cleared his throat. "Mr. Ta'set, I advise you to take your seat."

My entire body trembled with the need to rip the cloaks from their heads and wrap my hands around their throats. "If you want me at the head of this system, then let me do it my way. She stays."

The female pushed past Deep Voice, knocking him aside on her march to shove the guards in front of me away. She leaned in close. "You maintain a precarious balance, Mr. Ta'set. I encourage you to find solid footing before you fall.

"She's Kryon. One of us. You can't just have her killed!"

Deep Voice came forward. He motioned for the guards to step back. "Kazan no longer meets Kryon standards. Surely you can see that."

He gestured for the female to also back away. "Under you, the Narvan has prospered. Its people are safe and wealthy in both credits and knowledge. We want the same things you want for your people. We want your attention undivided. Anastassia Kazan is no longer fit to stand beside you. She is a liability to us, to your people, and to you."

Hollowness threatened to swallow me. "No."

Deep Voice reached into his cloak and drew out a still frame. He dropped the film onto the floor at my feet. "I did mention we follow through on our threats?"

I stared at the woman in the image, one I'd thought hidden from the eyes of the High Council and everyone else, safe from any further harm I might inflict on her. I closed my eyes rather than look at her innocent smile for another second. Sonia.

Chapter Twenty-Six

I left Sere feeling that my legs had been cut off at the knee. If I stalled in taking Anastassia out, how long would the High Council allow Sonia to live? My stomach churned as I considered the possible death of an innocent woman, a mother, a woman I'd once cared a great deal for. The thought of killing Anastassia brought me to a stop to empty the contents of my stomach into a public trash bin on the way to Fa'yet's house.

He'd avoided me since Anastassia's sentencing and, while he'd seemed pleasant enough upon her return, he'd told me he'd watch over Sonia. Now the Council had her.

"This is an unexpected visit." Fa'yet cut off the noise of the outside world with his heavy door, leaving us with only our muf-fled footsteps on his thick carpet. "You look like you could use a drink."

He walked over to his liquor cabinet. Bottles clinked together as he made his selection. "Problems with Anastassia?"

I sank down in one of his chairs. "They want me to kill her."

The clinking stopped. Fa'yet spun around. "The Council? Anastassia? No. You must have misunderstood."

"They were quite clear." I pulled Sonia's still frame from my coat and held it up. "You promised me she was safe."

The bottle he clutched in his hands shook.

"How did they even know about Sonia? What did you tell them?"

He maintained his distance and put the bottle down, freeing

his hands. "I didn't tell them anything."

Had they taken the information from me when they'd made me play dead?

"But how could they ask *you* to kill Anastassia?" he asked.

"With words. The same way they ask me to kill anyone else." I glared at him. "Either pour me a drink or bring me that bottle."

Fa'yet grabbed the bottle he'd set on top the cabinet and two glasses. He set them on the low table in front of me and took a seat.

"But to ask such a thing of any man..." he said.

"She killed them. They exacted their punishment, and now they no longer find her useful. They want her gone." I opened the bottle and filled a glass with opaque blue liquid.

"But you're bonded to her. You can't!"

"I could." I took a drink. The sweet, heavy liquor did little to wash the distasteful words away. "Killing her would dissolve the bond, and I'd maintain control over the Narvan and stay in the Council's good graces."

Fa'yet's jaw clenched and his nostrils flared. "You can't truly be thinking about this."

I took another gulp and considered pouring the entire bottle down my throat. I wanted to be numb to the universe and the Council's demands for a few hours.

"Which makes me less damned, letting an innocent woman die or the one I'm bonded to?"

Who else would they go after if I let them take Sonia and still refused to act? I downed the rest of the drink and poured another.

He hesitated. "Why ask you to kill her? Why not someone else?"

Remembering the conversation after Deep Voice had dropped Sonia's image at my feet, my voice shook. "They were going to kill her for me. I demanded to have her back."

"I can't let you do this." He stood and pointed a gun at my head. "I'm sorry, but if I take you out, I save Sonia and Anastassia keeps her life and her position."

I'd had quite enough guns in my face for one day. I threw the glass at his head.

Fa'yet fired, but his shot whizzed past my ear. The glass shattered on his forehead and blue liquor splashed over his face. Blood gushed from a shard lodged between the bridge of his nose and his left eye.

I threw him against the wall and wrenched the gun from this hand. "I didn't say I *was* going to kill her, you hasty ass."

I tossed the gun aside and then picked him up by the collar of his coat, slamming him against the wall again. Blood poured down his face. I let go and plucked the glass from his nose, tossing it on the floor. He grimaced.

"If I don't kill Anastassia, Sonia dies, and I probably lose the Narvan." I sighed. "I need to know what that would mean for our people before I make any decisions. We're talking far more than two lives at stake here. Who would get my position?"

"I don't know." He brushed the glass from his shirt. "They don't discuss this sort of thing with me. I do my required work like everyone else."

"Yeah, and they invited you to their inner circle because they liked how you dress." I snorted. "I need to know whose hands the safety of our people would be in if not mine."

Fa'yet wiped at the blood on his face. "There are plenty of others that have systems like you. They might combine leadership. Maybe they have someone else in mind. It wouldn't be me. That's all I can say for sure." He went to the cabinet, pulled out a towel and held it to his nose.

"How long do you think I have before they go after Sonia?" I asked.

"If they didn't parade her in front of you, they're just watching her. She's fine. Take a deep breath and give me a couple days to move her to safety."

He gave me a blood-smeared reassuring smile. "Go watch over Anastassia. I'll let you know if I come up with anything."

I Jumped to the Merchessian house. Merkief, Jey, and Anastassia sat talking in the common room.

She caught sight of me in the foyer and gestured upstairs. I went to my room and checked over a few of my weapons while I waited.

I held a gun in my hand. All it would take was one bullet. She wouldn't expect it from me. Not now. No chance for her to fight, not in the condition she was in. One shot and all the people of the Narvan could go on thriving. Sonia would live. The Council would be satisfied.

Anastassia might get back up to Kryon standards eventually, but we couldn't work together now, when it mattered, not like we had before. The only one who benefitted from keeping her alive, was me. I'd made a selfish choice, and as much as I didn't want to follow orders this time, it was the responsible thing to do.

If I made it look like an accident on a contract, I could keep Jey and Merkeif beside me. They wouldn't expect this of me either. They knew she wasn't in top form. They'd buy it.

I began to form a plan.

Anastassia ducked into my room and closed the door behind her.

"I've been thinking." She bit her lower lip.

"About?" I slid the gun I'd chosen for the job back into its holster.

The natural connection between us surged to life at long last.

"Us," she said.

Now, with plans to terminate her swirling in my head, she wanted to discuss us?

"What's wrong?" Concern etched the faint lines around her eyes.

"Nothing. Just thinking about a meeting."

She glanced at my hands and her nose twitched."Blood and liquor. Must have been an interesting meeting." Our connection swelled with a wave of pleasure-filled sensations.

My body reacted immediately. "It was. What are you doing?"

She opened my coat to run her hand down my chest and over the front of my pants. "I think it's pretty clear."

"Shouldn't we go somewhere else? Merkief and Jey are right downstairs." A change in location would give me the pause I needed to delicately put her off. As much as I wanted this, it would only make what I had to do even harder.

"I turned off your room feed on my way up. We'll just have to be quiet." She pulled my coat off and draped it over the chair by my desk. Then she pulled off her shirt.

Watching Anastassia undress distracted me from the thoughts of Fa'yet, Sonia, my plan, and for a few enjoyable moments, even the High Council.

She sat down on my bed, naked and grinning. "Are you going to join me?"

Dammit, if I was going to go through with taking her out, I deserved a taste of what I was giving up. I made quick work of removing my weapons and clothes while her mind toyed with mine. My body's physical reaction to the sensations she sent proved to utterly muddle my efforts of both physical and telepathic reciprocation, leaving me to fumble about on all levels.

"Maybe we should focus on one thing at a time so we can both enjoy this," I suggested.

Anastassia raised an eyebrow. "One thing? Hmm. How long have you been waiting?" Her fingertips trailed over my chest and then downward.

My heart pounded, and I let out a strangled sigh as her fingers found their target. "Too long."

She looked up at me and grinned. "Well then," she licked her lips. "Let's see if you can keep quiet."

ᕉ

Six hours later, I woke with Anastassia's naked body pressed against mine. The muffled moans and gasps of our activities must have been suitably subdued if Jey or Merkief hadn't burst in on us by now. Her soft breaths against my arm assured me she was still asleep, as I would have been, if not for a urgent thought that permeated my pleasant dreams, waking me with a heart-in-my-throat lurch to alertness.

I contacted Fa'yet. *"Did you move Sonia?"*

He took his time answering. *"I'm sorry. They must already have her. She wasn't there."*

I grabbed a fist full of blanket and strangled it. *"Where would they take her?"*

"Even if I knew, you couldn't go after her. Vayen, if you violate their trust like Anastassia did, you'll be in the same situation she is."

"Then you go after her. You promised me you'd protect her."

"I tried. I thought I had. Dammit, you can't ask me to throw my life away for her. You have Anastassia. Keep her close, keep her safe."

I needed to do something to assuage my conscience. *"Tell me what her family needs. I'll see they get it. Credits, anything."*

"They don't need your credits! They need to be left alone and have no contact with you. Forget about her and them and concentrate on what you have." He cut contact.

I was too late. Tears rolled down my face.

Anastassia stirred. I wiped my cheeks, not wanting to explain what her presence next to me had cost or what I had to do to keep it from costing more.

She stretched and yawned, then slid back against me and smiled. "Good morning." She kissed me.

I thought of all the mornings I'd woken exhausted and craving a stim to get through the day. Could I go back to that, alone with nothing but work to drive me?

I kissed her back with equal intensity but my wandering thoughts prevented me from acknowledging her intentions further.

If I knew the Narvan would be safe, that the peaceful direction Stassia and I had set out for my people would be maintained, I could step away and let the High and Mighties play their games with someone else. But I also wasn't delusional enough to pretend they'd just let us walk away to enjoy our lives.

Anastassia propped her head up on her elbow. "You seemed to be having plenty of fun last night. What's the problem?"

"Sorry, I have a lot on my mind." I scrambled for a logical reason to keep her at bay for a few hours while I tried to figure things out. "We should be a bit safer about this next time. I hardly think we're parent material."

Anastassia threw her head back and laughed. "That's what's got you looking so forlorn? As if I'd rely on a man to think of that beforehand? I've learned that lesson."

She rolled away and swung her feet over the other side of the bed. "We should probably get up and get working anyway."

Not two minutes after Anastassia had dressed and left my room, an insistent presence invaded my head on the Council's link path. Acknowledging the High Council contact, I received a flashed location.

A male voice said, *"This is your second warning."* and then he was gone.

"Stassia, I have to leave for a little while. Stick with Jey and Merkief until I get back."

Static accompanied her voice. *"We've been doing this body-guard thing for years. I know how it works without you telling me every time you walk out of the room."*

I couldn't tell if she was amused or perturbed, but I didn't stick around to find out. I Jumped to the location I'd been given. The buildings looked mildly familiar, but nothing stuck out as wrong.

As I walked out into the open, the Artorian pedestrians watched me with curiosity and maintained their distance. Racking my brain for anyone I might know in the vicinity, I glanced upward into the bright afternoon sky. The skyline struck me. I was only a couple blocks from home.

Who would the High Council go after here? Neighbors and those I might call family friends wouldn't even know me by sight anymore. Sonia was personal. I didn't imagine they'd go for someone more general this time around. Maybe the entire neighborhood?

I kept walking, my stride lengthening the closer I got to my family home. No smoke, no alarms, no chaos.

As I rounded the street corner, I saw it. Nothingness. An empty lot, wiped clean as if my home had never existed. Even the wild space of greenery was gone. All of it a blank slate of bare dirt. The homes nearby stood untouched. Children played in their yards. Birds soared overhead as if nothing was wrong.

Slack-jawed and standing in the middle of the street, I stared at the void where my memories had lived. My father's favorite chair. My mother's kitchen. The still frames documenting my childhood that hung on the wall. Chesser's uniforms, still waiting in his closet. The lone little bot I'd repaired on my last visit.

Everything gone.

For the second time in one day, tears ran down my face.

My wooden legs made their way back to the shadow of a building where I could Jump without being seen. I stepped out of the void into the foyer of the Merchessian house.

Merkief acknowledged me with a nod from the couch in the common room. "Jey and Kazan are at a meeting on Karin. Should be back in an hour or so." His focus returned back to the vid he'd been watching.

Needing to think, I went to my room. I couldn't stand by and let the Council keep picking at me. I was going to have to do this.

When I heard Anastassia's voice in the common room and then coming up the stairs, I plastered a relaxed smile on my face and opened my door. "Are you up for a job in a few hours?"

She rubbed her temples and nodded, joining me in my room.

Jey's voice slipped into my head. *"Something's wrong with Kazan. She botched the Jump here. She's never done that. And I keep getting static when she talks over the link."*

I felt the smile slipping from my face. *"I'll look into it. Thanks."*

"If this is something to do with this bond business…" he said.

"I don't know what's wrong, but it's not that."

Anastassia closed the door and leaned against it. "He's telling you, isn't he?"

I dropped contact with Jey and nodded. "You haven't faltered on a Jump since I met you. What's wrong?"

"I've been having headaches since I came back. They've been getting worse." She shrugged. "I took a stim before we left. They've been helping, but not enough today, I guess."

"You've been popping stims? Why didn't you say anything?"

She stared at the floor. "I wanted to get back to work. I was so behind on everything and then trying so hard to catch up. Once the headaches go away, I will."

I'd been pushing her like all nine hells to get back into the swing of things in order to reestablish her worth with the Council. I pulled her away from the door and wrapped my arms around her.

She sagged against my chest. It was near impossible to consider my plan with her next to me even though I'd been full of resolve moments before.

Thinking of headaches triggered a memory. "Didn't you once say that Strauss had some magical cure for your headaches?"

"He did." She squeezed me. "That's a great idea. I haven't been to the station since I got back either. Do you have a few hours?"

With the warmth and calm of the bond flowing through me, I couldn't say no. "For you, yes."

"Thank you." She kissed my cheek and stepped away.

I Jumped to the station and turned to Anastassia. She wasn't there. What the hells? *"What happened?"*

"Nothing." Her voice shook. The static was louder than before.

I Jumped back to the house and took her hand. "Come on, maybe Strauss will have some answers for you on that front too."

I Jumped the two of us to her quarters on the Verian station. We walked to the medical clinic.

Strauss caught sight of us and his face split with his stupid wide grin. He acknowledged me with a hasty nod as he rushed over and threw his arms around Anastassia.

I wanted to rip his arms off, but I stayed right where I was. Determined not to let the damned bond rule me, I tried to pay attention to an attendant who walked past us and over to a woman who appeared to be very pregnant.

"Vayen." Anastassia disentangled herself from Strauss's embrace and glanced at me over his shoulder while he gushed about missing her and how wonderful it was to see her again. *"I can*

feel you going all Artorian on me. You suggested this, remember?"

"*Right. Sorry.*" I found a chair close by where I could keep an eye on them but not have to hear his every fawning word.

It was a shame I didn't harbor any favorable feelings toward the doctor. Maybe the High Council would have taken him out for me.

Strauss led Anastassia to an examination table. He ran a scanner alongside her body, then picked up a datapad and made notes. He touched her head, examined her ears and eyes, shook his head and made more notes. They talked.

Through it all, Anastassia's gaze darted to mine, looking more concerned each time. I wasn't sure if that was because of what Strauss said to her or if she thought I might leap up and rip him limb from limb at any moment.

Since she chose to keep silent on the matter for now, I figured she'd fill me in later. I didn't expect it would be anything the tank, laying off the stims and some rest couldn't cure. Not that she'd want to drop off the radar after just getting back into things, but hearing the diagnosis from Strauss would have more merit than coming from me.

My heart jumped. If I could convince her to lay low, to go into hiding, maybe we could con the Council. I'd just need to provide some form of proof of completion. But then I'd need to convince her that stepping away from the Narvan was necessary, and find some proof she'd be willing to part with, and... they'd expose the ruse if any of them got the urge to slip into my head. Fuck.

Strauss turned the scanner off and set the datapad down. They spoke again, the doctor with his arms across his chest, Anastassia chewing on her lip. Strauss turned to look at me. I stood and started toward them. Anastassia shook her head.

"*We'll be back in a few minutes.*"

I scowled but returned to my seat.

If he upset her again, as he usually did... My fists clenched. She didn't need this friendship or whatever it was between them. I'd needed the doctor to convince her to rest. That was all.

When they reappeared, Anastassia trailed behind Strauss. They made their way to me. He offered her a tight-lipped farewell. She gave him a lip-quivering promise to 'think about it'.

I grabbed her hand and hauled her out the door. "What in the nine hells was that about?"

Tears welled in her eyes. "Can we not do this in the corridor?"

I led her to a quiet spot out of the notice of the passersby and Jumped us to our quarters. "We're alone now. Talk."

Anastassia drew a deep shaky breath and let it out. "This bond, from what I understand it's some sort of monogamy control, right?"

"Among other things, yes. What does this have to do with Strauss or your link?"

She held up her hand. "You said you wouldn't hurt me. Is that you or the bond?"

"Both. Though neither one is guaranteed if you don't tell me what Strauss said," I made myself say, trying not to think about my initial plan to off her on her next contract.

"And the protective, possessive thing, the bond?"

"Yes. Why?"

"Would that also carry over to those I held dear?" she asked.

"If harm coming to them would thereby cause harm to you, then yes." Intrigued, I nodded.

She looked uncertain. "Sounds like a lot of aggravation on your end, what do you get out of this?"

I pulled her close and closed my eyes, drinking in the smell and feel of her until I found peace. "When we're close, this is what I feel," I opened my mind to her, hiding everything else, but sharing the intense calm of the bond.

Anastassia let out a soft, "Oh."

Despite the chaos in my head, I felt a grin forming.

"And what exactly would my obligation be in this thing?"

Was she serious? I examined our bonded connection more thoroughly. She seemed to be genuinely asking. "Quit stifling our natural connection. If you keep it open, you'll get some of this too."

"So there's no ritual, or ceremony or anything like that?"

"Technically, yes, but I meant what I said before. I don't expect you to go through with any of that. I'd be happy if you'd simply acknowledge it."

I hadn't envisioned a future in which I might be happy, not where she was concerned. Tolerated maybe, but not this.

Anastassia wrapped her arms around my neck and kissed me.

"Consider your bond acknowledged," she said. "Are you sure there's nothing special I need to do?"

"More of that would be nice." I pulled her tight against me.

"Maybe later." She pushed me back to look me in the eye. "Does this bond mean I can trust you without reservation?"

"You always could, but yes." As long as she didn't ask me to divulge the fact I was supposed to be killing her rather than herding her toward a bed.

Anastassia pressed her open palm to my chest, halting my efforts. "I need to show you something."

"Right now?" Unless whatever it was happened to be in the bedroom, it didn't fit in my itinerary of sex, rest, and then discussing the doctor's assessment of her link issues. Followed soon after by figuring out how to keep her and Sonia alive and the Council off my ass.

She nodded, holding out her hand.

Damn. I took a deep breath and willed the pleasant sensations in my head to cease.

The calm of the bond enveloped me. I took her hand and followed her out the door.

We walked along the same path we'd just traversed, right back through the doors to the medical clinic and into Strauss's solemn stare.

What the hells was she going to show me here? The results of her scan? My nerves tingled.

"I'm glad you've seen reason," said Strauss. "Someone needs to know in case something happens to you. You wouldn't want him back there, alone and forgotten."

Him? I made an effort to keep my snarl to myself. "Someone mind filling me in?"

The doctor gestured for Anastassia to lead me to the lab at the back of the facility where I'd watched the two of them disappear too many times.

Her palm grew cold and clammy in my grasp, but she trudged onward, stopping to enter a code and a scan at the door.

Lights flickered on as we walked in.

A row of six metal tubes several feet longer and wider than me, sat on carts at the far end of the room. Anastassia walked past the desk near the door, littered with food wrappers, datapads, and scribbled notes on actual paper. With her hand in mine, we passed a square table on which sat what looked like diagnostic scanners of several sorts in various states of disrepair.

My steps faltered. Visions of my brother's dead body or her brother or father, preserved in a tube, flitted through my head.

"Over here." Her voice seemed hushed even in the dead silence of the room. She passed the first tube, pausing to touch the window, no bigger than my hands side by side, before moving to the next.

A dim light glowed from within. I glanced inside to see the light came from an array of displays on the far exterior side and also within the tube. They lit a Verian who could have been sleeping. I wondered what cure he was waiting for, how long he'd waited, and if Strauss was any closer to an answer for him.

Anastassia tugged my hand. She came to a stop at the last tube and laid her shaking hand on the window.

I peered inside to see a baby with Artorian coloring.

At a loss for words, I looked to Anastassia.

She kept her gaze locked on the tiny body inside. "This is Daniel. Your brother's son."

Chapter Twenty-Seven

I forced my gaping mouth to work. "You have a son?"

Anastassia smiled weakly. "I gave birth to him anyway. I had him for all of three days before I realized I couldn't do it and begged Peter to put him in stasis."

"Couldn't do what? You have a child." I knew I sounded stupid, but I couldn't help repeating the fact.

"You were right about me not being parent material. Chesser died before I confirmed the pregnancy. He never knew. I didn't know who to turn to."

This was who she'd done everything to protect. There was no other man between us. My brother had a son. I had family.

"If he's Chesser's son, why did you keep him from me?"

"I had to be sure you wouldn't use him against me."

Her doubt stung and suspicion crept in. "Is that why you accepted the bond, because of Daniel?"

Her gaze held mine. "Partly."

"And because your link is malfunctioning."

Was nothing about this real? Were we only addiction and necessary concessions at the core of it all? I stared at the baby rather than face the truth in her eyes for another second.

She took my hand in both of hers. "Hey, I said partly. If we're going to attempt to make some level of this bonding thing work, we should be honest with each other."

It was much easier to lie with a nod. Sharing my truths would end it all in seconds.

"You put a perfectly healthy baby in stasis for no reason other than fear of being a bad mother?"

Her voice wavered. "Peter had talked me into putting him up for adoption with a Verian family, but I needed time to think about Daniel's safety. I told you how I was treated among the Verians, never quite one of them even with the telepathic gift they so revered. I didn't want that stigma for my son. We compromised on stasis, but it was only supposed to be for a couple weeks."

"Stassia, it's been years!"

"You think I don't know that?" She looked at her son, guilt plain on her face. "I went to work for Kryon, thinking that in a position with them, I'd be able to assure Daniel's safety and provide for him."

I snorted.

She nudged me with her hip. "I seem to recall you were just as naïve when I hired you."

The object of my naivety now sat in the High Council's manipulative hands. At least Daniel was safe.

"Can he be revived after so long?" I asked.

"Peter says he can do it."

"Do you want him to?"

Anastassia looked away. "I can't even fully protect myself. What good would it be to wake him now?"

My brother's son lay within reach, his eyes closed, tiny face serene.

"You can't leave him like this forever. He deserves a chance to grow up. I can protect him."

"I hope so. That's why you're standing here."

A chill ran through me. "Stassia, what did Strauss say about your link?"

"That I need to rest and not overtax it. He's consulting his research and the rest of the results. He said he'd let me know if he comes up with anything definite."

"That damned field did this, didn't it? All their testing damaged your link." And the high-and-fucking-mighties knew it. Now she was damaged goods and they wanted to throw her away.

"No wonder the tank can't fix it. Screw Strauss, we need to get you to the University so the LEs can set their nanites on the problem and get you back up and running like they did for me."

"Your link malfunctioned too?"

"I fried it just after you left while we were fighting the Fragians. If they could fix mine, I'm sure they can get yours working again too.

Anastassia stepped closer and wrapped her hand around my arm. "Give Peter a chance."

If she wanted to lean on Strauss for a little while longer, I couldn't blame her, but this couldn't go on. The Council wanted her gone. If they got tired of waiting for me to do it, she needed to be able to defend herself.

What would her son be like? Would he favor Chesser or Anastassia, and in either case, was one better than the other? They were both stubborn with a need to be in control.

"Does anyone else know about Daniel?"

She shook her head.

"You're sure? They seem to have ways of knowing things."

"I don't give them a reason to think I have anything to hide. The only people who know are you and Peter. He delivered Daniel himself and has him logged under a different name."

"Surely people here saw you and knew you were pregnant."

"The logs show that I left two weeks after my return. I spent six months in those damned quarters pretending to not exist. I ate here with Peter, Jumping to and from this lab. I told him about the link, as much as I knew, and he kept my secret without question. He helped with the headaches caused by the pregnancy. Not to mention all the other hellish discomforts that came with carrying a child with different chemistry than my own. There's a definite reason you don't see many cross-bred Artorians wandering around."

I took in all the stats on the side of the tube, not following what half of them were. "Is he all right in there? No ill effects from Jumping during pregnancy?"

She pulled me away. "Let's get out of here before you start asking to take him out and play with him."

The fact that she didn't even try to Jump herself was a testament to the truth of her condition. I Jumped us back to her quarters.

She nodded toward her bedroom. "I suppose you're going to tell me to get in bed and stay there."

"You'd take a contract just to spite me. No. You do what you know you need to do. Just do me a favor. No more stims."

Anastassia smirked. "I don't suppose I could talk you into staying in bed with me?"

As much as I enjoyed basking in the new openness between us, the Narvan needed me and so did she, but not in her bed. "I can't."

She nodded as if she'd already known my answer. Fear edged her words, "Send them both."

"You'll be safe here." I kissed her quickly before we had company and then Jumped to my office on Rok where I could get some thinking done and sink deep into my link.

Halfway into outlining a contract of my own to two of my contacts on Moriek, a summons interrupted my link conversation. Dammit, I really didn't need any additional warnings or Kyron contracts shoved in my face at the moment.

The door to my assigned meeting room closed behind me. I took my seat and shoved all thought of Daniel into the furthest recesses of my mind. As much as I appreciated Anastassia trusting me with her son, it also gave the High Council a possible opening to an even juicier target.

Three cloaked figures parted to reveal the uncloaked blue creature. I swallowed hard.

Its raspy voice floated from the black box strapped to its upper shell. "You are being most obstinate. Perhaps we should hand your position to another."

"I'd rather you didn't do that." I wanted to spit in its face. If I had an idea where it's face was.

Its claws clacked faster.

The door behind me opened. A grey-clad guard held a hooded, struggling woman in his grasp. He brought her to stand beside the blue creature.

The creature's voice deepened. Its fleshy wings burst from its shell. "You could have saved this one. I thank you for not doing so. I am hungry."

"Leave her be." My pulse hammered in my ears.

The guard yanked the hood from her head. Sonia blinked several times and tossed the hair from her face. Her wide, terror-filled gaze locked on to me.

Something stabbed the back of my neck.

"A self-monitoring inhibitor," said one of the cloaked figures. "You violated our trust by speaking of our conversations with another operative. We will not allow that again. We would also caution you against Jumping. The restrictive field is active in this room and we prefer that you are fully aware of these proceedings."

The creature's wings glistened with caustic digestive fluids. "When we asked Isnar Fa'yet to provide us with a suitable motivation, he convinced us he'd chosen wisely."

Convinced? Provided? Shoulders had given them the information or this thing had skimmed my mind. That had to be where they'd learned about her. Fa'yet wouldn't betray me. My mind spun.

"If you would save this one, deliver Kazan to us, and I will dine on her instead."

Sonia sobbed, tears rolling down her cheeks. "Vayen, do something!"

The guards along the walls had their guns aimed not only at me but at Sonia. "Did Fa'yet bring you here?"

"He told me you wanted to see me. Please," she pleaded with the cloaked figures, "I want to go home!"

Anastassia had accepted my bond. Any thought of handing her over to the blue-shelled monster slipped through my mind like mist, refusing to solidify.

"I'm begging you, don't do this," I said.

The blue creature clasped its claws before it. The black box emitted a loud hiss. Its wings snapped forward, encasing Sonia in their slick membranes. The barbs on the edges of its wings sunk into her back, driving deep into her flesh. She screamed, a shrill piercing terror that drowned out all thought.

I found myself out of my seat, pounding on the bone-framed membranes, clawing with my fingernails to try to free her screaming, writhing body. Bullets pelted my coat but I didn't care. Then I was through. I had a hand on her. I formed a Jump for both of us.

Blinding pain tore through my brain. I fell to my knees in a puddle of thick, yellow fluid. Holding my head, I fought to block the pulsing agony as well as Sonia's muffled screams.

Her screams stopped long before my head cleared.

When I regained the strength to look up, the blue monster was gone. Where he'd stood, lay a puddle of tattered clothes and fluid. My hands burned, my skin red and raw. Blood oozed from my fingertips. My body shook and tears streamed from my eyes.

Two guards lifted me by my arms and dragged me back to my seat.

The female from my last meeting stepped away from the other two figures. "Mr. Ta'set, we warned you against Jumping. Defiance is not in your favor." Her cloak parted to reveal an arm, her skin the color of my own. A fellow Artorian.

She caressed my cheek, her fingers trailing through the wetness. "You will be given a single chance to redeem yourself. If you fail, we will no longer be able to help you."

She covered her arm and backed away. "Isnar Fa'yet has been outspoken among Kryon for years. We have tolerated his protests and belligerence. However, he is now sowing seeds of dissent among Kryon, hinting at our methods of operation and questioning the treatment of certain members."

Fa'yet may have handed Sonia to the High Council, but if he was creating enough noise on our behalf to aggravate them this badly, I was convinced some degree of our friendship remained intact.

"Your redemption is two-fold. Eliminate Anastassia Kazan and hand over her link implant as proof of completion. Also, you will eliminate Isnar Fa'yet and deliver his body to us with his head intact."

Because of him, Sonia was dead. I had few reservations about delivering Fa'yet to them.

"You are dismissed."

I formed a Jump to our house on Karin. As I rummaged through the medical supplies with trembling fingers, I cursed the High Council, Fa'yet, and myself.

With my hands coated in healing salve, I stood in the common room, waiting for the worst of the redness and irritation to go away. It didn't compare to the healing wonder of the tank gel, but I didn't have several hours for a dip and recovery time. The deep bruises covering most of my body would have to wait.

Red eyes stared at me in the mirror as I washed the slick salve away. I popped a stim to combat the throbbing in my head from the anti-jump field and the pain everywhere else. My ears still rang with Sonia's screams.

Screw courtesy, I'd been there enough to have a solid jump point. I Jumped directly into Fa'yet's common room. Alarms rang throughout the house. With a gun in my hand, I kicked in the door to the private section of his house.

"Vayen?"

I fired into Fa'yet's coat before I got my rage under control.

He staggered back, coughing until he regained his breath. "I suppose I deserve that."

"You lied to me."

"The truth wouldn't have made any difference other than you shooting at me then rather than now."

"Then you should have killed me when you had the chance."

A bullet in his head would have been far quicker than Sonia's death, but he didn't deserve any kindness and the Council wanted his head intact. I aimed for the same point on his coat and fired again. Three to four shots in the same position would weaken the armor enough for a bullet to get through.

As he took a second to recover, his hand flew to his chest, feeling his thinning armor. His voice shook. "They don't want you dead. Neither do I. I just did what I had to. You still have Anastassia."

"I trusted you, and you lied to me." I fired again.

From the grimace on his face, I guessed his armor hadn't deflected much of the impact that time. One more would do it.

I took aim.

He held out his hands. Empty. He'd made no move to defend himself. My finger rested on the trigger.

"Is this you or them? I don't know what they did or said to you, but killing me won't make anything better. I've been gathering support for Kazan. For you. Let me keep at it. We can make the High Council listen."

Words died on my tongue. Nothing I wanted to say, either to confirm or deny, came out. Damned inhibitor. I'd never felt so much a puppet as at that moment, no better than their grey-suited zombies.

Fa'yet paled, backing down the hall. "It's them, isn't it? Fuck."

"Not another step."

"Vayen, please. We're friends. Don't do this."

His pleading sounded far too similar to mine. Sonia's screams. The clacking of the blue creature's claws. The thumping of my fists pounding the bone of his wings. I shook my head, trying to clear the noise away so I could think clearly.

I kept my gun raised. "Run. Leave. Hide. I don't ever want to see you again." He could take his own chances with evading the High Council. His blood wouldn't be on my hands.

"Vayen, I can talk to them."

I shook my head. "You can't. Go." I aimed a hair to the left and fired.

Chest heaving, he dropped back against the wall. He crouched there, wheezing. After staring at me for a long moment he nodded.

I left him there and Jumped to the station to check on Anastassia. I desperately needed the calm of the bond.

When I appeared in the common room, Merkief took one look at me and rushed over. "Are you all right?"

"Later." I pushed past him and went into Anastassia's bedroom.

She sat on her bed, an array of disassembled weapons surrounding her. She saw me and dropped the cleaning cloth.

I scooped her up and held her tight. The screams in my head faded.

Anastassia gasped. "You're going to snap me in half." When I loosened my death grip on her, she put her hands on my wet cheeks. "What happened?"

The inhibitor silenced all mention of Sonia's death and the High Councils threats. "I can't..."

Her solemn gaze met mine. "You don't have to tell me, I can feel it. Since I agreed to this bond, it's like your defenses have dropped."

I took a deep breath and blew it out. "That's normal. Part of the process."

A sad smile formed on her lips. She wiped my tears away and kissed my cheeks.

"You're a wreck. Lie down."

"Stassia, I can't do this right now."

"We're not having sex, idiot." She pushed the weapons aside and pulled me onto the bed. "Shut up and lie down."

I stretched out on her soft blankets and tried to focus on the calm of the bond, letting it wash over me.

"That's it," Anastassia said softly as she sat behind me. She picked up my head and eased it onto her lap. Her fingertips ran over my scalp, settling on points and pressing with gentle pressure. "I haven't used my training in a long time, and I've never tried it on an Artorian before, but the Verians I used to work with swore it helped."

Her mind opened to mine like it had a thousand times before, but different now, filled with warmth and an overwhelming sense of peace. It was Anastassia and not her. A breath of ocean air carried away the smell of the puddle the blue creature had left. Soft whispers and laughter drowned out the horrific sounds. Sunlight burned away the nightmare that played behind my closed eyelids.

Her strong hands kneaded my neck and shoulders as the sensations swirled around and through me. Hair tickled my cheek as her lips brushed over mine.

"Looks like it's working just fine."

She sat up and the utter peace within me dimmed, but a sense of it remained, dulling the nightmare I'd witnessed. Her fingers stilled.

I wanted to lie there forever, but that wasn't an option.

"That blue thing, can it read minds?" I asked.

"It could control my link, but I didn't suffer any residual effects in that aspect, so more like a light probe, I guess. It never gave me the impression it could take anything without my knowledge. If it had, I don't expect we'd still have the tank at our disposal."

"True. Do they have anyone else who could?"

"Not that they've thrown at me, why?"

"Don't ask why," I said.

"I think I have a right to know after you showed up here like this and now are asking odd questions, don't you?"

"Sorry, I can't explain."

Anastassia slid my head off her lap and straightened herself. "As far as I know the only way they'd get into your head is to probe you. Knowing your usual level of defenses, it would have to be a deep probe and those are anything but subtle. You'd know."

"All right. Thanks." I sat up. The tank, Anastassia, and Daniel were safe as long as I avoided a probe. Fa'yet had said they didn't want me dead and they'd not gone for my head when I'd attacked the blue thing so he must have been telling the truth. They wouldn't risk a brain damaging probe unless they didn't want me anymore.

"Have you heard anything from Strauss?" I asked.

She looked away. "He can't save the link. He said it needs to come out, that it's causing damage to the surrounding tissues."

"So we'll go to the University and get a new one."

"There's too much damage." Her voice dropped to a whisper. "He doesn't think it can be reversed, even by the LEs. He says I can't host another implant."

Without it, she'd be unable to Jump or access the amount of information we needed. At least she'd still have her natural telepathy. But that would also mean she couldn't work with me. I couldn't Jump her all the time, especially not if we were divided in a fight. Without her link, she'd be unable to help run the Narvan, unable to track contracts or research targets. She'd be reduced to doing manual searches, consulting maps and clocks, vid calls, never knowing the current price on her head or receiving tips on who might be acting on it. She'd be little better off than Sonia had been, ill-equipped to deal with the threats against her.

"Yeah, that look on your face. That's it exactly. If it comes to removing my link, I might as well be dead."

I took her hand. "We're going to the University. The LEs are far better qualified than your station doctor."

She nodded, but doubt shadowed her eyes. I formed a Jump to one of my own points that was directly inside the University. Anastassia gave me a questioning look.

"We had a discussion while you were gone about where their funding comes from and my accepted level of access."

"I see you were taking notes during all those meetings where you lurked behind me."

Anastassia and I walked to the nearby security station. "We need an LE now. In fact, I want several of them on this," I said to the guard on duty.

I inserted my hand into the scanner and waited for my identity to come up on the vid. I knew the second it did as the guard snapped to attention and then fumbled with his terminal in a rush to relay my wishes.

We were escorted into the heart of the University. Guards stood aside and workers dodged out of the way. We passed the room where we'd first stayed when the three of us had received our links. I cringed. I had thought I had known who she was and my place in the known universe.

Our escort left us in a conference room with a promise that the LEs would join us within minutes. Three men arrived in less than two. One of them was the one who'd repaired my link. Anastassia sat beside me. In fact, she couldn't have gotten much closer short of sitting in my lap. Fear and dread seeped through our bonded connection. I rested my hand on hers where it sat in her lap.

I addressed Nanchet, the LE I knew. "Her implant is malfunctioning. You'll fix it. I don't care how much it costs, but you'll do it immediately."

"We'll need the details of the problem before we can discuss solutions." He launched into questioning Anastassia.

By the fourth time she'd repeated that she couldn't divulge the details of how her link had been damaged, they were all scowling. So was I.

"Does it matter how? Just find the problem and fix it. You

fixed mine. Hers shouldn't be any different."

"We'll have to do some tests," he said.

"So test."

"This might take awhile," he informed me.

The calm of the bond wavered as logic overrode it with warnings that the High Council could easily have agents watching for her here. They knew her link was damaged.

I was beginning to understand why Jey had resorted to shoving a gun in Nanchet's face to get my treatment rolling. "We don't have awhile. Get on it."

"We'll get a room prepared." The three men scurried away, leaving us alone.

"I don't like this," Anastassia said.

"Me either, but if they can save or replace your link, we need to know. If not, we need to make other plans."

She rested her head on my shoulder, hand tightly gripping mine. "Yeah, funeral plans. Promise you'll look after Daniel?"

"Of course I will, and so will you."

An insistent pressure in my head alerted me to a High Council message. I ignored it. Acknowledging my failure to off Fa'yet would only make them more impatient.

One of the staff came in to show us where the LEs were waiting. When I got up to join Anastassia, the woman shook her head.

"I'm going wherever she's going."

"Sorry, we need a sterile room." said the woman. "You'll have to wait here."

"Maybe you don't understand what I said."

Anastassia rested her hand on my arm. "Maybe you could walk with us and wait right outside the door?"

"That would be acceptable," said the woman.

I followed them out of the room and down the hall. She stopped in front of a door inset with a small window.

"You may observe from here. You," she turned to Anastassia, "will need to come with me and change. Leave anything valuable with him."

Anastassia shrugged out of her coat and handed it to me. She followed the woman into a room just down the hall. They were gone for hours. Or minutes. Too long.

I glanced up and down the hallway but found nothing out of place. A cleaning bot worked along the upper corner of the wall. The LEs, wearing their sterile blue robes and now masked faces, milled around an examination table, probably talking, but I couldn't hear them. A door opened inside. Anastassia entered, dressed in a loose-fitting ivory robe. She glanced at me, as if reassuring herself that I was there, before taking her place on the table.

The LEs pulled a ceiling-mounted scanner over her body from head to foot and back to her head again. They left it there, pointing at the display, nodding to one another and at one point, seeming to argue. I could see Anastassia's lips moving and I had no doubt she was giving them grief.

As the LEs continued their assessment, Anastassia seemed to relax. The tension flowing through our connection eased.

The woman who had taken Anastassia away opened the second door and approached me with wary steps.

"Well?"

"The host site is damaged. It's a wonder her implant is working at all. If she continues to use her link, the damage will continue to spread and you will notice violent mood changes followed by slurred speech and loss of motor functions which may be eventual or sudden. Left unchecked, and assuming the implant remains at least partially operational, which will continue to exacerbate the damage, I'd say she has about two weeks."

"That can't be right. When my link went haywire, all he did," I pointed to Nanchet, "was unleash some nanites on me and I was back to work a few days later."

"LE Nanchet has informed me that this damage is old and not isolated within the implant itself. She is also not Artorian, which is what our nanites are programmed to work within. If you wish, we could attempt to use them, but they will very likely cause more harm than good."

"If the damage is beyond the implant, can't they just do surgery to fix it?"

"Yes, of course." She held up a hand. "However, the site will be unable to host another implant."

"*Vayen,*" Merkief's voice intruded on our conversation, "*Where the hells are you? I was told to meet you on Sere an hour ago. We've got a rush contract.*"

"*So do it with Jey. I'm busy.*"

"*I can't get the details until you're here. I tried to pull Jey in but they were adamant that you needed to be involved.*"

They were trying to pry me away from her. Was this Deep Voice and his partner trying to cover for me? Send me on a job and have someone else take out Anastassia so I could go on with the Narvan in hand? And if I didn't play along, what would they do? Visions of Merkief being impaled by the blue creature's barbs brought sweat to my brow.

"You're not a room all by yourself are you?"

"I was waiting in the contract office. They gave me a meeting room a few minutes ago. I'm on my way there now."

"Jump. Now."

I lost contact. Either he'd Jumped or had been knocked out. Damned impatient High and Mighties. If they were willing to take Merkief out, how much longer did I have before they gave up on me?

"What would you like us to do?" asked the woman who, by her annoyed look, had probably already asked multiple times.

"What does she want you to do?"

"We are unable to ask her. She was quite obstinate during the testing. LE Nanchet had her sedated.

So that's why she had relaxed. Damn her, now I was supposed to decide her future?

"Then we're waiting until she wakes up so she can tell you what she wants to do."

"That could be several hours. You indicated you were in a hurry?"

How could she put me in this position? "If you remove the implant and repair the damage, will she be fine?"

"We don't know for sure. The LEs will do their best, but there are no guarantees."

"Will she still have her natural telepathic speech?"

"Possibly. Telepathic speech is controlled by the same area of the brain as the implant. It just depends on what the LEs will need to do to repair the damage and maintain her normal functions."

If she lost her telepathy, what would that mean for our bond? And would she want to face the prospect of waking up impaired or without any form of mind speech, knowing she'd never stand at the helm of the Narvan again? Protecting her if she were unable to Jump or communicate over any distance opened up a whole new box of problems.

If I was willing to let her body take it's natural declining course, I might be able to buy a couple weeks if I explained the situation to Deep Voice. I could spend that time with her. Jey and I could hold the Narvan knowing that Anastassia's blood wasn't on our hands. Was I being stupidly selfish by wanting otherwise?

I'd have her link to turn over to the High Council.

Either way, she'd be dead. One by reality and the other—she'd have to go into hiding. Would she want to hide?

Anastassia had once asked me if I could kill someone if she asked me too. I had. Lots of them. But not her. Never her. Not even if she was awake to ask me to.

I wanted her alive.

"Do it. Remove the link, fix what you can and don't let anyone in that room."

A direct High Council summons hit me. Had I lost my chance with them?

"I want to be in there. I need to watch, and I can't see anything from here." I'd hadn't seen them sedate her for Geva's sake.

"If you insist, there's an observation room over here." She led me to a door down near the one she'd taken Anastassia through. A bank of narrow stairs waited inside. The woman closed the door and left me in silence.

The stairs led to an enclosed area overlooking the operating room. The door at the top slid shut after I went inside. The space would have been crowded with more than three people and offered no comfort. Block walls, bare floor, no chair, not even a ledge by the window to wrap my trembling fingers around. A closet with a view.

Below me, the LEs stood conferring while two female assistants prepped Anastassia and the equipment.

A speaker tube funneled their muffled voices to me. Nothing they said sounded suspect, yet paranoia sent my heart speeding. Through the window, I took in every detail of the room below. The assistants draped cloths over Anastassia, leaving only her head exposed. Surgical implements, laid out in neat rows on trays, gleamed in the bright light of the operating room. A silver-plated med bot with its yellow neck lights blinking in the slow succession of standby mode stood beside the door below.

If I Jumped to Sere, would Deep Voice let me leave? I doubted it. Instead, I left him a message, telling him I was working on getting Kazan's link and I'd have it to him within a few hours.

Within minutes the pressure in my head eased as the insistent Council request faded. I pressed my eyes shut and forced myself to calm down.

I tried Merkief and found him alive and well. *Stick with Jey.*

I need you to work together until I figure some things out with Anastassia at the University. Stay away from Sere until you hear from me."

"*If you say so."* He sounded like he had a dozen questions but wisely, he kept them to himself and cut contact.

One of the assistants shaved the hair above Anastassia's left ear. I took a deep breath and let it out. How the hells were we going to keep Anastassia hidden from the High Council? If they were willing to take Merkief out, they'd be willing to do a full probe on him to verify the truth of whatever story I fed them. I'd simply have to not tell Merkeif or Jey the truth. I laughed to myself.

I imagined showing up to tell Jey and Merkief that Anastassia had died and everything was just fine, business as usual. Imaginary guns ended up in my face. They'd expect me to be injured, or dead, or at the very least, incredibly broken up about it. Could I fake a convincing show of grief in front of men who knew me really damn well?

The Council still might sacrifice Merkief to a probe just to be sure. We needed a believable story of her demise that no one would question. Someone who had been openly after her that I could wring some concessions from of my own. Someone the Council themselves had used against her. Kess.

He acknowledged my contact after a couple of minutes. *"I can't say as I expected to hear from you after how things ended last time."*

"I need a favor."

He chuckled. *"Are you sure you want to owe me?"*

"I'm repaying you right now. You wanted a way back into the High Council's good graces and to regain a name for yourself, right?"

"I'm listening."

"You're going to kill Anastassia on Artor later today."

Silence.

"I'm going to have her link delivered to you. *The High Council will want details. How convincing can you be?"* I asked.

"*Are you serious?"*

"They won't have any reason to probe you if your story leaves no room for doubt, and you'll have the link. Can you pull this off?"

"Yes," he said. *"I take it she'll still be alive and without a link after this lie goes public. Can you keep her safe?"*

I sure as all hells hoped so. *"You take care of your end. I'll worry about mine."*

"If I do this, I need a guarantee she's not going to pop up in a few weeks and make me the fool of the known universe."

"If she does, you get to expose my part in it, and the Council will rip me apart too. Fair enough?"

Silence stretched on again. *"I suppose that would be worth watching. When?"*

"When you get the link. Should be within the next few hours. Oh, and you'll leave me and my friends alone once this is done."

"Not a problem. Nice doing business with you." Kess cut contact.

I slumped against the wall. What was I going to do with Anastassia? I couldn't keep her at any of our houses. Jey and Merkief would pick up on that. She needed somewhere to hide where no one would look for her. The Narvan was out. Too risky. Same with Merchess, and I didn't trust anyone on Twelve. Merkief and Jey didn't know about her direct ties to Veria Prime, but the information was there if they talked to the right people and looked in the right places. Veria Minor might work. She knew the culture and even though she'd not meshed perfectly with the Verians before, maybe she would now that she'd done her part with the Narvan. She also had her Seeker training to fall back on if she chose to use it.

That would mean I'd have to visit Veria Minor to see her. Damned Verians. I tried to think of anywhere else I'd feel safe placing her and came up empty handed. At least on Minor, she'd be close to the station. Not that she'd be able to visit. Or see her son. I rubbed my hands over my face. I needed both of them in the same place or I'd never be able to make sure they were both safe. I didn't like the idea of having Anastassia so far from me and possibly out of contact, but knowing Daniel sat out there with only Strauss to defend him—that just wasn't acceptable.

The LEs stood around Anastassia, marking the display and indicating tools while one of them opened up the first incision into her scalp. What little I heard were simple requests for instruments or for one of the assistants to adjust the lighting. The med bot stood against the wall opposite me, out of their way and waiting to be activated if need be. The LEs opened the window for personal error, but I felt more at ease with eyes I could read than a faceless bot.

Nanchet glanced up at me every few minutes, but if he offered any hidden message of progress, I failed to pick up on it. I tapped my fingers on the wall beside the window, watching and waiting.

If I wanted Anastassia to survive longer than her surgery, I needed to make arrangements and that meant leaving her. I took out a knife and scratched a pattern into the wall so I could return unnoticed. Nothing seemed out of place below. Even so, I gritted my teeth and paced the tiny room for another five minutes before I worked up the resolve to Jump to the Verian station.

The damned lift couldn't go fast enough and too many people were in the corridors. By the time I made it to the medical clinic, my nerves wanted me back in the closet watching over Anastassia. But I couldn't go. Not yet.

Strauss wasn't in his office. I spotted him with a patient. Not wanting to gain too much attention, I asked one of his assistants to retrieve him. Once he saw me, he hurried over.

"I need you to wake him."

"Him?" Strauss jutted his chin toward the back lab. "Now? Why? Where's Anastassia? Is she all right?" His hands wrung together at his waist.

"No, she's not all right, but she wants to see him. Can you do it?"

"I'm not putting him back in there once he's revived. You understand that, right? That child deserves to live his life."

"I'll see that he does."

"Good." He stood straighter. "This isn't an immediate process. We're dealing with an infant, no less. It might take a day or two before he's ready to leave."

"You have three hours. Make it work. No errors, got it?" I glanced around to make sure no one paid us any particular attention. "And I'll need supplies. Packed tightly. Single bag. Any instructions you could include would also be helpful."

Strauss's forehead creased. "You're not planning on raising this child, are you?"

"Oh hells no."

It would be her raising Daniel. Dragging Anastassia away from her position was going to be hard enough without me thrusting her into the very future she hadn't wanted with my brother. I grimaced. We were out of options. Having her alive and pissed at me forever was preferable to her being dead.

"Then I'll do it," he said.

"I'll be back for him. Have him ready."

As the Jump back to the observation room formed in my head, it occurred to me that the LEs and the assistants could blow my story. If the Council learned that Anastassia's link had been removed at the University rather than by Kess, both of us would be in trouble. Killing them all would be a shame and likely raise more attention with the wrong people. Instead of Artor, I stepped out of the void into my office on Rok. Thirty quick steps down the hallway put me at Gemmen's open door. He glanced up and nodded at the empty chair across from him.

I didn't have time to sit. "That drug. The Fragian one you were working with. Do you have any ready?"

"We haven't handed it out to the men yet, if that's what you're asking. Has one of our missions been compromised?"

"No. Not yet." Great Geva, I had to be careful. One suspicious sounding word could sow doubt. Two could mean my story was blown. My guard would have to be up one hundred percent at all times. Even so, I would be a liability. I'd have to take the drug myself to make sure she and Daniel remained hidden.

My breath caught in my throat. I'd think she was dead, but the bond would remain active. I'd know it was a lie and I'd probably drive myself crazy trying to find her. I certainly wouldn't have the level of single-minded concentration it took to hold the Narvan together and balance the demands of the Council with my plans for the System.

"Everything all right?" Gemmen asked.

I forced my work face into place but panic lay right beneath it. "How much of a wipe does this stuff do?"

"Full dose is estimated at around three months. What kind of effect are you looking for?"

"I'm not looking for anything in particular."

Gemmen chuckled. "So that grimace at three months was meant for something else? Perhaps the cleanliness of my office?"

I couldn't even control my own fucking face anymore. I sat down. "Three days, three hours, something in between. Short term. How safe is this stuff?"

His eyes lost their spark of amusement. "Safe enough that I'd let you use it on yourself. Sounds like the small batch we made for testing would work for you. How much do you need?"

"Nine doses." I looked him over and sighed. "Make it ten."

"Mind if I make mine small? I've got a lot going on here."

"As long as you don't remember I was here."

He shook his head and whistled. "Even knowing I'll forget shortly, I don't want to know what you're up to."

"Good. How soon can you get this stuff? I'm kind of in a hurry."

He stood. "Give me fifteen minutes."

I sat, unable to move. Everything I did and said would be under observation once this was done. A fuck up was inevitable. The Council wouldn't take kindly when my ruse was exposed and neither would Kess. I needed to make sure the Narvan would be safe without me if it came to that.

Since the Council was so fond of threatening me with putting a Jalvian in my place, I'd point them at one. One with an Artorian at his side. If the Council was wise, they'd allow Merkief and Jey to take over uncontested, knowing that I'd likely have a safety net of my own.

I contacted the planetary leaders, dividing the worlds between Jey and Merkief if anything should happen to me and let my contacts know not to cause trouble if they took my place. Merkief became the backup advisor for the Jalvian world of Syless, along with Artor and Moriek. Jey received Jal, and Rok with the Artorian moon, Karin. Merchess was a handful on a good day. New to the demands of advising the system, they'd need to concentrate on the Narvan itself. Merchess could go its own way. That left Frique. Anastassia might hold it dear, but all the Friquen people wanted was to be left alone. They were tucked safely within the Narvan anyway and posed no threat. I left them out of the loop.

When I came out of the link trance, I found Gemmen sitting across from me. "That's dangerous, you know. Anyone could have wandered in here and slit your throat."

"I'd hope our security is a little better than that."

"Just promise me you won't do that sort of thing when you're elsewhere. Kazan's safety is in your hands. What would she do if she lost you?"

She'd be alone and unprotected, stranded in a Verian colony with a baby. Would she know through our connection when the ruse went bad and the council offed me? Would she turn to someone else to help her? Manipulating others to her needs was certainly a talent she possessed. But to find someone she could trust on that level and in a colony of peace-loving Verians no less, the odds were slim.

"She won't," I said.

"You sure about that? You've got this crazy look about you like you're about to do something really stupid. I know I said I didn't want to know, but if it will help, lay it on me."

"I can't."

He slid a tiny clear bag containing nine and a half white dots across his desk. "They take a couple minutes to start working. Once the slight nausea hits you've got about five before you start blinking and wondering how you got there."

I took the bag.

He grabbed my arm. "Really though, promise me you're not about to do something stupid."

"I don't have much choice."

His fingers dug into the sleeve of my coat. "You know better than that."

He released my arm and held out his hand. I opened the bag and put the half of a pill on his palm. He tossed it into his mouth and swallowed.

Gemmen gave me one last look of warning before pointing to the door. "Now get out of here so I can forget this conversation ever happened."

Chapter Twenty-Eight

The block wall held me up as I stared through the plaz at Anastassia. Tubes had been fed into her mouth and nose. Sheets masked any rise or fall of her chest. My gut clenched. The two other LEs and one of the assistants had left the room. The bot's lights now flashed orange, waiting for orders.

Nanchet glanced up at me and nodded, though what he meant by it, I didn't know. The assistant said something I couldn't make out. Nanchet ordered the bot to his side. Its arms extended, working inside Anastassia's skull. The LE sat on a stool at the head of the table and voiced directions while he kept an eye on the display. I willed the LE to finish and pronounce that Anastassia would be able to fully recover.

The assistant walked to a shelf on the wall just below me. I couldn't see what she was doing, but a faint hissing came from the sound tube.

The air around me grew heavy and sweet. I coughed and tried to form a Jump, but the gas muddled my concentration. I punched the door panel. It didn't respond.

I held my breath and pulled out a gun to beat on the window.

Inside the operating room, the assistant circled around behind Nanchet with a length of fine wire in her hands. She slipped the garrote around his neck and pulled it tight. He gasped, his hands clawing at the wire.

She spoke a single word, loud and clear. "Execute."

Red lights flashed on the bot. Its arms retracted to its side.

The plaz refused to break. I shoved the gun back in my coat and drew my pulse pistol. At least that wouldn't ricochet back at me. My lungs burned.

A different bot arm extended, a hair-thin surgical cutting laser sprang from its tip, slicing the floor tiles as it stretched toward the table and Anastassia.

The arm extended toward her head. The red beam cut through the edge of the table.

I fired. The pulse wave sucked the air from the tiny room as it blasted into the wall only a few feet away. I fell to the floor and covered my head as the bricks burst into powder. Plaz shattered, flying through the air like a thousand tiny knives.

My body demanded air. Dust and diluted poison rushed into my lungs. I gasped and leapt down into the room below. Landing with a heavy thud, I rolled through the debris and came to a stop on one knee.

With the flick of a setting pin, I switched the pulse wave to a focused beam and hit the bot with a full blast. Its chest and head caved inward as the wave knocked it back. The assistant ran out the door. The laser cut a swath in the wall and ceiling as the bot fell on its side with a metallic twang. The red beam went out.

I collapsed, fighting to fill my lungs with clean air. Once I could breathe again, I crawled forward until I'd gained enough energy to get to my feet. Nanchet lay across Anastassia's head and chest. The bot's laser had cut a trench across his shoulder. I rolled him off. His body had protected her face and the open hole in her skull. Not wanting to contaminate her further with any of the debris clinging to me, I stepped back.

After making sure the bot was inactive, I ran through the open door. I glanced up and down the hallway, the pulse pistol still in my hand. Seeing no immediate target, I went to the first door I saw and opened it. Empty. As were the next two. I glanced back at the operating room. It was silent.

The next door wouldn't open. I could hear voices inside. I pounded on it. The sounds of a physical struggle ensued. With my back against the opposite wall, I checked the remaining charge on my pistol. Two partial shots left. I fired another focused beam. The pulse wave ripped the door from the wall. It fell inward, a twisted scrap of metal.

Inside, the missing LEs and the other assistant scuttled backward on the floor. They cried out, shielding their faces.

The murdering assistant caught sight of me. "You're supposed to be dead."

The remaining pulse charge was enough to silence her. She dropped to the ground, limp and lifeless.

If this was a High Council contract on Anastassia, the effort was put together in moments with whatever connections they had on hand. The pre-programmed bot deepened my suspicions in their direction. They knew she'd come to the University at some point.

They'd authorized gassing me. Did they now want me dead too or would I have only been knocked out?

"Are you injured?" I asked one of the LEs.

He shook his head.

"Then get back in there and finish up. How much longer will this take?"

He stammered for a second before clearing his throat. "This particular instance is not typical. I really don't know."

"Then get in there and seal the door. No one gets in or out until I say so. Got it?"

He bobbed his head and the three of them fled down the hall and into the operating room. I followed.

"Sorry about the mess. And your friend." I pointed to Nanchet's body on the floor beside the table. "Don't worry. I'll stand guard out here."

"I pray that you will." He took a shuddering breath and took his place at the table with the others.

I made sure the door was locked, as well as the door to the observation room. The next hour and a half passed with me looking through the window, pacing the hallway and threatening anyone who came within earshot.

A knock sounded on the door behind me. "I'm finished. Is it safe to come out?"

I opened the door. The LE pulled his face mask away and smiled.

Warmth spread through me as hope blossomed. "Will she be all right?"

His gaze dropped to my boots. "She had significant damage and the chaos in there didn't help. I did what I could, but we won't know for sure until she wakes up."

"How long will that take?" With one attempt on her here already, I had little doubt the Council or someone else would try again.

"A few hours. Even in the best case scenario, she'll likely be prone to intense headaches. She'll never be able to host another link. As to her telepathy, I wouldn't hold out too much hope."

Headaches were something medication could treat. How she would deal with the loss of her telepathy, in addition to the link, worried me far more.

The other LE pushed Anastassia into the hall on a gurney.

Too many people knew where we were. "Bring her somewhere no one would look right away. Do you have an office or spare room we could use?"

"There's a lounge. No one would expect us to bring a patient there."

"That will work."

Thankfully the lounge was empty. I locked the door. We got her squeezed in between a couch and a table.

The LE headed out the door. "I should see to taking care of—"

I shook my head. "I'm going to have to ask you to stay until she's able to walk out of here."

"She just had surgery. She needs to rest. She can't be up walking around."

"Don't ever tell her what she can't do." I laughed to myself. "Besides, I'm not quite done with you yet. Have a seat. We might have a few hours to wait."

The LE settled in, casting disgruntled glances in my direction as I checked for sightings of me or Anastassia. Things were quiet on that front, which meant it had to be the Council after her or us.

I leaned against the wall at Anastassia's side, brushing her hair away from the fresh stitches on the side of her head. I hoped her hair would cover the bare spot when she let down what was left in her braid. The less attention she brought to herself on the way to her new life, the better.

We didn't have any jump points on Veria Minor. Being a sparsely populated planet of rudimentary colonies, we'd never had cause to go there. She'd need transportation. No more Jumping. I booked a cabin on a flight set to leave in four hours. If I had to carry her there, I would.

I rubbed my freshly scabbed hands over my face to find tiny particles of plaz embedded there. "Someone clean this up." I pointed at my face.

The assistant looked at the others and went to a cabinet by the door. When she returned, she had a med kit in her hands and got to work.

After she was done, I checked the time. Daniel would be waiting for me. With one attempt on her already, and the LEs painfully unequipped to deal with any threat, I needed Merkief to watch over her. I prayed Gemmen's pills would do as he'd said.

Merkief arrived and took in Anastassia's sleeping form with haunted eyes. His voice was hushed. "Will she be all right?"

The LE looked to me.

I nodded. "If I have anything to say about it, yes."

Merkief gave me a tired smile. "You look like you've had quite a day."

"I feel like it too." I raked the hair from my face.

He cleared his throat. "Jey would like to know 'what in the fucking hells is going on.'"

At least Jey was kind enough to not interrupt me and ask me himself.

"Would you like to clue him in or shall I?" Merkief asked.

"No, and no. I'll call him in when I'm ready to."

"Then would you care to clue me in?"

"No. Stay here and keep her safe. I have something I need to do."

He glanced at Anastassia. "Must be important."

"It is."

He nodded. "Go on then."

I took one last look at Anastassia and Jumped to the Verian Station. The Council plagued me with another insistent contact. Had their agent contacted them when she'd fled the room? If they knew that I truly had no intention of killing Anastassia, I didn't have much hope of making Kess's story believable. Taking a deep breath, I started toward the medical clinic.

One of his assistants spotted me as I entered and pointed me toward the back lab. I went in to find Strauss with a squalling infant in his arms.

"It worked," he said with a beaming smile.

"Thank Geva. Any complications?"

The doctor shifted Daniel to one arm and handed me a datapad with a display full of stats. "Everything checks out. I'm so happy that Anastassia will finally get a chance to hold her son. They've both been waiting for this moment for far too long."

I glanced at the datapad and nodded my agreement with Strauss' assessment. He was too giddy to be lying.

"Did you get the supplies?" I asked.

Strauss handed me a bulky shoulder pack. "I hope I haven't forgotten anything."

I took it from him before he got the notion to go through it and make sure. "Anything I need to know?"

He picked Daniel up and patted his back. "How much do you know about babies?"

"Not much."

Stassia had run the entire Narvan and cared for the well-being of billions of lives. How hard could one baby be?

He smiled. "You'll find a vid chip I give all new parents in the bag."

"Thanks." I tossed the bag over my shoulder.

Strauss fiddled with Daniel a moment, talking some nonsense to him and checking his wrappings. "He should sleep soon. You'll need to feed and change him when he wakes up."

I didn't have time for a lecture on baby care. "I'm sure we'll figure it out."

He handed Daniel to me.

Lighter than I expected, I almost dropped the blanket-wrapped, wriggling mass.

Strauss steadied Daniel in my arms. "There, like that. It just takes practice."

"I need you to do one more thing." I extracted a white pill from the bag. "Go to your desk and find a scrap of paper. Write: Daniel is safe. Burn this."

"Why would I—"

"Just do it." It would be better I didn't allow him any further knowledge of Daniel, but if he'd guarded him for years, I had a feeling he'd go as insane as I would to find his charge mysteriously gone from his life. I wasn't looking forward to that, and I couldn't afford to leave myself any notes.

He scrawled the words on a scrap of paper.

"Set it where you will see it and then take this." I handed him the tablet. "For Anastassia's safety. It will make you forget the last day or so. I hope you haven't had any great undocumented breakthroughs in that time."

Strauss shook his head and took the tablet. He swallowed and allowed me to check his mouth.

"Other than a blank spot in your memory, you'll be fine." I took a couple tentative steps to get a feel for the tiny weight in my arms. Holding him in one hand, I undid the latches of my debris-covered coat and tucked him inside. "Thank you for all of your help."

He nodded.

If Anastassia would need my help in getting to the spaceport, I needed to be inconspicuous too. I Jumped to the house on Artor and set Daniel in the middle of the blankets on my bed while I changed. Since he seemed calm for a moment, I ran into Anastassia's room and packed a bag with some of her clothes. I added her favorite knife and the neckband. Everything else would have to stay. Not only did I not have the energy to Jump anything else in addition to Daniel and his bag, but making it apparent that she'd packed with the intention of leaving would raise suspicion.

With the two bags and the baby in my arms, I Jumped back to the little half-destroyed closet in the operating room. All the Jumping with the extra items started my head throbbing. The Council's demand for contact only made it worse.

I made my way back to the lounge and contacted Merkief to unlock the door. He ran over to open it for me.

"How is she?" I asked.

"Nothing's changed." He eyed the bags. "What's all this?"

"Nothing you need to worry about. I need to sit down." I brushed past him to find an open chair away from the others. Adjusting my hold on Daniel beneath my coat while seated was more covert than doing so while standing. Merkief and the others kept their distance but watched me warily.

Despite Gemmen's warning, I needed to sink into my link again in order to set up accounts for Anastassia. I didn't have access to any of her credits. She'd never trusted me enough for that, but I had plenty of my own. I drew from several smaller accounts, mostly obscure investments under scarcely used aliases. Next, I got into Veria Minor's public systems. A house, supplies, new identity, everything she needed would be waiting when she arrived. Nothing was extravagant enough to gain undue notice, but it would offer her a comfortable life.

With Daniel securely wrapped inside my coat, I went to Anastassia's side. My free hand found hers. Maybe Gemmen was right. There was another choice. One that didn't leave her alone and that I'd already made a few provisions for. Not that it seemed any less insane.

I looked to Merkief. "I need you to do something for me."

"Only if you'll tell me what's going on. I've had it up to here with operating on nothing."

Even though I knew they'd soon suffer memory loss, there were too many eyes and ears in the room. "Get over here."

He came up beside me. "What?"

I turned from the others and opened my coat. "Keep an eye on him for me, will you?"

His eyes bulged. "Who in Geva's name is that?"

"No one you need to give any thought to. Just hold him. Get Jey in here too. I'll be back." I slid Daniel into Merkief's arms and strode across the room to grab an LE.

"Come with me." I near dragged him out of the room, all the while trying to convince myself that I wasn't making the biggest mistake of my life.

❧

The LE poked my shoulder. "Hurry, she's waking up. I put the envelope in your pocket as you requested."

The Council's insistent contact was gone and the warm, sleeping mound on my chest under my coat assured me Merkief had made an effort to keep Daniel as out of sight as possible. I sat up to see Jey and Merkief standing next to Anastassia's gurney. Keeping one hand on the baby, I got up and joined them.

Anastassia's eyes opened. It was a wonderful sight. She turned to me and smiled. "I take it I'm still alive?"

I nodded, the lump in my throat too big to allow words to form.

The three of us stepped back to allow the LE room to check her over. "Normal function seems to be fine. As to the telepathic aspect, time will tell."

Anastassia scowled. "What do you mean by that?"

I went back to her side. "I'll explain later. Right now, I need you to try and stand."

"I just woke up from surgery, idiot."

"I know. We're kind of in a hurry. You need to die in a couple hours."

Her brows rose. "Excuse me?"

"I'll explain later."

"I'm thinking right now would be good." Her face went white as she sat up.

"Can she handle a stim?" I asked the nearest LE.

He looked at me like I was crazy, but nodded.

I handed her my tin and then took Gemmen's bag from my pocket. Shaking out three pills in my hand, I turned to the two LEs and the assistant. "I need all of you to take these. It's for your own protection."

They eyed the pills as if they were poison. "They won't kill you. Hurry up." If I'd had my other hand free, I would have pulled a gun on them. Pointing a baby at their heads just didn't seem very threatening.

Merkief and Jey must have added enough additional threat by just stepping towards them because they quickly complied. I watched them swallow, and then checked their mouths.

"Vayen." Anastassia grabbed my arm. "What is going on?"

I wrapped my free hand around hers. Her grip eased but her insistent glower remained.

"Jey, I need you to Jump her here." I flashed him and Merkief one of the Jump points we used on Artor. Jey took Anastassia's bag. "Merkief you'll take me and—"

"Got it." His gaze locked onto Daniel inside my coat and the bag at my feet that he then grabbed.

We stepped out of the void and into a quiet corner of a park just outside an Artorian spaceport.

I pulled Anastassia from Jey's grasp and took both bags from them. "I'm afraid this is where we part ways."

Jey made a grab for Anastassia's arm. I dodged between them, making sure to keep her out of his reach. He would have nearly as hard of a time letting her go as I would have.

"None of you will thank me for this, but it's the best I could do." I pulled Daniel from the safety of my coat and handed him to Anastassia.

She gaped and then quickly took him into her arms.

Merkief and Jey's stunned faces mirrored hers. I snapped my fingers. Their gazes returned to me.

"I split the Narvan between you in the event of my demise. Which will be in the next few minutes."

The absolutely stricken look on Anastassia's face convinced me that her acceptance of the bond wasn't entirely based on concessions. "Please, Vayen, tell me you didn't make a deal with the

High Council."

"Quite the opposite actually." I turned back to Jey and Merkief. "The High Council should be approaching one or both of you for the Narvan position. Stick together. Do what they say, but keep our people safe."

Merkief shook his head. "What are you talking about?"

"I'm pulling myself out of play. I have to keep them safe."

Jey's gaze darted to Anastassia, Daniel, and I. "But your link, won't they just pelt you with summons until you come back?"

"I need you to say goodbye to Kazan. Quickly." I took Daniel from her so the three of them could share a confused and hushed farewell.

The envelope the LE had placed in my pocket clanked in my hand. I handed it to Merkief. "It is extremely important that you bring this to Kess at his office on Twelve."

Merkief stammered, looking at the envelope.

"Open it."

He peeked inside and emptied the contents into his hand. Two link implants.

"They're both fried. Hers naturally, mine suffered a pulse wave. They won't be readable for anything beyond establishing identity."

With both our links to work with, Kess could make his story far more convincing. The three of them stared at me.

Anastassia found her tongue first. "Have you lost your mind?"

"Probably."

I gave Merkief a shove. The stim wouldn't hold Anastassia over very long. She needed to rest and recover somewhere safe.

"Go right now. I need to know it's done."

"You're giving credit to that bastard?" Merkief clenched the links in his fist.

"The High Council knows we've been at odds for years. They'll buy it."

"Just do it," said Jey.

Merkief gave me a tight nod and Jumped.

Already, I felt lost and claustrophobic without my link. I didn't know the time or the current price on my head, the weather on Veria Minor, or if the supplies I'd ordered had arrived. Everything was still happening, but I'd fallen out of sync with it. A cold sweat broke out on my forehead. The pain medication the LE had given me was already wearing off. Anastassia had to feel far worse than

I did, even with the stim. Daniel started to cry.

"You're sure about this?" asked Jey.

"The Council likes you well enough. Merkief should pick up his half of the system pretty quickly since you won't have the chaos we had last time. I trust that the two of you will do what's best for our people."

"That's not exactly what I meant," he said.

Merkief reappeared, saving me from having to answer.

I took two pills from the bag and handed them to Merkief and Jey. They stared at the white specks in their hands.

"Take them."

They looked at each other and then to me. Jey swallowed his first. Merkief followed.

I needed to get Anastassia and Daniel on our flight before anyone made note of us standing around. "I'm sure you have a hundred questions, but you won't remember the answers anyway."

Jey's stricken face told me he'd come to the realization first. "We won't remember we said goodbye."

"The important thing is that you don't remember what happened between when you arrived at the University and when you heard about Kess killing us."

Merkief's voice broke. "We'll think you're both dead."

"Then we'll be safe."

Anastassia tugged on my sleeve. "Vayen, please. I don't want to leave. Certainly not this way."

Seeing the grief on their faces, it was hard not to allow them some small written hint. But they might be probed and any hint would leave room for doubt. Doubt would mean death. The real kind.

"I know this is not what you wanted, but I'm not about to kill you or let anyone else, and that's what the Council has decreed. I said I'd protect you and I will."

I pulled her close, and with the bags over my shoulder, and Daniel in my arms, we backed away.

I fought for the words to say farewell, to offer them luck with the High Council and the Narvan, but my throat was thick and the tablets would wash away my words within minutes. I settled for an apologetic nod and hurried Anastassia toward the port where we could lose ourselves in the crowd.

I thought of Sonia's letter. She'd managed to find happiness in the midst of the abrupt change I'd thrust into her life, even if only for a short while. I prayed to Geva that we would fare better.

Unable to stop myself, I turned to look at the men who had been my friends. My mind placed a smiling Chesser between them. Jey raised his hand to wave.

Though this was not the future I'd imagined with Anastassia, I did have her beside me. The bond stirred, still there, emanating warmth and comfort. I had my peace. I squeezed Anastassia's hand, and she smiled through her tears.

About the Author

 Jean Davis lives in West Michigan with her musical husband, two attention-craving terriers and a small flock of chickens. When not ruining fictional lives from the comfort of her writing chair, she can be found devouring books and sushi, weeding her flower garden, or picking up hundreds of sticks while attempting to avoid the abundant snake population that also shares her yard. She writes an array of speculative fiction.

She is the author of several books including _A Broken Race_, _Sahmara_, _The Last God_ and _Destiny Pills and Space Wizards_. As an author who's been both self-published and traditionally published, she appreciates all reviews as they help readers discover good books.

Read her blog, _Discarded Darlings_, and sign up for her mailing list at www.jeandavisauthor.com. You'll also find her on Facebook and Instagram at JeanDavisAuthor, and on Goodreads and Amazon.

CPSIA information can be obtained
at www.ICGtesting.com
Printed in the USA
LVHW040437100320
649438LV00004B/202

9 781734 570106